Where the Sun Hides

SEASONS OF BETRAYAL BOOK ONE

BETHANY-KRIS
LONDON MILLER

ISBN 13: 978-1533525246
ISBN 10: 1533525242
eISBN 13: 978-1-988197-15-9

Cover Art © London Miller
Editor: Nina S. Gooden

This is work of fiction. Characters, names, places, corporations, organizations,
institutions, locales, and so forth are all the product of the author's imagination, or
if real, used fictitiously. Any resemblance to a person, living or dead, is entirely
coincidental.

Dedication

For Kaz. We love you, you little shit.

Contents

Prologue

There were days when Alberto Gallucci thought it would be easier to have the mind and ideals of a child. Children didn't concern their little selves with worldly things or the issues of men. As long as their tiny hands were filled and their mouths were distracted with food or talk, the rest was unimportant.

The small things didn't bother children.

Alberto couldn't remember what that felt like.

Except for his Violet.

She was not like most children. She wanted to know everything—all things. Her questions never ended, and her innocent curiosity couldn't be contained. Most times, he didn't mind indulging his daughter with her constant chattering, or giving into her demands when she stomped her foot and pouted.

Violet stood at her father's side; her bob of golden curls haloing her features. She barely reached above his knees in height. Sometimes he worried that her tiny size was a sign of some health problem, as his son had stood nearly to his waist at the same age, but the doctors assured him that Violet was completely, entirely normal.

He didn't think she was at all—she was far too special for that.

She grabbed a fistful of his slacks and tugged hard. "Daddy?"

Alberto patted Violet's head, hoping she would stay quiet for just a little while longer.

He shouldn't have bothered.

"Daddy?" Violet asked again, pulling firmly on his pants.

"Hush, *topina*," Alberto murmured, running a hand over her hair.

There was a chill in the air, the shifting colors of leaves giving way to the promise of fall. And even the rolling gray clouds, obscuring the sun on what was meant to be a clear day, were a grim reminder as to where Alberto and his daughter waited.

Cross Hills Cemetery—the poor man's graveyard.

Over the years, there had been a number of meets, many of which had taken place in far worse locations than the one he was currently standing in, but Alberto would wager this was one of the most important.

How long had they stood there already? Watching. Waiting. But above all, anticipating. His first attempt at reaching out to the man he was meeting had gone unanswered. And why wouldn't it? They were on opposite sides, both fighting for a piece of something each wanted to possess. It wasn't until much later, with a simple spark in the air, that both men had ultimately been brought around.

The rules for this meet were simple. No weapons, no men, and as a show of good faith, Alberto suggested bringing along the children. No man, not even those as unstable as the Russians, would dare plan an attack at the risk of a child being hurt.

It'd been the harming of a child that had ultimately brought them to this place ...

The familiar wave of guilt washed over Alberto, knowing the error he had made and what it nearly cost another man.

Children were so important in *la famiglia*, much like wives, mothers, and grandmothers. Hurting children was unacceptable, even in the midst of a brutal, bloody street war that had no time or concern for loss of life. After all, that was the only thing street wars were really good for, in the end.

He was regarding a tombstone to his left, a bouquet of dying roses resting in the vase beside it, when something—or someone rather—caught his attention, forcing his gaze from the stone to the man that was now entering the graveyard.

Alberto's hand found the fur-trimmed hood of his daughter's coat as the other man came a bit closer to his spot. He wanted to keep Violet still for the moment. She had been bouncing and chattering away, ready to jump out of her damn shoes. She very well might bolt forward, at the presence of someone new. His daughter was open in that way. She was too young to understand that their visitors were not friends.

Russians and Italians could never be friends.

At the man's side, a young boy stayed close. The boy's hand was firmly enclosed within the man's, and he wore a pair of black, thick-rimmed glasses with shades too dark to see beneath.

Alberto winced internally, knowing the cause of those sunglasses on the boy, who had been just one part of his men's mistake.

"Daddy?" Violet asked.

For what, the millionth time?

Alberto touched the back of Violet's head gently. "What is that game we always play, *topina*? The one when we need to be quiet, hmm?"

Violet's gaze drifted between her father and the newcomers. At four, she was far too perceptive for her own good. He hoped that later in life, her inquisitiveness would be a virtue, and not something liable to get her into trouble. As it were, he already knew there would be no hiding his activities from his children.

But he would like for Violet to stay ignorant for a while longer.

Once the newcomers were only a few feet away, the man released the boy's hand. He bent down and muttered a few low words—Russian words—to the boy. His hand skimmed the dark, short hair of the boy, and then he patted him on the side.

With a nod and nothing more, the boy walked a few steps off the stone pathway, his hands held out, as he couldn't see with those sunglasses of his, and came to a stop at a cracked, weather-beaten, marble bench. The boy sat down, and stared off to the side, silent.

"How's his eyesight?" Alberto asked.

The Russian man's gaze cut to Alberto with a flash of pain. "Better, but it's difficult when he's outside. The brightness of the day makes his eyes hurt. Frankly, the brightness of *any* light hurts his eyes."

Alberto cleared his throat. "Your other boy, why not bring him?"

"He's too old. He understands much more. He favors his uncle."

Alberto nodded. "Your girl, then? I heard you had a daughter, Vasily."

The Russian's stare dropped to the blonde, green-eyed girl at Alberto's side.

"She was occupied," Vasily murmured.

Alberto chose not to push, but he believed Vasily's reasons for not bringing another one of his children to the meeting were different from the ones he had given. Perhaps because the sight of a ten-year-old boy wearing sunglasses to protect his damaged eyes caused by a bomb that Alberto had ordered to be set was enough to cut at even the hardest and coldest of men.

Children should not be brought into the affairs of the mafia, if it could be helped.

After half a decade of fighting between the Markovic *Bratva* and the Gallucci Cosa Nostra, a street war that killed nearly thirty men between their respective organizations, a single bomb had quieted the streets.

But not in the way Alberto wanted it to.

He'd intended to stop the fighting, to reclaim part of the Brooklyn streets leading into Little Odessa that had always been the Gallucci grounds. A great portion of his family's business was tied into the warehouses and connections they had made. When the Russians started to push back against the Gallucci's demands, it had all snowballed from there.

A shouting match led to a sit-down.

The sit-down led to name-calling.

Italians and Russians simply didn't work well together. They were two entirely different criminal organizations, following codes that might have seemed similar on the surface, but were actually quite different in some ways—from family dynamics both in and out of their respective organizations, and even from the way the two conducted business. Cosa Nostra was steeped in tradition and smothered by rules. Working with other organizations outside of their systems and beliefs was practically impossible.

Alberto brushed off his inner thoughts, knowing they weren't important now. "Violet, what's that game I asked about?"

His green-eyed daughter was staring at the quiet boy twenty feet away on the marble bench.

"Counting clouds," Violet said in her childish, sweet voice. "We count clouds to be quiet."

"Why don't you go do that for a bit, huh?" Alberto was going to tell his daughter to leave the boy alone and find her own spot to play—Violet had a knack for annoying others at times—but she was already making a beeline for the bench. "Well, at least they will be entertained."

Vasily's lips curled up at the corner in what seemed to be disgust, but he quickly tampered back the reaction when his son patted the bench as Violet approached with her quiet hello.

"Kazimir is a guarded boy ... even for his age." Vasily glanced to the side and took in his son, who was openly chatting away with Alberto's daughter. "Or he usually is, anyway."

"Violet doesn't let people have walls," Alberto replied, chuckling. "She barrels right through them with a smile."

For a moment, one second of suspended time, they were just two fathers taking in the sight of their children enjoying the company of each other. It was simple. It was innocent. It was peaceful, something both had longed to provide them with.

But in the end, the pair had come to this place with a purpose. One that Alberto could no longer put off.

"Why were you the one to finally accept my offer of a meeting?" Alberto asked. "I expected your brother. He is the boss, isn't he?"

Vasily bared his teeth when he flashed a smile. A cold smile. "Gavrill has no intention of backing down against your family."

That was not what Alberto expected to hear. It set him on edge instantly, and he once again found himself sweeping the graveyard with his gaze, looking for something he might have missed. Had he made the wrong choice in doing this with the Russian?

"Worry not, comrade," Vasily said like he could read Alberto's mind. "The graveyard was a good choice to meet up. No one would ever desecrate the final resting place of so many souls, no? And our children, of course. I wouldn't have brought my boy along, had I thought for a second that you might hurt him."

Again, Alberto added silently.

10

"Forgive me," Alberto started to say, shrugging, "but we haven't exactly been amicable in the past."

Vasily tipped his head to the side like he was brushing the statement off. "I accepted your offer because I believe the best thing to do is stop the fighting."

Alberto had to agree.

When street wars got to the point that innocents were involved, it had already gone too far.

"You just said—"

"I came here without my brother's knowledge or permission," Vasily interrupted before Alberto could finish. "I know his intentions, and that he wishes to open the Markovic *Bratva* territory beyond the streets of Little Odessa. To do that, the feud between our families will have to continue. My interests are not aligned with my brother's, but at the moment, it seems ours are, Alberto."

"So it seems," Alberto echoed.

Out of the corner of his eye, he watched Violet point to an oak tree filled with colorful leaves that were just beginning to fall from the thick branches. The boy at her side shook his head, and Violet frowned with her pout firmly in place.

"I assume," Alberto said, still watching the two children, "... that if your interests are not tied in with your brother's, then that will be a problem you'll have to deal with. Won't it?"

Vasily sighed, tossing his hands into his pants pockets. "Perhaps, but I don't want to keep fighting for possession of something that doesn't belong to us. And if I did, at what cost will it come to me? You nearly took my son from me the last time."

Alberto flinched. "That was a mistake that never should have happened. The bomb was intended for your brother."

"A mistake that would have resulted in a war far greater than you could imagine." Vasily's tone never changed from one of casual indifference, but Alberto could still hear the warning behind his words. "And you call us Russians savages."

Alberto was on guard, waiting for the moment when the Russian would strike. The Markovic brothers were volatile by nature. It didn't take much to set one off.

Even so, he kept his composure as he said, "It was a mix up of cars, and certainly not intentional on my part."

Vasily met his gaze. "Nonetheless, you came too close."

He had.

Even Alberto knew it.

"How do you intend to fix the little issue of your brother's interests, if they don't fit with what you want, then?" Alberto asked. "That's a bit of a mountain to climb over, considering he's the boss of your operation."

"*Pakhan*," Vasily corrected. "We call him *Pakhan*."

"Same thing, isn't it?"

"About the same as someone from the outside addressing you as Don, Alberto," Vasily said.

He wondered, if briefly, whether the Russian was intending to be offensive, or if it was just his nature. "Understood."

"And my brother ... He seems to be a problem for us both, no?"

Alberto took Vasily's seemingly innocent statement in, absorbing what the man might be alluding to. Often times, discussions where business was forefront were held with a sort of vague secrecy surrounding them. A man should never come right out and say what he wanted or needed done, but rather, hint at it and let the other side draw its own conclusions.

"He's certainly a problem for me, if he intends to make his way any farther into Brooklyn than where he already is," Alberto said. "As it is, he's severely cut off some ties my Capos have to warehouses that we use for storing things needing to stay hidden for a while. I don't like losing out on money because someone wants to play keep away with my streets."

Vasily chuckled. "You don't have other storage facilities to use?"

"None close enough to keep attention away from the fact that things are traveling," Alberto answered, not giving away much else.

His hand in the cocaine trade had long been a source of debate between his syndicates and other Cosa Nostra families that he sometimes did business with. Cosa Nostra liked to tote themselves as upholding standards, but also keeping away from being the moral police.

Yet, when a Don decided to handle substances as a way to make money, someone always took issue.

"You didn't answer my question," Alberto asked.

Vasily lifted a single brow high. "About what I intend to do with my brother, you mean."

"*Sì*. About him ..."

The Russian smiled again, in that cold way like he had earlier. "I was hoping we could work something out that would be to both of our benefits where Gavrill is concerned."

Alberto stood a little straighter.

Were they actually getting somewhere now?

"Keep going," Alberto pressed.

Vasily passed his son and Violet a glance before quickly turning back to Alberto, his face a mask of passive indifference. "As I see it, we really only have one option, Italian. You don't want to keep fighting, and neither do I. Given that this is a triangle with my brother being the peak, we have to consider him, too."

"He does want to keep fighting."

"Yes."

Alberto weighed his options, and the Russian's actions. Vasily had accepted the offer to meet. He'd followed all the rules—came alone, brought his son, and was amicable.

Even respectable, to a point.

Vasily hadn't needed to do any of that. His organization was slightly smaller than the Gallucci syndicate, but as both families had already proven, they were more than capable of making the streets of Brooklyn a living hell. It needed to end.

Alberto finally found a Russian who seemed like he might be willing to do just that.

"No problem is unfixable," Alberto said.

"My thoughts exactly," Vasily agreed. "And I know, being the *Sovetnik* that I am to my brother and our organization, that not everyone is happy with his ... choices."

"One more dead man might correct all of that."

Vasily shrugged. "It could, as long as it didn't create problems within the *Bratva*."

"And how would that work?"

"Don't you already know, Don?" Vasily asked.

That time, Alberto could hear the snideness in Vasily's words. The man hadn't even tried to hide it. He let it go.

"You want me to pave your way to the top, is that it?" Alberto asked.

Vasily grinned. "Win-win, Italian."

Would it be?

The fighting would stop.

No more dead men.

Alberto found his daughter sitting beside Vasily's son, ruffling the tulle layers of her pink dress under her long coat.

He would be able to breathe when his children left his home.

"I will still take the blame for it, despite the fact you're asking— without really asking—me to do it," Alberto murmured. "And that concerns me, because that leaves me open to retribution when you suddenly decide that your brother's death needs avenging. Isn't that how the mafia goes? An eye for an eye."

Vasily barked out a laugh. "You do not have very good insight into the *Bratva*, comrade. We are not like the Italians and sometimes the one death is enough to end it all. We don't feel the need to keep spilling blood after it's already stained the ground."

Well, then ...

"I want a guarantee, if I agree," Alberto said.

"I'm listening."

"The Markovic *Bratva* stays out of Brooklyn, barring Little Odessa, of course. Even your businesses and your men's businesses. I know you simply use Little Odessa as the home base to your operation. You don't need territory, being an arms trafficker, Vasily. Most of your work is done out of state and country."

"I'm fine with that demand," the Russian said. "As long as Coney Island can remain a no man's zone. No one owns it, so to speak. And while Brooklyn remains your territory, I want a guarantee we can still come and go for personal reasons … *safely*."

It didn't escape Alberto's notice that Vasily hadn't confirmed or denied his hand in the arms trade, but he didn't bother to call him on it.

"Of course, I'll steer clear of you and yours, and this," Albert said, and gestured around them, "will never have to happen again."

A nod from the Russian.

What Vasily was asking for, would be no easy task to complete. Alberto knew firsthand the level of protection one needed as the boss. If Gavrill were half as smart as Alberto thought he was, the man would be surrounded at all times. It wouldn't be easy, what Alberto was agreeing to, but if it meant his city would finally sleep, he was willing to take the risk.

That, and more.

Alberto also knew that no one could ever know about what had transpired between him and the Russian in this cemetery with their children playing just feet away. It would look shameful for an Italian Don to work with a Russian for any reason, even if it was to his benefit. And he strongly believed that Vasily would feel a similar shame from his people, should it come out that he had worked with an Italian to have his brother killed so that he could take the man's spot in his organization.

No one could know.

"I'll see it done," Alberto said.

Alberto extended a hand, waiting for Vasily to accept and seal the deal between them. With the slightest of smiles, if the dark amusement on his face could be considered one, Vasily gripped his hand. For the first time, Alberto noticed the spider inked on the back of his hand.

It was only a second before Vasily was pulling his hand away, but the sight of it sent a shiver of apprehension through him.

Along came a spider …

Alberto had only heard the saying once, but it had never resonated in him the way it did just then. Some spiders were innocent, but others … others were deadly. The Russian's chiming phone had him stepping off to the side.

Alberto quickly made his way off the path and strolled toward his still-animated, happy daughter. She was kicking her legs to and fro, her head tipped back, and her smile was so wide it could outshine the sun. The boy at her side was smiling, too.

"It does not," he heard the boy say.

"Does too," Violet said in her sing-song way. "Brown, red, orange, and yellow. Everywhere."

Alberto stopped walking, confused. What was his child doing?

"What about the sky?" Kazimir asked.

"Gray—like your daddy's eyes."

Kazimir's brow puckered. "But the grass is still green?"

"Very green. Like your jacket."

Violet closed her eyes, still kicking her legs and smiling.

"Where is the sun, then?" the boy asked.

"I don't know."

"You don't know?"

Violet laughed. "I closed my eyes, so now I can't see it, either."

"But you were supposed to be helping me see, Violet."

Alberto watched his daughter's eyes pop back open instantly.

"It's hiding behind the clouds," she said. "But we'll find it again."

Alberto didn't quite know what to think. Children weren't like adults. They didn't understand the boundaries between cultures, and surely not ones as difficult as Cosa Nostra and *Bratva*.

But there his girl was, helping a Russian boy to see, in her own little way.

It was still time to go.

"Violet," Alberto called. "It's time to go have some gelato."

Kazimir frowned.

Violet jumped off the bench without argument. "Next time, Kaz."

"Okay," the boy agreed, his frown fading.

Alberto didn't correct the children.

Life would teach them.

It always did.

Her father was going to kill her, if the alcohol didn't first.

Violet Gallucci had waited for this day—the day she finally turned twenty-one—counting down until she was able to taste the freedom that her birthday brought. Until now, she had been confined to the places her father deemed appropriate. And when it wasn't him breathing down her neck, it was her brother, Carmine.

And she had toed the line, doing exactly what was asked of her, even as she had rebelled in small ways.

But tonight, she was pushing the boundaries as far as they would go, teetering on the edge. Violet might have known what her father would say if he knew where she was headed, buckled into the backseat of the cab with two of her best friends, but what he didn't know wouldn't hurt him.

Amelia was to her left, texting away on her phone. She was oblivious to everything around them, her brows drawn together as she read whatever excuse her boyfriend, Franco, was feeding her as to why they wouldn't be able to hang out later.

Then there was Nicole to her right, whose gaze was rapt on the passenger window, watching the city pass them by as they sped toward the outer limits of Brooklyn to Coney Island. She was the quietest of the three, and the one most anxious about where they were going, but being the good friend that she was, she'd dutifully come along.

And right in the middle, was Violet. She had been nervous before they left, but a shot of raspberry tequila had fixed that and now she was just bubbling with excitement. It wasn't just the club they were heading to that had her adrenaline flowing, it was the risk—the thrill of something she knew was against the rules.

But, she never outright broke the rules her father had set forth, merely bent them a little.

"Franco is an asshole," Amelia muttered with a frown as she locked the screen of her phone and dropped it in her lap. "Remind me again why I put up with his shit?"

"Because you love him?" Violet asked.

"Because he's the only one of your boyfriends that your father approved of," Nicole supplied, finally looking away from the passing scenery and to her friend.

"That's not entirely true," Violet said. "He liked … what was his name, Ben?"

Amelia made a face. "Because he was a political trust fund baby."

Violet shrugged. "He still approved."

Amelia scowled as her phone buzzed again, her attention on whatever message had come in. Nicole tossed Violet a look, rolling her green eyes.

"Still loves him," Violet said, too quietly for Amelia to hear.

Nicole shook her head. "Not the kind of man to love."

Amelia didn't seem to notice her friends' discussion, or she just didn't care, with her phone in her hand and Franco giving her his time.

The three girls had been friends for longer than Violet could remember. She had memories of playing in the middle of a giant pile of tulle ballet skirts, dressing up with her mother's shoes, and stealing the makeup from her vanity. All those memories featured Nicole, Amelia, or both, in some capacity.

In a way, her best friends had been picked for her.

Violet knew it was true.

Alberto, her father, kept Violet on a leash that was shorter than anyone actually knew. Sometimes it didn't seem like it was there, but it was. Her friends were just one example of that.

The Gallucci family had a lot of rules, but only one was really important for Violet to follow: she didn't see, hear, or know a thing. From the time she was young, she knew that was the only thing her father really cared for her to learn. The rest of the rules came along after.

But some things couldn't be ignored. And with readily available Internet at Violet's fingertips, and her family being a sort of dynasty in New York, there was only so much pretending she could actually do. When new people learned her name, or even her father's, she answered their questions with a shrug and a smile.

She knew who her father was.

She knew what he did.

She just wasn't supposed to.

Cosa Nostra wasn't meant for girls, after all.

Both Nicole and Amelia were the daughters of her father's right and left-hand men. And because of that, they had been placed in Violet's path from the time she could walk. They were respectable, acceptable, Catholic,

Italian girls that understood the secret, sometimes smothering, lifestyle that Violet was surrounded by.

They lived it, too.

"So ... where's your brother tonight?" Nicole asked.

Violet passed her not-so-subtle friend a look. "I don't know. Why?"

"Curious."

"You should drop his ass before it becomes a habit," Violet said.

Nicole lifted a single shoulder in response. "He makes it easy."

Because he was easy.

To anything with legs and tits.

Violet forced herself to swallow those words back. She wasn't particularly close to her brother, being that he was six years older than her, but his attitude didn't help most days. Carmine felt like it was his personal duty to make sure his sister was staying out of trouble and keeping her nose clean.

Nothing irritated her more.

Nicole was the perfect example. If it was Violet who was running around with some guy, her brother would probably take offense. But his choice to run around with a girl was perfectly acceptable and none of her business.

Not that Violet wanted to know what Nicole did with her brother.

"You're not telling Franco where we're going, right?" Violet asked Amelia.

Her other friend glanced up from her phone again. "Why, so he can gain himself some brownie points with my dad and yours by ratting us out?"

"Just asking."

"Don't worry," Amelia said. "I was only trying to get him to meet up with me later."

Violet checked out the window, looking for a sign of how close they were to their destination. It couldn't be far—maybe another ten minutes.

Then she could forget about how she was failing several of her classes, how her father was going to flip when he found out, and about everything else that was stressing her out.

She just wanted to party a little.

That's what being twenty-one was for, right?

Who cared if Coney Island was no man's land and off-limits for a *principessa della mafia*?

18

The loud crunch of bone was enough to make even the strongest of men flinch, but as Kazimir Markovic—or Kaz, to those that knew him well—straightened, flexing the fingers of the fist he had launched into the man's face, he didn't look bothered at all.

"Was that really necessary?" Abram asked from his position in the corner, arms folded across his chest as he regarded the scene with thinly-veiled amusement. "He was just about to tell us the good news, isn't that right, Marcus?"

Kaz and Abram both looked to the man sprawled on the floor, one hand cradling his face as he groaned in pain. His shirt was wrinkled from Kaz's former hold on him, and spattered with his own blood. His nose had already been broken, the soft cartilage giving way beneath Kaz's strength.

Contrary to popular belief, Kaz wasn't as violent as people made him out to be. He much preferred using rationale and reason to get the things he wanted from others, and that had served him well over the years.

But tonight, he was in no mood.

The last thing he wanted to be doing was tracking down men like Marcus to find out where his money was. He liked to think he was a patient man, giving those that owed him a chance to pay their debts before he came to seek them out.

Except, Marcus had chosen to duck and dodge him for the last three weeks, practically a ghost in a city where no one could hide—at least not from Kaz.

When he had gotten the phone call from Abram that Marcus had been found and instructions were needed, Kaz had to postpone the meeting with his brother to deal with this bullshit.

And if there was one thing Kaz hated, it was being late for a prior engagement.

So, no. His patience was gone, and the last thing he wanted to hear from Marcus was another excuse.

"I-I've got your money," Marcus stuttered out, holding an arm out in front of him, as though that might help ward off any more blows from Kaz. "Please, I can get you—"

"*Zatknis*—shut up." Reaching into his coat pocket, Kaz pulled out a crisp, white handkerchief, tossing it down on the man. "Clean yourself up."

The portly man rushed to obey, his hands shaking with fear of what Kaz might do next. It wasn't often that a man broke your nose, and then gave you something to clean up the blood.

"Here's how this works. Abram here is going to escort you to your office, your home, or to wherever the fuck it is you keep your money. You hand him over what you owe, plus twenty percent for wasting my time, and I won't cut off your fingers. Understood?"

Marcus nodded, still holding the handkerchief to his face. "Good."

Kaz glanced back to Abram, who looked far too amused by it all and gestured with a tilt of his head for the man to follow him toward the exit. Neither had to worry about Marcus trying to make a run for it, though it would have been entertaining to watch.

"See this done. I have a meeting I'm overdue for."

Abram nodded once. "Right. Take it easy, Cap."

Kaz frowned as he watched the man head back toward Marcus, whistling beneath his breath. He had always hated that nickname, 'Cap,' but Abram insisted on calling him that—his idea of showing him respect since he was a *brigadier*—or Captain—in the Markovic *Bratva*. And no matter how often Kaz asked—or demanded, depending on who you asked—he still did it.

Putting Marcus out of his mind for the time being, Kaz headed out into the night, breathing in the cold air as a wind blew over the vacant parking lot. Across the way sat his baby, the one thing that never failed to make him smile. It had been a present to himself after he'd received his stars.

A matte black, fully customized Porsche Carrera GT.

It was ostentatious to say the least, and when his father had seen it for the first time, he hadn't approved, but he didn't bother trying to tell Kaz to get rid of it—he knew the request would go unheeded.

Hitting the unlock button on the fob he carried, Kaz slid inside. He slid the key inside the ignition and started her up. The low hum of the engine was like music to his ears as he pulled out of the lot, heading toward his brother's nightclub in Coney Island.

It was rare that Kaz visited him there, especially when Sonder was open for business. He wasn't usually one for the nightlife scene, but whatever his older brother asked of him, he usually provided.

He owed him that much …

Kaz had only been driving for a handful of minutes when his phone rang. He took one hand off the wheel, dug his phone out, and read the name that flashed across the screen. He thought of not answering and letting it go to voicemail, but Vasily Markovic was not one to be kept waiting. And even if he did ignore the call, Vasily would just call back until he answered.

Sliding his finger across the screen, he connected the call. "Kaz."

"What have I told you about this?" His father's voice came in loud on the stereo of his car. "Your mother named you Kazimir, act like it."

This wasn't the first time they'd had this discussion, and probably wouldn't be the last. Then again, there was very little about him that his father didn't take issue with.

"Have you seen to the new storage?"

That was code for: 'Did you make Marcus regret not paying on time?'

"It's under control."

"Good. And the shipment from Dulles?"

"Secured."

That was the way these things worked. It was one thing to say that Kaz was a shit son, but no one could ever say that he took his position in the *Bratva* lightly. Not anymore. This was what he lived and breathed, the only thing he was sure of lately.

Truthfully, the *Bratva* was the only thing he and Vasily had in common.

His earliest memories were of Vasily's role in the *Bratva*. From the time when he was his brother, Gavrill's, *sovetnik*, or right hand, to when he became the acting *Pakhan*, the boss, after Gavrill's death. Sometimes, Kaz thought Vasily was a better boss than he was a father—and there was a strong chance that Vasily felt the same way about him.

To say that they didn't get along outside of their mutual responsibility to the *Bratva* was an understatement.

"You're meeting with Ruslan soon, no?" Vasily asked.

Kaz heard it, even if he didn't want to, the derision in his father's tone when he said his brother's name. For those that didn't know the man, they might have missed it, but Kaz had his whole life to study him. He could practically see the slight curl to his lip that Kaz was sure would be there if they were in the same room together.

But Kaz never called him out on it, he bit his tongue.

He bit his tongue about a lot of things.

"I am."

Vasily was quiet for a moment. "Be careful out there. Stay mindful of where the lines lay."

He received that warning any time he ventured anywhere near Brooklyn, although he did go further in from time to time for personal reasons. Back when he was younger, before he could understand what the *Bratva* meant, a truce had been called between his father and Alberto Gallucci, head of the Gallucci Crime Family. The years before it had been wrought with tension, the animosity escalating to heights of which people hadn't seen since the Valentine's Day massacre.

Even Kaz had felt the unforgiving hand of what an escalating turf war could do to a city. Sometimes, as he lay awake at night, he could still feel the heat of the blast on his face.

Hear the sharp cries of alarm as the car that had been not too far in front of him had blown up into a cloud of black smoke, the ensuing fire raging for hours.

No, in that regard, Kaz had no interest in testing the boundaries set before him.

"Yeah," Kaz said drifting back to the present. "I got it."

Vasily hung up then, without a goodbye.

Tossing his phone on the passenger seat, Kaz gunned through traffic, just spotting the glowing blue lights through his tinted windshield that shone from the club's exterior.

Sonder had been a pet project of Ruslan's, something he'd worked on for the better part of a year before he had even thought to try and open it— but that was his brother. A perfectionist. He went over the details numerous times, working through any problems that might arise, and making sure he had a solution before he ever got started. Ruslan didn't believe in failure.

There was already a line forming at the doors where Ruslan and Nathaniel stood like sentinels, ensuring that only those they deemed worthy stepped foot inside. Despite the late hour—or maybe because of it—the line stretched down the block.

As he came around the corner, eyes shifted to his car, some in amazement, some in envy, but he paid none any mind as he parked in the alley next to the club. Climbing out, he pocketed the key and headed around the side to the entrance. The thumping bass of the music playing inside echoed out to the street and alley. Kaz drummed his fingers against his thigh to the beat.

At the front of the club, he didn't bother to get in the mile-long line. He walked straight to the doors where his brother and Nathaniel were standing.

Ruslan caught sight of Kaz and smiled, holding out a hand. Kaz took it, and his brother brought him in for a one-armed hug before releasing him just as quickly. He was the only person Kaz would allow to do that shit.

"*Brat,*" Kaz greeted.

"Brother," Ruslan replied in English. "Did you finish out your business?"

"Mostly."

"Then you deserve a drink."

Kaz laughed. "The business wasn't drink-worthy. But talking to Vasily, after, certainly was."

Ruslan's lips drew into a thin line at the mention of their father. His brother, more than anyone, understood just how exhausting it could be to even have a simple conversation with Vasily Markovic.

Between the two Markovic brothers, Ruslan took after their father more than Kaz did in appearance. Ruslan had a good forty pounds of muscle over Kaz's lean, tall one-eighty-five. His brother would make the perfect linebacker, with wide shoulders and a chilling stare ready to silence anyone who looked at him the wrong way. At six-foot-six, Ruslan had three inches of height on Kaz. Ruslan sported their father's squared jaw and thin lips, while Kaz had taken his mother's sharp lines and fuller smirk.

Anyone who didn't know Ruslan always took a step back when they first met him. He was as intimidating in stature as he was in behavior. But Kaz did know his brother, and he didn't find him intimidating at all.

Ruslan put a hand on Kaz's shoulder and squeezed. Then, he turned to Nathaniel.

"I will be back after I get my brother a drink," Ruslan said.

Nathaniel didn't look up from the tablet in his hands, which contained what looked to be names he was scrolling through. The man was always around. Wherever Ruslan went, Nathaniel was right around the corner. Kaz didn't mind him all that much because he stayed out of his business, and Ruslan's, for the most part.

"Sure, Rus," Nathaniel replied.

Kaz gave Nathaniel a nod that was returned as he passed. The music instantly became louder as the entrance doors of the club opened under Ruslan's push. Walking in behind his brother, Kaz took in the floor of the club. He noted the moving bodies going from the bar to the dance floor, and between the tables and booths.

The place was packed, but it wasn't shocking. Ruslan had created a high-energy atmosphere with constant movement and total sensory pleasure with the music, lighting, and modern setup. The club scene wasn't Kaz's thing, but he could appreciate the effort and talent it took for his brother to pull something like this off.

Not to mention, make it a success.

"Looks full," Kaz said, coming up to his brother's side.

Ruslan shrugged, but pride radiated in the action. "Trying to keep it under fire code limit. We don't need that problem."

Kaz chuckled. "No, we certainly don't."

The brothers came up to a bar that stretched from one wall of the club all the way down to the other, the background made of mirrors that reflected the glistening bottles lined up there. Ruslan caught the gaze of one of the bartenders, and waved two fingers high.

"Two vodka. Neat."

The bartender nodded, and turned to ready the drinks, abandoning the one he was already prepping for someone waiting at the bar. Ruslan spun around to face the crowd and Kaz followed the action.

"So, Vasily was his usual self, yes?" Ruslan asked.

Kaz forced his scowl away. "Same old."

"The twins' birthday is in a couple weeks."

Shit.

Kaz had forgotten about that. Their fifteen-year-old sisters would be soon turning sixteen. Vasily and Irina, their mother, had probably planned something for the girls. Vera, their other sister who was one year older than Kaz, would come in from the city for it.

But Ruslan …

Blyad.

"Don't worry about it," Ruslan said.

"I'll talk to him—he shouldn't exclude you with the family."

"It's easier."

"But you want to go, no?" Kaz asked. "See the twins, and Vera? Irina, too."

Ruslan frowned. "It's been a while for all of them."

Kaz was aware of just how long it had been since Ruslan had been allowed to any family event. Vasily kept up appearances well enough, for show and nothing else, but he made every effort to keep Ruslan away.

He hated that for his brother.

"I'll talk to him," Kaz said again, offering nothing more.

The brothers turned at the sound of glasses clinking down on the bartop.

Kaz picked up his drink and tilted it toward his brother. "*Za zdorov'e, brat.*"

Ruslan returned the sentiment before tipped his own glass back and emptying it in one go. Kaz took his a little bit slower, wanting to enjoy the taste of good vodka.

His brother clapped him on the shoulder after he'd discarded his empty glass to the bar. "Stay and drink. Watch the people. You never go out unless it's for the *bratva*. I'll be around."

Kaz thought about it, and decided maybe he would stay. He'd only promised to come and see the club in live action, given how much work his brother put into it, but he did like the place.

"Find me after you're done vetting people at the door," Kaz said.

Ruslan laughed. "Unless you've already found some *krasivaya kiska* to take home."

Well, Kaz chose not to respond to that.

But he did grin.

Before long, Kaz was milling through the throng of people, his gaze sweeping the floor for anyone he might recognize or for some problem that might show up all of the sudden. It wouldn't be a surprise if some fool thought they could try something. He was sure that Ruslan had a dozen different plans at the ready, in case an issue came up, but the habit was hard to break.

Kaz didn't know how to break his habits.

He stayed to the far walls and corners as he strolled around the joint. His front to the people, his back to the wall—always. Cowards had a way about them. They preferred to hit a person from behind. So even if the club was lively with no threat in sight, Kaz couldn't help his instincts.

Back to the wall.

Front to room.

Out of the corner of his eyes, he saw a flash of blonde that drew in his attention. Just as quickly as he saw the woman, she was gone, swallowed into the dancing, swaying bodies.

Still, he looked again.

Sonder was hot.

And not just a great club that was filled with patrons. No, *hot*.

Violet could barely breathe when the music turned up, and the people started moving faster around her. She had already tossed back a few drinks and danced with her friends until her feet hurt in her heels. She still wasn't ready to leave. She shrugged off the leather bomber jacket she wore overtop of her cherry-red, bodycon dress. At the same time, she leaned forward and took a sip of the green-colored drink Nicole offered. The sour sharpness of the liquid burned the whole way down, but she barely even noticed.

"Good, right?" Nicole asked.

"So good."

Violet looked around, trying to find where Amelia had disappeared to in the swarm of drunk, sweaty bodies. She quickly found her, right in the middle of the dance floor, surrounded by other people with drinks held high and grinding together.

"I think she forgot about Franco," Violet mused.

Nicole snorted. "I guess so. Not like that's a loss. Want another drink?"

Violet knew she should refuse the offer. As it were, she felt light on her feet and a little hazy in the head. But she hadn't risked her father's wrath and traveled all the way from Manhattan to Coney Island for nothing. She planned on having a damn good time, partying it up to celebrate her twenty-first birthday, and nothing more.

"Yeah, get me another," Violet said.

Nicole spun on her heel and made a beeline for the bar again. Violet cut through the people toward where Amelia was still dancing in a group of strangers. The beat of the music pumping through the venue pulsated from the floorboards and into the soles of her heels.

Violet loved to dance.

Moving to the rhythm was as easy as breathing. One of the purest forms of pleasure for her. She had danced since she was young. Ballet, jazz, contemporary and whatever else her father could put her in to keep her out of trouble and add to her Gallucci profile. As an adult, she didn't get to dance as much as she used to when she was a younger girl.

Focuses changed.

School became more important.

So when she did get the chance to let loose with her friends, especially in a club that seemed specially designed for people to have the best time they could, Violet didn't take it for granted. There was the bar area that had a number of stools lined up along the front with three bartenders ready to take orders. A DJ's booth was set up against one wall with the dance floor stretching out as far as the eye could see. Soft lights lined the floor, but not so much that it took away from the setting.

Violet joined her friend to dance as the song switched to a faster, smoother beat. She linked hands with her friend and ignored how the swell of people seemed to grow, getting even closer to her and Amelia. The strangers that Amelia had been dancing with before Violet joined in came back, one wrapping around her friend while the other tried to slide in behind her.

She wasn't having too much of that, but she let the guy get close enough that she could move to the beat with him.

Before long, Nicole was back. She balanced two drinks in one hand while she sipped on her green concoction from the other. Violet took one of the two red drinks from Nicole's outstretched hand, immediately tipping the drink back for a long pull of the tartly sweet mixture that reminded her of strawberries but with the harsh kick of rum.

"Slow down," she heard Nicole say, laughing right after.

Violet paid her no mind. She was already taking a second drink. Amelia wasn't far behind, grabbing the drink that Nicole had brought for her. The music kicked up again, lights flickered, and Violet was lost to the visceral sensation of the club's atmosphere.

There was no mob boss's daughter here.

No *Italiano principessa*.

She was just another face in the crowd.

No one could possibly understand how precious that was to her.

Violet leaned forward, away from the man she was dancing with when he tried once again to kiss the back of her neck. She didn't mind dancing or flirting with him, but she wasn't up to letting the guy think he was taking her out to his car, or wherever.

Unfortunately, the fool had a handful of her wavy blonde hair wrapped in his fist and he tugged her right back in place. A faint sting radiated over her scalp from his pull, but Violet's senses—diluted with alcohol—was numbed to the pain.

"Back off," she said, turning to push her hand against the man's stomach.

His lips pulled into a smirk and he chuckled, but thankfully, let her go.

"A tease, then?" he asked.

Violet narrowed her gaze, refusing to dignify that with a response. Why did men automatically think because a woman rejected their advances, that woman was suddenly playing games?

"Go find someone else to feel up," Violet told the guy. "I've had enough."

He took a step toward her, and Violet forced herself to stay in place and not back up. She gave a little sigh in relief when he shrugged her off and walked on past into the rest of the dancing people.

It was only then that Violet realized she had lost her friends.

Shit.

She quickly scanned the patrons, searching for Nicole and Amelia. Between several more drinks, songs, and random strangers wanting to dance, the girls must have gotten separated. Pushing through the faceless strangers, Violet tried clearing her thoughts enough to resemble being sober.

Drunk and lost was not a good look on a woman.

Violet scanned the people at the bar, and didn't recognize the backs of the people or the dresses she knew her friends were wearing. She was just about to turn and go back onto the dance floor, but a buzz coming from inside her small clutch stopped her.

She pulled out her phone, and sighed at the name lighting up the screen.

Nicole's message scrolled across the touch screen: *Near the entrance. Help.*

Violet shoved her phone back into the clutch and changed directions toward the front of the club. She found Nicole and Amelia together, but one was looking a hell of a lot worse for wear than the other. Nicole was holding onto their friend, and pushing the hair out of Amelia's eyes, trying to talk to her.

Amelia wasn't responding all that well by the looks of it.

Violet knew they had all drank quite a bit, but not that much.

"What happened?" Violet asked, bending down to help straighten Amelia's short dress.

Nicole huffed as she forced a slurring, confused Amelia to lean against her side. "I don't know. One minute we were laughing, I danced with a guy and turned my back on her, and the next …"

"She was like this?"

"She was on the floor and some guy was laughing as he tried to pick her up," Nicole said, scowling.

Violet shuddered at her friend's implication. "She was fine before?"

"A little drunk. We all are."

True enough.

"Did she take anything?" Violet asked.

It wouldn't be such a shock if that's what Amelia had done. They weren't entirely innocent. Sometimes, they experimented with different things, but they were always careful about it and stayed together.

Nicole shook her head. "She would have said something. Someone might have dropped something on her. Can we just get her out of here before something else happens?"

That sounded like a good idea.

Violet moved forward, grabbing Amelia's arm and helping Nicole to move their friend away from the wall. It wasn't easy, considering Amelia seemed to have the balance of a baby that couldn't walk.

"You girls need some help?" came a voice from behind them.

Violet glanced back at the person who had asked the question. It was the same fool from earlier, who had tried kissing her neck after she'd told him not to. He had "bad" written all over him—and not in a good kind of way.

"No, we're—"

Violet's words cut off when someone slammed into Nicole from the other side of their three-person chain. She went sprawling to the floor, along with her friends. Above the music, people, and someone's apologies, she heard what sounded like the crunch of glass.

"Shit," Violet muttered, reaching for Amelia.

Nicole was doing the same, but a thick streak of red dripped down her arm, and she had tears in her eyes. "Someone dropped a glass," her friend said in explanation.

It looked pretty bad—deep.

Chances were, Nicole needed to get that checked out.

Great.

Like Nicole could read her mind, she said, "Let's just worry about getting Amelia out of here, okay?"

Violet nodded, and the two got Amelia back on her feet and moving toward the door again.

Unfortunately, a bull of a man stepped in front of them, stopping the girls entirely. His thick, tall build forced Violet to look up at gray eyes and a scowling face. He pointed at Amelia.

"What's wrong with that one?" he asked.

Violet's mouth clamped shut.

Nicole spoke instead. "Nothing, she's drunk."

"She would have been escorted out already," the man said.

The hint of an accent colored up the man's tone, making his words sharp and quick. She didn't recognize it right away, not with his first question. But with his second, his r's sort of rolled off his tongue, and that was when Violet knew exactly what accent the man sported.

She had only heard it a couple of times in her life, and never firsthand. *Russian.*

"She's on something, yes?" the man asked.

"No," Violet argued. "And we're leaving."

"You're not leaving yet. I won't have the cops showing up here because some girl got mixed up and found herself in the hospital after being at my club."

Violet straightened, panic swelling in her throat. "We're taking her—"

He pointed at Nicole. "She is bleeding."

Thank you, Captain Obvious.

Violet really just wanted to get the hell out of there.

"Can we just go?" Nicole asked, her voice betraying her panic, too.

"Yes," the man said.

Violet let out the breath she'd been holding.

"Shortly," he added with a cold smile.

Wonderful.

The man jerked his head to the side and said, "Take them to my office, and we'll go from there."

Violet didn't get the chance to ask what he meant before someone was grabbing her arm from behind and separating her from her friends. She chose not to fight against the bull-like man wearing all black as he pulled her along through the curious crowd that had suddenly quieted and was watching the show.

At least they were getting their money's worth for the entrance fee.

After a short walk through a back hallway, Violet and her friends were shuffled into an office that was far bigger than what she was expecting, considering how it looked from the outside. There was a couch along the back wall, two stuffed armchairs, and a large mahogany desk that dominated the space. Bookshelves were built into the walls with rows of books and tombs on various subjects lining them. Though the decor was understated, there was definitely a masculine feel to it.

The man who had stopped them earlier waved at his counterparts, and the three men who had escorted the girls into the space disappeared before the office door shut. Amelia had been placed on a couch, and Nicole moved to sit beside her.

Violet figured her friend had Amelia handled, so she faced the man who wouldn't let them leave.

"I—"

"Quiet," he uttered. "What did she take?"

Violet clenched her teeth. "I don't know. That's why we were leaving."

"Does she need a hospital?"

"She needs a bed and water," Nicole interjected.

"You need stitches," he said, glancing down at Nicole's arm. "You're bleeding all over my couch."

Nicole just glared.

Violet held back her grin, knowing it wasn't the time.

"We're really sorry," Violet said, hoping to appease the guy so he would let them go without any more trouble. "We just wanted a good time—this club is supposed to be the hottest thing on Coney right now, and someone must have spiked our friend's drink. We don't want problems. We *really* don't want the cops involved, so if that's what you're worried about, don't be."

The man's lips drew into a thin, grim line as he looked the girls over. "I will make sure you all get home safe and sound."

Violet didn't like that idea at all. She could still hear her father in the back of her head, repeating his warnings. *Keep out of Coney Island, don't go too deep into Brooklyn, and stay the hell away from Russians.*

It was more likely that whoever this guy was didn't have anything to do with the kinds of Russians her father demanded she stay away from, but Violet knew where the lines were drawn with Alberto Gallucci. She often tested them, occasionally even jumping over them when her father wasn't looking.

Russians were not one of them.

"We can take a cab," Violet said. "We took one here."

The man didn't look all too impressed with that idea. He opened his mouth to speak, but the office door opened from behind Violet, stopping whatever he was going to say.

"Everything good, *brat?*"

Violet turned fast on her heel at the new voice.

And froze.

He was tall—over six feet—and built like he ran a ten-K every day. The black suit he wore hugged his frame, but the jacket was left unbuttoned, showcasing a white silk dress shirt that was pulled taut across his chest.

The man was cut.

Violet swallowed hard and met the man's stare.

Gray eyes, like the other man's but more intense, looked her up and down with a slow, predatory fashion. His face was framed by a strong jaw dotted with a couple days' worth of scruff and sharp cheekbones. His lips, full enough to draw in her attention, curled up at the edges into a grin of sorts.

She thought it looked more like a smirk.

He raised a hand and ran it through his short, dark hair that was tapered at the sides but a little longer down the middle.

But it wasn't so much the action that caught her attention, but the black ink marked on his hand. An upturned spider that looked to be crawling up under the sleeve of his suit jacket rested upon a web.

Her gaze cut back to his when he dropped his hand back to his side.

He looked familiar. She was sure that she should know him, but in her semi-drunken state, she was coming up with nothing.

The man's smirk quickly faded into a mask of cool, calm nothingness. He looked past her to the man behind her and said one word that chilled her entirely.

"Gallucci."

"Someone's on the wrong side of the bridge," Kaz said casually, almost smiling at the way her mouth twisted. Turning his attention to his brother, he switched to Russian, ensuring that the Gallucci girl and her friends wouldn't understand. "What's the damage?"

"*Fuck* the damage," Ruslan returned in the same tongue. "She needs to leave. Now. I have enough problems without having to worry about who else is going to show up at my door looking for her."

He had a valid point. There was a reason for the lines that divided their two organizations, and Kaz didn't doubt that she knew where those boundaries lay—she was the only daughter of Alberto Gallucci after all. There was no doubt that the Italian boss wouldn't look too kindly on his daughter and Kaz being in the same room together.

Glancing over at her, he had to wonder if that was what she'd wanted by coming here tonight. There was always the chance that she hadn't known who this club belonged to, but what were the odds of that?

And if she did … well that made her a little more intriguing to him. It made him wonder what other lines she was willing to cross.

"Don't worry, brother." Clearing his throat, Kaz switched back to English. "Nathaniel is going to take you ..." He gestured to the girl with the bleeding arm who was actively scowling at him.

"Nicole," Violet supplied quietly.

"Right. Nathaniel is taking you to the hospital."

Before Kaz could go on, Violet interrupted him. "We don't—"

He silenced her with a look and whatever she'd thought to say, she swallowed it back. "Ruslan, get the other one home."

The one needing the stitches—Nicole—looked to Violet then, an emotion in her eyes that Kaz couldn't read, but he didn't expect an answer from her, he waited for the Gallucci girl to explain.

"That's unnecessary. Like I said, we can catch a cab."

Now it was Kaz's turn to scowl. "That's not how we work. Take a look," he said pointing to her friend. "She can barely hold her head up. Do you really want her out in a cab where she can't protect herself? My brother wouldn't touch her."

He waited for another argument, or at least another excuse, but when she remained quiet, he went on. "Address."

Hesitantly, as though it was being forced out of her, Violet rattled it off. Kaz nodded to Ruslan, giving him the go ahead. He didn't argue, but he did send Kaz a look before he helped the girl to her feet and called Nathaniel for Nicole.

When it was just Kaz and Violet left in the office, he studied her, admiring the way she kept her chin tilted up, as though she was looking down her nose at him though he was a good few inches taller.

She was a pretty girl, beautiful really, with wide expressive eyes a shade of green that lightened toward the pupils. With a dainty nose, and pouty lips that were currently turned down at the corners, she was perfectly fine with letting her irritation show. Blonde hair that looked soft to the touch tumbled down around her shoulders in waves, and if not for the fact that he knew the legacy she came from, he might have thought her benign.

But looks were deceiving. He knew that better than anyone. Kaz hadn't been sure, not at first. He hadn't anticipated anything more than to find three drunken girls way over their heads waiting in his brother's office. The last thing he had expected, or even wanted, was Violet Gallucci standing there staring him down.

"And me?" she asked breaking the silence stretching between them.

Pulling his keys from his pocket, he held them up for her to see. "Looks like we're taking a ride to Manhattan."

Somehow, in the span of a little more than thirty minutes, Violet's night had turned to shit in the worst way. This was supposed to be her night, the one where she could be free, forget about the carefully controlled life she lived, but not anymore.

Not when she was about to climb into a car with the one person she knew she *really* shouldn't be around. But what other choice did she have? It was only a matter of time before her father found out where she had been, especially with Nicole on her way to the hospital.

The man who'd walked right in and taken charge was leading the way out the back and around the side of the building toward a monstrosity of a car that was parked there. While she might not have known much about cars, she could tell that this one was expensive just off the brand alone.

She might not have liked *him*, but his car was another story.

The lights flashed as he unlocked the door, and though she had expected him to climb into the driver's seat, he surprised her as he came to her side first and opened the door, gesturing for her to climb in with a tilt of his head. It was unexpected because she hadn't thought of him as a gentleman, not in the slightest.

When she was safely inside, and he'd closed the door, rounding the front of his side, she took in the sleek interior. All black leather, chrome detailing, and while it was only a two-seater, there was plenty of space to stretch her legs out.

There was a moment as he climbed in—inserting the key and starting it up, the blue lights of the dash cutting through the darkness—that she became all too aware just who she was seated beside.

And that she didn't really know him at all.

"It's a good hour and a half, maybe a little more, of a drive back to Manhattan," he said, his tone gruff. "Settle in."

Violet tossed him a look from the side, admiring his profile. "You seem to know a lot about me, but I don't know a thing about you."

He flashed a smile—white teeth and sinful in a blink.

"Shouldn't that be something you learn before you get into a car with a man?" he asked.

"You didn't give me a choice."

"You had a choice."

Violet's brow furrowed. "I don't think so."

Not the way it played out, anyway.

"You did," he assured, never taking his gaze off the windshield as he pulled the vehicle out onto the road. "That choice, Violet, came for you when you came this deep into Brooklyn and made your way to Coney."

Well, then …

Violet looked away when he cut her with a hard look. "I wasn't doing anything wrong."

"Yes, you were."

"No, I—"

"How old are you now, about twenty-one, yes?"

Violet blinked.

He knew her name.

Her age.

That she lived in Manhattan without even asking.

He *knew*.

She ignored the drip of panic slicing through her middle. Despite the darkness that colored up his aura, he didn't scream entirely bad to her.

And Violet knew bad.

"Turned twenty-one today," she admitted.

His hands tightened around the steering wheel, drawing her attention to his tattoos again. It was only when he spoke that she finally tore her gaze away from the spider and its intricate web.

"I am sure there are far more places in Manhattan or Brooklyn for you to enjoy your birthday, other than my brother's club," he said. "No doubt, your father has made it perfectly clear where you are and are not allowed to go in New York, Violet."

She liked the sound of his voice, and the way his r's rolled a little harder than his brother's had back at the club.

But she really liked the way he said her name. It came out a little differently than how most people said it. Instead of just the "i" following the "v" in her name, he said with a hard "o" following the "v".

She shouldn't have liked it at all, but she did.

Violet chewed on her inner cheek. "It's not fair that you know my name, but I don't know yours."

"You know it," he said, smiling in that way of his again. "But I'll remind you."

He held out a hand, palm up, while keeping his other hand firmly on the wheel. Violet glanced between his hand and his face, unsure of what he wanted her to do.

"Shake politely like you've been taught," he urged.

She glowered at him. "No, thanks. Only civilized people shake hands."

He cocked a brow. "And what does that make me, a savage?"

Violet couldn't have missed the heat in his tone even if she tried. Deciding she had pushed her luck enough for one night, she slid her smaller hand into his waiting palm, and ignored the way the heat of his rougher skin seemed to siphon straight into her smoother flesh.

His fingers circled around her hand before she thought better of touching the man, and squeezed just hard enough to make her look up at him.

"A savage man—one not like me—wouldn't have bothered to get you inside a car, *krasivaya*," he said, his timber dropping to a lower note. "He would have done what he wanted when he had you alone in an office."

Violet tried to tug her hand out of his grasp, but he held tight.

"Kazimir Markovic," he said, squeezing her fingers once more. "But I prefer Kaz. It's very nice to meet you again, Violet Gallucci."

Finally, he released her hand. Violet sat back in the seat fast, confused.

"Again?" she asked.

Kazimir—Kaz, he'd said—resumed driving like nothing had happened. "We met once, a long time ago."

Violet didn't remember that at all.

"When?"

"A long time ago," Kaz repeated quietly. "You were helping me to find the sun that day, if I remember correctly."

He was talking in gibberish.

Violet was sure of it.

Then, she had a more pressing realization. It settled hard in her gut, thick and heavy. She knew the surname Kaz mentioned only because of who she was, and who she was supposed to stay away from. Occasionally, that name was whispered between men at her father's dinner table, but never discussed for very long.

"Markovic?" she asked. "Like the ... Brighton Beach Markovic family?"

She thought better of saying Russian mafia, but just barely.

Kaz didn't take his gaze off the road as he chuckled. "Ah, she finally understands."

"Answer my damn question."

"We prefer to call it Little Odessa," he said. "But yes, one and the same."

Oh, God.

Violet went from being pretty sure she had fucked up, to knowing she was in such deep shit there would be no digging her way out of it.

"Drop me off at the next intersection," she said quietly.

Kaz laughed. "What?"

"I can't be in this car. So you need to let me out so I can call a cab and go home."

"No," he said simply.

Violet's mouth popped open. "No?"

"That's what I said, Violet. No. You made your way down to Coney, knowing that you shouldn't be there, and now I'm going to make sure you make your way back to Manhattan and you stay there."

Her father was going to *kill* her.

Violet's frustration boiled over in a slew of words. "How do you even know where I *live*? Do you realize how creepy that is?"

Were the Russians watching her or something?

Her family?

Did her father know?

For a brief moment, Kaz's indifferent, handsome mask cracked and he frowned. "I am not so different from you, Violet, despite the culture shock."

"Can you stop talking me in circles for five fucking seconds?"

"You're awfully combative for a woman who grew up in the house of an Italian mafia boss," he said.

Violet glared. "My father didn't raise a doormat."

"But I suspect he did raise a lady."

Ouch.

Point taken.

Violet tampered her rudeness for a second. "What did you mean when you said that you're not so different from me?"

Kaz tipped his head in her direction, and a small smile played at the corner of his lips. "I know where I should and should not be going, Violet. I grew up being told where it was safe to play, so to speak. I don't suspect your raising was much different, which is why finding you on Coney Island was such a shock."

"I know what they say about Coney," she mumbled. "It's nobody's land."

"Maybe so, but the fact remains, it's too close to Odessa."

Violet didn't bother to argue. She knew he was right.

"But that still doesn't explain why you know where I live," she pointed out.

"Quick girl," he murmured.

Violet ignored the way that sounded like he was praising her. "So explain."

"If there are places I am not allowed to go being who I am, then there are reasons for those rules."

Reasons being people.

She understood his unspoken words.

"It took me a second to recognize you," Kaz added, "but you can't exactly hide who you are to someone who makes it his business to know all that he can about a certain family that doesn't like us all that much."

"What, like safety?" she asked.

"If you want to look at it like that. Let's put it this way, Violet. There are places that I can go but I know I'm toeing a line. Then there are places I can go and while it's probably safe, I still shouldn't be there. And then there are other places, like Manhattan, where it's a goddamn death sentence."

Oh.

The territory lines had never quite been explained to her in that way before.

Maybe if they had, she wouldn't have went down to Coney Island.

"I still think you should drop me off and let me grab a cab," she said. "To be safe and all that."

Kaz smirked, shaking his head. "No."

Violet just stared at him. "Even after what you just said?"

"Even after that," he confirmed.

"Why?"

"Because I'm not that bad of a guy, even for a Russian," he said with a grin, "and I was taught that every lady deserves to be treated like one. Even if she isn't being a very nice lady."

Violet decided after that statement to sit still, be quiet, and hope the rest of the hour-and–a-half-long drive went by as smoothly as possible. It was probably unlikely that her father wouldn't somehow find out where she had been, but maybe—just maybe—she could keep Kaz and the fact that he drove her home a secret.

Maybe.

When they finally did get into Manhattan, Violet didn't have to say a thing about where she lived. Kaz navigated the streets like he had done it a hundred times before.

If she had to guess, she would say he had spent time where he wasn't supposed to.

Just like her.

Park Avenue was a great deal quieter in the middle of the night than it was during the day. There was still traffic, but it wasn't nearly as bad as it usually was. Besides the occasional passerby, the street was practically empty.

Violet didn't say a thing when the car rolled to a stop in front of the apartment building that belonged to her father. The fifteen-level complex held several condos of varying size and expense. It was older, the exterior lending credence to a time when gold detailing and warm shades were all the rage. Hers was one of the biggest and most costly, and at the very top. Her parents had used it on and off for years, but once she starting taking classes at Columbia, they handed the keys over to her to make travel easier.

"Thank you," Violet said.

Kaz smiled. "Don't say a thing about it."

"Quite literally, huh?"

His laughter came out dark and rich.

Violet chose that moment to get out of the car before her errant, half-drunk thoughts might notice something else about the man she found attractive.

Wasn't his appearance, attitude, and charm enough?

"Until the next time," Kaz murmured from inside the vehicle.

Violet's hand tightened around the passenger door. "There won't be a next time."

She heard the smirk in his tone when he replied, "There wasn't supposed to be a next time after the first time we met, and look how well that turned out for us both."

Violet blinked awake at the hard hammering coming from her left side. At first, she thought it was the throbbing in her head that was making all the noise, but she quickly figured out it wasn't.

Right about the time her brother cursed from outside her bedroom door.

"*Cazzo Cristo.* Violet, I swear to *Dio*. Get your ass out of that bed before I come in there and force you out of it."

Violet pushed up from her pillow using one hand, but everything swam in her vision and the massive beating her head seemed to be taking increased enough to make her sick. She dropped right back down to the bed with a groan, burying her face into the pillow.

"Go away, Carmine," Violet grumbled.

"Oh, good. You're up."

Her brother's snarky, arrogant self was not what Violet wanted to deal with first thing in the fucking morning. Wait—was it even morning? She couldn't tell what with the way the light coming in from the window seemed to burn the eyeballs right out of her skull.

Hangovers were the devil.

"Violet, stop making me stand out here like a fool," Carmine barked.

Violet glared at the bedroom door, willing her brother away. She turned over in the bed, hoping her silence and lack of response would make him think she had gone back to sleep.

It didn't work.

He started banging again.

Louder.

"Oh, my God," Violet mumbled. "Stop, Carmine."

"I will if you get up."

But getting up meant being sick and dizzy.

The bed was better.

"No deal," she said loud enough for her brother to hear. "And no one said you could just come into my condo whenever the hell you wanted, asshole. That's not why Daddy gave you a key."

Carmine scoffed. "That is exactly why he gave me a key, princess. Get up, or I will open this door up myself. You have exactly three minutes, Violet. Don't test me. I will break it down."

Violet briefly considered ignoring her brother. Carmine was a lot more mouth than he was action, and he wasn't allowed to be a dick without some kind of good reason. She wondered why he was even there at her place as she crawled out of bed with enough slowness to rival a snail.

Her mouth was dry, but she quickly found the glass of water and two Tylenol tablets she had left sitting on her bedside table the night before. Popping the pills back, she chugged half of the room-temperature water before setting it back down.

Maybe it was the placebo effect of having taken something, but her headache lessened almost instantly. Glancing down at herself, Violet realized she had managed to put something appropriate on before falling into bed.

Her brother started pounding on the door again.

"Are you up?" he asked loudly.

Violet's irritation shot up another few notches. Enough to make her stomp over to the bedroom door, unlock it, and swing it open regardless of her very hungover, less-than-perfect appearance.

"Listen, you stupid ass. You don't get to come into my place this early in the damn morning demanding that I—"

Carmine cocked a brow, shutting Violet's rant up instantly. The fact that there wasn't even a hint of amusement on his features only made Violet's stomach roll a little more.

And it wasn't from the alcohol she drank the night before.

Her brother was pissed. She could see it in the way his familiar brown eyes darkened as he looked her over.

"You look like shit," Carmine said.

Violet balled her hands into fists. "I went out last night for my birthday."

Her makeup was probably a mess, and she was scared to touch her hair for fear she might feel a rat's nest going on up there.

"How much did you drink?" he asked.

"A bit, Carmine. Why, is that a problem? Because you drink yourself nearly to death every damned weekend."

Carmine's gaze narrowed. "Maybe I do, but I sure as fuck don't go down to Coney Island when I do it."

Fuck.

The events from the night before flooded Violet's memories. Her friends, their stupid choice to go to the hottest new club in a place where they shouldn't be, and the events that followed.

Kaz.

More than anything else, she thought about Kaz.

Violet realized her silence was not what her brother was looking for, so she tried a different approach. "How mad is Daddy at me?"

Carmine sneered. "He's spitting bullets."

Shit.

"I just wanted to have a little fun," she tried to say. "I didn't go into Brighton Beach, I promise."

"No, but you did leave your friends with a bunch of Russians to take them home, and then skipped out with another Russian yourself," Carmine said.

How did her brother know all of that?

"And both Nicole's and Amelia's fathers are ready to …" Carmine trailed off, scowling. "Never mind, let's go. Dad wants you in Amityville before nine."

Violet's throat felt like someone was squeezing it. "Just let me take a shower and get dressed."

"No, you can come like that."

She glanced down at her sleep pants and too-large sweater ensemble. Not to mention, she knew her face and hair was a mess.

"Carmine, I am not going out on Park Avenue looking like—"

"You spent the whole night partying?" her brother interrupted.

So this was how he wanted to play that game, huh?

"Daddy will have a fit if I show up to the mansion looking like this," Violet warned.

Her father was a stickler for appearances. From very young in her teenaged years, Violet had been taught what foundation was for and just how to use a makeup brush. Clothing had to be the latest styles, and she needed to look the part of her father's daughter each and every time she stepped out of her condo.

No matter what.

"Actually," Carmine drawled, still sneering, "he thought this might be a good lesson for you."

"What?"

"A good lesson. Shaming him with your behavior also means you're shaming yourself, after all. Get your coat, sis."

The Gallucci mansion had never felt quite as foreboding to Violet as it did when her brother parked his Mercedes in the driveway. She recognized the other vehicles in the circular driveway as belonging to her parents, and another white Lexus that belonged to Nicole's father, Christian, who was also her father's consigliere and his personal doctor.

Her nerves picked up a notch when her brother turned off the car and stepped out without a word, slamming the driver's door behind him. He likely knew that Violet would follow behind when she was ready to face the music. After all, with a protective iron gate behind them closing, there was no where she could go unless her father let her back out.

Violet pulled down the visor and stared at her reflection in the mirror. Embarrassment bubbled through her as she took in her messy, disheveled appearance. Her makeup was smeared, she needed a fucking toothbrush, and her hair looked like it had been put through more than one round of ...

She shook her head, wanting to get away from all that.

As quickly as she could, with nothing but her fingertips to work with, she tried to soothe the waves of her hair enough to be presentable and wipe the bits of smeared makeup away from under her eyes and around her mouth. It didn't help all that much.

Fuck Carmine for not letting her make her face and hair more presentable.

Maybe she finally understood her father's goal when he demanded she feel the shame she had caused him by her reckless actions. It still pissed her off.

Getting out of the car, Violet hugged her bomber jacket a little tighter to keep out the chill of the wind. She kept her head down as she walked across the large driveway and up the intricate marble entryway of her parents' four-level, two-wing mansion.

The front door was already open.

Inviting, almost.

Violet just wanted to turn around and bolt.

The cold air forced her inside where she knew was warm. Violet was greeted by a long, empty hallway that led into spiral staircase wrapping around the entrance of the mansion. The stairs separated off into one of two wings. She thought for sure that her father would be waiting to meet her, but not even her mother was there.

And her brother had already disappeared.

Violet took her time to remove her shoes and coat, before putting them away in the large closet with the rest of the outerwear. She walked slowly through the ground level of the mansion, finding the large kitchen and dining room empty, as well as the entertainment room and living room.

If her father wasn't waiting for her in one of those rooms, then she knew exactly where he was.

His office.

That didn't bode well for her at all.

Violet decided not to put seeing her father off for any longer than was necessary. It was only drawing out the inevitable bitch-fest he was sure to level on her. Better to get it done and over with so she could get back was to her condo and sleep this awful day off.

It was only when Violet was up onto the third floor of the second wing and standing outside of the large oak doors that led into her father's office did she realize how much trouble she was really in.

His office was closed.

Which meant closed to her.

Alberto, in all of her twenty-one years, had never once closed his office doors to her when he called upon Violet for something. A thick lump lodged in her throat as she stared at the doors, knowing what her father wanted her to do.

Knock.

Wait.

Enter only at his will and direction.

Not like she was his daughter, who could come in any time and was always welcome, but instead, like one of his men who had to be deemed worthy enough to be seen.

It was like a punch to her gut.

Violet had always been her father's little girl, even when she was an unruly child. Alberto often proclaimed her to be his favorite between his two children, even if he did so in a joking manner. He spoiled her with anything and everything she asked for.

He had never shunned her.

Not like this.

Violet took a deep breath, hoping it would calm her nerves. She again smoothed out her hair and swiped her thumbs under her eyes. Stepping forward, she raised her hand and knocked on the oak doors hard enough that she knew it would be heard within.

Silence answered her knock.

She didn't knock again. Instead, she waited like she knew her father expected her to do. Her back straightened a little more as minutes ticked by, and tears started to well in the corners of her eyes when yet another couple minutes passed in total silence.

Alberto's message was clear: she was not worthy of his time or attention, not yet.

Her father's lesson was being learned, if the shame compounding in her heart was any indication.

By the time the doors finally opened to expose her mother, Andrea, standing behind them, Violet had been left waiting for fifteen long minutes.

Yeah, she had counted.

"Ma," she greeted quietly.

Andrea raised a perfectly manicured eyebrow as she took in her daughter's appearance. Wearing one of her signature blue dresses that she personally designed, her mother was the picture of beauty and grace. If only Andrea's inner self reflected what she portrayed on the outside. Violet refused to let her mother's silent disapproval add to the shame she was already feeling.

"Violet," Andrea said smoothly. "Your father is waiting inside."

Not saying anything else, Andrea moved gracefully out of the office, leaving the doors opened behind her. She didn't even glance over her shoulder back at Violet as she glided down the hallway toward her own private office.

Violet hesitated at the entrance of her father's office, unsure and wary in her heart.

Alberto quickly remedied that when he boomed, "Do not keep me waiting a second longer, Violet."

She took the three steps needed to enter the office, trying to hold her head high at the same time. Inside, she found her father sitting behind the large, cherry oak desk that dominated the room. He sat in his high-back, black leather office chair. Behind him, a painting of her grandfather rested proudly. In the painting, Alberto Sr. drank from a glass of cognac, barely an emotion on his face, as he stared the person painting him down.

He looked exactly like her father did at that very moment while Alberto stared her down.

Alberto's spacious office was decorated in warm, earthy tones with bookshelves lining one entire wall from floor to ceiling. A sitting area with a leather loveseat and matching chairs sat in front of a floor to ceiling window that nearly covered another wall and overlooked the entire front of the property.

As a child, her father's office had always been a safe place for Violet. She would hide under his desk as he made phone calls or shuffled through papers. She remembered being about six and finding him counting stacks of money; he gave her one so she could count, too.

The office did not feel like that safe place today.

Sitting on the loveseat were her brother and her father's consigliere, Christian. While her brother was looking over his phone in his hand, Christian was scowling into his glass of whiskey.

"How do you feel?" her father asked.

Violet found her father's brown stare to be cold and hard as he looked her up and down, taking in the mess she clearly was. Swallowing hard, she felt the wetness prickle at her eyes again, and she dropped her father's stare.

"Awful," she admitted.

"Fifteen minutes was long enough, I suspect," Alberto noted. "You have another five to explain exactly what happened last night that led you, Nicole, and Amelia down to Coney Island where you are well aware you are not permitted to go."

Violet didn't even hesitate to start talking like her father wanted. Alberto's tone brokered no room for argument, and when he was in that sort of mood, it was not time to start testing her father's limits. As it was, she had pushed them enough.

"After we had dinner here for my birthday, we went back to my place," Violet said.

"And?" her father pressed.

"Amelia—"

Alberto held up a hand, stopping her.

"What?" she dared to ask.

"Do not put blame on one of those girls, Violet. Do not tell me that they convinced you to do something you already knew was wrong. Years, *ragazza*. I have explicitly forbade you for *years* from entering the lower part of Brooklyn. And if, for one second, you say it was someone else's fault that you went down there—knowing that you could have refused and chosen a venue I approved of—then we're going to have a problem."

Violet corrected herself immediately. This was not the man she was used to. Only a handful of times in her life had she come face to face with this man.

He wasn't Alberto Gallucci, her father.

No, he was Alberto Gallucci, Cosa Nostra Don.

"We decided to go to the club in Coney," Violet said quietly. "It's a new place. Everyone is talking about it. We didn't know it was owned by the Russians. I swear, Daddy—"

Again, Alberto held up a hand. This time, he stood slowly from his desk, keeping his sharp, cold brown eyes on her all the while. Violet flinched away from her father when he walked around his desk and came a little closer to her. Even when she was an unruly child, he never raised a hand to her.

She shouldn't be afraid of him.

But right then? Yeah, she was.

"Violet," Alberto said harshly, coming close enough to grab her chin and force her head up. "You will look at me right now while we're speaking. Do you understand that?"

She nodded.

"Continue," he ordered.

"We took a cab because we knew we were going to be drinking. And after we had been there a while, something happened with Amelia. Like, somebody spiked her drink and we were trying to get out to come home."

Alberto pursed his lips, clearly unhappy. He released her chin, and Violet immediately put her head back down. "I already know what came after that, thanks to both Nicole and Amelia."

"She's okay?" Violet asked.

She hadn't even gotten the chance to call her friend that morning, and all of her calls from the night before had gone completely unanswered.

"Do you care?" Alberto asked, seemingly calm. "Because when you allowed your friends to be toted off by strange men—"

"I wasn't exactly given a choice," she interrupted softly.

Alberto scowled. "Get out of my office right now."

Violet's head snapped up. "What?"

Her father wasn't looking at her. He was waving at the two men sitting on the loveseat. "Out, I said! *Adesso, stoltos!*"

Carmine and Christian discarded their glasses on the black coffee table and left the office without needing to be told again. Once Violet was alone with her father, the sickness in her stomach only seemed to increase even more.

"I am so sorry, Daddy," she said.

"You are a mess," Alberto murmured.

Violet cringed. "I know."

"I have never been so disappointed or more embarrassed by you than I am today, Violet."

46

"I'm sorry. We didn't know, Daddy."

Alberto tipped her chin up again with a softer touch than the first time. "You didn't need to know, *dolcezza*. You shouldn't have been down there in the first place. As you already know."

"You're right."

"Of course I am." Alberto sighed, eyeing her smeared makeup. His thumb swept the corner of her mouth like he wanted to will the smudge of lipstick there away. "And now, because of your actions, I have to answer to men who are beneath me for their daughters' injuries and other problems."

Violet's brow furrowed. "But Nicole and Amelia wanted to go. I didn't force them."

Alberto shrugged. "You seem to forget your place in my life, Violet. You're my daughter, and when you are with other daughters of made men, their behavior is reflected from yours. Not the other way around. You will always be the one responsible because you, above anyone else, were raised far better."

"I'm sorry," she said again.

"I don't doubt that." Alberto let go of her, taking a step back. "The Russian just dropped you off and nothing else, right?"

"*Si.*"

"Such a shame," he muttered low.

Violet blinked away more prickling tears caused by the disappointment she knew her father felt.

"It won't happen again," she said.

"I should hope not." Alberto flicked a wrist at the oak doors. "Go to your old room and find something suitable to wear. Fix your face and your hair before you leave this house again. Apologize to your mother for your appearance and behavior."

"Okay."

Was he finally done?

While it might not seem like her father had done a lot to punish her, it was the emotional impact that hurt Violet the most.

"You're forgiven," Alberto murmured softly. "But I won't forget this, *topina.*"

Violet sucked in a hard breath, not knowing what to say.

"You have never given me a reason to distrust you before," her father continued sadly. "And this was not a good way to start testing my limits with you. I overlook your weekends at the clubs, and your sometimes boyfriends that I don't approve of because I knew you are too smart to end up in a bad situation or one that might shame our family and my legacy."

God.

"It won't happen again," Violet repeated, stronger the second time.

Her voice was still fucking weak.

"You've never given me a reason," Alberto said, "until last night."

"Are you out of your fucking mind?" Vasily demanded.

Kaz had barely had the phone to his ear before his father's voice was raging in his ear. Groaning as he rolled over, he rubbed his tired eyes, casting his mind back to the day before to remember what he had done to warrant a pissed off phone call this early in the morning.

There was Marcus—no one gave a shit about Marcus—and he'd already told Vasily about that, then there was the club, his chat with Ruslan, and then …

Shit, right.

Violet Gallucci.

He hadn't forgotten her. How could he when the smell of her had lingered in his car even after he'd dropped her off? But he had put it out of his mind.

It was inevitable that Vasily was going to find out, nothing stayed hidden forever, but he hadn't thought he'd learn—Kaz glanced over at the clock on his bedside table, reading the time—before nine in the damn morning.

"Is this where I pretend like I don't know what you're talking about?"

Kaz almost laughed as Vasily spat curses, but even as he found humor in a situation that really wasn't funny at all, a part of him knew that there was a problem. This wouldn't be the first time he had done something his father hadn't approved of, not even the second, but those times had never warranted a phone call. His silent displeasure, sure.

"My house, one hour."

With that parting demand, Vasily hung up—he never was good with the proper way in ending a conversation.

Throwing the covers off, Kaz swung his legs off the bed, getting up to his feet as he headed toward the en suite bathroom on the other side of his room. With a flick of his wrist, he had the multiple showerheads turned on, raining water from the tiled ceiling.

He didn't bother waiting for the water to heat before stripping out of his boxer-briefs and climbing in, letting the coldness wake him up further as he scrubbed a hand down his face, feeling the whiskers covering his jaw.

Grabbing the soap, he bathed quickly, deciding that it was probably best not to keep Vasily waiting. If he had to guess, the man was a little more than pissed off, and his tardiness would only make it worse.

It wasn't like Kaz hadn't known that by taking the Gallucci girl home—fuck, even just talking to her—there would be a problem. He knew better. But that hadn't stopped him from getting her in his car and taking off. Sure, it was innocent, definitely not something worth starting a war over, but even he could see the implications of his actions.

Like waving a red flag in front of a bull.

Back out again, Kaz toweled off, next rubbing it through his hair before he tossed it on the counter and headed into his closet. And despite his lackluster attitude in terms of everything else in his life, there was one thing that Kaz definitely cared about.

His attire.

A lot could be said about a man that broke the law for a living, but more could be said about one that made sure he looked good while doing it.

He chose a black-on-black ensemble—seemed appropriate—before he dressed and ran his fingers through his hair to push it back out of his face. Heading back into his bedroom, he grabbed the Beretta M9 he kept beneath his pillow, holstering it at his back, then smoothing his jacket over it.

Grabbing his keys, he was out of his place and heading down Oceana Drive in no time. The drive to Vasily's beachfront mansion was only a fifteen-minute drive away, twenty-five if there was traffic, a distance that felt far too short for Kaz most days.

The house he was driving to hadn't been the only residence in Little Odessa that Kaz lived in. Before, they—he, his parents, and siblings—lived in a more modest two-story a little ways away. Vasily had moved the family after Kaz's eleventh birthday, and some months after Vasily had become the new *Pakhan*.

As he turned onto 296 West End Avenue, typing in the code to get through the gated entry, Kaz could already see the fleet of cars parked in the driveway. Most were of his father's collection—all luxury, but none as bold as Kaz's Porsche—and one, he knew, belonged to his father's attorney, Gerald Tansky. Since the man got paid even if he was only stopping by, Kaz had to wonder why he was there.

Pulling around, he parked a good distance away from the other vehicles, because family or not, if you scratched his car, he'd be pissed. Exiting, he dug his hands into his pockets as he headed for the front door, checking his surroundings as he always did before raising his fist to knock. He took a step back, waiting, listening to the soft click of heels as they neared the door. His smile, a genuine one this time, was already curling his lips before she even had the door open.

Swathed in a peach-colored dress that ended at her knees, Irina Markovic looked every bit of the housewife that she was. Never a hair out of place, the brown strands were twisted into a knot at the nape of her neck, showing off the simple diamond earrings adorning her ears.

"Kazimir," she said warmly, already reaching to draw him into her embrace.

When his father called him that, it annoyed him, but he never minded from her. "*Privyet*, Mama," he spoke softly, pressing a quick kiss to her cheek. "How are you?"

"Very well. Your father is waiting for you in the kitchen."

He could tell just by the look on her face that Vasily was definitely angry with him and she was curious as to why, but she would never come right out and ask. She followed the rules in that way.

Waiting at her side as she closed and turned the locks, he figured since he was there, he didn't have to rush. He was on time after all.

"How are you, Kazimir? You look tired," she said looking up at him, even in her heels, as they headed for the kitchen.

"Fine, Mama. It was just a long night." And an early morning, but he didn't bother mentioning that. To say he was not a morning person was an understatement. Thankfully, a lot of his business could be done at night.

"And your brother, how is he?"

This question was asked softly, so low that Kaz knew the question was meant only for him to hear, and that fact annoyed him. Not because she was asking the question at all, but because she felt she had to sneak to do it.

"Good."

"You'll watch after him, yes?" she asked reaching for his hand, squeezing it lightly.

Ruslan didn't need looking after, plus he was the oldest, but because she rarely saw him, she made this request whenever Kaz came around. Since she couldn't dote on Ruslan, she made sure at the very least, Kaz watched out for him. Sometimes, Kaz felt like he was the oldest.

"Of course, I—"

"Kazimir, get in here!" Vasily called out, his voice echoing.

The booming sound might have been enough to frighten a lesser man, but Kaz merely rolled his eyes, looking back down to his mother, who was smiling apologetically.

51

"Go on, you don't want to keep him waiting."

As he bent at the waist, giving her a chance to kiss his cheek and wipe away the trace of lipstick before she disappeared around the corner, she made herself scarce for their talk. Kaz hardened himself as he always did, heading into the lion's den.

The kitchen was a cavernous space, made that way after his mother had made the request. Vasily, who loved to dote on his wife, gave her exactly what she asked for. Bay windows made up one wall, allowing an unobstructed view to the beach a mere walking distance from the house. The sunlight shining in through them made the white cabinetry seem brighter, and the gray marbled flooring stand out more.

Gerald was seated at the dining table, a newspaper in hand as he read the front page, acting oblivious to Kaz's appearance. Vasily, on the other hand, was glaring at Kaz from his position behind the island, a tumbler filled with amber liquid in his hand.

Unlike Kaz who was dressed in all black, Vasily was dressed in a pin-striped suit, a blood-red shirt beneath it, with a matching handkerchief in the breast pocket of his jacket. His shirt was unbuttoned at the collar, revealing a delicate gold chain that hung around his neck. His once-dark hair was mostly gray now, and thinning in the middle, but he kept it styled where one could hardly tell.

"A little early for spirits, no?" Kaz asked, careful to keep his tone as respectful as possible.

"With the shit you pulled last night," Vasily started. "I could be drinking from a bottle." Downing his drink, in one swallow, he set the glass on the counter. "Tell me, what were you thinking?"

It was scary, how quickly Vasily went from angry to calm in a couple of seconds. Kaz could still remember a time when that worried him, when he had no idea what to expect, but now he was older, and his father's anger didn't faze him as much.

"They—those girls—were in the wrong place."

"You knew better," Vasily said after a moment, already reaching for the carafe of Brandy resting behind him on the marble countertop. "You could have dropped that girl off the second you were out of our territory."

Kaz took a seat at the bar, unbuttoning his jacket as he did. "I thought it best to make sure they got home safely, as opposed to letting them leave Odessa where we couldn't guarantee that."

His father knew what he meant, and that he was right, even if he didn't voice it. Had they taken a cab home—as Violet was so adamant they should have done—and something were to have happened to them on that trip home, the Markovics would have been blamed. It was their territory after all, and nothing happened without their knowledge.

And for whatever reason, the idea of Violet Gallucci getting hurt didn't sit well with him.

"Even so, you have created a problem for us." Vasily poured two fingers, and instead of throwing this one back as well, he sipped. "Alberto Gallucci called me this morning."

It had been a while since Vasily uttered that name. While the two were more ... neutral toward each other than Gavrill and Alberto had been, that didn't mean the two would ever do business together.

"Oh?"

"Apparently that car of yours was seen leaving a building on Park Avenue." Vasily gave him a dry look. "I don't think I have to mention *whose* building it belonged to, no?"

"Like I said, I made sure the Gallucci girl got home safely. Nothing more."

"And the other two? Their fathers were not too pleased either."

Kaz tapped his index finger against the marble. "Ruslan would—"

Vasily made a noise that could be described as a mix between a grunt and a snort, a sneer working its way onto his face.

Kaz, who was doing his best to keep a level head, went from zero to sixty in a moment, that familiar rage he welcomed like an old friend coming to life inside of him. His hand clenched, his body grew tense. There were some things he was willing to put up with from his father.

His need to dominate any room he walked in—Kaz gave him that. He was the *Pakhan* after all, it was his due.

The snide comments made to and about Kaz—again, Vasily was the boss—but more than anything, Kaz didn't give a shit.

But one thing that he had never been able to stand was the blatant disrespect Vasily always showed whenever Ruslan's name was brought up.

"Careful," Kaz said before he could check the impulse, and even if he'd been able to, he didn't think he would have restrained himself.

With the command resting between them, Vasily paused—the glass he was bringing to his lips suspended in the air—his gaze moving to Kaz. Even Gerald looked up from his reading, where he was acting as though he was not listening to the conversation.

That was the thing about having one's father as the boss as well. The lines blurred as to which persona you got. It was one thing for Kaz to speak out of turn to his father. Though still disrespectful, it could be excused. But to speak to a *Pakhan* as though he were equal, that was an offense not taken lightly. It didn't matter that Vasily's vocalized response was one of a father's feelings toward his son, the discussion at hand was between a boss and his soldier.

Placing his glass back on the counter, Vasily laid both hands down, leaning his weight into them as he narrowed cold eyes on Kaz. His displeasure bled out of him. "What did you say?"

Kaz had a choice, everyone always had a choice, just as he'd told Violet last night. He could repeat himself, risk his father's wrath, or he could bite his tongue and stay silent. Knowing his mother was still somewhere in the house, Kaz chose the latter.

"Nothing." It took a lot for him to even voice that—Kaz wasn't usually one to back down from a fight.

A heartbeat's time. Two. Then, Vasily's shoulders relaxed as he straightened. "Finish what you were saying."

"Ruslan took one home." Kaz didn't remember the girl's name, or had he even bothered to find out? "And Nathaniel took the other to the hospital. Undoubtedly, you already know this. So, instead of wasting time on what we already know, how about you tell me the real reason you called me here."

Vasily frowned. "Why?"

"Why what?"

"Why was any of that necessary?" Vasily elaborated. "What happened before this?"

Truthfully, Kaz hadn't thought much of what had ultimately caused the girls to be in Ruslan's office. The only thing he remembered hearing was a glass breaking near the bar, and the girls' cries of alarm from where he'd stood with Ruslan.

While his brother had immediately went to help the women, Kaz had lingered behind, making sure the broken glass was cleaned up and that no one else was hurt, *then* he went to see if his brother needed any help with them.

"One had too much to drink, I assume. I didn't see it all."

That did nothing to placate his father, however. He still looked baffled, and a bit annoyed by it all. "You knew better," Vasily said again, shaking his head. "How many times have I told you that Brooklyn is off-limits to you? And that you were to never be around the daughter of Gallucci."

The first he had said so many times that Kaz thought his head would bleed. And the second had been repeated a few times, but not nearly as much as the first. It wasn't as though Kaz had had any interest in Violet before last night. He had never given the girl a second thought.

"Plenty."

"Then don't let it happen again. The last thing I need is Alberto Gallucci giving me shit because you're making moves on that daughter of his."

Kaz sat back with a shrug. "Duly noted."

The front door opened with a crash, the sound of two giggling teenagers breaking up the somber mood that had settled in the kitchen. Just as before, Kaz let down his guard as his two younger sisters, Dina and Nika, came barreling into the kitchen, oblivious to the tension that had just been there.

Of the two, Nika was the more outgoing. Dina let her sister lead, waiting her turn as Nika immediately came over to him and wrapped her arms around him. Getting to his feet, Kaz returned the embrace, reaching to bring Dina into the fold as well.

"Kaz, what are you doing here?" Nika asked, smiling up at him.

"Just visiting," he returned smoothly. "And coming to ask what the two of you wanted for your birthday?"

From the corner of his eye, he could see Vasily nodding.

Nika looked to Dina, and Dina back to her before they both looked to Kaz and said simultaneously, "Clothes."

"There's this new place over on Sixteenth Street," Dina said in a rush, picking up on her sister's excitement. "We've been dying to go, but because Nika is having trouble in school ..."

"Dina!"

"What?" she returned with an arch of her brow. "It's not like he won't find out from Dad."

"But you didn't have to be the one to tell him!"

And there they went, arguing as though there was no one else in the room.

Remembering that their birthday was only two weeks away, reminded Kaz of their party and the conversation he'd had with Ruslan the night before. In the chaos of everything that had gone down, he'd forgotten this, and the fact that Vasily hadn't bothered to send Ruslan an invitation.

What better time to bring it up than right then?

"No worries," he said, interrupting their banter. "I was just talking to Ruslan about your party and—"

Nika gasped, smiling widely. "Is he going to come? Dad said he couldn't get in contact with him."

"Darling," Vasily interjected quickly, coming around the island to stand before them, his eyes gone cold as he stared at Kaz, even as he addressed her. "Ruslan is very busy. I've told you this, no?"

"I'm sure he could make it," Kaz said, making sure to keep the smile on his face. "After all, nothing's more important than family, right?"

Vasily wouldn't deny that, not in front of the girls, and though he was probably boiling with anger, it was his turn to bite his tongue.

"So how about this," Kaz said giving each of them a squeeze. "You give me a time and a place and I'll make sure he's there, even if I have to escort him here myself."

"You're the best, Kaz," Dina said as she and her sister started out of the kitchen, probably in search of Irina. "And we'll text you the name of the store."

"Do it now so you won't forget."

She yelled her affirmation as they disappeared around the same corner Irina had taken earlier, leaving Kaz standing with a newly pissed off father.

Would it ever be any other way?

"You pull that kind of stunt again," Vasily muttered. "I won't be as forgiving."

"Duly noted. We done here? I've got things to take care of." He had fuck-all to take care of, but he was more than ready to get away from Vasily. If they spent too much time together, tempers were bound to flare.

Dismissing him with a wave of his hand, Vasily said, "Get out of my sight."

Kaz was almost to the mouth of the kitchen when Vasily called out to him once more, making him pause and look back.

"Stay away from the Gallucci girl. I mean it."

Offering him a salute and nothing more, Kaz went in search of his mother to say goodbye, knowing that despite his silent agreeance, he couldn't make that guarantee.

Violet kept her head bent down and her hands joined with her friends on both sides. Her father, at the head of the table like always, finished saying grace with his usual solemn thanks and little else. Violet had always thought that when it came to their family, religion was more for show than having actual faith in a higher power that protected them.

After all, her family wasn't exactly what she would call good people.

Well-dressed, sure. Nicely cultured and polite, absolutely. Rich, yes.

Sin was still sin, underneath it all.

"The opening collection for your mother's designs is next week," Nicole said to Violet's left.

Violet reached across the table for a bowl of mixed vegetables to add onto her plate. She didn't respond to Nicole because she hadn't asked her a question, but instead, she had stated the obvious.

"We decided on what we're wearing," Amelia put in.

Nodding, Violet continued filling her plate. Scrapes of utensils echoed in the dining room, along with murmurs from several voices. It was common for her father to have large dinners, and to open his doors to his closest men and their families. Most times, these dinners happened last minute, and Violet would receive a simple text, telling her a time to show up.

Today had been the exception.

Her father sent a car.

Clearly, Alberto was still a little pissed off.

Her stunt, nearly two weeks before, with the club in Coney Island was not being overlooked.

Each time she had tried to sit down and talk to him since it happened, he hadn't seemed to have a word to say back to her.

Actually, he mostly ignored her.

"Okay, what gives?" Nicole asked.

Violet's fork, filled with a cut of prime steak, froze midway to her mouth. "I beg your pardon?"

Amelia sighed to Violet's right. "You've been quiet since we got here. You can't be that pissed off at us, Violet. We didn't do anything that you didn't do."

Violet was still confused as hell. "Again, what?"

"Telling our dads what happened," Nicole supplied.

Ah.

Violet shrugged. "I'm not angry."

"Then why aren't you talking?" Amelia asked.

"Because I don't care about my mother's reveal for her upcoming collection or what anyone wears to it," Violet said.

Yeah, maybe she was a little pissed at her friends, if she thought about it. She understood her father when he explained that she was the one responsible for her friends when they went out because of who she was, but her friends knew better.

And she didn't feel like pretending that they were innocent.

"Wow," Nicole muttered.

Violet frowned, feeling just a little bit guilty. Maybe the girls hadn't done anything that she wouldn't have done if put in their position. And they'd been her friends—since forever.

"There's a shop on Sixteenth Street," Violet said, deciding she didn't want to play the bitchy game with the girls. "Ma mentioned it. Anything she says is good has to be gold, right? Maybe I'll head over there and check it out, see what I can find."

The thought of sitting through another one of her mother's collection reveals was almost revolting, but Violet didn't have much of a choice. Her friends weren't the first to bring it up.

Alberto was.

And since Violet needed to get back in her father's good graces, she would do whatever he wanted. Including spending a day at a place she hated, doing something that bored the shit out of her.

"Want us to come?" Nicole asked.

Even Amelia looked happy at the prospect.

Violet, on the other hand, figured she could probably handle picking out a dress on her own. "Next time? I have a busy week with school, and I'm just going to fit it in sometime in between that."

"If you're sure," Amelia said.

"Yeah. I'm sure."

Thankfully, her friends dropped the topic. Violet's week was actually panning out to be pretty slow. She had some catch-up work to do for the classes she was failing, but that was it. If she could at least get her grade point average just beyond the failing mark, her father wouldn't have such a fit.

That's all she wanted to focus on right now.

Keeping her father happy.

"Of course you wait until the last minute to find a gift."

Kaz didn't bother to dignify that remark with a comment, knowing that his brother would only give him shit, no matter what he said. "I had shit to do."

He didn't bother to mention he knew fuck-all about women's clothing. Sure, he could appreciate a woman in a figure-hugging dress—more so, if he were the one to take it off her—but actively going in search for women's apparel, especially since it was for his younger sisters … well, he was a bit over his head.

He'd been up early that morning, handling business down at the docks, making sure shipments were coming in on time and the right people were compensated for their time. Afterward, he'd made his way out of Little Odessa into the city, heading toward the boutique his sisters favored. He called Ruslan along the way to make sure he knew that after he finished there, he would be on his way to pick him up.

Last week, he had called, letting him know that he'd talked to Vasily, and that he was welcome to attend the party. Kaz hadn't bothered to mention the way he had went about it. Then, Ruslan had seemed to accept him at his word, but now that it was the day of, he had felt the need to call and check in.

"He might have agreed," Ruslan said over the line, "but he's never been one to hold back how he feels."

Kaz was silent for a moment, concentrating on the traffic in front of him. The street was packed tight with cars, making it hard to find a parking spot, and it was only worse for Kaz because his car drew more attention and made people stop and stare. Eventually, after circling around, he found a spot a couple blocks up. Swinging in smoothly, he cut the engine and pulled on a pair of sunglasses before climbing out, and heading down the street.

"Don't worry about Vasily," Kaz said. "He won't make a scene, not in front of the twins."

If there was one thing to be said about Vasily, he cared about his image. While in the privacy of his own home, he was prone to violent outbursts and making sure his thoughts were clear in blatant, brutal honesty, but he was always quite careful when there were others around. At the twins' party, friends from their school, along with a number of their own associates would be in attendance. Vasily had always presented the idea that they were the perfect family. He wasn't going to fuck that up.

No matter if Ruslan showed ...

Even in a city as densely packed as Brooklyn, where celebrities, tourists, and the common person all mingled, Kaz stood out. It might have been his height—six feet, three inches—or the way he presented himself, but people tended to give him a wide berth as he walked, stepping out of his path before he'd even had the chance to get close.

Worked for him.

"Maybe so, but do you remember the last time we were in the same room together?" Ruslan asked.

How could Kaz forget?

There was always a tension when the two Markovic boys were in the presence of their father, if for different reasons. While Vasily would act annoyed by Kaz's antics, he completely ignored Ruslan, going so far as shunning him when he dared speak to the man. Ruslan never voiced his feelings on the matter, not to anyone, and certainly not to Vasily, but Kaz knew his brother.

"You trust me, no?" Kaz tried another tactic, wanting to calm his brother's doubts. "Everything will be fine. And before I forget, what happened with the girl? The one you took home?"

Kaz had already told him about the Gallucci girl, though he did refrain from telling him about the conversation they had in the car—that felt private in a way. He *had* mentioned Vasily's anger about it, and the ensuing warning he'd received later.

"Was no problem," Ruslan responded, probably with a wave of his hand as that was what he usually did. "Had to practically carry the broad inside, but she was fine when I left her."

About what he'd expected.

The boutique at the end of the corner, *La Fleur* as was the name written in gilded ink on the door, was charming in its simplicity. Fresh tulips, even in this weather, rested in a metal container hanging on either side of the entryway. With a sharp twist of his hand, he had the door open and was stepping inside as a gust of wind blew in behind him.

All eyes turned in his direction, a few even gawking in open admiration. He took a moment, clocking in every person inside the place— mostly women, though there was a man in the corner looking terribly bored with one hand on a massive stroller in front of him—before he removed his sunglasses.

He hardly spared anyone a glance as he headed toward the back wall where dresses hung in an assortment of colors. While he wasn't quite sure what he was getting just yet, he knew at the very least that he had to pick two very different items. Though Nika and Dina were twins and had a habit of finishing each other's sentences, their styles were polar opposites.

"What the fuck were they doing on our side anyway?" Ruslan asked with an edge to his voice. None of the Markovics were very trusting of any Gallucci. "They know the rules."

Kaz had wanted to believe that it was done on purpose, a blatant display of disrespect, but if Alberto had wanted to send that kind of message, he would have sent one of his soldiers, not the daughter he loved more than anything. And after the short time he'd spent in Violet's presence, Kaz doubted it had been anything more than happenstance.

"Sonder's fairly new, not many know that it's yours."

"And you believe that?" Derisiveness had crept into Ruslan's tone.

What choice did he have? "Doesn't matter. It won't happen again. I'm sure of that."

Kaz had only been browsing for a short time, shaking his head at some of the choices, knowing that they would be too revealing for two almost-sixteen-year-old girls, when the door was opened again. He couldn't say what made him turn to look—simple curiosity or just a need to be precautious—but when he did and caught sight of Violet hurrying in, pushing curling blonde strands back out of her face, he was almost glad he did.

What were the odds?

Once could be considered a coincidence, but twice? In a city this size? It was almost like the universe was laughing at him.

She didn't notice him immediately, and unlike him, she seemed to be on a mission, heading for another rack of dresses some distance away. Unlike the last time he'd seen her when she was slightly drunk and teetering on too high heels, today she was perfectly put together.

As the daughter of a Gallucci should be.

He was surprised, expecting to see a guard of some sort come in behind her—or at the very least, be able to see one through the windows waiting for her outside—but there was no one. She was alone.

Kaz would have expected Alberto to be a little more responsible than that ... but it wasn't his business.

His father's warning rang in his head, he could even hear the way the man's voice would lower an octave as he told him exactly what *not* to do, and Kaz could have heeded it. He could have ignored her, stayed where he was and finished perusing the selections. Or even left and came back another time—as his father probably would have wanted him to do—but where was the fun in that?

"Rus, I'll see you in an hour."

Kaz didn't wait for a response, hanging up before his brother could get another word in, tucking his phone away. Undoubtedly, he would be hearing about that later, but for the time being, he put it out of his mind.

Abandoning his current selections, Kaz headed directly for her, not hesitating in the slightest. There was a moment, right before he was in her space, right before she could turn and see him approaching, that he could have walked away. No one would know he had almost approached her—that would've just been his little secret—but for reasons he wasn't yet ready to consider, he didn't stop himself.

She was too busy eyeing a red number to notice that he was behind her.

"Which do you prefer?" Kaz asked.

Violet jumped, spinning around to face him, eyes gone wide as though she couldn't believe he was standing there. Her gaze skirted past him, looking around as though she were expecting someone else to walk up behind him.

"Just me," he said, answering her unspoken question. "Or were you expecting someone else?"

She seemed flustered for a second and he wondered whether she would continue to speak with him, or if she would run away as she probably should. At the very least, she would wonder what his intentions were, but even he didn't have an answer to that.

Schooling her expression, she stood a little straighter, brushing her hair over her shoulder. Ah, and there it was, the steely backbone of a woman who knew she had nothing to fear.

How very wrong she was ...

"What?"

"What was it about what I said that was unclear?" he asked, waiting to see the fire in her eyes—she didn't disappoint.

"You asked which do I prefer. Of what?"

He gestured with a lift of his finger to the store around him. "All of it."

Violet's eyes drifted over him from head to toe, unabashed in her study of him. Anyone else might have been uncomfortable under her scrutiny, but he stood his ground. "I doubt you'll find something in your size."

"Fair enough, but it wouldn't be for me. It's a gift."

Her lips turned down as a coldness seemed to wash over her. "Oh?"

He nodded. "Two, in fact."

Kaz could tell from her expression that she thought the gifts would be for women in his life, girlfriends maybe, and it wasn't like he hadn't offered that impression. He'd wanted to see her reaction to that ... and it looked like Violet wasn't as immune to him as she pretended to be.

"I'm sure someone that works here would be willing to help you."

The subtle edge to her voice made him smile. "Undoubtedly, but I suspect you have a far better fashion sense than the lot of them, considering who your mother is."

At the reminder that he knew more about her than she probably knew about him, she took a step back, her gaze darting to the entrance. "I should go."

She'd only taken a step before he was calling out to her. He should have let her leave, it would have been the right thing to do, but he wasn't ready to walk away yet.

"My sisters. They turned sixteen today." That information wouldn't be hard to find out should she have asked anyone else, so he didn't find it imperative to keep it a secret. "They asked for something from here, but as you can see, I'm ill-equipped to pick something out for them."

"I'm not sixteen," she returned with a lift of her brow.

"No," Kaz said, his lips curling up in one corner. "You're definitely not that, but you were once."

Now it was his turn to drink her in. She wasn't wearing a dress that conformed to her curves like that night, but she was wearing skinny jeans that molded to shapely legs, and a cream-colored blouse that dipped in the middle to reveal a tantalizing view of her breasts. Even though it was her, or maybe even *because* it was her, Kaz felt a stirring of lust.

"Fine. Have you anything to go on? Did they say what they wanted?"

"Lady's choice."

Violet chewed on her lip for a moment, like she was contemplating whether to go through with this. After all, she would be actively engaging with him as opposed to it being forced on her.

Ultimately, she agreed, nodding once, just the slightest tilt to her head, before she was moving quickly through the racks. Though, she did keep a sizable distance between them. After asking for their sizes—he'd had to check his phone for an answer—she was silent as she picked up an assortment of dresses, skirts, blouses, putting some back, eyeing others, and those she deemed worthy, she handed to him.

By the time she finished, they had gone through nearly every garment in the place and his arms were laden with items. Even Kaz, whose wardrobe was arguably large, was a bit surprised by how much she had chosen.

"This is a bit much, no?"

To that, she gave him a sparkling, if not sarcastic, smile and waved his words away. "A girl only turns sixteen once, right?"

While he took his items to the register, setting them on the counter and picking out a number of gift boxes that were complementary with any purchase, Kaz looked back to where Violet had disappeared to. She was still looking at the red dress from earlier, but now she was comparing it to another that wasn't nearly as nice.

"Sir? We can have someone bring your purchases to your car, if you would like," the sales associate offered politely, drawing his attention back to her.

"Yes, that's fine."

When it was all rang up and carefully placed in boxes, Kaz paid, gesturing for the man that was now carrying them to follow behind. Before leaving, however, he stopped at the last moment and went back over to Violet. And this time, she was all too aware of his presence as she turned before he even got close.

"Is there something *else* I can help you with?" she asked, almost like she was wary that his answer might be yes.

He gestured to the dresses she held. "The red one, I like it."

Violet looked down, almost like she was surprised to find the dresses there, or maybe surprised that he had noticed in the first place. She sounded almost wistful as she said, "Yeah, I like it too." Even as she said the words, however, she hung it back up. "But no one can look better than my mother at her own event."

That might have been the stupidest shit he had ever heard, but he wouldn't tell her that. Without thinking, he took a step closer, taking her hand into his own as he lifted it to his lips, brushing a lingering kiss to her knuckles.

"You can't help that though, can you?"

Her lips parted, her gaze shooting up to his own. It was there, if only for a moment, the naked desire she couldn't quite hide. Maybe he was playing with fire, but for once, he didn't care.

"*Spasibo*—thank you," he said finally releasing her. "For everything."

He left her there, going back out to his car, tipping the man as he carefully arranged the gifts in his passenger seat. Ultimately, they would have to be moved once he picked up Ruslan, but he didn't think about that for the time being.

His thoughts were on Violet and the way her skin felt against his own.

Unlike Kaz who had an apartment right in the heart of Little Odessa, Ruslan liked his privacy, taking up residence in one of the row-style houses on the outskirts. Though it was older, he had made repairs—the roof, the fence surrounding the property, and a new paint job—and took meticulous care of it so that it didn't look its age. Though their father would not step a foot inside—it wasn't up to his standards—Ruslan loved the place.

Pulling up outside, Kaz parked alongside the curb, laying on the horn as soon as his foot hit the brake. Since his brother always insisted he call to announce his presence—as opposed to coming straight up to the door—Kaz elected to ignore that decision and do what he wanted, even as he respected Ruslan's request.

It was the little things, Kaz thought as Ruslan swung open the door, flipping him off before disappearing back inside.

Five minutes later, he was back, dressed quite similarly to Kaz, though his suit was navy with a crisp, white shirt. This wasn't out of the ordinary for the oldest Markovic, but Kaz could tell that he'd put in an extra effort with his appearance.

"You said an hour," Ruslan commented as he folded his big body into the car. "And you couldn't drive your Range Rover today?"

Though Kaz had customized the car, paying far more than any rational person would to make sure it would fit his impressive height, Ruslan still barely fit.

"What? I love this car."

Though his eyes were shielded by a pair of sunglasses, Kaz could practically feel Ruslan's eye roll as he looked out the window.

"Yeah, the whole world fucking knows it, too."

"Someone's in a surly mood … Didn't get any last night?" Kaz was smiling, oblivious to the glare Ruslan was shooting in his direction. "I've been meaning to ask, how does that wor—"

Before Kaz could even get the question out, Ruslan slammed a meaty fist into his shoulder, making Kaz bark out a laugh, even as he quickly straightened the wheel when they nearly swerved into the next lane.

"Are you trying to kill us?" he shot in Ruslan's direction, still fighting a smile.

"Just you."

Kaz shrugged, unbothered. "At least you're honest."

"No, but seriously. Where the hell were you? You're never late."

The last thing he felt like doing was explaining to his brother who he had run into at the boutique—and more, that he had even talked to her—especially after having Vasily on his ass about it. Ruslan wouldn't usually care who Kaz talked to, but if it was somebody like Violet Gallucci—*especially* because it was Violet Gallucci—he wouldn't bite his tongue.

"Had to get the twins' their gifts. Just took longer than I thought." One thing Kaz wouldn't do was lie—he didn't believe in it, but he could omit parts.

"Yeah, right." Ruslan might not have believed him, but he didn't pry. "Tell me … What's the likelihood that the day won't fall to shit because of this party?"

Turning on Oceana drive, knowing they were only about ten minutes from the place they both rarely enjoyed going back to, Kaz shook his head. "We're not even on the scale."

Unlike the rest of the guests that were steered around to the back of the mansion from the driveway, Kaz and Ruslan went through the house instead, knowing that Irina would be in the kitchen. If they could put off seeing their father for as long as possible, they would.

There were decorations all around, balloons and glittery things that made the space look more like a family lived there instead of a showroom. Sure enough, Irina was in the kitchen, overlooking the caterers as they plated food and put the finishing touches on a massive birthday cake with a candle depicting 16 resting at the top. She was just about to give instructions to a girl holding a platter of shrimp when she caught sight of her sons.

And more importantly, Ruslan.

Irina didn't even bother to finish her request before she was crossing the floor and pulling Ruslan into a tight hug. Kaz didn't mind that the attention wasn't on him. After all, he'd seen her two weeks prior, and

Ruslan … he couldn't remember the last time Ruslan had seen their mother.

"I'm so happy you could make it." Pulling back after a moment, she touched his face in motherly affection, looking him over for any changes since the last time she'd seen him. "You look thinner. Are you eating?"

Only Irina would be able to notice that Ruslan's massive size was *smaller*.

"I'm fine, Mama."

"What are you eating? You can't just eat at that club of yours, *syn*."

When she called him 'son,' Ruslan smiled, soft and fleeting. "It's not so bad."

"Nonsense. I'll make you something before you go."

"Where's Vasily?" Kaz asked, butting into their conversation.

Irina frowned, her joy at seeing Ruslan deflating like a balloon. "Out back entertaining."

Giving Ruslan a pointed look, Kaz said, "I'll go and speak."

At least then his brother would have more time with Irina.

Clapping Ruslan on the shoulder and kissing Irina's cheek, Kaz headed out the back, scanning the crowd below from his position on the deck. He could spot the twins with ease as they were at the center of a group of girls, huddled together as they talked. Parents mingled, most with drinks in hand, and on the outskirts of it all was a number of Vasily's men. They were careful to be present, but unseen.

It was what they were good at.

And off to the side, smoking a Cuban was Vasily, holding court amongst a group of men as though he were the king of them all. In his head, he probably was.

On his way down, Kaz ran into the one person he wasn't expecting to see.

Older than him by a year, Vera was the sibling he was closest to since they were so close in age. She looked like a younger version of their mother, though she did have Vasily's eyes. Most confused them for twins.

Unlike Kaz and Ruslan, who were deeply involved in the life, Vera wanted no part of it. And the day after she turned eighteen, she had moved out and put as much distance between her and Vasily as possible. The only time she came around was during holidays and birthdays. Otherwise, he went to her.

Vera might have looked annoyed as she came up the stairs—though this was just what she looked like—but she smiled when she noticed Kaz. "I'm surprised you didn't forget about today, Kaz."

He had … but he wasn't going to tell her that. "How's my favorite sister?"

"As well as to be expected, considering present company."

While Kaz didn't have the best of relationships with Vasily, Vera and Ruslan's was worse—the second by his own actions, and the former because Vera just downright loathed the man. Sometimes Kaz thought he understood why, it wasn't like they had the best of childhoods, but other times, Kaz didn't think he knew the gravity of Vera's hatred for their father.

"And your business?" he asked.

Vera had started an interior design business, and was quite successful. "Everything's good. How are *you*? Mama says you might have gotten into trouble …"

While Irina wouldn't ask, Vera would. "It was nothing."

Though it was starting to seem like it was something …

"Be careful, Kaz," she said, lowering her voice. "Don't give him a reason."

Kaz inclined his head, the only response he was willing to give to that. "Rus is inside," he said instead. "He'll be happy to see you."

Vera knew exactly what Kaz was saying as they both looked over in Vasily's direction, whose attention was on them. "Right. We'll catch up later, Kaz."

She was gone in a flurry of maroon, leaving Kaz to start across the yard toward his father. He didn't immediately recognize a few of the men standing around Vasily, but his father didn't waste a second in introducing him. Kaz nodded, the most he ever did when around people he didn't know.

If he didn't know them, he didn't trust them.

That was how he'd stayed alive this long.

"You're late," Vasily said after he'd excused them, and they stepped off to the side. "You know better."

"I had to buy birthday presents," Kaz said by way of explanation.

Vasily was quiet for a moment. "And is that the only reason?"

Kaz knew what he was really asking—whether it was somehow Ruslan's fault that they were tardy, and he was merely covering for his brother. It wouldn't be the first time he had, and probably wouldn't be the last, but on this particular instance, Ruslan wasn't to blame.

"It's a nice day," Kaz said gesturing out with an arm around them, a smile lighting up his face in case any others observing their conversation. "Let's act like it, yes?"

While Vasily might not have liked Kaz's words, judging from the scowl on his face, he wouldn't call him on it. Not today. "Have you been doing what I asked, regarding that girl?"

How long had Kaz gone without any mention of Violet, but now it seemed like she was brought up every chance Vasily got. If he was meant to forget about her, pretend like she didn't exist, that was hard to do when he was reminded of her often.

"Of course," Kaz answered easily.

It wasn't a lie, not really. He hadn't expected to see her that morning, so he wasn't seeking her out. That had to count for something.

Vasily looked skeptical, but ultimately accepted his words. Changing the subject, he said, "Don't forget tomorrow."

On the third Tuesday of every month, there was a meeting between Vasily, and the higher-ranking members of the *Bratva*, their tribute of sorts, where money changed hands and any concerns were addressed. If there was one thing Kaz wouldn't forget, it was the meeting. Attendance was mandatory, and only once had he seen what happened when you were late—that man still had a limp.

"No worries. We'll be there."

It didn't matter that Vasily and Ruslan were at odds. Ruslan was still expected to show.

"Rus! You made it!"

Kaz turned just in time to see Nika hurrying across the backyard, throwing herself at Ruslan as he stepped down to their level. Vera was right behind him, along with Irina, and a number of caterers that were bringing out the last of the food.

In a way, Ruslan had come out prepared with his own little army.

Vasily wouldn't cause a scene, not with the number of people at the party, and especially not with Irina, the twins, and Vera in attendance—he saved his savagery for when they weren't around.

Dina was right behind her sister, barreling into Ruslan as he caught them easily, his lips moving, though Kaz couldn't make out what he was saying.

Vasily's scowl grew worse as he looked over at his eldest son, and with fire in his eyes, he took a step in their direction, as though he meant to pull them apart if he had to.

"Ah, I wouldn't do that," Kaz said easily, not taking his eyes off his siblings.

"You can't save him from me, Kazimir," Vasily returned in a dark voice. "You shouldn't try."

Kaz nodded, his lips turning down at the corners. "Maybe so, but then who would save you from Vera?"

Vasily had chosen wisely in a wife. She was quiet, knew when not to ask questions, and kept her opinions of how he treated their children to himself—even the twins took after her in their quiet manner.

But Vera, on the other hand, she didn't bend to Vasily's whims. If she thought he was wrong, and that was more often than not, she called him out on it, but only in regards to his parenting. When it came to the *Bratva*, she let him run it as he saw fit.

Unlike with Kaz, Vasily was careful to mind his words around Vera in regards to Ruslan. Maybe he was trying to mend the relationship with his eldest daughter, but even Kaz knew that he wouldn't be able to fix something that wasn't there.

"Give him today," Kaz said from his position at his father's side. "Tomorrow, you can hate him again."

For the first time in what felt like ages, Kaz thought he saw his brother's shoulders relax, like the weight of his burdens had finally been lifted.

... if only for a short while.

Violet kept her attention focused entirely on the textbook in her hands, and not her father sitting across the room behind his large desk. She knew he was watching her, he always had at least one eye on her.

Earlier in the day, her father had called with a simple request for her to come over and have lunch with him. He offered nothing more when he called, and made it clear his request was not up for debate. Violet dropped the lunch plans she had with Amelia and Nicole, and found a driver waiting outside of her Manhattan condo, ready to drive her across the city to Amityville.

After eating lunch with her father, Alberto invited Violet up to his office to sit and talk for a while. She ended up on the couch studying while her father scribbled on papers in a folder. Very little talking was being done at all.

It was unnerving.

"How has Gee been treating you?" Alberto asked.

Violet finally lifted her gaze from her reading, and found her father had dropped the pen he had been writing with. Gee was her driver—her new not-so-much best friend.

"Fine, Daddy."

"He says you've been following the rules and only staying in the upper part of Brooklyn."

Violet shrugged. "That's what you wanted."

"Only when he drives you, right?" Alberto pressed.

"Of course."

She was not planning to defy her father again. Her lesson was well learned. Even driving anywhere now was impossible to do by herself, because Gee had been given the second set of keys to her car and was not permitted to hand them back to her until her father allowed it.

"Have you seen the Russian since the club incident?" her father asked.

Violet hesitated before answering. Her father's sharp eye looked her over, searching for any proof that she was about to lie. Her encounter just a couple of days before with Kaz Markovic had been nothing more than chance. She didn't think he was purposely seeking her out, and in fact, she hadn't even noticed his flashy car parked anywhere outside of the shop before she went in that day. Then again, her driver had been in a fit over the smothering traffic and just wanted to find a place to park, so maybe that was why they hadn't noticed him.

While she didn't understand why the man would risk going so far into Brooklyn just for the sake of shopping for his sisters' birthday, she wasn't going to get him in trouble for doing so.

"No," Violet said quietly. "I haven't seen him or anyone else from Brighton Beach."

Alberto's lips pursed, and Violet recognized the action immediately. It was her father's way of considering her words, and whether or not he wanted to believe them.

Before the club incident, he might have taken her words as instant truth with no questions asked. Now, he was not as forgiving.

Violet didn't drop her father's gaze, knowing that if she did, he would find her lies.

Alberto was the first to look away. "I worry, that's all."

"I was the one who went into their space, not the other way around," Violet replied. "It was a mistake, and they seemed to understand that."

"Russians seem like they understand a lot of things." Her father scoffed loudly. "Then they turn on you the first chance they can. You can't trust them, Violet. Don't you understand that?"

She nodded, but she didn't entirely believe him.

Kaz didn't seem untrustworthy.

Not when he looked at her.

Not when he kissed her hand, and smiled like he had.

Violet ignored the tightening sensation in her throat, and the heat dripping down her spine all of the sudden. She certainly understood her interest in the Russian, as far as that went. Not only was he seemingly charming and good-looking—extremely so—he was also entirely off-limits.

She would have to be stupid and blind not to be a little curious.

"What would happen if they did?" she dared to ask quietly.

Alberto raised a single brow high. "Did what, *ragazza*?"

"Came further into Brooklyn, or beyond Brighton."

"Some of them often do," Alberto said offhandedly, almost like it didn't matter at all.

71

Violet's brow furrowed. "But—"

"You're a girl, you see, so you have no need to be involved with the affairs of men and their deals. I simply made sure as you grew up that you knew where my limits and lines were for you to follow and not cross, Violet. As far as the Russians go, we often allow them into Brooklyn beyond just Brighton Beach. We turn cheek to them being there, because they are neither doing business, nor creating business for themselves. And therefore, not encroaching on our business. Whatever the Russians demand of their people as far as territory goes, I cannot say."

"Is that why you always warn me to stay out of the lower parts of Brooklyn?"

"Exactly why."

Violet fingered the pages of her textbook. She didn't really understand what the Russians did for business, and she didn't think that asking her father would get her any answers. She wasn't even entirely sure she understood what her father's Cosa Nostra did to make money.

Girls weren't allowed to know.

"Vasily Markovic," Alberto started to say.

Violet's head snapped back up at the surname, curiosity instantly simmering through her blood. She knew the name, and who the man was, but she decided to play stupid for her father's benefit. "Who is that exactly?"

"The Russian boss. He has a daughter that lives in the upper part of Brooklyn. I overlook her residence because she has no real connection to her father's business, and she is simply working to build her brand. Vera is her name; she's quite a successful interior designer. If she weren't Russian, your mother might have had her come in to design that new studio she wants. Apparently, the woman has a good eye for spaces."

Vera.

That meant Kaz had at least three sisters, and a brother. Violet filed that information away with the rest of the little bit she knew about him.

It wasn't much.

She shouldn't want to know anything about the man at all. Not with who he was, the people he was affiliated with, never mind her father's very obvious dislike of the whole bunch.

Yet she did.

She still *did*.

"But Manhattan," her father continued, drawing Violet out of her thoughts. "Amityville, even. Those places are off-limits to the Russians entirely. No matter who they are, or how docile they seem."

"I haven't seen them again," Violet repeated, hoping her father believed her.

"I only want to keep you safe, Violet."

"I know, Daddy. And I'm doing what you want."

"I'm aware." Alberto sighed, pushing up from his desk. He reached over into a glass bowl and pulled a pair of familiar keys from it. "I have something for you."

Violet tried not to smile at the sight of her car keys. "Okay."

"I don't like not trusting you, *dolcezza*. But you've done well for the last little while, and it leads me to think that maybe the club incident was just bad judgement on your part. So these," he said, shaking the keys, "… are conditional."

She dropped her textbook in her lap in just enough time to catch the keys when her father tossed them at her.

"How so?" Violet asked.

"Manhattan is a free zone for you. You can drive yourself wherever you please. Brooklyn is not. I expect to you have Gee drive you, or follow you, depending on where you're planning to go. Lower Brooklyn is still—"

"Off-limits, I know," she interrupted quickly. "Anything else?"

She was just happy to have a little bit of freedom and her keys back.

"Yes, there is," Alberto said, chuckling. He quickly sobered. "As much as I want to trust you, I can't entirely do that without feeling like you might pull the wool over my eyes in some way, Violet. Once you've treated me like a fool, I won't give you the chance to do me wrong again."

Violet swallowed back her denial, knowing it wouldn't help.

"To be sure you're following my rules, I will have Gee pick you up from wherever you are whenever I deem it suitable for him to do so. I will call you, and you will answer, no matter what. Depending on where you are to where he is, you will have that amount of time to be ready for him to pick you up, and drive you to … whatever. Dinner, one of your mother's showings, or something else."

Jesus.

That essentially meant Violet was still chained down depending on her father's demands and schedules. And she wouldn't exactly be able to lie, either. If she said she was somewhere else, somewhere she was allowed to be, and Gee showed up to get her but she wasn't there … it wouldn't end well.

Still, she had her keys.

And her father had actually spoken to her after ignoring her for weeks.

It was something.

Violet chose not to question it.

Violet found her brother perched on the kitchen counter, chatting away to their mother as Andrea checked on the progress of a soup she was cooking.

"Not yet," her mother said. "Give it another year, Carmine. My God. You're still young."

Violet held off from entering the kitchen completely. She was just out of their view, but she could see them. If there was one thing Violet never understood, it was the closeness her brother and mother seemed to share. Growing up, her mother had always felt a little distant to her in most ways. Andrea never had time to feed into her daughter's whims, never mind indulging Violet's many games and quirks.

That had always landed on her father.

Alberto hadn't seemed to mind.

But it did leave a lasting effect on the relationship between Violet and her mother. She always saw the woman as cold and unapproachable. She felt like her mother wouldn't care about her problems or thoughts. It wasn't like Andrea gave her the impression that she wanted to know those things about Violet.

And then there was Carmine.

Andrea, quite literally, doted on her son constantly. Despite the fact that Carmine was twenty-seven and more than capable of handling his own business, their mother made sure to visit his apartment several times a week to pick up after her son and make sure his fridge was full of food. As children, Andrea would be quick to take Carmine with her on her many trips in her rising career as a clothing designer, while she left her daughter at home with her father.

It was just ... an entirely different dynamic.

Violet wasn't jealous. She had a close relationship with her father, after all. Maybe even closer than the one Carmine shared with Alberto. But the same thought always lingered in the back of her mind whenever she saw her mother and brother together: What had been so different about her as a child that her mother couldn't even be bothered to *try*?

"There's just no point in waiting, Ma," Carmine said.

Andrea reached over the counter and cupped her son's cheek in her palm. "You're young. Do you really want to settle yourself with a woman and babies right now?"

Carmine chuckled. "I can still have my fun when I'm married."

"Carmine."

"What?" Carmine flashed a smile. "I've waited too long as it is. I'm not going to wait anymore for the perfect woman who suits what you want me to have, Ma. I just need an appropriate enough wife."

Andrea scowled. "For your father, you mean."

"And for me. I *have* waited too long."

Dropping her hand from her son's face, Andrea grabbed a dishtowel and wiped at the counter. "What does your father think of this?"

"He thinks she's appropriate."

There was that word again.

Appropriate.

Like the only way a woman could possibly be worthy enough was if she met a certain set of standards determined by those around her. It irritated Violet in a way she couldn't explain.

"But you don't love her," Andrea said.

"I don't have to, Ma." Carmine pushed off the counter, and grabbed an apple from the fruit tree. "I just need the ring and the license."

"I don't like this."

"You like Nicole," Carmine pressed.

Well, Violet figured her friend would be happy at least. Carmine was finally going to settle Nicole into some kind of permanent relationship, even if he had no intention of being committed to it. It wasn't like Nicole didn't already know Carmine was a manwhore in every sense of the word.

"I liked what she was good for," Andrea muttered. "And you know exactly what you used the girl for. I know what you're doing, son. You're trying to butter me up to get your grandmother's engagement ring for Nicole, and I won't give it to you. Buy her one, for all I give a damn. She's not having my mother's."

Carmine scowled at his mother before turning on his heel and storming toward the entry of the kitchen. To hide the fact that she had been eavesdropping on the conversation, Violet stepped into the space at the same time her brother was just about to leave. He was too pissed off to care she was there if the way he brushed past her with a grumble and a glare was any indication.

Andrea didn't give Violet a second look either before she was back at the stove, tending the soup again.

"I wanted to say goodbye before I left," Violet said.

Her mother waved a hand over her shoulder, and nothing else.

Violet wasn't surprised. It probably didn't help that her mother was now in a mood over Carmine's choices regarding marriage. Andrea wasn't going to be able to dote on her son like she did now once he was a married man.

"All right, bye, Ma," Violet called over her shoulder as she turned to leave.

"Violet, wait," Andrea said.

She stopped. "Yeah?"

"I forgot to tell you earlier, but I left a few dresses from my new collection upstairs in my studio office. I know your friends liked them, so I kept them for you to have."

Violet was shocked her mother had even cared enough to do that. "Okay, thanks."

Andrea simply waved her off again.

Wanting to get back to Manhattan before the sky started to darken, Violet quickly made her way back through the mansion and up to the wing where her father's and mother's offices were located. She found the dress bags her mother mentioned easily enough, and slung them around her arm. She was just leaving the studio when she realized she had also forgotten her textbook in Alberto's office.

Violet shifted the few dress bags to her other arm as she stopped just outside of her father's office. The doors had been open all the way earlier when she left, but now they were closed except for a couple of inches. She could clearly hear her father and brother talking inside.

"I can't make your mother give you the ring," Alberto said, almost sardonically.

"I know you can, Papa."

"It's her ring to do with what she wants. It didn't come from my family. Do you want my family's ring? I have that one."

Carmine grunted something unintelligible.

"She's spoiled you rotten, and that is exactly the problem," Alberto said with no sympathy in his tone. "She denies you one thing and you go on a rampage. Did you consider that's why she did it?"

"I don't want to talk about it anymore."

"You don't want to hear the truth, Carmine."

"No, we have better things to discuss."

"Indulge me," Alberto said, sounding bored all of the sudden.

"The Russians."

"It's handled."

"Then why don't you sound pleased with that fact?" Carmine asked.

Alberto sighed heavily. "I worry about your sister, that's all. She liked the one all those years ago—made fast friends with him in a very short amount of time. I don't need that happening again."

Violet's brow furrowed. She remembered Kaz saying they had met once before, but she hadn't believed him. Her father wouldn't mingle with Russians, not guessing by the way he so easily dismissed and insulted them every chance he could.

But here Alberto was, saying Violet had met Kaz when they were children.

"Do you think the Russian boss will keep his end of the deal?" Carmine asked. "It's been years. He could decide with recent events that it's just not worth the peace of mind, anymore."

Alberto scoffed loudly. "Peace of mind, Carmine? My God, son, you are a fool. You walk around in a bubble of your own making half of the time, believing that because of who you are, the rest of your life will be an easy road to travel. There is no such thing as peace of mind here, and that meeting brought neither me, nor Vasily Markovic, any peace, either."

"Didn't it?" Carmine asked. "The fighting stopped."

"For a price," Alberto muttered.

What price was that?

Inside, Violet knew she was too curious about something that clearly wasn't her business to begin with. Still, she moved a little closer to the doors, wanting to hear every little word if her brother and father decided to talk quieter.

"My point," Alberto said, "is that I worry about your sister. When she finds something she likes—someone—she trusts them too easily. She has too many friends as it is that I don't approve of."

"You could fix the problem by getting rid of it altogether."

Violet's heart stopped for a split second.

It only lasted as long as her father's silence.

Alberto barked out another one of his bitter laughs. "See, there you go again, Carmine. You shoot off at the mouth like you understand how this works, like there will be no consequences for your rash decisions. No, I cannot justify the war and bloodshed it would cause me if I killed the son of Vasily Markovic."

"Papa—"

"Once again, son, you managed to prove to me in very few words how unprepared you are for a position you think belongs to you, simply because you were born a boy."

Ouch.

Even Violet flinched at that.

Clearly she wasn't the only one who had disappointed their father lately.

"What about Franco?" Carmine demanded.

"What about your foolish friend?"

"He deserves some kind of retribution for what happened."

Something smacked against something hard, making it echo out to Violet's spot in the hallway. "Goddammit, I am not getting into this again. I said no to that. The answer is no. If that enforcer defies me simply because he is your friend and he thinks he can get away with it, I will cut his fucking heart out."

Violet had no idea what her father was talking about, but she decided in that moment her textbook could wait. She didn't want to be caught listening, and she really didn't want to hear anything else.

She couldn't get out of the mansion fast enough.

"You look wonderful," Alberto praised, taking Violet's hand as she approached him. "I see you managed to find a dress."

Violet smiled, and pretended like there wasn't a hell of a lot of eyes watching her at that moment. The long stage meant for the runway and models was lined on either side by six rows of seats from one side to the other. The ballroom had been converted for the fashion show's use. Black and chrome accents hung from the ceiling. Music pumped through the place courtesy of the high-profile DJ set up near the entrance of the runway where the models would come out of. Media people, flashing their badges and cameras to keep out of the hands of security, bombarded the venue from every angle.

While this very scene of high-life and socialites was exactly her mother's thing, it wasn't Violet's. She didn't feel comfortable in front of a large crowd being photographed and asked questions about her mother's latest designs and the event that was sure to turn heads.

But her father demanded she show, and so she had.

"Thank you," Violet told her father.

"Where are your friends?" Alberto asked.

"Coming. They got caught up in all the pretty lights outside."

Alberto caught onto what she was saying, and chuckled. "For some people, the shininess of a red carpet and paparazzi doesn't wear off, Violet."

It wore off for her about ten years ago.

When she was a kid, it mostly just scared the hell out of her.

"Sit," Alberto said, waving at one of the empty chairs beside him.

Violet followed her father's demand. It wasn't long before Nicole and Amelia joined her in the front row, along with her brother on the other side of her father, and a few familiar faces behind them. They had some of the best seats in the house nearing the very front of the runway.

BETHANY-KRIS & LONDON MILLER

Taking a quick look around, Violet picked out a good dozen celebrities that had been handpicked for invitations from her mother, a few musicians that had a taste for fashion, as well as high profile individuals from all across New York. Each event was a little more important than the last, Violet knew. Her mother's name only grew, and her celebrity status lifted higher with it.

Gallucci was more than just a dynasty.

It was a goddamn *brand*.

When the lights dimmed and loud voices turned into hushed murmurs, Violet relaxed a little more. She didn't have a lot of interest in her mother's shows, but she did enjoy watching the models.

Once, she had even entertained the idea of becoming one. She certainly had a way in, if she wanted to try.

The music changed tempo slightly, just enough to signal something was about to happen. Lights flickered, drawing in the crowd's attention to the entrance of the runway. Andrea stepped out of the sheer black curtains with her blood red smirk and a single hand held high. Her hair had been piled high on her head in a messy up-do. She wore one of her signature black dresses, detailed along the smooth lines with chrome to fit the theme of the event.

Then, as quickly as her mother had come, she was gone.

The music changed again just as the first model stepped onto the runway. Andrea Gallucci fashions weren't about being crazy and out there. Her mother liked class, and style. Simple was sometimes the sexiest. She wanted to see each and every woman in one of her designs ... if they had the luxury of being able to afford one of the pieces.

Violet figured they were probably half-way through the first run of the collection when her father tensed in his chair beside hers. She shot him a curious glance, noting he was looking down at the phone in his hand. Instantly, his confusion melted into a simmering rage that danced across his scowling lips and narrowed eyes.

She tried to look at his phone, but he quickly hid it.

What was wrong?

Alberto leaned to the side, toward his son. Violet watched her father's lips move fast—too fast for him to be happy.

It wasn't like Alberto to cause a fuss on a day that was meant to spotlight and showcase their mother, never mind the public attention on their family.

Something had to be bad for him to do that.

People were taking his picture, catching his visible anger.

Alberto would never risk that being caught—not like this.

"I didn't," she heard Carmine say.

"Bullshit."

The one word from her father might as well have been spit from his mouth. And it hadn't been quiet, either.

"Daddy," Violet said softly. "People are watching."

Alberto straightened in his chair, glanced around and fixed his jacket.

"Papa," Carmine started to say.

Alberto held up a hand, silencing his son. "I warned you."

Violet still didn't understand what was going on. Her father stood from his chair, seemingly oblivious to the people watching him all over again with their curious gazes. People knew who they were—who her father was.

"Apologize to your mother for me," Alberto said.

He had directed his comment to Violet only, not Carmine.

"Sure," she said.

Her father offered nothing else before he disappeared into the crowd. Carmine cursed on the other side of Violet, but she ignored him. A heavy feeling had settled in her gut.

"What was that all about?" Nicole asked from Violet's right.

"I don't know," she admitted.

And she didn't know if she wanted to.

Kaz was on his back in nothing more than a pair of jeans, as he lifted the cigarette to his lips, dragged in a lungful and held it, letting the nicotine burn before releasing it. It was rare that he smoked, only indulged a handful of times when he wanted to take the edge off.

The day had come and gone, filled with long hours of business with the men that answered to him, and some that didn't. Now that he was finally home, he was ready to call it a night. Try and get some sleep before he needed to be back up and doing that shit all over again.

He had just ground out the cigarette in the ashtray on his bedside table when his phone's vibrations cut through the silence. He contemplated ignoring the call for only a handful of seconds before he saw who was calling.

Ruslan.

The party had gone well a few days ago. Vasily had left him be, though he hadn't spoken to him once. Even the monthly meeting had been easy enough. And while they didn't talk every day, Kaz and his siblings, when they did call, he never ignored their calls.

"Rus, what's up?"

"We've got a problem."

Kaz sat straight up, already on his feet before Ruslan could get out another word. It was his tone, the hardness that was twined around his words, that made Kaz move without question. His brother was fully capable of handling himself, had been for far longer than Kaz was alive, so if Ruslan was calling him, it was serious.

"Talk to me." Kaz grabbed a shirt from the closet, not bothering to pull it on as he snatched his keys from the counter and practically ran out of his apartment. "Are you at the club?"

"Yeah. I got a call from one of my guys, said they saw an Escalade driving around. I didn't think much of it until he called again and said he saw it again circling the club. Once is a coincidence, and twice …"

He didn't have to finish that statement for Kaz to know what he meant. Twice meant somebody was trolling.

But who the fuck was stupid enough to be so obvious about it?

"I'm on my way." Climbing in his car, Kaz started it up and sped out of the parking lot, ignoring the speed limit as he gunned through traffic. "You armed?"

"I'm not a fucking idiot, Kaz," Ruslan returned, sounding as though he was walking. "I got this."

"I'm ten minutes out, *brat.*"

"Probably somebody trying to flex their shit," Ruslan returned. "By the time you get here, I'll be out back to check the perimeter. It's probably not—who the fuck are you?"

Kaz knew the question wasn't aimed at him as Ruslan's tone had changed from annoyance to outright anger. There were only certain people that inspired that kind of reaction in him. His father and Italians.

"You fucked up, Russian," someone said, their voice carrying over the line loud and clear.

"What the fuck are you talking about?" Ruslan asked, his voice softer, as though he'd taken the phone away from his ear.

Whatever response that might have been said was lost as a grunt sounded, then the phone dropping. Kaz heard all of this, and knew with absolute certainty that it was Ruslan's grunt that he'd heard.

Fuck.

Pressing down on the gas pedal a little further, Kaz's back hit the seat as he did ninety the rest of the way.

His tires screeched as Kaz came to a stop in front of the club, barely putting the car in park as he jumped out, grabbing his M9 from the middle console as he went. Abandoning his car—even with the keys inside—Kaz ran, throwing caution to the wind.

At this hour, there was only a few drunk stragglers left, but they seemed oblivious to anything and anyone around them, including the fact that Kaz was carrying a gun for anyone to see.

Kaz was just rounding the corner, spotting the giant lump on the ground that he immediately could see was Ruslan, his face bloody and nearly unrecognizable.

It felt like a punch to his chest, the rage that filled him, and though his first instinct was to go to his brother and make sure he was breathing, the sound of peeling tires and the smell of burning rubber made his head jerk up. He just caught sight of the Escalade driving out of the lot, and when he did, his gun was up and aimed without a thought, bullets splitting the air as he fired.

He ran, even as he pulled the trigger, shattering the back windshield with a bullet, embedding another in the trunk, and a final one in a tail light before the truck disappeared out of view.

"Rus!"

Kaz jogged back to his brother, two fingers already going to his pulse as he carefully rolled him over, scanning him for any bullet wounds, but it seemed the blood coating his shirt was mostly from his face. Feeling the firm, but slow heartbeat beneath his hand, Kaz sagged in relief, using his free one to tug the phone out from his back pocket.

"You're going to be all right, Rus," Kaz said, dialing the number for the man they kept on their payroll for this kind of thing. Ruslan hated hospitals and avoided them as much as he could.

"What the fuck happened?"

Kaz let go of Ruslan only to pick up his gun and point it back at Nathaniel as he appeared at the back entrance, holding the door open. At least until he saw Ruslan on the ground, then a rage the likes of which Kaz had never seen fell like a mask over his face as he ran over.

"What—"

Before he could repeat the question, Kaz asked one of his own. "Where the fuck were you?"

Nathaniel blinked, then blinked again as he seemed to become aware of the gun that Kaz had trained on him. He was no stranger to Kaz's surly nature, but never had Kaz blatantly held a gun to the man's head.

"I was doing inventory in the freezer," Nathaniel explained, sounding far too calm in the face of Kaz's anger. "I didn't hear shit—not until the shots."

Hanging up—the good doctor hadn't answered—Kaz finally withdrew his weapon, already dialing another number, getting to his feet.

"Stay with him."

Nathaniel didn't question the command, just did what was asked of him and remained where he was. Just as Kaz had done, Nathaniel checked him over for injuries.

Turning away, Kaz was brimming with fury by the time Vasily picked up, and when he did, he didn't waste a second. "We've got a fucking problem."

Once again, Kaz found himself with a cigarette between his lips, fighting the urge to do violence. He had expected the nicotine to help, if only for a spell, but it did nothing. But he wasn't out committing murder, so it must have been doing something.

Back inside his house, Ruslan was getting checked out by Marcus Fray, their resident doctor, and one of the few men that knew secrets about them but wasn't officially a part of their organization. Kaz had stuck next to Ruslan the entire time, at least until his brother had demanded he go away once he'd come around.

That'd been ten minutes ago, before Kaz's cigarette, and—as the door to his place opened—before Vasily's arrival.

Tossing the butt over the railing, Kaz headed back inside.

Ruslan's face was clean of blood, though the bruising was bad, as was his chest. Now that his clothes were gone—doctor's orders—it was far easier to see what all had been done to him, considering he was already bruised and it had only been an hour.

It wasn't just fists that had been used on him—Kaz knew firsthand the kind of impressions those made on the body. A bat, probably, judging from some of the large markings, especially along his back. But despite the obvious pain he had to be in, Ruslan didn't complain. That wasn't his style.

Vasily glanced in Ruslan's direction, taking in the multitude of his bruised body before he frowned. "What happened?"

Ruslan, who had grown used to Vaily ignoring his presence entirely, was slow to realize that Vasily was asking him the question. Kaz leaned against the island in his kitchen, folding his arms across his chest as he waited for the answer he wanted to know as well.

"There were five of them in front," Ruslan explained. "One came at me from behind with a fucking aluminum bat."

It seemed Kaz was right about that. "Did you recognize them?"

"Not immediately, but they were fucking Italian. That was clear enough before the idiot in the front introduced himself. Can you believe that shit?" Ruslan ran a hand over his mouth, scowling when he caught sight of the blood on the back of it. "Said his name was Franco."

Kaz was mildly impressed. Even he didn't go about announcing his name when he came to make a point, but he didn't think it had anything to do with arrogance—which Kaz had in spades—but more to do with stupidity. "What the fuck was his problem?"

"Something about a girl—his girl, apparently." Now, it was to Kaz that Ruslan looked, a hint of accusation there. "The girl, whatever the fuck her name was, that I took home that night, she told him I drugged her."

No one spoke a word—there was no reason to. If there was one thing they all knew, even Vasily, the likelihood of him drugging a woman was nonexistent.

"What are we doing about it?" Kaz asked, cutting to the chase.

All eyes turned to Vasily, waiting for his response.

After a brief hesitation, he gave them their answer. "Nothing. You'll do nothing."

"Are you out of your fucking mind?" Kaz asked pushing off the island to cross the floor and stand toe-to-toe with Vasily. He didn't care that the others were quick to excuse themselves, knowing what was coming next. "You make your point about boundaries and lines, getting on my ass about it, but now you want to let this go? Fuck that."

"I've allowed your blatant disrespect—ignored your petulant behavior. If you want me to treat you like a child, Kazimir, I will. When I say stand down, that's exactly what I mean. *Stand down.* I am not to be questioned. This is not a fucking democracy. You do what I say, when I say it, or so help me, Kazimir—even if it breaks your mother's heart—I will put a bullet in your fucking skull. Now mind me and *leave it.*"

With that parting remark, Vasily took his leave.

Once the door was shut, leaving Kaz and his Ruslan alone, Kaz looked to his brother. Before he could speak, Ruslan shook his head, coming over to sit on the couch, wincing as he slowly sat.

"One day he's not going to be so nice," Ruslan warned, grabbing the remote and reclining back like he hadn't just had the shit beat out of him. "You shouldn't goad him."

"Fuck him." This wouldn't be the first time Kaz had said those words. "You know I'm right."

"You may be, but you can't change his mind. I don't see why you try."

Ruslan was always the rational one, imploring logic even when Kaz didn't like to hear it. That was why, after all, he was the older brother.

"How are the ribs, *brat?*"

"They'd feel better if someone pried them the fuck out of me," Ruslan admitted.

Damn.

Kaz took a seat beside his brother, careful not to drop down too fast and cause Ruslan more agony. "The girl, they said."

Ruslan didn't take his gaze off the television. "That's what they said—he said. Just the one spoke."

"Franco, yes?"

"Apparently. What kind of fool goes around introducing himself like that?"

"One that believes he is just and untouchable," Kaz said.

He filed the Italian's name away. Before morning, he would know exactly who this Franco was. Regardless of Vasily's opinions, Kaz wanted to know why the Italians thought they had any right to be in Coney, never mind attacking Ruslan.

A boss would have needed to give some kind of approval for that, considering it could start a damn war.

"Stop," Ruslan said.

Kaz's knee quit bouncing instantly. Sometimes, when he was overthinking shit, he got that way in his daze. "I'm not doing anything, Rus."

"You're thinking about doing *something*. That is enough."

"I'm supposed to be okay with my brother being jumped by a bunch of Italians over some female's lies? You want to be like Vasily and tell me to look the other way?"

Ruslan grunted under his breath. "Leave it alone. Maybe now they'll fuck off, yeah? They made their point, Kaz."

Kaz didn't think it was that simple, but given the state of his brother, he wasn't about to argue the point with him. Ruslan was all about keeping the peace where other people were concerned. He didn't put himself into shit that would cause problems, and he didn't like to make others uncomfortable if he could help it.

While Kaz typically appreciated that in his brother, he didn't find it to be a virtue when Ruslan looked like he'd just gotten stomped on by a bunch of horses.

A bit of guilt swam through Kaz as he looked his brother over again. It was, in a way, his fault that Ruslan had been put in this situation at all. If it hadn't been for him ordering Ruslan to take the girl home, she wouldn't have been able to lie about who had drugged her.

Following that guilt was a hell of a lot of irritation and rage.

Her friends had to have known the truth. She was fucked up in that office, and long before she entered it, too—if their stories that night were any indication to go by. While he didn't know much about the other two girls, Violet Gallucci didn't seem like the type to throw others under the proverbial bus to save her own ass.

But if she knew her friend was lying to her boyfriend to save face, then that's exactly what she had done to his brother.

And that pissed him off.

"If you're going to keep that bouncing shit up," Ruslan said, still flicking through channels on the television, "then I am going to make you leave."

Kaz stilled again. "You'd think after having your face beat in, you'd be a little quieter."

Ruslan laughed, a wince following right behind. "Yeah, you'd think."

But that wasn't Ruslan's style.

Out of the corner of his eye, something on the television's guide caught Kaz's attention. "Wait, go back."

"I am not watching fashion shit, Kazimir. If you suddenly took possession of a vagina between your legs, feel free to go home and watch it on your own flatscreen."

"Shut the fuck up. No, there was one—Gallucci Fashions, it said. Go back."

Grumbling under his breath, Ruslan did what he was told. Sure enough, it was a live shot of Andrea Gallucci's latest collection she had released. Beside him, his brother sighed and muttered on, but Kaz was too busy scanning the faces in the crowd behind the models.

Front row and center, he found her.

Violet.

The camera quickly left her position as it continued following the model's walk, but what he had seen was enough for him to consider a few things.

Her friends had been sitting on one side of her. Her brother on the other. An empty chair was between them, probably reserved for Alberto himself.

Except the man wasn't there.

Fury filled Kaz's throat with a sickening taste all over again, and he clenched his fists tight enough that his fingernails bit into his palms.

Had the Italian boss decided to forgo his wife's show because he had better business to attend to, say like making sure his orders were followed through?

Kaz wasn't sure, but he didn't like the look of it.

"Are you done watching this?" Ruslan asked.

"Yeah, whatever."

Ruslan changed the channel, but not in quick enough time for Kaz to miss the camera's next shot landing directly on Violet and her friends again. It lingered a bit longer the second time—long enough for him to see her perfectly coiffed like she always seemed to be whenever she was out in public.

That wasn't what irritated him the most, however.

It was seeing her with the other two—mostly the one who lied and caused his brother to be beaten like an animal. She had to have known her friend was saying falsehoods about what had happened that night, and yet, she didn't correct the lies.

And those who didn't correct other's lies were just as bad as those who spoke them.

No, she was sitting right there with the other girl, even as she wore that fucking red dress that he'd chosen at the boutique. It was almost like she was taunting him, even if she couldn't have possibly known that he was going to see her wearing it.

He wanted to know *why*.

If Kaz wasn't allowed to go after the Italian who attacked Ruslan because of his father's orders, Vasily had said nothing about Violet.

... for once.

Kaz stood from the couch, still simmering in his fury and settled on his decision. Manhattan might be a warrant for his death, but he was willing to risk it after tonight.

"You'll be all right, yes?" Kaz asked his brother.

Ruslan glanced up, a knowing glint burning behind his eyes. "Stay in Brighton, Kaz."

"I'm not planning on going anywhere. You heard Vasily—I was told no ... and called a child."

"That doesn't mean you'll listen."

"I'm going home, *brat*."

Ruslan let out a heavy breath, turning back to the television. "Sure you are."

Violet snatched a flute glass filled nearly to the rim with champagne and tossed the bubbly drink back in one long pull. She knew it didn't look well on her to be drinking like that with so many people around to watch, but her nerves were frayed enough to make her reach for a second glass as soon as she finished the first.

Just holding the second one was enough.

It was there if she needed it.

Out of the whole event of her mother's fashion shows, the one thing Violet usually enjoyed the most were the after parties. While she could get an up close view of high profile people and celebrities sitting along the runway at the actual event, during the parties afterwards, she was rubbing elbows with those same people.

Most of the time, it was surreal.

Tonight, she was not in the mood.

It didn't help that her friends had all but deserted her after arriving to the rented private upper-Manhattan loft space that her mother preferred to use for her after parties. Both Nicole and Amelia were gone off into the crowd of guests somewhere, putting their faces in front of the right people and smiling just the way they had been taught.

Violet knew the game. She used to play it, too.

Not tonight.

Glancing around the loft, she took in the black with chrome detailed decorations that matched the theme of her mother's show. Chandeliers full of glittering crystals hung low from the vaulted ceiling. Most of the people had changed attire from what they had been wearing at the show, to sexier nightwear that they could move and dance in. Music from a DJ filled the space.

Violet's mind was somewhere else entirely.

BETHANY-KRIS & LONDON MILLER

Her father had yet to come back. It wasn't like Alberto to leave his wife hanging on a night that was as important as this one. Andrea was pissed off to the high heavens, but she was hiding it well enough, with her usual smile plastered on and a hand held out, ready to accept praise for her latest designs.

Violet was still worried. It put her on edge, which meant she just wasn't in the mood for the party or the people. She would much rather be back at her condo where she could at least feel safe.

Maybe that's what it was.

Maybe she just didn't feel safe out in the open like this when something was clearly wrong.

Turning her back to the crowd, Violet stared out one of the loft's many floor-to-ceiling windows as she tipped the flute glass up for another drink. The alcohol settled in her blood with a heavy quality, numbing her senses enough to take that edge off for the moment.

She wasn't stupid enough to think it would last for long.

"There you are."

Violet turned on her heel at the sound of her mother's voice. Andrea's smile was wide, but her eyes spoke of irritation as they narrowed in on Violet.

"What are you doing over here in the corner by yourself?" Andrea asked low, careful not to talk loud enough for others to hear. "I found your friends, but you weren't with them. Do you know the people who are in here tonight, Violet? You should be out there talking to them."

"I can do that on another night, Ma," Violet said. "You'll have another two shows this year alone."

Andrea's lips thinned. "What is the problem?"

"Nothing. I'm just tired."

"Well, get untired," her mother snapped.

Violet bit back her retort, knowing it wouldn't do anything except piss her mother off further. Andrea's bad mood was only caused because of her husband's absence. Otherwise, she would leave her daughter alone.

"Aren't there people who want to talk to you?" Violet asked.

"Yes, but at the moment, I'm busy chasing after my *daughter*."

"It's not like you want to be doing that, so why are you even bothering?"

Andrea straightened, her hand clenching tight around the flute glass she held. Violet stood still and strong in the face of her mother's barely-hidden anger. She felt a little proud of herself for having stood up to Andrea for once, because she usually wouldn't, and instead, would let her mother criticize her as much as she wanted.

Maybe Violet was just growing up from that sort of nonsense with her mother. As a child, and a young teen, she had constantly tried to seek her mother's approval in any way she could. While she loved attention from her father, she had always wanted some sort of affection from her mother as well.

Andrea's affection only came when she approved of something, and not in between.

She was the very definition of conditional love.

Violet just didn't care anymore.

"What did you just say to me?" Andrea asked.

If she held that glass any tighter, it very well might shatter.

Violet nodded at the glass. "Careful. We all know how quickly spilled blood can end a good party."

Andrea's hand loosened a bit. "Fine. If you want to leave like your father did, then go. God knows you're doing nothing for me standing here in the goddamn corner."

She smirked, knowing her mother's words were only meant to hurt. For the majority of the night, her mother had ignored her, more so after hearing her daughter be complimented on the dress she'd chosen to wear. She hadn't missed the looks Andrea had shot in her direction when she thought Violet didn't notice, either.

The red dress Kaz picked out.

Unable to stop herself, though she knew she shouldn't, Violet brushed her hand across the skirt of the red dress and said, "Even standing in a dress like this?"

Andrea's jaw ticked. "Especially in a dress like that. You're dressed like a whore."

"You never did like it when someone looked better than you, Ma."

Her mother didn't respond to that. Instead, she clenched her teeth, turned on her heel, and stormed back into the flood of guests.

Violet was already heading toward the door.

Tapping his thumb against the steering wheel, Kaz stared out the windshield, watching and waiting for the moment that Violet Gallucci appeared. He knew she wasn't home yet—he'd been out on the street long enough to know that much. But he was a patient man ...

In his other hand, he turned a cigarette over between his fingers, thinking of how the nicotine within would take the edge off and give him peace of mind. For now, he was jittery with anticipation. There was a certain thrill to be where he was, especially knowing that he courted the wrath of more than one man if anyone knew where he was, or worse, what he had planned.

There was no guarantee what this night would bring—it wouldn't be the first time he had made a mistake—but by the end of it, and of this he was sure, his point would be made, whether the girl he was waiting on liked it or not.

Glancing over at the illuminated dash, Kaz checked the time once more, then as he contemplated withdrawing his phone, just to keep himself busy, blinding headlights caught his attention. The town car they came from slowed down in front of Violet's building.

The rear, passenger door swung open, and after a moment, the very person he'd been waiting on for more than an hour stepped out, slamming the door shut behind her. Before she could get far, however, the passenger's window rolled down and a masculine voice called out to her. She turned, a flash of annoyance in her eyes as she went back, bending over to see inside the car and listen to what was being said.

The position made the material of the dress pull tighter across her backside, drawing his attention there and down the length of her legs.

Kaz might have hated the girl at the moment, but he could still appreciate the sight she made.

After a rather brief conversation, one that had Violet nodding, she was finally allowed to walk inside, and only when she was through the doors did the car pull away.

Stepping out of his own vehicle, Kaz tucked his cigarette away, making his way to the entrance. There was no guarantee that the doorman would let him in. Though the man looked ancient, he probably remembered a face and knew that he didn't live in the building, but that didn't stop Kaz.

Deftly, he pulled a hundred-dollar bill free from his suit jacket, holding it between two fingers as he offered it to the man without question. "I'm here to see the Martins on fifteen," he said by way of explanation.

Whether there was an actual Martin family, or the man just wanted the money, Kaz was let through.

There was no sight of Violet in the lobby, but there was no need. Knowing men like Alberto Gallucci, he wouldn't just allow his daughter into any apartment. No, it would need to be at the top, and one with a fair level of privacy, in case he or any of his associates were to visit.

Arriving at the bank of elevators, he checked the numbers. There were four, with two having never left the lobby floor, and another only going up to the second floor. The last, however, had stopped on the 26th floor— which must have been the one Violet had taken.

Boarding one, he pressed the number, watching the doors close as he drummed his fingers against the railing. After a while, he curled his fingers around the cool metal, needing to get his shit together. He had too many tells—the bouncing of his knee, drumming his fingers—like no matter how carefully controlled he tried to force himself to be, his nerves always manifested themselves.

When the bell dinged—the doors opening once more—Kaz stepped out, glancing down the hallway. To his surprise, there was only one unit on the floor, the door at the end. As he stopped in front of it and knocked, he didn't bother covering the peephole, but purposefully took a step back so that she would have a clear view as to who stood on the other side.

He waited. And waited. Then considered the logistics of kicking the fucking door in before it swung open, Violet standing on the other side of it, wide-eyed like she had never seen a man before.

The cameras hadn't done her justice, not even a little. In person, he could see the warm glow of her skin, the way her dress hugged to her curves. She looked beautiful, stunning really, enough that it made him want to drink her in further, and that annoyed the fuck out of him.

His brother had nearly gotten his head caved in because of her shit, because she and her friends decided they wanted a little trouble and wandered over to their side to fulfill it.

His anger renewed, when she opened her mouth to speak, he snapped, "Don't speak."

Surprisingly, she heeded the command, her lips slamming shut. He didn't give her a chance to contemplate her actions before he was grabbing her arm, dragging her back into her apartment, and slammed the door shut behind them. He swung her around to stand in front of him.

"Kaz, what the hell are you doing?" she asked after he'd let her go, looking down at her arm as though it hurt.

But he hadn't gripped her hard, of that he was sure. "What did I say?"

"Wait, wha—"

"Violet!"

She jerked violently at the sound of her own name, her gaze lifting to his immediately as fear clouded them. Oh, was she getting it now? Was she understanding that he wasn't under her father and wouldn't treat her like she was fucking glass?

"Tell me, when you stood in that office with me, worried about that little *suka*, what did I say?"

She swallowed, the sound almost audible as her eyes flitted to the side and back again. "That she would be fine with your brother, but I—"

When he took a step toward her, she took one back, and they repeated this dance until her back was against the wall and he was merely inches away. He shouldn't have been delighted in her fear, but the sight of it—the way she trembled slightly, her breath catching in her throat—called to the darker urges inside of him.

"Imagine my surprise when fucking Italians show up and beat my brother to shit because your *friend* told them that he drugged her."

"Amelia woul—"

"Who is Franco?" He really wanted to know, and despite his promise to his brother that he wouldn't be going after the Italians, he would at least have an ending place for his rage once he got the green light.

Understanding seemed to light up her eyes. "Amelia's boyfriend, but he—"

"Is that what you do?" Kaz asked, interrupting her once more, dragging his gaze down her front like he couldn't help himself. "You and your little friends. You go out, get fucking slaughtered on drinks, and then cause problems? Is this some kind of game for you? Is that what you want, someone to fuck with?"

She was just standing there, staring up at him as though in a daze, but he was too pissed for that shit.

Slamming his open palm against the wall to get her attention, he said, "Answer me, you little *suka*!"

"Fuck you!" She exploded, shoving two hands against his chest and pushing him away.

Her strength was laughable compared to his, but he did take a step back, waiting to see what she would do next, because while her fear called to him, that fire in her eyes excited him more.

Violet clenched her fists at her side, staying pressed against the wall as she glared at Kaz. She was grateful he had taken a step back from her, because it let her take a second to think, but it didn't offer much more.

She could still see him. The tightness of his jaw, the darkness in his features, and the anger radiating over his entire body.

He was so pissed.

At *her*.

And he still looked good.

She kind of hated him for that, too.

"Who do you think you are?" she asked him.

Kaz cocked one eyebrow. "I—"

"No, you get to listen now." Violet's anger forced her away from the wall where she felt a little more grounded, and right back at the man who thought he had some kind of right to storm into her apartment, demanding answers like she was the only one who might have them. Her finger snapped into his chest hard, making his gaze drop down to her hand. "Fuck *you.*"

He chuckled—dry and deep.

Violet ignored the way it rocked his chest and her hand. "I don't care who you are. You don't get to come in here like that, putting your goddamn hands on me and dragging me around like some doll."

Again, he just smirked.

That time, he bared his teeth a little, but he was still watching her hand.

It irritated Violet like she couldn't explain.

"Look at me!"

Kaz did, instantly. "What?"

Violet stilled. The one word had been practically spat from between clenched teeth—like she was nothing to him, and she wasn't worth his words, looks, or attention.

She didn't believe it, though.

He'd come here.

That meant something.

"You don't get to do that," she repeated quieter.

"Your friend got my brother's head bashed in—do you not understand that? Your little lies—saving face, whatever the fuck it was— nearly took his life tonight. If you think you don't deserve to be called out on bullshit like that, I have news for you."

Violet shook her head, frustrated. "I don't know what you're talking about. I told my father what happened."

"Lied," Kaz corrected.

She jammed her finger at him again. "I did not!"

Kaz, like she was an annoying little fly that kept touching him, brushed her hand away from his body. "Don't do that again."

Violet barked out a laugh. "Why, because you don't like it? But it's completely okay for you to grab me like a piece of property and haul me the fuck around. *Right.*"

She poked him again.

"Fuck you," she muttered.

Kaz's jaw clenched, and his gaze narrowed. "Stop."

Violet didn't drop her hand, but she didn't poke him again. The heated anger in his tone was enough of a warning to say she had pushed him to a line and he was teetering on it. His fists, balled tightly at his sides, said he was holding back.

"I did not lie," she said quietly. "I told my father what happened at the club with the drinks and Amelia."

"With the addition that my brother was the one to do that, yes?"

Violet's frustration exploded again, but this time, she didn't let it blow up at him. She turned away, throwing a hand high in his face as if to wave away his stupidity and his assumptions.

She didn't even get to turn around completely or drop her hand before Kaz had grabbed it tight in his own and spun her back around.

"Don't you fucking walk away from me right now—don't put your hand in my face like you're fucking dismissing me!"

Violet's back met the wall with a hard smack. The air left her lungs with a gasp when he grabbed her other hand and pushed it down at her side. Kaz clouded her vision—all of him—dark, angry, and ready to *hurt*.

Strangely, she wasn't scared that time.

Swallowing hard, Violet refused to meet his gaze. "Let me go."

"I like you right where you are."

But he was too close to her.

Close enough for her to smell his cologne and see the flecks of blue in his gray eyes. Close enough that she could feel the tremor crawling over his arms and the way his muscles jumped when he pressed against her.

Too close.

She shouldn't be turned on by a man who did to her what Kaz had done.

"Tell me the truth," he demanded. "You lied."

"I didn't."

Violet didn't even know how to begin explaining her situation to Kaz, but his assumptions were entirely wrong.

"Do you understand the gravity of lying about a man like that in this kind of business?"

She blinked. "Yes."

His hold on her wrists tightened to an almost painful point. "And you still did it!"

Violet's head snapped around, her gaze cutting to his. "I did not!"

"Standing by and doing nothing as someone else lies is the same thing, Violet."

"I didn't do that either, asshole."

He released her one arm, and pointed a finger right in her face. It almost reminded her of a gun ready to blow as it came closer.

"You did, you fucked us over when all I did was try to help you that night. But I suppose I shouldn't be surprised, right? Rich little *sukas* like you have to get your kicks somewhere when you're bored of draining your daddy's pockets dry."

Violet's mouth dropped open, and a pain sliced straight through her heart.

He didn't know her.

He knew nothing about her.

And his words *ached*.

Reaction from pure fury alone was the only excuse Violet had for her next actions. With her hand free, he had left himself exposed. Before she could properly think over what she was doing, she smacked his hand out of her face with a huff.

Kaz dropped her other hand, surprised.

She was raising it just as fast.

When it cracked across his cheek, the sound reverberated in the condo.

Nothing else made a noise.

He didn't even breathe as he took a single step back, his thumb stroking his jaw as his stare focused in on her again.

She didn't move an inch.

Violet knew better than to hit a man when he was in a rage. A normal man would walk away, but a man prone to violence might not.

She opened her mouth to speak—not to apologize, but to tell him to leave—but she didn't get the chance to say a thing. Kaz was on her before she had even blinked.

His hands were at the top of her throat, forcing her head up as he crowded her to the wall again. Violet's eyes widened, her heart racing as she felt his long fingers tighten just enough to scare her.

"Don't hit me," he said.

Violet tensed as his hands began to move down her throat with a slowness that made her shudder. Maybe it was the roughness of his skin, or the heat of his palms dragging down the column of her neck, but his touch didn't quite feel threatening like it first had.

She sucked in a deep breath when his thumbs rested against the hollow of her throat. He didn't press to cut off her windpipe, but rather, just let his thumbs rest there like they could hurt her with her next blink.

"I didn't lie," she told him. "And I didn't know she did."

Kaz's gray stare never wavered from hers. "It's easier for me to believe otherwise."

"That's something you'll have to deal with, I guess."

Her words were bravado, and very little else. It was getting more difficult by the second to ignore the shake in her hands or the pulsing ache between her thighs.

This was not good at all.

"This could be so easy," Kaz said, still watching her in that way of his. "Just a little press of my fingers right here, and then what you did is answered for."

"Except I didn't do it."

His lips parted to speak again, but he hesitated.

"I didn't," she repeated. "And you won't hurt me for not doing anything at all."

Kaz's mouth curled at the corners, and he flashed his white teeth in a mix between a sneer and a grimace. She felt his fingers tighten to her throat and his thumbs press against the hollow just enough to make her stand a little straighter, freeze under his hands, and *wait*.

She didn't have to wait for long, but his next move was not what she was expecting.

Violet blinked and Kaz's mouth was crushing down on hers rough, hard, and demanding. The shock of his kiss made her gasp, and his tongue instantly sought out the heat of her mouth. His hands never left her throat, but they had loosened enough that she relaxed. And when his tongue struck hard against hers, she was already fisting his jacket and pulling him closer.

He groaned against her mouth, the sound originating from somewhere deep in his chest. Violet's eyes were locked on his, only shutting for a brief moment when his teeth sunk into her bottom lip.

The shock of pain was *electric*.

Jesus.

She whined low, and pulled him closer again.

There was no hiding how she shook and he let out a ragged sigh as his forehead rested to hers.

Silence echoed.

He watched her like that, saying nothing.

She didn't mind—she no longer wanted to move.

A heartbeat's time passed before Kaz moved away, fighting to get himself under control. This wasn't the first time he had ever kissed a girl, and even if it had only lasted for no more than a minute, his cock was harder than it had ever been.

She didn't take her eyes from him, not even when she licked her lips, just a quick swipe of her tongue that made him ache all the more. Would she look like that when she was on her knees? Would she be as excited to have those pretty little lips wrapped around his cock?

Shit.

He shouldn't have been thinking of her, not that way, but he couldn't get the image out of his head, and the more he stood there staring at her as she did him, the more he thought about getting her exactly as he wanted.

Reaching down, he palmed his erection, shifting it into a less painful position. Violet's eyes followed, a flush blossoming in her cheeks as she watched his actions.

Knowing that it wasn't going to do him any favors by watching her reaction to him, Kaz turned away, taking a breath as he contemplated where to go from there. It wasn't like he could pretend like it didn't happen—he didn't want to.

He had learned rather quickly that she had already managed to dig her way under his skin, and at the moment, he had no intention of trying to get her out. So since she was already there …

Turning back to her, he got himself under control long enough to ask, "Hungry?"

Maybe it was the confusion of all that had just happened, or perhaps because he sounded so unaffected that she frowned, her brows drawing together. "What?"

"Are you hungry?" he asked again. "For food, I mean."

That, at the very least, wiped the confusion from her face, only for a scowl to replace it. "Why are you asking?"

"Let's grab something to eat."

Violet looked like he'd sprouted a second head. "Are you joking?"

Kaz shrugged a single shoulder. "I'm quite serious."

"You have to be joking … Kaz, are you forgetting who I am? Who *we* are? We can't be seen together, let alone *be* together."

It sounded more like she was afraid of being seen with him as opposed to not wanting to go with him at all. "Come with me. We'll get out of Brooklyn, I'll take you to a little place I know that'll keep you out of trouble, and we can have a moment to ourselves. What do you say?"

Violet looked nervous, unsure even, but as he expected her to decline, maybe even talk more about the risks, she nodded.

Kaz waited in the living room as Violet disappeared into her bedroom to change. While he hadn't gotten the chance to fully appreciate that dress on her, that would have to wait for another time.

Another time …

He was already reading too much into the situation.

It shouldn't have mattered that they kissed, or even that she made him feel something he couldn't explain. She was still a Gallucci, and he was a Markovic—the two families just didn't mix. But as he waited for her to reappear, that distinction didn't seem to matter to him.

Taking in her space, he eyed it carefully—the soft gray walls, the mixture of fabrics and textures, something Vera would have pointed out, if she were there. His sister always liked to point out things whenever they were together, like she couldn't control the impulse. For the most part he tuned her out, but sometimes he picked up on smaller details.

Kaz had only been waiting a few minutes when Violet reappeared, dressed in a pair of jeans that hugged her hips and contoured to her legs, along with a simple white tank-top beneath a bomber jacket. Despite how understated she'd attempted to be, she still stood out. She had even gone so far as to pull the long length of her hair up into a ponytail, and washed the makeup from her face.

It almost felt like he was dealing with another person entirely—like seeing another side of her. He had never seen her this way, so … vulnerable.

But he liked it all the same.

"Ready?"

Nodding without a word, she grabbed her purse and a set of keys, exiting her apartment first before he followed. The ride down to the lobby was quiet and uneventful, but when they stepped off the elevator, she hesitated, looking over at the desk attendants before making a decision about them and turning to go out another exit at the side of the building.

"They answer to my father," she said softly when they were outside and the metal door was swinging shut. "Since he pays their salary, they're more willing to tell him what I'm doing."

Made sense that she wouldn't want them to be seen leaving together. Earlier, they hadn't come in together, so there was no reason for the clerks to report to Alberto about who they had seen coming in.

Reaching the mouth of the alley, Violet scanned the street. "Where's your car?"

Withdrawing his own set of keys, he hit the button on the fob, the headlights to his Range Rover briefly flashing in the darkness of the night. "Probably best that I hadn't brought it, no?"

She didn't respond, not verbally, but he could tell she was thinking something.

Going around the front of his truck, he opened the passenger door, offering her a hand as he helped her up and inside. One she was situated, he hurried around to his own side and climbed in, starting it up, and turning on his lights.

"Are all of your windows tinted this way?" she asked, gesturing to the windshield with a wave of her hand.

"I like my privacy."

And that was the truth. All three of his cars had the same window treatment, and though his apartment faced the beach, he was so far up from the ground that with the sun reflecting on the glass, no one could see in.

Pulling out onto the street, Kaz was mindful of where he was and who he was with. It didn't matter that he wasn't driving the car everyone associated with him, it only took a single person to fuck this up.

His eyes were on the road, his attention focused when Violet called his name. When he looked in her direction, she looked uneasy all of a sudden, but was turned in his direction.

"I'm sorry about your brother. I didn't know anything about what Franco was going to do, honestly." She was quiet for a moment before continuing. "I can't speak for anyone else, but I never said anything negative about him, or you for that matter."

Kaz contemplated her answer, rolling her words around in his head. Before he had been too angry to see reason, and hadn't really wanted to listen to a word she said, but now that he was slightly more rational, he believed her. It could still be that the kiss they shared was frying his brain, but for the time being, he accepted her word.

"Is he … is he okay?"

"He'll be fine," Kaz said softly. He didn't bother to mention that Ruslan had suffered worse under the hands of someone that was meant to love him. And before he could talk himself out of it, he added, "Thank you though, for your concern."

She nodded, and for the rest of the time, they rode in a comfortable silence. When they reached the outskirts of Brooklyn, and closer to his territory, she sat up a little straighter, becoming more aware of her surroundings.

"Don't worry, *krasivaya*. I won't let anything happen to you."

Reaching across the seat, he lifted her hand, stroking his thumb along the back of it to calm her. He could understand her fear, not knowing what to expect, and placing trust into a person that she'd probably always been told was the enemy.

But he did hope, as foolish as it might have been, that he could change her opinion of him.

After another couple of miles, Kaz finally caught sight of a hole-in-the-wall diner that looked like it was one step above being closed down, but while the outside wasn't much to look at, the interior was little better on the eyes, and the food was fucking amazing.

The only question was whether or not Violet would be okay in a place like this.

"I know the outside doesn't give the best impression," Kaz said as he parked the Range Rover.

Violet gave him a look. "Understatement."

"Don't go all spoiled princess on me right now." He smirked when she scowled. "I promise the food is worth it, if you turn cheek to the appearance. Sometimes the best things come in the most unlikely of packages." .

Violet pursed her lips in an attempt to hide her smile. "Fine. But only for you."

"I'll take that."

Before she could say another thing, he had turned the truck off and was getting out. She barely had time to unbuckle her seatbelt before he was opening her door.

Like any good gentleman would do, she mused.

Kaz offered her a smooth smile and his hand. She took it, but that familiar heat siphoned from his palm straight into hers as he helped her out of the large vehicle.

"When you're not driving the car, I see you feel the need to drive something that's big enough to mow trees over," she said.

"Cheap shots about my vehicles will get you nowhere."

She doubted that.

It would probably get her something like that kiss from earlier if she irked him enough.

Violet wasn't looking to do that, however. As it were, she had taken a lot of risks just to give this man a few hours of her time—and it was precious time, considering how much trouble she would find herself in if they were caught. She wasn't about to ruin it by seeing if she could provoke him into another moment.

But as she stared at him from the side while he locked the Range Rover, she knew somehow that she probably wouldn't have to try at all if she wanted him to kiss her again. She probably just needed to grab him and pull him closer ...

Kaz cleared his throat, making Violet's attention snap from his mouth to his eyes in a flash. "Food, right?"

She rapped her fingernails against her thigh. Why did it sound like he was offering something else? Like all she had to do was ask, and he would follow through.

"Food," she agreed.

The inside of the diner was slightly better than the outside. It almost seemed like a throwback to the fifties diners in design with booths lining the walls, a main bar across the front crowded by stools, and the white and black checkered floor and walls.

An older couple ate at the far corner booth in the right, while a younger couple chatted animatedly on a pair of stools. Only a woman wearing a white-and-yellow ensemble stood behind the cash register, counting money. She didn't even look up as Kaz and Violet approached.

"Food or coffee?" the woman asked.

"Food," Kaz said.

"Find a place to sit. I'll be with you in a second."

Violet turned to find which booth she wanted to sit in—one that wouldn't put them directly in the view of the windows—but she stilled in place when Kaz's hand slid into hers. She hadn't been expecting the gesture, and he didn't give her much time to think on it before he was pulling her along at his side.

"I like to sit back here," he said, directing her to the exact opposite booth from where the older couple were sitting.

It was tucked away in the corner where the lights were a bit dimmer and they had more privacy from the few diners. Kaz let Violet slide in so that her back was to the wall. She expected him to sit across from her, but he surprised her by tipping his chin as if to ask her to move over.

Violet did, laughing when he slid in beside her.

"Always sit here, huh?" she asked.

Kaz shrugged, pulling off his suit jacket and tossing it into the booth seat across from them. "People don't usually like to sit in the darker spot of a restaurant unless they're going for that kind of mood."

"And you like your privacy."

"You don't?"

Violet wet her lips, nodding. "I do. I'm just not given very much."

"Ah, point taken."

Kaz quieted as the woman dressed in yellow and white approached with a smile on her face like she recognized him. Violet wondered how often he actually came here to eat.

The woman held no menus in her hands. "The usual, Kaz?"

He flashed a smile.

Violet ignored the pinch of jealousy flaring up in her middle. It wasn't the time, and the waitress wasn't exactly anything to be concerned about, considering she was a good fifteen years older than Kaz at least. Maybe it was the fact that the woman seemed friendly with him, as if she knew him.

And Violet didn't.

"Usual for me," he said. "Same for her."

"About twenty minutes, okay? Daniel is just getting off his break."

Kaz waved a hand. "No problem."

When the woman was gone, Violet asked, "What's the usual?"

"Something you can't go wrong with. Burgers. Fries. Coke. I can change it, if that's not—"

"It's great," she interrupted quickly. "How often do you come here?"

"Are we playing twenty questions now?"

Violet glanced away from the teasing, light grin he sported. It didn't help the walls she was trying to keep up. At least if she tried to keep them up for a while, it might be harder for this man to tear them down.

Her father had always said she made friends too easily, and without care.

"Hey," he murmured.

Violet kept staring at her hands on the table. It was only when she felt a finger slide under the line of her jaw, stopping at her chin and pressing a little to make her turn her head, did she look at him. "What?"

"You're acting stiff. Why?"

"You're not worried, not even a little?" she asked. She wasn't ready to admit that she actually thought she *liked* him—not even to herself.

Withdrawing his hand, Kaz seemed to study her before giving an answer. "I'm cautious by nature, Violet, but that doesn't mean I'm foolproof. So of course, there's a part of me that wonders what will happen if someone walks in here, but what is life without risks? I'm willing to risk it."

And more, Violet thought. While she wasn't completely sure of what her father was capable of, she knew if he ever caught her with Kaz, it wouldn't end well for him.

"Are you telling me to relax?"

Kaz winked. "Live a little, *krasivaya*."

Violet couldn't help but notice how that Russian word seemed a lot more affectionate than the one he had called her earlier—whatever it was.

"What does that mean?" she dared to ask.

For the first time, he managed to look slightly uncomfortable. "It's a term of endearment."

"That doesn't tell me what it means."

Kaz chuckled. "Good, you're quick, too."

Violet pretended like he hadn't said that. "Stop deflecting. Why won't you tell me what it means?"

"It's not that I won't. It means you're a beauty, or beautiful. Take it either way, depending on how it's used and said."

Oh.

Violet hadn't thought it would mean that. "And the other thing?"

Kaz eyed her from the side. "I didn't—"

"You did. Before you put your hands around my throat."

His lip curled up at the side as he said, "Can I just apologize for that one without an explanation?"

"Not now."

Kaz sighed heavily. "Bitch."

Violet tried not to glare—she really did.

And failed.

"I'm sorry," Kaz said quickly.

Violet wasn't sure it helped. "So basically you called me a spoiled, rich bitch."

"And now I'm taking you out to eat. Do you see how these things work out?"

"You called me a *bitch* and then you kissed me," she muttered.

"You're not making this easy right now," he replied.

"No one ever said I was easy, Kaz."

Kaz laughed, deep and heady. "Fair enough. I am sorry."

"I'm not sure that's enough ..."

"What do you want, then?" he asked, resting his elbows on the table as he leaned toward her. "What can I do to make it up to you?"

She matched his posture. "What are you offering?"

Kaz smiled and the sight of it, so brilliant and open, made her return it. "Ah, there's the Gallucci in you."

Usually there was some derision to his tone whenever he made reference to her family's name, but this time, it sounded almost complimentary.

Violet tapped her chin with a nail, pretending to think over her answer though there was really only one thing she wanted. "How about another kiss, but without the bitch this time?"

A surprise burst of laughter left him, but it was over in a second as his face turned serious. Curling a hand around the side of her face, he pulled her closer, his face just a breath away. She waited, more than a little ready for what he would do next, but he didn't come any closer.

Then, he whispered, "Take what you want."

A flood of heat swept through her at his words, but she didn't waste a second thinking on his words—she just did exactly what he said.

This time, it was her kissing him, pressing closer, wanting to eliminate all the space between them. Despite how hard the rest of him was, his lips were soft, but unyielding. For a time, she was the one in charge, taking what she wanted, but very soon, he was taking over, tilting her head to the side as he deepened the kiss, putting her exactly as he wanted her.

His other arm slipped around her waist, drifting beneath the edge of her shirt, the heat of his palm almost shocking. In one firm pull, he had her closer as their lips found a familiar rhythm that shouldn't have been familiar at all. His fingers pressed into her skin, teasing and promising at the same time. She hummed a contented sound against his mouth.

Kaz smirked, pulling away slightly. "Was that what you were looking for?"

"Better without the bitch."

He lifted a brow. "Why do I hear a but in there?"

Violet shrugged. "But your hands. On my throat. I liked your hands the last time, too."

Kaz's grin spread a little wider, and he shook his head. "Killing me here."

She wasn't trying to.

His tone had deepened with a huskiness that made her mouth dry. She was not alone in this strange attraction. Not in the least.

Violet needed a second to breathe, never mind the ache between her thighs. "How did the birthday party go?"

"That's what you want to talk about right now?"

"Distance?"

He seemed to get what she said, and what she didn't. "My sisters loved the clothes. Thank you for that, again."

"Sixteen-year-olds are not so hard to figure out."

"These ones can be," he said, laughing.

106

Violet cleared her throat, still hyperaware of his hand on her back and how close he was to her. "All right. Enough."

Kaz's brow dropped in his confusion. "Enough of what?"

"Distance."

She leaned forward, and kissed him again.

Kaz liked bending rules, but never outright breaking them—he thrilled in it—but as he exited the diner with Violet on his arm with every intention of taking her back to his place, there was no doubt that he wasn't bending a rule, but obliterating the fucking thing.

But he didn't care. It was the last thing on his mind as he opened the passenger door and helped her into his truck. He was, however, wondering how they had got to this point, or rather how *he* had gotten here.

When he had set out for her place, ready to do murder, he hadn't for a second thought they would end up here.

Nor had he imagined that he would have kissed her. Not once, not even twice, but a number of times that had all blended into one.

There was just something about her … something he hadn't expected from a girl like her. Kaz had had his fair share of spoiled, rich girls, and had grown bored with them fairly quickly after only a couple of weeks. They were all the same: immature, weak, and only valuing what a person would buy or give them.

But Violet … there was a fire in her, a burning passion that he wanted to ignite further, just to see what would happen. He wanted to see her come alive beneath his hands.

It was dangerous, not just her, but the implications of what would come if anyone found out about this.

This could no longer be considered innocent.

And with what he planned to do to her, it definitely wouldn't be.

Sliding in the truck, Kaz buckled up, the lights on the dash illuminating the dark interior as he started it up. Violet was turned in his direction, her expression open, her eyes seeking an answer that he wasn't quite ready to give.

They had only been driving for a short while when that expression changed as she said, "This isn't the way to Manhattan."

He couldn't quite contain the smirk that was fighting its way free. "No, it isn't."

She grew quiet again, making Kaz glance over in her direction. "You can always say no. I'll take you home right now, and we'll never have to talk about this again," he said. It was the last thing he wanted to do, but he would if she asked it of him. Right then, he'd give her anything she wanted.

"I've wondered what your place looked like," she murmured, like the comment was more to herself than for him.

That was the only answer he needed, and more was what was left unspoken between them. He wasn't the only one to receive warnings, he was sure, so she was taking just as much of a risk coming to Little Odessa with him as he was. Violet was trusting him, believing that he would not only keep her safe, but ensure that no one would catch them together.

Kaz wouldn't break that.

The rest of the drive was spent in silence, and though she sat a little straighter when they got into the heart of Little Odessa, making him reach across the seat and rest his hand on her thigh, his fingers curving around. It was silent, his reminder that she was with him, but it was enough to get her to relax.

Pulling into the parking structure attached to his apartment building, he drove around to the back, parking next to his Porsche, and the set of service elevators nearby. Kaz rarely went through the lobby anymore—especially when there was no guarantee what he would look like when he got home.

As they boarded, he pressed the button for his floor, and stepped back, looking to Violet as the doors closed.

There was no going back now.

Heart hammering, butterflies fluttering in her stomach, Violet tried to act normal as Kaz walked ahead of her once the doors to the elevator reopened. Like her place, his seemed to be the only one on this floor, but his had added security. After sticking the key in the lock, he pressed his thumb to an electronic key pad, the locks clicking open audibly.

At least she knew no one would just be walking in uninvited.

He opened the door wide, nodding his head for her to go in ahead of him.

She didn't know what she was expecting when she walked in, a bachelor's pad maybe, or a barren space that looked like it wasn't lived in, but as she looked around, she remembered that his sister was an interior designer, and it was clear that she had used her skills on his place.

The floors were a dark hardwood, his walls painted a soft gray. Floor-to-ceiling windows on one side of the room were shielded by dark gray drapes, though they were parted just enough that she could see the beach through them. A large sectional divided the living room and the open concept kitchen.

His place, though decorated with just about everything a person could want, looked inviting rather than cold, like a store room display.

"I have to make a phone call," Kaz said. "Look around if you want, but not too deep."

Violet raised a brow at his words. "What, scared I might find all your secrets, skeletons, and fears hidden in your dresser drawers?"

Kaz didn't even blink. "Exactly that."

"Closets are open, then?"

"Only a stupid man hides skeletons in the closet. Everyone always looks there first."

Violet laughed as Kaz pulled his phone out and made a beeline for the hallway opposite to the large living room. She milled around, noting that while the place was decorated and beautiful, there weren't many pictures to give insight to the personal life of Kaz or his family. In the kitchen, she found a haphazard stack of mail piled in the middle of the table, and smiled to herself.

Apparently, she wasn't the only one who just let her mail fall wherever it dropped.

After another couple of minutes without Kaz coming back, she decided to go in search of him. Down the hallway he had disappeared earlier, she found several doors. All of which were closed but for one. Standing in the doorway, she realized it was his bedroom.

Unlike the living room, his bedroom actually looked like someone regularly used it. His bed was left unmade, the sheets in disarray as though he hadn't been able to get comfortable in them—she briefly wondered whether he slept without clothes on. Twin nightstands, and a bookcase along another wall made up the last of the furniture in the room.

The muffled, one-sided conversation coming from behind the closed door directly across from the bedroom made her pause, and stopped her from entering Kaz's bedroom any more than she already had.

"Hey," she heard Kaz say. And then just as quickly, "Just wanted to check up on you, Rus."

Guilt flooded Violet almost instantly. The anger was quick to follow. She didn't want to believe that Amelia had told Franco a bunch of lies about what really happened that night at the club, but it seemed that was just what her friend had done.

And in the process, a man who had only tried to help them had gotten hurt.

So yeah, that pissed Violet off.

"Good, *brat*," she heard Kaz say. "No, I told you I was going home … Shit, do you want me to call you from my house phone? Hang up and I'll do that. We can play that game if you want to, Ruslan."

At that point, Violet decided to leave Kaz to his private conversation with his brother. She didn't feel right spying on him like that, after all. He had already told her to look around. Wasn't that enough?

As she stepped further into the bedroom, flicking on the lights as she passed the switch on the wall, her nervousness returned. She knew better than to be here—knew this was ten shades of stupid, and getting worse by the second.

Violet had worked particularly hard to make her father feel at least slightly more comfortable with trusting her again. She hadn't intended to disobey him, not like she currently was, but something in the back of her mind wouldn't let her drop Kaz. While her father made every effort to act as if the Russians didn't matter in their world, it seemed like fate had entirely different plans what with the way it kept throwing Kaz back into her path.

Or rather, the way he kept putting himself there.

She was starting to think she didn't mind.

Even if it was *wrong*.

And maybe Violet knew that if she really wanted to follow the rules set out for her, and please her father in the process, she should have told Kaz to leave hours earlier, when he showed up at her place. She shouldn't have indulged his argument, or let him touch her or kiss her. She definitely shouldn't have let him take her into Brooklyn, never mind Little Odessa.

Each time she didn't say "no" to something, she broke the rules a little more with something else. She pushed those boundaries a little further.

She was saying "fuck you" a little louder.

But what was she really doing wrong?

Violet was just a woman. Kaz was just a man.

She didn't really understand why their last names had to factor into it at all.

A peek of gray marble caught Violet's eye as she passed the unmade bed. A door, only slightly open, made her curious. What was it that he had said about closets?

He didn't hide his skeletons in there.

Violet found a connecting bath when she pushed the door open the rest of the way, but another door had been left wide open at the other side of the bathroom, and a light was left on. She could tell it was a closet of sorts, and once again, curiosity got the better of her.

Before she knew it, Violet was looking over an assortment of watches. She had kicked her heels off at the doorway, and she discovered that Kaz had a taste for black clothes and a small collection of Converse.

She wouldn't have taken him for the type, all things considered.

"What are you doing in here?"

Violet didn't start at Kaz's voice coming from the doorway connecting to the bathroom. She just continued admiring his vast closet.

"You have more clothes than I do," she said.

"I doubt that."

"Don't. You do."

Out of the corner of her eye, she saw him grin. "I like things."

"Things like watches and Converse?"

"Yes, on the first, and when I was a bit younger and could get away with them, for the second."

Violet nodded, more to herself than him. "And you've never thought to get rid of them?"

"Why would I get rid of them?"

His question had come out sounding so confused that she couldn't help but laugh.

"You don't wear them, you said."

Kaz shrugged. "I'm not seeing your point."

"You're one of those, then," Violet said.

"One of—what?"

"You probably have something in this closet from at least ten years ago, but because it might still fit and you may wear it again someday, you won't get rid of it."

"Wrong," he said.

Violet straightened, turning to stare him down. "I bet I could find something. I probably already did, but overlooked it because your Converse *collection* distracted me."

"I never said I didn't wear the Converse, just that I don't wear them as often. And I bet you own at least thirty pairs of shoes, if not more, so I'm not sure where this conversation is going."

"Ten," Violet said.

Kaz leaned against the doorjamb. "Ten what?"

"Ten pairs of shoes. Two of which are black because it goes with everything. One pair of flats. Sneakers. Two sets of kitten heels, pink and red. And four other heels that make my legs look great. Nice try, though."

"Huh."

"Surprising, is it?" she asked.

"Considering who your mother is, it kind of is."

Violet tossed him a simpering smile. "Surface appearances lie, Kaz. You should know that better than most people. But, to be fair, those ten pairs of shoes can interchange at any time depending on weather, season, or how pissed off I am at any given thing."

"And what do you do with the old ones?"

"Unlike you, I don't keep them."

He laughed, hard and loud. "So did you find what you were looking for?"

"Hmm?"

"You couldn't have started in here," he said. "I'd be disappointed if this was all you got around to."

"You have quite a stack of mail to sort through," she replied.

Kaz grinned. "That I do."

"And your living room looks like a show floor. I suspect you don't spend much time in it."

"Busy," he offered.

Violet took his word for it, but she thought it might be a bit more, too. Like maybe he was too high-strung on any given day to sit down and just enjoy his surroundings. He was probably always on the go, and this apartment was simply the place he stopped to rest and not much else.

"Are my drawers safe?" he asked.

Violet tipped her chin up, defiant and coy. "I'll never tell."

"If anything goes missing, I know where to find you."

His joking tone took away what little anxiety might still have been lingering inside of Violet.

"Aren't you scared I know all of your secrets now?" she asked.

Kaz shook his head. "Not at all."

"Let me guess—because you don't leave them lying around for anyone to find?"

"No, this place is full of surprises to find. It's got tighter security than even my father's house. That's not why at all."

Violet's brow furrowed. "Then why?"

"Because the only thing that I'm really concerned with keeping hidden at the moment is standing just a few feet away from me."

Oh.

She fidgeted with her manicured nails as Kaz finally took a step into the walk-in closet—although it was big enough to be a small bedroom—she suspected that's exactly what it had been at one time, before he remodeled—and shrugged his jacket off. As he grabbed a garment bag down from the many sections of bars meant for hanging clothes, her gaze was drawn down to the ruddy, smeared stains at the middle of his white shirt.

Violet knew better than to ask, but her mouth worked faster than her brain. "Is that blood?"

Kaz didn't even look down to see what she was talking about. "Yes, my brother's."

She flinched inwardly. "Sorry."

"There's nothing to be sorry for if you weren't the one telling lies, remember?"

"I told you that I didn't do that, Kaz."

"And I believe you," he murmured. "Otherwise, you wouldn't be here right now."

Violet didn't quite know how he wanted her to respond, nor how she wanted to, so she chose not to say anything at all. Kaz side-stepped her as he lifted his wrist slightly, and unlinked the cuff of the watch he wore to place it into an empty slot in one of the many turning displays.

As she watched him begin to undo the buttons on his shirt, Violet took a quick breath. She had known the moment that he hadn't directed his vehicle back toward Manhattan that a suggestion was in the air, hanging silently between them. He had only confirmed it further when he told her she could ask to go home at any time, and he would take her there.

She wasn't a dumb woman—she heard his unspoken words loud and clear.

Violet figured she had answered them just as clearly, simply by being where she was.

And yet, seeing Kaz readying for the evening like he was done for the day, only seemed to heighten her realization of just how far she had gone with him already tonight.

Violet chewed on her bottom lip.

What was a little farther going to hurt?

He had her so curious—what would feeding it do?

"What?" Kaz asked.

Violet's gaze jumped up to him. "Pardon?"

"You've been staring at my hands for the last two minutes."

Had she?

"Thinking," Violet supplied.

It was only then that she realized he hadn't finished undoing the rest of the buttons on his shirt, and had only gotten through the first two. But since the very top two had already been undone before he began, her eyes were drawn to the barest hint of ink under his shirt that was peeking out.

There was no denying the fact that Kaz was a sight to be seen with his tall, fit form, his darkly handsome features, and an attitude that almost screamed for someone to back off.

Subtly, Kaz tilted his head, still watching her like he could read her mind. That unsettled her just a bit—enough to put her off balance, and nervous under his eye.

"Don't do that," he said quietly.

Violet stilled on the spot. "Do what?"

"That—overthink and worry. I wouldn't take you for the kind of girl who turns shy when a man looks at you. Don't you know how beautiful you are?"

That was not what she expected him to say.

"I'm not shy," Violet said.

"Good. Because I lack the couth it takes to make a woman comfortable in her own skin. And I don't want to, either. You shouldn't need me to—not looking like you do."

Well, then …

Violet didn't feel as unnerved under Kaz's heavy gaze as he regarded her for a second time, letting his stare wander down her body and back up again. Almost imperceptibly, his gray irises darkened, his lips edged up in one corner, and his tongue snaked out to wet his bottom lip before disappearing again.

It made her aware of his intentions fully.

And it made her *hot*.

She knew what he had done immediately.

He lied—he had the couth to do it, he just didn't want to, and so he did it in his with his own style.

"Well played," Violet whispered.

Kaz winked. "I thought so."

He continued his work of undoing the buttons on his dress shirt as if she wasn't watching him like it was the most interesting thing she'd seen all day and he wasn't the least bit bothered by her attention. Or that she had a better view of the tattoos on his fingers, like the circle with a dot in the middle, or the cross on a dark background—she wondered what they meant. As he pulled the shirt off entirely, Violet's mouth went dry. The white fabric hung loosely from his fist as Kaz turned slightly, giving her a full view of the artwork she had only gotten a bare glimpse of earlier.

There were the twin stars inked just beneath his collarbone, one on either side of his chest, but what captured her attention the most were the three Russian cathedral domes tattooed on his chest. They were tattooed with incredible detail, as though the artist had spent hours painstakingly crafting each one. But despite how much space the tattoo took up on his chest, it was the only one she could see besides the stars.

Despite how easily she could get caught up in his tattoos and what they might mean to him, her gaze was quickly taking in the rest of his bare chest, too. The slight tease of his shirts stretching across his pecs and hinting at what was beneath did not do him justice. The man was cut— defined ridges and a hard "V" where his pants hung low on his hips that demanded exploring, especially that light dusting of dark hair that disappeared below his waistline.

Jesus.

Kaz was goddamn gorgeous.

She decided the eight-pointed stars were her favorite, though.

Kaz caught her staring again, but Violet wasn't the least bit ashamed. "See something you like?"

His arrogance was amusing. Most men thought themselves as confident, mysterious, and cocky all rolled into one, but they just came off as assholes. Kaz didn't even have to try, he was all those things rolled into one—including the asshole, sometimes—and Violet liked it a lot.

"Yes," she said, shrugging.

"Straightforward, are you?"

"I'm not a liar, Kaz."

What else did he expect?

"Do they mean something?" she asked, her stare dropping down to his tattoos again.

"Yes," Kaz said.

"What?"

"It's a story. Maybe I'll tell you someday."

"What story?" she asked.

"Mine."

Violet stilled when Kaz moved directly in front of her, almost crowding her. He lifted his right hand, and his fingers skimmed under the collar of the bomber jacket she wore.

Quietly but surely, he asked, "Can I?"

She nodded.

Kaz pulled at the collar of her jacket until it started to fall down her arms. Once the item hit the floor, his attention was back on her. His fingers grazed her neck with a soft touch, surprising her.

"Not shy," he said, almost like a reminder.

His softness was gone just like that. The pads of his fingers pressed into her collarbones and traveled lower to the neckline of her tank-top, wicked and promising. A huskiness colored up his tone, making her shiver.

Violet shook her head. "Not shy, Kaz."

How could she be shy under his regard when he was making it seem like she was the one and only thing he wanted to look at?

Again, Kaz stepped closer. He was so close that she could feel the warmth of his chest brush her arm as he leaned slightly to the side and tossed his white shirt into a small garbage bin behind them.

"Blood doesn't wash out," he said, more to himself than to her.

Violet was still listening. "Shame. I liked that shirt."

She could almost see his smirk when he replied, "I think you liked the person wearing it more."

"Maybe. But maybe not."

"You'll never tell, huh?"

Violet turned her head, catching his eye with her own. "Nope."

Apparently, that look was all Kaz needed. Violet barely took a breath just a blink before his mouth was on hers. Her lips parted the second his tongue struck at the seam, demanding entrance. His hand landed to her waist as his other caught her right under her jaw. Her back hit a row of shelves as her hand grabbed the belt at his waist. He tipped her head back, and his hand slid lower on her throat.

Because those hands—she liked his hands.

But it was his tongue seeking hers, and his groan building deep in the back of his throat that made her ache.

Kaz pulled back, just enough to let her take in a sharp breath. He was still close enough that his stubble scraped her lips as he watched her under dark, lowered lashes.

What was he waiting for?

What did he want?

Violet didn't have the patience to be tampered and teased. She let her fingers unfurl from his belt, and her fingernails dragged down his stomach, insistent and firm. Kaz crowded her again, letting her feel the hard length of his erection digging into her body.

"So sweet," he murmured.

Violet blinked. "Am I?"

"Your mouth. It makes me wonder what else might taste sweet on you."

She swallowed hard. "Care to find out?"

"I'll get there."

His words sounded like a promise.

Entirely.

Violet's fingers dug into the railroad path of Kaz's abdominal muscles when his lips found hers again, rough and hot. She suddenly felt hyperaware of his hands as one traveled down her side and the other moved from her waist to the hem of her shirt. She let him fist the material of the top and pull it up. He only broke the kiss long enough to toss her shirt somewhere behind him on the floor.

Those hands of his, so insistent and wanting, pushed her shoulders, driving her harder into the shelves. Violet didn't even mind, she just yanked him closer.

"Off," he demanded, fingers curling under her bra straps. "Let me take it off, or you do it. But it comes off now."

Here would have been the best time, she thought, to tell him to stop.

Before he took anymore from her—before she gave him anymore. Before he had the chance to see or have parts of her that weren't supposed to be meant for him, and that she wasn't supposed to show.

It should have been the time, but it wasn't.

Violet's smaller hands enclosed his, letting him pull the straps down around her arms. Kaz's gaze lowered when his palms slid across her sensitive skin, and pushed the lacy cups of the bra away. She sighed when the pads of his thumbs brushed over her pebbling nipples once, then twice.

At the third swipe, her exhale was a little more ragged than the last.

"Those sounds," he said low.

Violet looked up to find him staring at her mouth.

"What about them?" she asked.

"I want more of them—louder."

"Louder?"

"Yes," he said. "I'd like to remember them in the morning."

Violet wet her bottom lip. "I suppose that depends on how this next part goes, huh?"

Kaz smirked. "That, I'm not worried about."

She didn't get the chance to respond before he was pulling her away from the wall without a word. Her bare feet stumbled over the jacket, and she fell into him. Kaz had her spinning around just as fast, and backed into the open door connecting to the bathroom. His next kiss was harder than the last, his teeth dragging over her lips as his hands worked at the clip on the front of her bra, taking it off, too. She tugged at his belt, getting it undone and loose enough to yank it from the loops.

A whine escaped from her throat when his teeth sunk into her jaw as he lifted her against the door. The fast movement shocked her for a second, leaving her breathless when she realized she wasn't touching the floor anymore.

He lifted her easily—like she was a fucking feather and it was nothing for him.

With her legs wrapped tight around his waist, the insistent push of his hips against her center brought her attention right back to the erection under his pants and the throbbing between her thighs. It was enough to make her arch into him, wanting to feel more, and wanting less space and clothing between them.

"Fuck," he mumbled into her neck.

Violet shuddered. "Yeah."

Her back came away from the door, and she grabbed his jaw as he walked through into the bathroom, still holding her tight. His fingers dug into her backside hard enough to leave fingerprints behind. She pulled him in for another kiss that seared her from the inside out, his roughness leaving her skin stinging and her heart racing.

She couldn't even feel the counter hit her ass until Kaz took a step back and let her go. But just as fast as he moved away, he was right back on her, fingers working at the button of her jeans until it was undone and he could pull the zipper down.

"Up," he said hoarsely.

Violet complied, lifting up and using her hands on the counter to keep balanced as he tugged her jeans down her hips and over her legs. His hands met her bare thighs, fingers biting into her skin as he pulled her to the edge of the counter. A small tremor worked its way through her body when he eyed the blue lace panties that matched the bra he'd already pulled off.

"I swear women buy delicate shit like this just to see if a man will rip them off."

Oh, God.

Violet's teeth sunk into her lip. "I bought them because I liked them."

Kaz lifted a single brow, watching her. "Then I won't ruin them."

"Should I thank you?"

"I won't ruin them this time," he pressed on.

That lump returned in Violet's throat.

This time …

Because there would be more.

He wanted more.

So did she.

"Up," he repeated.

Violet lifted again, allowing Kaz to peel her panties down her legs with a slowness that said he enjoyed taking them off a great deal more than he had when it was just her pants. She couldn't help but hold her breath as his fingers grazed her skin. His gaze followed the path of her legs straight up to the junction between her thighs, and he moved forward again.

His hands were already back on her thighs the second her panties dropped to the floor. The softest tap of his palms to her inner thighs voiced his unspoken request. She answered it, widening her legs for him, and resting her trembling hands to the counter.

She thought he might take his time to look her over, take her in, entirely naked like she was. And he did, for a brief moment. Long enough to heat her blood, and make her think he had found exactly what he wanted, just by the way he opened his mouth to speak, and … nothing came out.

Violet had been with men before—not a lot, as far as that went. More times than she cared to count, her beauty had been praised as an asset she should be proud of. It had never been admired—she had never been treated—like it was something that a man was proud to have.

And it stunned her.

The way Kaz watched her, his fingers sweeping her skin and exploring like they were, stunned her.

"You're doing it again," she heard him say.

Violet fell from her thoughts with a bang. "Doing what?"

"Overthinking."

She didn't think so.

Not this time.

Slowly, like he meant for her to feel every press and caress of his fingers, they came closer to the junction of her thighs until his knuckles grazed her center. She jerked at the light touch, feeling the shock it caused begin to spread from her sex to her middle.

Heat pool when he stepped closer, fitting between her legs, and stroking her again.

More the second time.

Harder.

Closer.

Violet's thoughts slipped away when two of his fingers glided over her slit, sinking into her pussy without him saying a single word. Her responding cry came out high and broken.

Because fuck … he curled them on the first thrust and she couldn't breathe.

Kaz's white teeth flashed in a sinful grin as he watched her, knowing. "There …"

"*Yeah.*"

Measured, but fast enough to make her shake, his fingers worked her sex. Violet's mouth went dry as the sounds crawled from her throat without her permission. Her fingers curled against the counter, her nails biting into her palms. She was hot under his touch, mindless, and it was wonderful.

"So wet," he told her, bending down so that their noses touched and his lips swept hers as he spoke. "Tight and wet around me, Violet. Jesus."

She still couldn't fucking breathe.

"Oh, my God."

"Give it to me," he demanded.

His words came out clipped and dark—rough like his fingers that were digging into her inner thigh. That bite of pain was enough of a shock to make her gasp in a lungful of air.

"Come on," he urged.

His fingers stroked faster, harder. Then his thumb flicked up, driving into her clit as his digits curled on the next thrust.

Violet shattered. She was gone in a flash—suspended in a moment where she couldn't feel anything at all, and she couldn't hear the words Kaz was saying. Sensation started to hit, and it started from her center and swiftly worked its way through the rest of her body.

Like a live wire, her nerves snapped from the intensity.

"*Kaz …*"

"Just like that," he said. His voice was dark and heady in her ear as he kissed the spot under her ear. "My name, just like that, Violet."

She panted, letting her fingers uncurl from their tight fists. They literally ached from how hard she had pressed them into the counter. Tilting her head back to the mirror, she reveled in his soft lips as they moved over her neck with ghosts of kisses. Every so often, his tongue would strike out and taste her for just a second before his teeth nipped at the same spot.

But it calmed her.

Even as that heat started to build again, and his fingers left her body, a fire burned.

Bright.

Hot.

So dangerous.

Kaz Markovic could quickly become a complication for Violet. One she didn't need.

Like a fucking addiction she couldn't kick, swimming through her veins.

He might already be one.

Violet admired the sight of the small wave rushing up on the beach from the floor-to-ceiling windows inside Kaz's bedroom. Not a second after he had yanked her off the counter in the bathroom, a phone had started ringing somewhere outside of his bedroom, and after a quick internal struggle as to whether or not he was going to answer, he'd deposited her on his bed with a quick "Stay", as though there was anywhere else she would rather be as he left to answer.

She hadn't followed his instruction, not really, choosing to go over to the windows and look out, wanting to see whatever he saw when he stood in the same spot.

Stories had been told to her of Little Odessa, but from what she could see, it wasn't anything like those. It was beautiful at night, the stars glinting off the water, waves crashing into the sand. Lights lit up the buildings outside of Kaz's apartment, making her eyes stretch across the sprawling buildings, going on as far as the eye could see.

No, Little Odessa was nothing like she had been told, but neither was Kaz.

Pressing her hand against the glass, she leaned closer, looking everywhere she could, at least until she saw Kaz's reflection suddenly walking toward her through it. She didn't turn to look at him however, merely enjoyed the view.

"Do you like what you see?" He asked, a rough hand sliding along her hip and around to rest on her stomach.

"Yeah." But not as much as she enjoyed the sight of him. There was no need to tell him that, though—his ego didn't need it.

She could see people walking along the boardwalk, some even on the beach despite the hour. For a moment, she wondered whether if they looked up, would they be able to see them standing there in front of the

122

windows—her mostly naked, besides his shirt he had given her before leaving the room, and him in his pants.

And even as the thought crossed her mind, she still didn't move.

"They could see you," he said like he was reading her mind. "If the lights were on in here."

Violet raised a brow, musing over the people enjoying their evening. "Huh."

She shivered as Kaz's hand slid lower, his fingertips tapping a gentle beat against her pubic bone.

"I thought I told you to stay put," he said in her ear.

"And I didn't."

Kaz stepped closer, his chest molding to Violet's back. Again, his fingers danced lower until the tips were brushing the spot just above her clit.

Teasing, she knew.

"But since they can't see me," she started to say, grinning, "I think I like it here."

Kaz hummed a deep, lovely melody that rocked Violet straight from her toes to her fingertips. And all the fucking spots in between. When his hand tangled in the hair at the nape of her neck, she tilted her head as he tugged lightly. His lips grazed the back of her neck, peppering the side of her throat and the part of her shoulder where his shirt had fallen down with kisses.

Violet let out a soft sigh.

"I was right, you know," he told her.

"About what?"

"You do taste sweet elsewhere."

Violet laughed, feeling out of air already. "You're too good at this."

"Hmm," he replied, the sound vibrating against her pulse point, "Only if the effort is worth it."

She met his gaze in the reflection of the glass. "Was it?"

"You tell me."

Violet opened her mouth to respond, but the words melted into a quiet moan when his hand dipped between her thighs. Softer, and less insistent than on the bathroom counter, he stroked her pussy until she was shaking and gasping, but not quite on the edge where she might find that sweet bliss again. No, he took his time, like he wanted to learn her body with just his fingers alone, and hear all her sounds as he did.

Dark and husky whispers crawled over her skin, his words soaking through her nervous system like a drug.

So soft and *Like that, yes?*

Dirtier and harsher when her legs began to shake and her hands found the glass, wanting purchase on something.

Ride my fingers and *Fucking come, Violet.*

She did … all over again. It wasn't as fast and unrelenting as that first time. It built up slower, clawed through her deeper, and she felt every single second of it.

Violet barely heard the rustle of clothing behind her as she desperately tried to come back down from yet another high. It was only the crackle of foil that made her turn around. Kaz, condom in hand, was just stepping out of his pants, and shoving his black boxer-briefs down at the same time.

A sound—some crazy cross between a squeak and a groan—died on her lips when his gaze snapped up and landed on her. She couldn't help but look down again, finding his hand circling his erection and palming the length with slow strokes. Even in the dimness of the bedroom, she could still see the thick vein on the underside of his cock pulse with each tug.

It made her throat tight.

Her stomach clenched.

"Yes," she said as he took a step forward.

Kaz chuckled. "I didn't ask anything."

"You were going to. Yes, I like what I see."

The sexiest grin bloomed on his face, reminding Violet yet again that regardless of who Kaz was, he was still just a man underneath it all.

A man that, right then, wanted her.

A man she wanted.

What was so wrong with that?

Violet's back met the cold glass of the window as Kaz stepped out of his boxer-briefs. She stayed silent and still, thoroughly enjoying the sight of him naked.

Because he was a *sight*—something to admire.

Kaz make quick work of tearing the foil packet open, and sliding the latex condom down his length. All the while, his eyes never left her. She was still stuck watching his hand closing back around his shaft, and the way his thumb swept the head of his cock every time he came to the tip.

His hard body pressed to her softer figure, and she swore she could feel his heartbeat thrumming with the pulse in his shaft as it rested against her skin.

Violet blew out a slow breath when Kaz's hand caught her under the chin, and urged her face upward.

"If you like it here—the window—we can stay right here," he said.

She nodded.

At that point, she didn't think she was capable of much else.

Violet straightened a little when Kaz's free hand slid along the small of her back, down over her ass, and then grabbed firmly to her thigh. He bent down a little, just enough to hold onto her, and lift her up effortlessly. Like earlier, it seemed she weighed nothing to him. Her legs tightened around his hips, holding him there. Her one hand found his shoulder, while the fingers of her other wrapped into the hair at the nape of his neck. His mouth replaced his hand on her chin as he kissed up her jaw, across her cheek, and then nipped at her bottom lip.

Between her thighs, his cock slid against her pussy with every movement, spreading her silky wetness through her folds and rubbing along her clit.

"Breathe," she heard him whisper along the seam of her lips.

Violet took that breath when he demanded it, feeling his free hand slide between their bodies. It was just the movement of his hand, the slight shift of his hips, and he was there …

His length pressing against her entrance, the thick width filling her full as her body stretched open to take him in. There was no resistance when he flexed his hips again, and she was filled entirely.

Too full, even.

But it was fucking glorious.

Even the slight sting from him entering her as fast as he did was quickly replaced with a deep, burrowing need digging its way through her bloodstream.

She heard his sharp exhale muffled into her ear.

Time stopped—just like that.

A heavy relief, not quite as cloying as her release had been, but no less intense, settled into her bones at just the feeling of him inside her, her walls flexing and fluttering around his cock with each jostle of their bodies.

"Shit," he breathed.

Violet's fingers tightened in his hair. His forehead hit her shoulder a second before his cock was withdrawing from her sex, and then slamming right back in again. Her shoulders hit the glass—hard.

Over and over.

Each thrust drove her closer to the precipice again.

His teeth embedded into her shoulder while a shudder racked over his entire back.

Violet arched into his rhythm, wanting his fingers squeezing her even harder, his bite stinging her even sharper, and his cock fucking her even deeper.

She wanted all of that, but she couldn't get the words out to voice it.

The only sounds she made where a mixture of moans and whimpers that matched his thrusts. Apparently, she didn't have to say anything, because he just knew.

Like he always seemed to.

His fingers on her thigh dug in, pushing her legs open more and making her muscles burn. On the next thrust, he took her hard enough for it to hurt, but in the best fucking way.

"*Oh*," she mumbled.

Kaz's hand left her waist and slid from her stomach up to her throat. Violet gulped hard as his fingers curled around her throat, and he finally lifted his head.

Gray eyes found her green ones. His jaw, tight and hard, ticked under her palm. She thought he was beautiful like this—more so than any other time. A little raw, maybe. Wild, even.

Colored dark around his edges as he chased a high with her.

So beautiful.

"Harder," Violet told him.

Kaz bared his teeth, his grimace mixed heavily with pleasure. "Come and I will."

"I want it harder."

"Come," he growled.

Violet whined, feeling his fingertips bite into her throat a little rougher than before. Her lips parted with a high cry, his name following right behind. That seemed to do the trick for Kaz, before he leaned close enough to lick her jaw before his teeth embedded into the same spot.

She came.

So hard.

Violet didn't even feel the cold glass leave her back as Kaz pulled her away from the window.

But her knees felt the messy bedsheets when he tossed her onto it. He wasn't done with her it seemed.

Not even close.

Deft, calloused fingers danced over Violet's naked side, tracing the curve in her waist, skipping down along her hip, and then back to the small of her spine. She shivered, holding back giggles at the slight tickling sensation running over her skin.

"Stop moving," she heard muttered above her.

Violet tried not to squirm, but as Kaz's fingertips grazed over the crease of her knee, she couldn't help but move.

"You make a terrible bedfellow what with all your jittering and giggling," he said.

"Stop tickling me."

"Not tickling. Learning."

Violet pressed her lips together, amused and confused at the same time. "Learning?"

"You," Kaz said, his voice thick with sleep. "I'm learning you."

Oh.

She hadn't expected him to say that. Suddenly, the exploration of his fingers on her skin as they laid close to one another under sheets in the dark didn't feel quite the same as it had. The ticklish sensations gave way to a much more contented, deep-thrumming need with every slide and caress of his fingers.

She stopped moving.

Her giggles ceased.

Tilting her head up, Violet found Kaz with his eyes closed and a lax, lazy smile curving his lips upwards at the edge. He looked so relaxed, like there was no other place he wanted to be right then.

"Better," he whispered. "Sleep."

Violet knew it would probably be a good idea to go home right then, and not wait until morning when she was more likely to be caught in Little Odessa—never mind with Kaz. But strangely, she didn't want to say a thing, and she really didn't want to move an inch. She liked the feeling of his arm resting over her side, his fingers grazing her skin, and the comforting familiarity that was seeping into her consciousness the longer she spent time with Kaz.

Somehow, a simple hookup had turned into them tangled up close to one another in his bed, and what should have been over as quickly as it started, was looking like it would end up continuing well into the morning.

Violet still didn't care.

She let his wandering fingers soothe her to sleep.

Violet liked the sun. It was hot and bright and pretty. Her father liked to say that she was a lot like the sun—lighting up people's days. She didn't understand what he meant.

He also said she asked a lot of questions.

She didn't think she asked a lot of questions.

When the sun was out, she could play all day and never get cold, wet, or sad. She couldn't be sad when the sun was high and shining down.

Lifting her head up and closing her eyes, Violet felt the sun warm her cheeks. She knew it wouldn't be very long before the cold came, because the leaves were already turning different colors.

Reds. Browns. Yellows. Oranges.

All sorts of colors.

But as quickly as the sun had peeked out from behind the clouds, it was gone. The wind picked up, cooling her warm face.

Sighing, Violet opened her eyes again.

She glanced over at her new friend—Kaz, he said.

Kazimir.

He didn't like Kazimir.

He liked Kaz.

His glasses hid his eyes, but she knew he was watching her, waiting.

"Well?" he asked.

"It's gone again."

"But didn't you see it before it went?"

Violet kicked her white sneakers to and fro, rocking the bench she was sitting on with Kaz. "Nope."

Kaz laughed. "You're supposed to be watching, Violet."

"Can't you try?"

"No," Kaz said.

"Because your eyes hurt, right?"

Kaz nodded. "A lot."

Violet frowned. "Will they always hurt?"

"I hope not," he muttered.

Violet glanced around the quiet place. She really didn't understand what it was, but she remembered being at a place like this once a few months ago when her Grandmama got sick, went to sleep, and didn't wake back up. They put her Grandmama in a big, shiny black box with latches and bars on the side, and then put her in the ground. Lots of people came and they cried.

She hadn't seen her Grandmama since, and her Grandpapa was always sad now.

All the stones in the quiet place were mostly shiny, but some weren't. Letters and words covered them all. Violet could read a few small words, but not the big ones.

"What does ... rest ... mean?" she asked Kaz, finding one word she could pronounce because of the letters.

"Um, my dad says resting means relaxing. Being quiet, still. Sleeping, sometimes."

Violet nodded. That made sense.

This was the quiet place. It was a good spot to rest.

Her father had told her to be a good girl when they first arrived at the quiet place. He said other stuff, too, like "respect" and "graves".

Violet didn't really know what all that meant.

But she figured that since she was sitting with Kaz, and not running around, she was being a good girl, and respecting the graves.

Whatever those were.

Suddenly, the quiet place brightened again and Violet's cheeks warmed with the rays of the sun.

"Sun is back," Kaz said.

Violet was already looking up, but she closed her eyes again. It only lasted a few seconds longer than the last time, but her face stayed warmer for longer, too.

After the sun was hidden behind the clouds again, Kaz asked, "Well, what does it look like today?"

Violet shrugged. "I don't know. I closed my eyes again."

"You're supposed to be helping me see."

She was.

Violet smiled. "The sun keeps hiding and it doesn't stay for long."

"What do the trees look like, then?"

"Pretty."

"Pretty?" Kaz asked.

"Colorful."

"What colors?"

"All the colors," she said, giggling.

"Tell me more," Kaz replied.

Violet started describing everything she could see for her new friend.

Because he couldn't see.

And that wasn't fair.

She didn't mind.

Kaz was smiling.

Kaz came awake slowly, then all at once. The sharp rays of sunlight peeking through the drapes of his bedroom were too fucking bright this early in the morning. With a groan, he rolled over, putting his back to the windows, his arm stretching out beside him, but coming up short when he was met with soft skin.

There was a moment of confusion as his foggy mind tried to catch up with what his hands were feeling. Nevertheless, he continued on, letting his fingers slide down and over feminine curves. Memories of the night before slammed back into him as his eyes opened and he took in the sight of blonde hair fanning out along his sheets and pillows.

From what he could tell, Violet was still sleeping, her chest rising and falling with even breaths as she remained unaware to his movements. How many hours had gone by as he had familiarized himself with the very curves he was tracing once more? Did it matter? He still felt like there was so much left to learn.

Even more so when it came to the woman herself.

Slipping out of bed, careful not to jostle her, he headed in the direction of the bathroom, leaving the lights off as he went. After relieving himself and washing his hands, he splashed water on his face, trying to further wake himself up. He had only been gone a handful of minutes at most, but as he reentered his bedroom, he could see that Violet was awake, though she hadn't moved from her spot in his bed.

And, oh, what a sight she made.

She was naked beneath that gray sheet she held against her chest. Her hair rumpled and in disarray, she *looked* like she had spent the night getting fucked. He might have smiled at that thought, but for the way she was looking at him with a mixture of confusion and dawning realization.

Curious, he asked, "Why are you looking at me like that?"

"I remember you," she said just soft enough that he almost didn't hear her. "We were in a graveyard? I think? I'm not really sure—it was all fuzzy."

It wasn't fuzzy for Kaz. He remembered that day well, mostly that he didn't want to go. After the car bomb shortly before, Kaz had hated any kind of light, the sight of it making his head hurt instantly, even with the thick, opaque sunglasses Vasily had bought for him.

His father hadn't told him much of what was going to happen that day, only that he was expected to be there, and to be on his best behavior. Even at ten years old, he knew better than to disappoint his father, especially on a day as important as that one, even if he didn't know it at the time.

It had been one of the few times that Kaz had seen Alberto Gallucci in person, and the lone time he had seen Violet in person before a few weeks ago. More, it wasn't the Italian Don, or his father's excitement after the meeting had taken place, that he remembered most about that day.

It was Violet.

She had to have been no more than four at the time, but she smiled and talked to him like they were the same age. There had been no fear in her when she spoke, talking about things he couldn't see as she described them for him.

It was the sun, she had said, that shined the brightest …

Thinking back on it, he wasn't so sure that was true.

"Yeah," he finally responded. "It was a graveyard."

She ran fingers through her hair, trying to tame it as best she could, even as she looked away from him, trying to remember a past that he knew all too well. "Why were we there, though?"

That was one answer even Kaz didn't have. He had asked Vasily once, what he and Alberto had discussed that day, but his father had never given him an answer, and even forbid him from asking about it again. Until recently, he had abided by that—truthfully, he hadn't given a shit to ask again—but now, he was a little more curious.

"I don't know."

She didn't seem surprised by his lack of knowledge. "That was what you meant then, when you said we met before?"

Pushing off the wall, he crossed the floor in a few, quick strides, and stretched out at the foot of the bed, tucking his hands beneath his head. "It was."

"Funny that no one's ever mentioned that," she said almost absently, shifting in the bed so she was sitting up.

Especially with the way Vasily talked about the man, as though he was the scum of the earth. One would think that the two men had never seen eye to eye on anything, but at one point, at least for a time, they had. There had been no bullets fired that day, nor had any voices raised above pleasant conversation level.

Strange. All of it was fucking strange.

But the last thing Kaz wanted to be doing presently was thinking about his father, and hers, knowing that if either of them knew what was happening at that very moment, Kaz would be a dead man.

Reaching out, he offered her his hand, and she accepted it without question, letting him pull her across the bed, dragging the sheet along with her. As she straddled him, his hands drifted beneath the fabric that covered her to rest at her hips, and he felt content, enjoying the visual she made on top of him.

He could have never anticipated this, that he actually *wanted* her exactly where she was, but he did. And though he had business to attend to, he wasn't ready to give up this moment. He'd hold onto it for as long as he could.

"Now it's you," she said with a smile, drawing his attention back to her. "You're overthinking."

He merely returned her smile, reaching up to let the strands of her hair drift through his fingers. She leaned down further to give him better access, but the moment she did, he stole a kiss instead, feeling her contented sigh against his lips.

One hand drifted around to the back of her head, fisting the hair there to keep her in place, the other palming her backside to keep her steady. It was only supposed to be for a moment, just a quick kiss to remind him of what she tasted like, but it soon spiraled into something else as she ground down on his cock, making him grip her ass just a bit tighter.

Kaz was hard, had been since the moment she climbed on top of him, but at the feel of how wet she was, even the slight tremor that worked its way through her body, it became almost painful.

Last night hadn't been enough. No matter how many hours were spent rolling around in his bed. He was quickly learning that when it came to her, he was insatiable, the need almost making him crazed. But as he had half a mind to grab a condom from his nightstand, a ringing phone made him pause.

It took him a moment, thinking it was his phone, but as Violet shot up, scrambling off of him to go in search of it, he knew their moment was over, and at worse, their time was up.

She hadn't been gone long before she was right back in his bedroom, the phone to her ear, her face devoid of color. "Hey, Daddy."

There was nothing quite like the sound of her saying, 'Daddy,' that made his cock shrivel up, but he didn't move from his spot on the bed, not wanting to even breathe in her direction.

"In *thirty* minutes?" Violet said, the anxiety in her expression making Kaz frown, wondering what they were talking about. "I won't be ready by then. I've only been awake for a few minutes. I need to shower, do my hair—and you know how long it takes me to do my makeup, I—"

She grew quiet again, and he could almost hear her father's muffled voice on the other end.

"No, no. An hour is fine ... right, I'll see you soon ... bye."

The second she ended the call, she turned her panicked eyes on Kaz. "My dad is sending a driver to my place in an hour. We need to go." She spun around, rushing back to his bathroom where he had thrown her clothes all over the floor.

Fuck.

It was already hell trying to get through Manhattan traffic on a good day, and that was on top of the hour and a half drive that it took to get there from Little Odessa. To get her there in less than an hour?

Kaz grabbed the first pair of pants he could find, then a shirt, and finally shoes before he had his keys in hand and was ushering Violet out the door. Down in the parking garage, he unlocked the doors to his Porsche with a press of the button, but as he walked toward it, Violet hesitated.

"What?"

She bit her lip. "Everyone knows this car ..."

True enough. "But if you want to get back to Manhattan anytime soon, it's the Porsche—the Rover will be too slow."

He didn't have to say anything further before she was sliding into the passenger seat. He barely gave her a chance to buckle in before his foot was on the gas and he was shooting out of the garage and onto the street, ignoring the blaring horns he left in his wake.

Shifting into second gear, he bypassed another set of cars, barely making it through a yellow light before it turned red.

"You know, if I die in a car wreck," Violet started, her fingers white-knuckled around the center console. "That's not going to help us."

Kaz merely said, "I got this," before concentrating on the road again, the speedometer already approaching ninety miles an hour.

He hardly paid attention to anything else besides the cars surrounding him, and the time ticking by on his dash. Doing well over forty above the speed limit, he knew if he passed any police, he was definitely getting stopped, but that was the last thing on his mind.

Just sitting beside her, he could feel the waves of anxiety pouring off her, the fear that she wasn't going to make it in time, or worse ... that she would be caught with him.

But he couldn't—*wouldn't*—let that happen.

"You know," Kaz said, a sudden thought popping into his head. "I don't have your number."

Violet looked at him as though he'd grown a second head. "Are you serious?"

"About needing your number? Absolutely. The next time I show up to your place uninvited might not work out as well for me."

With one hand still on the wheel, he dug into his pocket for his phone, typing in the four-digit code before passing her the device. "Plug it in."

She didn't question his command, merely did what he asked, then went on to call her own phone so that she would have his number as well.

The hour mark had just passed when he made it into the city. The traffic was far worse there than it was outside of it.

Worse, he knew better than to pull up directly outside of her building. There was no guarantee that her father didn't have people watching the place, or even just in the neighborhood doing business. So instead, he turned on a side street, parking on the opposite side of the back of her building.

He didn't get a chance to say a word before she was whipping her seatbelt off and opening the door, but before she got out, she leaned across and gave him a quick kiss, surprising the hell out of him for a moment.

"See you later."

Violet was gone seconds later, dashing across the street in a flurry of blonde hair. Even with the circumstance being so dire, and the fact that he still had to make it back out of Manhattan yet, Kaz still smiled.

Violet had just come up to the back of her building when the phone in her purse started to ring. The sound was as insistent as it was dooming. Answering the call, she put the phone to her ear and hoped the background noise of the city went unnoticed.

"Hello?"

"Gee will be there in fifteen minutes," Alberto said, not even offering her a greeting. "Apparently, traffic is terrible in Manhattan this morning and he's stuck behind an accident that just happened two minutes ago."

Violet felt her heart finally rise back up from her stomach into her chest. "That's okay, Daddy."

"Are you already outside? I hear cars."

Shit.

"Yeah, just waiting on him out front. You said an hour, right?"

"I did," Alberto agreed. "You'll be a little late for breakfast because of the traffic, but it was semantics anyway."

Violet's brow furrowed as she dug for the access key that would let her in through the back emergency door of her building. She needed the front desk people to at least see her walk by them in case her father asked after her at some point.

"Semantics?" she asked.

"Your friends are here," was all he said.

She knew then what was happening. The events of the night before involving Ruslan and Franco had not gone unnoticed by her father. Amelia's lies had probably been exposed.

Alberto Gallucci was not the type of man to beat around the bush. She had told her father the truth of what happened, and there was no doubt in her mind that he would not have sent Franco after Kaz's brother, based on her side of the story.

But her father didn't know that she knew.

So, she feigned ignorance. "Why are my friends there?"

Alberto sighed, heavy and angry at the same time. "You'll find out soon enough."

Wonderful.

He hung up the call without a goodbye.

Violet managed to get inside her building, and took a quick look at the screen of her phone. She had another ten minutes to be at the front waiting, if Gee's estimate of time had been anything to go on. The man was known for his fucking punctuality.

His time was right and she knew it.

The decorative mirrors along the back hallway that led into the main floor where the elevators were stopped Violet. She grabbed the small toiletry case out of her purse, and did what she could to her face and hair with what time she had, and what products were in the bag.

She made a mental note to keep more in it next time when she was left with nothing more than a bit of color to her cheeks, red lipstick, and mascara. The single black elastic in the bag was more than enough for her to pull her messy hair back at the nape of her neck, and flip the hair up in and around to make it seem like she had put far more effort into the updo than what she actually had.

Messy was a style, after all.

Checking her appearance one last time, and pulling a few strands of hair out to let it frame her face, she grabbed her purse off the floor and headed for the front. She didn't give the front desk a second glance, and they didn't seem to notice that she hadn't come out of the elevators.

Her heart still pounded like crazy.

The building's front door just closed behind her when Gee pulled up.

Violet walked in on what she could only describe as a somber mood. The dining room table was filled with people—Amelia, Nicole, their parents, Violet's mother and father, and her brother. There was even a couple of other men standing in the corner of the room, gazes trained on Amelia, and faces as blank as stone.

"Violet," Alberto greeted, barely glancing up from the phone in front of him.

"Morning, Daddy."

He waved a hand at the free chair beside Nicole. "Sit."

The command was laced with the sound of his obvious irritation. Violet chose not to argue, and grabbed the chair to sit as fast as she could. Her father looked her over, taking in her appearance quickly before his attention was back on that phone again.

Silently, Violet let out a breath of relief.

If Alberto hadn't been satisfied with the way she looked, he would have said straight away, regardless of who was around to hear him criticize her. She figured what with the adrenaline rush the entire morning had been, she probably looked fresh-faced and wide awake.

Maybe she should thank Kaz for driving like a freaking maniac.

Alberto swiped at the screen on his phone, and scowled.

"Nothing?" Christian asked from where he sat, directly across from his daughter.

Nicole flinched at her father's question, her head dropping a little lower.

"I'm sorry," Amelia whispered.

Vito shook his head, rubbing at his temples. "Boss—"

"Shut up. *Fermo, stolto*," Alberto barked, the volume of his shout echoing through the dining room. Even Violet dipped her head, and she knew damn well it wasn't her in trouble. "Do you know what your daughter has done now?"

"I know," Vito replied quietly.

"I cannot even get a response from the Russian. It's bad enough when I do have to speak to any of them, but let me just say it is far worse when *he* will not answer a call."

Violet's head snapped up, finding her father seething mad, but with a bit of panic lingering there as well.

"And for what?" Alberto asked, waving at Amelia. "So she could make that *idiot* jealous?"

Amelia sniffled, using the heels of her palms to press against her eyes. Violet wanted to feel some sort of sympathy for her friend … but she couldn't find any. Amelia had always liked to play stupid games with Franco, things that would draw him back to her before she pushed him away again. Ruslan had probably been another one of those stupid games.

But it wasn't a game.

Those kinds of lies killed people.

Amelia should have known that.

So no, Violet didn't feel bad as both Alberto and Vito started shouting between one another, and at Amelia.

Violet passed Nicole a subtle look at her side. "Did you know?"

Nicole shrugged, but her expression said that no, she hadn't known a thing.

"Explicitly!" Alberto roared. "I explicitly forbade Franco, and you—" He turned on Carmine. "You, I told you the answer was no because her stories didn't line up with the other two."

"Dad," Carmine started to say.

Alberto pushed away from the table, taking a single step toward his son. "Say that again, Carmine."

It didn't even come out like a question.

Carmine tipped his chin down. "Sorry, boss."

Violet blinked, confused and stunned at the same time. She knew her brother had long been mixed up in the family business, but inside their home, she had never heard him address their father as anything less than "Dad" or "Papa". Certainly not "boss".

Alberto, seemingly satisfied with Carmine's correction, turned back to the table and pointed at Amelia. "A man very nearly lost his son last night because of your lies. And if I didn't know you as well as I do, if I didn't care for your father as much as I do, it would be you taking the punishment for what happened, and not Franco."

Amelia sucked in a sharp breath, saying again, "I'm sorry."

Vito said nothing, and neither did his wife beside him.

Violet wasn't surprised at their lack of a response. They were *la famiglia,* and a blood relation didn't have to factor into that at all. Alberto was the head of the family, a family they were a part of, and like he always had done, he made the calls and doled out the punishments.

This was just another one of those times where he had to step in.

"Get out of my face," Alberto said, far quieter than before.

Violet was up out of her seat before anyone else.

The others sat there, looking stupid, as she made a beeline for the exit.

Alberto Gallucci was a lot of things, but a quiet man was not one of them. And when he was quiet, when he spoke softly through thinned lips and clenched teeth, it was a very bad thing.

"Now," Violet heard her father say behind her. "But do not leave the property."

She was already heading toward the back door.

The further she could get from her father in that moment, the better she thought it would all be.

Standing beneath the spray of water, Kaz ducked his head, letting the shower wash away the night before. He hadn't minded the scent of Violet clinging to his skin, reminding him of just how long he had spent learning every inch of her, but business was calling, and he had to get a move on.

He had only been upstairs for little more than thirty minutes before he was heading back down. With his phone in hand, he looked over the messages he had ignored earlier, but came up short when he caught sight of Raj, one of Vasily's soldiers, standing next to his car, his hands in his pockets.

This wouldn't be the first time that Vasily had sent a man around to see him, especially when he was indisposed, but he saved Raj for special occasions. Kaz knew all too well what the man was capable of, especially when he was feeling inspired. And while Kaz feared no man, he still gave *him* a wide berth whenever they were in the same room together.

Catching sight of Kaz, Raj's expression didn't change, that permanent scowl he usually sported still etched firmly onto his grisly mug. "The *Pakhan* wants to see you."

Kaz tapped his thumb against his phone, then said, "He couldn't call me himself?" It wasn't like the man was incapable of using a phone—he had just seen him the day before. And if Vasily was going underground for any reason, Kaz would have been one of the first to know.

But despite his inquiry, Raj didn't offer a response—not that Kaz was expecting one. Raj didn't question orders, just did what he was told and nothing more. He was a good soldier in that way.

And maybe if he hadn't spent the night between the legs of someone he knew was off-limits, Kaz might have been a little less suspicious as to why Vasily was calling him in.

He was careful to keep his expression neutral as he slid into his car, watching Raj through the windshield as the man jogged the short distance back to his own vehicle. The moment Kaz was sure he couldn't see him anymore, he dialed someone he thought might have answers. While he and their father might not have been the closest, Ruslan still heard things, sometimes even before Kaz did.

"It's early for you, no?" Ruslan said the moment the call connected, sounding like he was still in bed.

"Vasily wants a meet," Kaz explained, driving far more cautiously than he had some hours before.

There was a sound of movement, and his brother's muffled voice as he spoke with whoever he was with before Ruslan was back on the line. "What the fuck did you do this time?"

Ruslan wasn't far off. The last time Vasily had called him in this early was because of a shipment Kaz had fucked up and needed to fix. "Nothing that I'm aware of." The last thing he was going to mention was Violet.

"I haven't heard anything, if that's why you're calling—can't help you this time."

Kaz only had a few minutes before he would be outside of Vasily's residence, so there was no point in him asking for information anywhere else. He would just have to go in and pray to whoever the fuck was listening that he wasn't walking to his death.

"How's the face?" he asked changing the subject.

Ruslan made a disgruntled noise, sounding almost annoyed as he said, "Looks worse than it feels. I'll probably need to avoid Mama for a while. You know how she feels when she sees that shit."

Irina wasn't clueless. She knew all too well what the men in her life were doing, even without the specifics, but she never liked when it was staring back at her. That just made the reality of it all sink in a little more. If they could help it, they didn't show her that side.

"Do that."

"Right. Well, call me after your meet."

Yeah, if he lived to see the end of it … "Will do."

With a quick farewell, Kaz was off the phone, tossing the device in his passenger seat as he pulled up to the gate, punched in the code, and waited for the metal doors to swing open before he pulled in and parked. At first glance, he could already see that Irina wasn't at home, nor were the twins. One of the two matching BMWs that Vasily had bought them for their birthdays was missing.

He might have been inclined to think of this as a good thing. Kaz didn't want to believe that Vasily would kill him under the roof where Irina and the girls slept, but knowing his father the way he did, he would have him cleaned up long before any of them got home.

Grabbing his gun from the glove compartment, he checked the clip before holstering the weapon. It was now or never.

The front door was open when he tried the knob, not all that surprising since it was pretty well known who the house belonged to.

He crossed the floor to the spiral staircase, heading upstairs to the second level where Vasily's office was located. Though the door was pushed closed from what Kaz could see from down the hall, the gruff, but soft voices could still be heard.

Rapping his knuckles twice against the door, he pushed the door open and stepped inside. There were five men in attendance, his father included. Raj stood off to the side looking disapproving—probably because Kaz had arrived after him, though they had left from the same place. Two more men were seated against the back wall, not speaking. And last, there was Andrei who was standing across from Vasily, his gaze shooting to Kaz the moment he entered the room.

"Good of you to finally join us," Andrei said, condescension dripping from his tone.

Kaz's brow rose as he regarded the man, but he kept his mouth shut. He and Andrei had never gotten along, in part because the man felt Kaz didn't deserve the spot he had. Andrei had been a part of the brotherhood for more than two decades, had even spent a tour in a Russian gulag back during the fall of the Soviet Union, and yet he was still occupying the same position as Kaz.

Of course, he couldn't voice his anger to Vasily—not if he wanted to live—but he lived to make Kaz's life difficult every fucking chance he got.

"Sorry, Mom," Kaz said. "Next time I'll call to let you know when I'll be late for dinner."

Chuckles arose, making Andrei's face mottle with red. "You little—"

"As entertaining as this has been," Vasily interjected. "We need to get to business. Take a seat, Kazimir."

Kaz quickly surveyed the available spots left in his father's office to sit, noting the only seats would put his back to someone else, or a window. Standing where he was, his back was only to the door, and that was better than it facing men he didn't trust all that much.

"I'll stand," Kaz said.

Vasily passed him an indecipherable look, but settled on a nod. "Fine. Last night—"

"I still think we should send a message to the Italians," one of the two men standing against the wall said.

"I'm going to speak without interruption, or the next time someone jumps in on my conversation, I will have their tongue removed and bronzed for a paperweight," Vasily said rather dryly.

Any and all sounds in the office silenced instantly.

Vasily wasn't known for idle threats, and he always had a certain flair when it came to making a point.

"Good," Vasily said, pleased with the quietness around him. "As I was saying, I wanted to revisit the attack on Ruslan last night, and what I have decided to do about it."

Kaz shoved his hands in his pockets, curious but wisely choosing to stay quiet. It would do him no good to open his mouth at that moment, and he was well aware of that fact.

"And, what of it, boss?" Andrei asked.

Vasily picked up a mail opener from the desk, and fiddled with the dull knife. He spun the tip against the pad of his index finger as he spoke again. "You have to understand the way the Italians work, especially one like Alberto Gallucci. A man like him understands the value and weight of a proper apology."

Kaz's irritation jumped a notch.

His father seemed entirely unfazed by what had happened to Ruslan the night before as he set the letter opener down, and picked up his phone. Swiping at the screen, Vasily passed it a look before turning it off and setting it back down with a nod.

"And while I would usually send out a message of my own after something like this happens, I have chosen not to this time," Vasily said, eyeing each man, but lingering a little while longer on Kaz when he finally came to him.

It was like his father knew the rebuttal was right on the tip of his tongue.

"Do you have an opinion on that, Kazimir?" Vasily asked.

Kaz kept his cool demeanor firmly in place. "I have an opinion on my brother being attacked, yes."

"That's not what I asked."

That was the only answer Kaz was willing to offer.

His nonresponse to his father stretched on for a long while until Vasily let out a heavy, annoyed breath and rested back in his large chair.

"I have reason to believe the attack was misguided, and appropriate action will be taken," Vasily informed.

"By whom?" Kaz dared to ask.

Vasily smiled. "Men who understand the value and weight of an apology. Only if I do not receive what I want, then I will revisit this discussion and Ruslan's attack again."

Kaz didn't like that statement at all, but what could he say?

His father made the calls.

And if, after everything was said and done, and nothing happened to Ruslan's attackers, Kaz could always handle the issue himself. If he felt the punishment he might receive for doing so would be worth the reward in the end.

Vasily drummed his fingers to the desk and said, "For the next little while, I want everyone to be careful and quiet about business. Be mindful of the territory we have, as there is no need to begin pushing against someone else's lines when we are perfectly capable of working within our own. At least until the dust settles, and I have gotten what I wanted."

Kaz cocked a single brow. "And what is that?"

Vasily didn't answer.

No one else seemed to want to question the *Pakhan* on his decisions, or what was really going on. Kaz was left to the task.

"What exactly are we waiting for?" Kaz asked.

Picking his phone up again, Vasily turned the screen on and checked it. He then placed it back to the desk before clasping his hands together and looking straight up at his son.

"A message."

Violet hugged her bomber jacket a little tighter when the wind picked up. She usually enjoyed walking around her parents' large property because it was so quiet and calm. Over the years, her father had several different landscapers come in and add pathways, small bridges, and seating areas throughout the many acres of wooded property behind the mansion.

It was the peaceful place in her otherwise hectic life. There were no rushing cars, beeping horns, or hordes of people all around when she strolled through the woods.

Just her, the trees, and rustling leaves.

She could remember being maybe seven or eight before her father finally allowed her to walk the pathways by herself without someone supervising her. But even then, Violet knew there had been someone watching. Alberto never let his young children go unattended for very long, not with who he was and his position.

"Come back here, Olly!" Violet shouted as a flash of beige hair disappeared around a turn.

A few seconds later, the dog trotted right back like he had been told. It was one of the only things the Golden Retriever had going for him—he listened. Olly was Carmine's dog, and while Violet mostly tried to avoid her brother, she did like Olly a lot. He was a good companion to walk with, but today he was restless and kept running ahead of Violet.

That wasn't like the dog.

Usually, he would stay right at her side, no matter what.

It was one of the many demands Alberto had made when Carmine got the dog just after his twenty-first birthday. Their father made it clear that if the dog was going to come and go from his home when Carmine was busy or out of town, then Olly needed training, and he needed to listen to commands.

143

Carmine agreed. Alberto allowed Olly to come and go from the Gallucci mansion after one year of constant training with a professional dog trainer.

Violet took a seat on a wicker bench, keeping a hold on Olly's collar as his head lifted high and he sniffed the air again. She didn't want him bolting off. God knew if he did and didn't come back, Carmine would blame her.

It wasn't even her responsibility to look after his damn dog.

But she hadn't been given much of a choice.

Ever since her father called Violet to the Gallucci mansion three days prior, he had refused both her and her brother's requests to leave. It wasn't often that it happened—a situation where Alberto locked his family in just to be safe, but this was one of those times.

She knew it had to do with the attack, the Russians, and what might come of it.

Alberto had said nothing except, "Just to be careful."

That was it.

He didn't offer anything else, and he refused to explain to Violet why she had to miss classes. She couldn't even have a driver take her off of the Gallucci property.

But if it was a matter of safety, then she chose not to argue.

Almost daily, she did stare at the contact on her phone for Kaz, considering making a call or sending him a message. But given how someone was always around—her father, Carmine, her mother, or even one of Alberto's men—she didn't feel safe doing so.

Anyone could pick up her phone and despite it being locked, messages still flashed on the screen. She didn't want to take the risk.

Standing from the bench, Violet pulled on Olly's collar to make him turn around and follow her back to the mansion. He refused to budge, still pointed in the other direction.

"Time to go back to the house," Violet told the dog. "Come on, Olly."

The dog's ear flicked.

Carmine had been absent from the mansion for the better part of the morning, and Alberto hadn't given much of an answer as to why or where her brother was. He'd simply said that Carmine was around, and had business to attend to. Apparently, that business had lasted for most of the day.

Because Violet had been stuck entertaining the asshole's dog all damn morning and afternoon.

"Olly," Violet muttered, tugging lightly on his collar again. "Aren't you hungry?"

At the mention of food, Olly would usually run straight for his bowls, wherever they may be. Violet didn't even get an ear flick out of him for that one.

Then, the dog's head picked up higher, like he had heard something farther beyond in the pathways. She supposed he could have, knowing the dog had far better hearing than she did. But Alberto had been clear when she said she was going for a walk.

Stay on the stone walkways. Not beyond.

After a certain point in the woods, the pathways turned to dirt instead of stone. There were a couple of small cabins toward the back of the property that they sometimes used for parties in the summer and things like that, but it was too cold for anyone to be in them now.

Olly lurched forward with a bark, and Violet went with him, her hand slipping out of his collar just at the last second. It saved her from taking a tumble to the ground, but barely.

"Olly!"

Her shout did nothing. The dog was already gone.

Cursing under her breath, Violet righted her jacket and jogged after the dog. She wasn't going to put up with Carmine's nonsense if she lost his dog because it wouldn't listen to her.

Before she knew it, her sneakers crunched on dirt as she called out for the dog again. It would be a good half hour, maybe even a forty-five minute, walk back to the mansion from where she was now.

And she had already gone too far, so there was no point in turning back now.

Violet had just caught a flash of beige fur when she noticed that the lights to one of the cabins were on, making her pause. Normally Alberto would have told her if anyone was staying in them, and since they were supposed to be empty, she didn't think twice about going up to the door, ready to knock.

But something made her pause ... Instead of knocking as she had planned to do, she walked around the side, peeking through the windows there. The furniture was still covered in sheets, the place empty of anyone as far as she could see, but even still, that feeling of unease didn't fade.

She was almost to the back of the cabin when she finally found Olly standing next to the small, rectangular window that looked into the basement. She hissed a command for him to stay, not raising her voice above a whisper, but it didn't matter, Olly wasn't moving. Whatever had made him run off was there in the basement, it seemed.

Getting a firm grip on his collar this time—she didn't need him running off again—her curiosity got the best of her as she crouched down to see whatever it was that held his attention.

Carmine was in the room, along with two others that Violet couldn't make out from where she was standing, but what surprised her the most was that Franco was in the room as well. Except, he wasn't there by choice.

A steel table had been set up in the center of the room, a plastic tarp placed beneath it, and on that table was Franco, his arms strapped down on either side of him, his legs cuffed in the same way. A light sheen of sweat was covering his face and naked torso, and if Violet wasn't mistaken, he was shaking as well.

There was nothing to cover his head, so his panicked, frenzied gaze was clear for them all to see. She knew she should have walked away then, put everything she was seeing to the back of her mind and act as though it had never happened. But she felt stuck, almost frozen in time as she watched the scene play out before her.

Franco wasn't the only one in distress, however. Carmine, while off to the side, was pacing the floor, scrubbing a hand down his face every few seconds, as though he too were still trying to make sense of what was happening. He wasn't wearing the same clothes he'd been in earlier—instead, he was in a pair of wrinkled jeans and a shirt whose logo was so faded, the original design couldn't be made out.

He shook his head hard, muttering something that Violet couldn't hear, but one of the men he was in the room with could. The man gestured to Carmine first, then to Franco who was now pleading, his hands in tight fists as he tried to break free of his restraints.

It was rare, Violet thought, for her brother to display such anguish. Alberto had never been easy on him that way, always demanding that Carmine act like a man, even when he was a boy. So, to see this emotion in him made Violet's own heart seize with worry.

What was happening?

It took some convincing, or rather it was a sharp slap to the back of Carmine's head, that finally had him crossing the room, picking up an instrument from the table near the wall. Violet crept a little closer, squinting her eyes to see better, but there was no need, not when Carmine came right back to where he had been standing, and she could now see what he was holding.

The glint of silver drew her gaze down to his hand, to the small blade she might not have noticed otherwise. It was thin, almost concealed entirely, but it was the sharpened tip that told her what it was.

A scalpel.

It was time to leave. She needed to *leave*, but no matter how loud the words were screamed in her own head, she remained in place, though her grip on Olly's collar tightened just a little more.

Carmine approached slowly, as though this was the last thing he wanted, his face reflecting each plea that was shouted from Franco's mouth. He stopped just at the edge of the table, and though he was looking at Franco, he couldn't meet his eyes—that was one place he refused to look.

He raised his instrument, his hands shaking as he brought it down to Franco's chest, resting it right in the middle, but he didn't cut, not yet. Or at least not before he mouthed an apology that would mean nothing in the next few seconds. Because once he finally dragged that blade down, blood welling immediately as Franco's skin split open, he screamed, a blood-curdling yell that even Violet could hear.

One of the other men in the room rushed forward, clamping a hand over Franco's mouth to muffle his cries of pain, even as he used his substantial weight to hold a thrashing Franco still. Carmine didn't remove the blade until he reached the man's abdomen, then backed away, his face a little greener than it had been before.

But that was only the first, because very soon, that scalpel was replaced with bolt cutters, and Carmine had to return to his once childhood friend.

Nausea churned heavily in her stomach, threatening to spill out of her in a moment's notice. Finally, when she saw Carmine position the metal around one of Franco's ribs, she squeezed her eyes shut just as he snapped it free.

Scrambling backward, Violet dragged Olly with her as she hurried away, breathing heavily through her nose as she tried to quell her need to vomit what little she had eaten that day.

Maybe it was the fact that Olly sensed Violet's distress, but the dog didn't fight to return to the cabin as she pulled him back to the pathways. She couldn't run fast enough, couldn't make her mind forget the images burning their way into her retinas.

Even when she closed her eyes, it was still there.

All of it.

Swallowing convulsively, she desperately willed the vomit to stay away. The burning prickle of tears stung her eyes, but she blinked them away.

Once her sneakers hit the stone pathways again, she took a deep breath. It didn't help. She might have been back in the safe zone, but she felt anything but okay.

How was she supposed to sit at the dinner table later with her brother, knowing what she did, seeing what she had?

Oh, God.

Violet was three-quarters of the way back to the mansion when she nearly rammed right into her father as they both came around a blind turn in the path. She was moving much faster than Alberto was.

"Slow down, Violet," her father said, chuckling.

It didn't sound true.

She schooled her features, knowing her panic and fear had to be written on her face as clear as day.

"Daddy," she greeted fast.

Too fast.

Too high.

Too breathless.

Alberto frowned. "What's wrong, *dolcezza?*"

Violet shook her head, her gaze dropping down to the item her father held in his hands. It looked like a white gift box with a top that could be removed. It even had a fucking bow on it.

Why did he have that?

What was he going to put in that box?

"Violet," Alberto said harshly.

"Nothing is wrong," she said quickly. "Olly got away from me, but I caught him. I just thought I should bring him back to the house."

Alberto looked over her shoulder, down the pathways. A dark distance colored up his eyes as he asked, "You didn't go further than I approved, right?"

"Of course not."

"And Olly?"

"He was chasing a squirrel. He gave up at the wicker bench."

Alberto still didn't look pleased with her answer, but Violet had the distinct feeling her father wouldn't question her on the lie. After all, he would have to explain what she saw. He would need to confirm it had happened.

He wouldn't do that, she knew.

"Supper is almost ready," Alberto said. "Go back to the mansion and wash up. You look tired—are you sure you're okay?"

"Fine, Daddy," she assured.

Lies.

She was so far from fine it was ridiculous.

Violet's gaze dropped to the box Alberto held again. She knew better than to ask, but with the shock of the day, her mouth worked before her brain could tell it to stop. "What's that for?"

"A gift," Alberto said simply, offering nothing else. "I need to collect it."

Jesus.

Usually, more than an hour in his father's presence and Kaz would be more than ready to go anywhere else, but for once he didn't feel that pressing need as he sat opposite the man in the warehouse they used to do business. It wasn't often that the pair were in this place at the same time, liability and all that, but for whatever reason, Vasily had demanded that Kaz come along.

And he had invited Ruslan.

Since Vasily already seemed to be in a mood, not to mention the cryptic shit he had spoken earlier, Kaz hadn't asked why. And for the first time in ages, he didn't question the order when it was given to him.

Now as he sat at the table occupied with a few of the higher ranking members in the *Bratva*, he let his thoughts wander, and it was of no surprise to him that they went to Violet. It felt wrong almost—thinking of her, considering present company—like his thoughts of her would be written all over his face.

But he couldn't help himself.

Already, he'd pulled his phone out, scrolling down to her contact and staring at the number, tempted to shoot her a text, but for whatever reason, he had been unable to do it, at least not yet—not when he was in a room full of men that, while sharing his oath with the *Bratva*, he didn't completely trust.

He had learned the hard way about who to give his trust to.

Years ago, back when he was first trying to earn his stars, Kaz had confided in a man by the name of Vadim. They had been around the same age, both trying to work their way into Vasily's good graces—because in the end, it didn't matter that Kaz was his son, if he didn't do the work, he would never become a part of the *Bratva*, despite what people thought.

It wasn't that the information Kaz had shared with him was of any importance, at least not to anyone but Kaz himself, but Vadim had taken it upon himself to share Kaz's words with Vasily, thinking that it would earn him favor from the *Pakhan*.

It hadn't. If anything, it only exposed the man for what he was.

But it *had* taught Kaz an important lesson, one that he hadn't really understood until that point.

There was no honor amongst thieves.

Ruslan's arrival dragged Kaz back to the present, and to the fact that he hadn't arrived alone. There was another man coming in before him— Ruslan rarely let anyone walk at his back—carrying a gift. Kaz nodded to Ruslan as his brother took the seat beside him, but most of his focus was on the white box wrapped with red ribbon that the no-name soldier was carrying over to Vasily.

When his offering was placed on the table, he made his leave rather quickly, though it was clear he wanted to stay and see what was inside of it.

This, apparently, was what Vasily had been waiting on. There was a note tucked into the bow of the ribbon, but as Vasily plucked it free, he didn't bother with the box at all, merely opened the note and began to read.

"Sacrifice," his voice rang out amongst the quiet of the room, "is at the heart of repentance. Without deeds, your apology is worthless. Bryan Davis."

Who the fuck was Bryan Davis?

"As you may all have been aware, one of our own was attacked two nights ago," Vasily said, dropping the note on the table, his gaze sliding over every man in the room—well at least everyone besides Ruslan.

But no one would have noticed that, no one except Kaz. Kaz also didn't miss that Vasily hadn't personalized his words—"our own" instead of "my son".

"I am not one to allow such acts to go unpunished, but I have learned with great patience comes great reward. There was no need for retribution," Vasily said, this time his gaze lingering on Kaz. "Not when we do not have to dirty our hands. We are *Vory v Zakone*, others do our work for *fear* of what we may do next."

Kaz had to stifle an eye roll. Vasily was known for his dramatics, but this was just over the top, and more than anything, he was just ready for the box to be opened so he could see what was inside.

"This," he went on, pointing to the box in front of him, "is a gift given to me, but I believe that it is one worth sharing—and after all, this gift is as much Ruslan's as it is mine. So please, Ruslan, if you would do the honors."

Ruslan had never liked the spotlight, much preferring to blend into the background, but as all eyes turned to him, he cleared his throat and stood, hand going out to catch the box as Vasily slid it across the table toward him.

His brother didn't waste time with theatrics, just pulled the ribbons free, then the top and tossed it on the table, his eyes searching the contents.

There was a moment of disbelief, as though he couldn't believe what he was seeing, then he was reaching inside, drawing out the bag inside, holding it up for them all to see.

Red.

That was the first thing that popped into Kaz's head as he saw the package, but as he blinked, his brain finally catching up to what he was actually seeing, he rubbed his own chest.

The Italians had sent them Franco's heart.

With a heavy huff, Violet dropped her messenger bag onto the seat and took the other right beside it. Nicole barely looked up from the laptop she was typing on, and Amelia, sitting beside her, kept her eyes down on her phone. Both girls already had to-go cups of lattes sitting in front of them, and another was waiting for Violet.

She picked the cup up, taking a sip of the Chai latte and letting the sweetness of the drink roll over her taste buds.

"Damn, thanks," she said as she pulled the cup away. "I needed that."

Nicole didn't look away from the laptop. "How'd the test go?"

Violet rolled her eyes. "Terribly, no doubt."

Whether she liked it or not, Violet was going to have to let her father know that her grades were slipping in school before the college gave him a call because she wasn't keeping up the average he demanded. The school wouldn't want to lose out on his regular donations, after all. With everything that was going on around her, she just couldn't focus like she needed to.

Alberto wouldn't be pleased.

It didn't help that Violet wasn't sleeping well nearly a week after witnessing a man's chest be cut open at her brother's hand—a man her friend had been involved with for a good year.

Violet passed Amelia a look, noting the dark circles under her friend's eyes, and her slightly disheveled clothes. Obviously, her friend wasn't sleeping well, if the way she looked was any indication to go by.

"Your dad is going to be pissed that you're flunking the semester," Nicole said.

Violet barely held back her scowl. "Thanks for the memo."

Nicole tipped her head in Amelia's direction. "Not the only one, though."

"Does Vito know yet?" Violet asked Amelia.

151

Her friend acted like she didn't even hear her question.

Nicole openly frowned, glancing at the phone in Amelia's hand. "Still no answer, huh?"

Finally, Amelia gave a response. Just a shake of her head, no words.

"Who?" Violet asked.

Nicole mouthed, "Franco."

Oh.

Damn.

All it took was Franco's name and Violet was right back to where she started a week ago when she watched from outside the cabin as his blood spilled to the basement floor. She tried to counteract the automatic reaction of panic and disgust swelling up into her throat, threatening to send the Chai latte back out of her stomach.

Violet cleared her throat, and glanced away.

"I don't understand," Amelia said quietly.

Her voice ...

So soft, pained, and confused.

It hurt Violet.

While she was angry with her friend because of what she had lied about, and what it caused, she didn't think Amelia deserved to be left in limbo like she was. Why hadn't someone—Amelia's father, even—spoke up and told her the truth about Franco?

That he was dead.

His punishment was his life.

"He never waits this long to text me back," Amelia said, looking up from her phone.

Nicole passed Violet a look. She wondered if her other friend knew the truth like she did. Nicole couldn't have possibly seen what she had, obviously, but she could know Franco was dead.

Violet just couldn't bring herself to tell Amelia.

"He's probably lying low," Nicole said, her tone thick. "Keeping out of trouble after everything."

Amelia nodded, but she didn't look like she believed it.

Violet didn't blame her.

Chances were, Amelia knew exactly why Franco wasn't answering her calls and messages. But given the relationship she had with him, Amelia wasn't willing to let him go.

It wasn't the first time a man had gone missing from the Gallucci ranks without so much as a word or a goodbye to the people who loved him. Others had suffered a similar fate for reasons beyond Violet's knowledge. For a while, people wouldn't talk about the man, simply turn cheek to the disappearance and hope he returned eventually.

And then a body might show up.

Washed up on a river bank, hands cut off.

Found in a garbage bin, dismembered into pieces.

Resting in a shallow grave, a bullet between his eyes.

Franco wasn't the first, but he was the only one that Violet had been privy to seeing happen. With the others that had gone from their family's ranks, she hadn't been all that touched by it because it was like a passing moment to her. Something that happened, but didn't really affect her because she hadn't been a part of it.

This time was not the same.

She knew what happened, and she couldn't forget it.

No matter what she did, it was there.

Violet scrubbed a hand down over her face, careful not to mess up the makeup she had taken an hour to apply that morning before school. Her first class was the test, and for the hour after, she had a free study period. Which was why she had met the girls at a cafe on campus for a quick coffee and some study time.

She couldn't even be bothered to bring out her textbook or laptop.

It was no wonder she was failing miserably in school.

Hoping her face was unreadable, Violet said, "Maybe you could talk to your dad, Amelia."

Amelia openly scowled. "Yes, because he's so happy with me right now."

Ouch.

While Violet knew how shitty it was to have your father disappointed in you, she didn't think she had warranted Amelia's attitude. It wasn't her who had lied and gotten them all in trouble. It wasn't her who had put Franco in the situation where he found himself. It wasn't her who did any of that.

"I was just trying to say—"

"Well, I don't want to fucking hear it," Amelia interrupted sharply, standing from her chair abruptly. "It's not like you tried to help at that breakfast, anyway."

Violet blinked, stunned at her friend's sudden change in demeanor. "Hey!"

Even Nicole seemed too surprised to speak.

"I didn't tell you to lie to Franco," Violet said, her gaze narrowing. "You did that all on your own, Amelia."

Her friend just glared, slammed the chair into the table, and stalked off. Violet wished she understood what had just happened, but she really couldn't even begin to comprehend it all.

"Cut her some slack," Nicole finally said after a moment.

"I didn't do anything," Violet replied.

"Well ..."

Violet crossed her arms over her chest. "Well, what?"

Nicole shrugged, refusing to meet Violet's eyes. "I mean, this did all start because you wanted to party down in Coney and—"

"Whoa," Violet snapped, leaning forward. "Stop right there. We all wanted to do that, not just me. And while I was willing to accept the bullshit my father threw at me for getting us all mixed up in trouble that night, I am not going to take shit from you, too. You wanted to be there. Amelia wanted to go. And now, just because we're all suffering the consequences of being caught, don't think I'll sit here and let you throw it on me, Nicole. That's not how this is going to work."

"I was just saying."

"A bunch of crap."

Nicole frowned. "You could have a bit of sympathy for Amelia, that's all I'm trying to say."

Violet did.

She had remorse and sadness in the bucketfuls for her friend, but this wasn't her fault.

"You don't know how I feel," Violet said quietly. "You can't possibly understand how I feel right now."

Because Nicole didn't know.

No one did.

And Violet couldn't tell her.

"Whatever," Nicole muttered, slamming her laptop closed and shoving it into her bag.

"Where are you going?" Violet softened her posture as her friend stood. "I thought we were going to study or something."

"I just ... need to take a break."

What?

"A break," Violet echoed.

"Yeah," Nicole replied. "From all of this. Carmine has been acting strange lately. You're being weird. And I just have better things to do."

Violet's jaw fell slack.

Oddly, as she watched Nicole pack up the rest of her things and sling her bag around her shoulder, Violet just knew ... this was the end of something. Or maybe it was just the beginning of an end.

A friendship that had started when they were just kids was running its course. And for what?

Because no one really understood.

Violet watched her friend leave the cafe without a backward glance; she felt more alone than ever.

She didn't want to feel this way at all.

Placing a bundled stack of twenty-dollar bills on the corner of his desk, Kaz stuck his hand back in the duffel bag at his side, pulling out more and laying them out to count. He had been at it for little more than an hour, but counting money was almost like therapy for him—it helped clear his mind, even as he concentrated on the numbers in his head.

This was his happy place, at least it usually was until Abram had walked into his office, dropping down on his couch like the weight of the world was on his shoulders. He didn't usually mind when it was Abram—but at the moment, he would have rather been alone.

"Can I help you with something?" Kaz asked, not taking his gaze from the money in his hands.

"I think I fucked up, Cap."

It wouldn't be the first time someone in the *Bratva* did—they all did shit that wouldn't necessarily be considered *good*. But they normally kept it to themselves. Abram had always been the sharing type though.

"What'd you do this time? Lost a shipment? Cut off the wrong thumb? What?" Kaz finally looked up when Abram didn't immediately answer, then he noticed the legitimate fear in the man's eyes. "What the fuck did you do?"

"Do you remember Stacey?"

Kaz turned the name over in his head. "The bird over in Hell's Kitchen? I thought you stopped seeing her when she tried to set your fucking car on fire the *first* time …"

Abram waved those words away as though they meant nothing. "She was just mad. You know how it is?"

No, Kaz didn't, and he really didn't want to find out either. "That still doesn't answer my question."

Like he had to force the words out or he wouldn't be able to say them, Abram answered, "She's pregnant."

Setting the money he'd been counting on his desk, Kaz sat back. "Yeah, you fucked up."

There were rules in place for a reason. In most cases, no one gave a shit where you stuck your dick, unless you were forcing it on someone, but with *sukas* like Stacey, who would happily fuck shit up just because they were in a mood, it mattered.

Kaz's phone chimed with a new message, but he ignored it for the moment, his attention on Abram. "What are you going to do?"

Abram shrugged, scrubbing a hand down his face. "I don't know."

"You need to figure that shit out," Kaz said, plucking his phone off the desk when it chimed again. He read the name, a beat of confusion hitting him as he tried to figure out why he would have saved someone's number under "Converse".

Then he remembered, and all thoughts of Abram and his newest problem were out of his mind.

How long had it been? A week? Maybe longer? He had kept himself from reaching out to her, fighting the urge, wanting her to come to him this time. He had made his interest in her clear, even if he hadn't outright said it, and while he knew she felt the connection, felt the spark that ignited between them when they were together, that was no guarantee that she would have been willing to risk it.

Apparently, he had underestimated the Gallucci girl.

Abram was still talking, rambling on about what he planned to do, but Kaz was too busy opening up the message to actually hear what the man was saying.

I'm at the border.

No one else could have known what that message meant, but Kaz did, and before he even realized he was doing it, he was texting her back to let her know he was on the way.

"Finish up in here," Kaz said gesturing around them to the money on the desk and the rest in the bag. "Have it done by morning."

He was heading for the door when Abram called back, "But what about my problem?"

Kaz paused. "Marry the girl. Take care of the kid, if that's what she wants. Just hope the *suka* doesn't get you killed."

Leaving the warehouse parking lot, Kaz tapped his thumb against the steering wheel as he drove toward the bridge that led out of Coney Island. He was nearly there, his headlights cutting through the darkness of the night when he saw her. She looked up in his direction the moment he got close, then grabbed the messenger bag that was sitting on the ground next to her feet, and hurried over, sliding into his car with ease, like they had done this a dozen times over.

Turning his body in her direction, he looked her over, taking in her appearance, and the almost sad expression on her face. There was a reason she had sought him out, Kaz knew, he just wondered if she was going to share.

"Where to?"

There was no hesitation as she said, "Your place."

Violet watched familiar streets pass her window by. Strange, she thought, how only one trip to Little Odessa before this one could make the drive to Kaz's place familiar.

"Why so quiet?"

She didn't turn away from the window. "Tired, maybe."

"But maybe not," Kaz pressed.

Violet didn't reply, but she relaxed a little more in the seat when his hand found her thigh and squeezed just under the hem of her dress.

"Tell me," he said, "are we going to get another phone call where I have to rush you back to Manhattan?"

"Probably not."

"Probably is not a no, Violet."

She shivered just a little at the way her name rolled off his lips. Like he'd been thinking about saying it for days, but keeping it to himself. And when he was finally able to say it, the word spilled out like a prayer.

It was too much.

For her, she liked it too much.

"It's a most likely not," Violet said, shrugging. "My father had some sort of thing in New Jersey he was going to, and he'll be there until tomorrow night when he drives back. My mother doesn't give a shit what I do or where I am, as long as I'm not within five feet of her. My brother has holed himself inside his apartment, which is where my mother has been for the last week, much to my father's dismay. And my friends ..."

She trailed off, scowling at her reflection in the passenger window.

"The girls from the club, yes?"

Violet sighed. "Yeah."

His hand tightened around her thigh again, making Violet swallow hard.

"Keep going," Kaz urged.

"I suppose it doesn't matter. All things have a course to run, and it eventually comes to an end, right?"

"Unless you're purposely being vague, I need more to go on."

Violet shook her head. "It's nothing. Just drive."

Kaz's hand left her thigh, and she felt the loss instantly. But just as quickly as it had gone, two of his fingers were stroking the side of her neck.

"You're sad," he murmured.

"A little," she admitted.

"Is that why you came down here looking for me?"

157

"Partly."

"And the other part?" he asked.

Violet finally spun in her seat to face him, slowly. His hand moved with her, fingers skipping down her jaw and under her chin.

"Well?" Kaz asked, still stroking her skin.

That was some of it, too. She thought about him a lot. Too much, really. She remembered his hands on her and how that felt, so maybe she wanted a little more.

But that wasn't all of it.

"I don't really know," Violet said.

Kaz nodded. "Yeah, me either."

It wasn't supposed to be this way.

At the very least, Kaz figured there would still be a little awkwardness between them as they entered his apartment. She had only been to his place once, but she moved around the space as though she had been there hundreds of times—like she belonged there—and as he tossed his keys on the table, shrugging out of his jacket, he found that he didn't mind it.

Kaz liked his space, his privacy away from the world, but with Violet around, he didn't mind not being alone.

Heading into the kitchen, he grabbed a bottle of vodka, and a bottle of wine Vera had given him as a housewarming present, holding them up for Violet to see. "What kind of night are we having?"

She pointed to the vodka.

Fair enough.

Grabbing two glasses out of the cabinet above his head, Kaz carried them and the bottle into the living room, his eyes on Violet as she got comfortable on the couch, kicking her shoes off and tucking her legs beneath her. He dropped down beside her, pouring them both a drink, then passed her a glass.

"Tell me," he said picking up his own drink.

He was sure she would deny him again, just as she'd done in the car as they drove over, but he was willingly to ask again. And even if she didn't give him an answer, he would just do it again until she did. He didn't like seeing her upset. Already, he missed her smile.

Violet hesitated, then tossed back a healthy amount of vodka without a single cough. "My friends are upset with me. They're blaming me—at least

Amelia is—for getting in trouble with her father when we came to the club that night. Then there's the fact that she hasn't seen F-Franco."

She stumbled over the word, but Kaz didn't think much of it as he tried to hide his own reaction at hearing that name. He didn't doubt that the girl hadn't heard from him, especially when they still had the man's heart. Vasily still had it in a cooler in the freezer of the warehouse—he was sick in that way.

"But they were here too, no? You didn't force them."

"Of course not, but they don't care about that."

"Sounds like your friends are selfish," Kaz said, finishing off his drink, then pouring another. "Are you sure those two are your friends?"

Kaz knew all about fake friends that ultimately betrayed you. Shit, he knew family that was worse.

"I think that's something we all learn after a while," he settled on saying.

Violet tipped back her glass, emptying the rest of the vodka in one smooth pull. She tipped the glass in his direction, and he refilled it for her. "What's that?"

"Not to depend on anyone else."

"That's … a little harsh, isn't it?" she asked.

Kaz chuckled. "No, it's life. When you depend on others for too much, your happiness, acceptance, or even approval, then you're already guaranteeing yourself unhappiness, rejection, and dissatisfaction from others and yourself. Better to go on seeking those things from yourself, than expecting others to hand them over to you."

Violet stared at him for a long while, saying nothing.

"Not what you were expecting?" he asked.

"I was … It makes sense," Violet said.

"Yeah, the hard lessons usually do."

"That must have been tough …"

Kaz threw back another drink before facing her. "What's that?"

"Having to learn that lesson."

"Is that your way of asking about me?" he questioned, canting his head to the side as he regarded her.

"Only if you're willing to tell me."

"Let me tell you a story." Kaz reached down, pulling her legs onto his lap, his fingers kneading at the muscles in her calves. If he was going to do this, he would need a distraction. "I had a friend once, my best friend I would say. Back when we were younger, he encouraged me to do reckless, outlandish things—he thrilled in the shit. I would be lying if I say I didn't enjoy it, but not like him. He got off on it."

Violet was listening, her face turned in his direction and laying back against the couch. And it was clear as he met that curious, worried gaze of hers that she wasn't just trying to placate him as he talked, but was actually listening. That encouraged him to go on, even if this was one story he refused to share.

Not even Ruslan knew.

"I was young at the time, sixteen thereabout, but we might as well have been men—we knew better—but I was a little shit and wanted the fuck away from Vasily, and if that meant doing bad shit—" He paused, smiling absently as his hands shifted to one of her feet and he pressed his thumbs into the arch. "—and not like the bad shit I'm a part of now. We smoked weed, drank heavily, and one night he even bought cocaine.

"That night, I was fucking wired, like I felt nothing, despite how high I was. We were sitting in the car outside of my old space in broad daylight, mind, but who gave a fuck? I am who I am. But what my friend didn't tell me was where he'd scored the stuff—and that he hadn't bothered to pay. Even as young as we were, it was easy for us to get by on names alone—my family is fucking infamous around these parts."

Kaz took a breath, holding it for a moment, and then he let it go once her legs shifted in his lap as she drew closer.

"Go on …"

"So we're sitting and laughing about nothing. It was all good. And maybe," Kaz said with a shake of his head, "just maybe, if he hadn't been ten fucking sheets to the wind, we might have noticed the men walking up. He might have noticed the guns in their hands. And maybe," said Kaz, his tone softening as he remembered that day, "just maybe, he could have prevented that little girl walking down the street with her mother from taking a bullet that was meant for him."

He was yanked out of his memories in a flash as Violet straddled his lap, her hands lifting to cradle his face. She looked so concerned in that moment that he almost didn't finish.

Before he could, she said, "It wasn't your fault, Kaz. Your friend, whoever it was, he should have been honest with you, or at least not have put you in that situation in the first place.

Ah, that was what he was hoping she would say. "So do you think he was a bad friend?"

She sat back. "Of course."

"You're right. I was a terrible friend."

"I don't understand."

Kaz sighed, resting his hands on her waist. "I was him. He was me. I went to the dealer, but didn't bother paying because the Markovic name was enough to strike fear in any person, but not in him. I was naive on that front, thinking myself beyond reproach, and worse, I knew I was bringing him down with me. And worse than that, someone had to answer for that child—not just to the mother who lost her kid, but to the police as well."

He could see it in her face just then, her fear as different ideas went through her head as to what might have happened to him as punishment, but as he remembered, he wasn't the one to suffer for it.

"Vasily made sure that the right people were arrested, but that dealer wasn't appeased. He wanted someone's fucking blood for what happened. He may be a bastard, but my father was never going to turn me over, even to teach me a lesson. To him, they weren't important enough to seek favor with, but because he owed a boon to their supplier, he compromised. Instead of me, he gave them my friend—even forced me to stick around and watch as they took him away."

He met Violet's gaze, letting her see the guilt in his own. "Because of me, two people lost their lives—one of which I care for like a brother. So these friends of yours, the ones that want to blame you for their own shit, cut them off while you can. Sometimes the consequences are much worse."

"Kaz ..."

His name, soft on her lips, was almost enough to make him smile. "You don't deserve bad friends, Violet. You deserve better than that."

The silence stretched between them, a heartbeat, even longer. Kaz was almost afraid that she wasn't going to reply, and was probably thinking exactly what he'd thought of himself since that day.

But instead, she moved toward him, her hands sliding around the front of his shirt and gripping the material. "Even with what you said, it's still not your fault. Now, I have a question for you."

"Ask."

"Is story time over?"

Violet let her hands travel a little lower on Kaz's body until she could feel the jump of his abdominal muscles against her touch. "Well, is it over?"

Kaz offered her one of his grins, sexy and sly. "It can be if you want it to be."

"For now."

"Oh?"

"I reserve the right to revisit this at a later time," Violet explained, tipping her chin up and teasing him with a smile.

Her words came out light, but she was serious, too. She wanted to know more about him—his past, why he chose the road he did, and how he got where he was now. All of those things fascinated her because they made up Kazimir Markovic.

He was far more than what everyone around her always said.

Russian. Savage. Scum.

There was a great deal more to the man behind the last name and the heritage he came from.

Just like her.

"Another time," Kaz finally agreed.

Violet reached up and stroked Kaz's jaw with two fingers, feeling the light stubble scratch along her fingertips. The motion made his grin melt into a softer smile, and the sadness lingering in his gaze began to depart. When he spoke about his friend, and his own mistakes, he was so sad. She didn't even think he realized how guilty he looked, like the weight of that one day wasn't ever going to leave.

She didn't want him to be sad.

Not when he was with her, anyway.

"Come here," Kaz demanded low.

Violet felt his fingers hook into the neckline of her dress and he pulled. She leaned forward until his lips were brushing against hers softly. Once, twice, and the third time, his teeth dragged across her bottom lip.

"There's a saying," Kaz began, letting his thumb sweep across her lax mouth.

"Hmm?"

"Once is a hookup, but twice makes a lover."

Violet's gaze snapped to his. "I hadn't thought of it that way."

"You probably should, if we're going to keep this up, no?"

He had a point, but maybe Violet just wasn't ready to quite go that way yet.

"I didn't actually come see you to fuck," she admitted.

Kaz laughed. "I'm not going to turn it down, Violet."

Yeah, she wouldn't either.

"Not my point," she told him.

His fingers glided over her lips again, a little firmer the second time. At the middle of her mouth, he pressed down, like he was asking her to open up. She did, parting her lips just enough for him to slide two fingers in. His teeth bit down on his lip as she sucked on his digits, letting her tongue roll around and flick at his fingertips.

"Shit," he muttered.

Violet let him pull his fingers free from her mouth, but not without dragging her teeth along his skin as he did. "My point, Kaz, was that it really wasn't my intention, but it's not like I mind."

"Clearly." He grabbed onto her waist tightly, making her sit a little more firmly on his groin. She could feel the length of his erection growing under her weight, and the sensation was enough to make her blood hot. "But you deflected what I said, and I'm not so much of an easily distracted man that I didn't notice."

Violet was pretty sure she could distract him from it if she wanted. Shifting her hips and widening her legs a little more, the skirt of her dress drove up her thighs. Kaz helped that along by pushing the fabric up further until he was staring at white lace.

"Still the same kind of delicate shit, I see," he muttered.

"I like this pair, too."

"I'm going to start ignoring that statement if you just like them all."

Fuck.

Kaz lifted a finger and circled it at her chest.

"What?" she asked.

"Take it off. I want to see if the top matches the bottom."

"It does."

"Still want to see," he said, entirely unfazed.

163

Violet laughed when he nodded at her again, as if he were telling her to hurry the fuck up. She tugged the dress up after he had pulled down the zipper at the back, discarding the clothing to the floor in a heap.

"Why do I have to be the one who's always underdressed?" she asked.

Kaz's mouth lifted at the corner. "Because the longer I stay clothed, the better it'll be for you, *krasivaya*."

She wisely chose not to push him on that, then.

His fingertips traced a circle around her navel, leaving behind a slight sheen of wetness from her saliva on his fingers. Up his exploration went between the valley of her breasts, over the hollow of her throat, and then against her collarbones.

The longer he touched her like that, soft, slow, and sweet, the harder it was to breathe.

How did he manage that without barely doing anything at all?

"It does match," he mused, his caress falling back to the top of her breasts. He skimmed his digits under the lacy cups of the bra, lingering on her nipples until they were tight and hard under his fingers, and her breaths came out sharper with every swipe and pinch. "Do they always match?"

"Yes, and I'm not a liar, Kaz."

He didn't act like she'd said a thing.

"Lift up," he said, taking his hand away.

Violet wanted it back. "What?"

"Up, I said."

She lifted up from his waist, and sighed the very second his hands traveled from her sides around to her backside. His fingers slid under the lace boy-shorts, his fingernails dragging across her skin as he pulled her closer.

Violet blinked, surprised when he fell down lower, moving his body beneath hers. His hands pushed against her ass again, making her hips tilt forward until she could feel every pulse of his warm breath hitting against the lace of her underwear.

"There we are," he murmured.

Violet's teeth cut into her lip as she hummed. "Better the longer your clothes stay on, huh?"

Kaz flashed his teeth in a wicked smile. "So much better."

He lifted his head slightly, tipping his chin up, and instantly, Violet felt like she had to find purchase on *something*. He hadn't even touched her, she was still covered by lace, but she just *knew*.

And then when his mouth was on her, covering her pussy over the lace, she was glad she had grabbed the back of the couch, and let her other hand thread into his hair. His tongue lapped at the material of her panties, and his teeth scraped over the same spot.

Testing.

Measured.

Slow.

A whine clawed its way out of her throat when she felt one of his hands move between her thighs. It wasn't a heartbeat later before he'd swept the digit under her boy-shorts, his tongue lapped at her clit overtop the lace again, and bliss raced down her spine.

"God," she breathed, tilting her hips into his mouth with another lick. "What are you waiting for?"

Kaz hummed a throaty sound against her body, his lips brushing against lace as he spoke. "Ask me."

"For what?"

"You know what."

Violet wet her lips, and let her eyes flutter closed. "You want to play the tease, then?"

"Not at all. I just want you to ask me for it, Violet. Ask for my mouth, my tongue, and my fingers. And I promise that you'll get it all, and you'll scream louder than you've ever done before."

Jesus.

"Why do you make that sound so good?" she asked.

Because it was fucking filthy.

"Ask," he repeated.

She let out a hard breath when his finger slipped between her folds, smearing her arousal over her sex. Instantly, her eyes were back on him. He dragged that finger out from beneath the lace and up to his mouth. Hot all over, and burning up with every passing second, she watched his tongue strike out to taste her wetness.

The throaty sound of approval that he let loose was sinful.

"Please," she whispered.

"Not what I wanted."

Violet's fingers tightened in his hair, but Kaz didn't even react if it hurt him at all. "I want your mouth, and your fingers, and your tongue. I want you to eat me. I want to come."

Kaz's lips split wide, his gray eyes dropping hers and going right back to her panties. "Now ... that's what I wanted."

Yeah, her too.

Violet didn't get the chance to prepare for what he did next, because she was far too focused on watching his mouth when it came dangerously close to her body again. His left hand slipped down between her thighs with his other one. She felt cool air kiss her folds as he yanked the lace to the side, and then hot breath washed over her center.

The first flick of his tongue along the seam of her sex had her back straightening. The second made her shout. When his tongue stroked against her clit, and two fingers buried knuckle-deep into her pussy without warning, she was lost.

Feeling. That's all there was.

Sensation.

The roughness of his stubble against her sensitive skin. His tongue driving into her throbbing clit. Fingers curling on the thrust and widening on the withdrawl.

Every time she sucked in a breath, his name followed it.

Each nip of his teeth to her folds made her shake.

"There," she managed to say.

Kaz's head lifted, just enough for his gaze to find hers. His fingers worked faster, his tongue flicked *harder*.

The coil twisted in her stomach, a pressure building at the base of her spine. She knew it was coming because the buildup left her weak and breathless long before the orgasm even crashed down.

But when it did …

When it did, she did exactly what he said she would.

Screamed.

So fucking loud.

The darkness of the bedroom stared back at Violet as she blinked awake. For a second, it was unfamiliar, but the feeling didn't last for long when a strong arm tightened around her waist, and pulled her into a warm, hard chest.

"Doing it again," she heard Kaz rumble behind her.

"Doing what?"

"Moving. You mumble, too, when you sleep."

Violet tilted her head when she felt his mouth skim the back of her neck, his fingers threading into her hair to keep it out of his way as he kissed her there, soft and insistent.

"I don't share a bed very often," she admitted.

Kaz chuckled. "Me, either."

That wasn't why she woke up, however.

The dreams—nightmares, more like it—were persistent little bastards that wouldn't let up.

His lips stopped moving against her neck.

"Stop," he whispered.

Violet stilled. "Pardon?"

"Tensing like that. Was it me?"

"No," she said quickly.

"What, then?"

"I've just … had a lot on my mind. I have dreams, and it's stu—"

"Not stupid," he interjected before she could finish. "That might explain part of the mumbling."

Violet swallowed the lump growing in her throat, willing Kaz to drop whatever he was thinking about saying before he went any farther.

He didn't.

"Carmine is your brother, yes?"

Violet squeezed her eyes shut. "Yeah."

"And … Olly?"

God.

"His dog," she confessed.

Kaz cleared his throat, his hand skimming over her naked hip and down to her thigh. Grabbing there, he pulled her closer into him again until their bodies were molded together and her legs were tangled with his.

"I wouldn't usually let a woman stay in my bed after she's mumbled another man's name," Kaz said.

"My brother's, you mean?"

"No, I knew that's who he was."

Violet pressed the heel of her palms to her eyes. She knew what he was getting around to saying. "Can you just … not do this right now?"

"If that's what you want, sweetheart."

The endearment rolled off his tongue far too easily for it to be meant simply to placate her. It held too much affection, and strangely, it hurt a little.

Before Violet could stop herself, she asked, "What else did I say?"

Kaz sucked air in through his teeth. "Things."

"Well, thank you. That explains everything."

"I think you know exactly what you were mumbling on about in your sleep, so I don't see why you need me to repeat it back to you, Violet."

She wiped at her eyes again with her palms, keeping the wetness at bay. It wasn't the time and she didn't want to cry, anyway.

"I fucked up," she said. "Went beyond where I was supposed to."

She could feel Kaz's frown press to the back of her neck. "And you're dreaming of it."

It wasn't even a question.

"A couple times."

Kaz sighed. "I'm sorry."

That was not what she expected him to say, but she shouldn't be too shocked. The man continued to surprise her.

"It doesn't matter," Violet said. "It'll stop eventually."

"It will," he agreed.

She could hear the "but" he left unsaid.

"What, Kaz?"

"But it bothers me to feel you twisting and turning, and going on like you were. Especially right now."

"It always seems to be there when I sleep," she said. "And I just want to … *sleep*. Not dream. Sleep."

Suddenly, Violet found herself spun around in the bed, facing Kaz. He grabbed hold of her wrists, tugging her up onto him wordlessly. Her thighs opened around his waist as her hands rested to his pecs.

"Sleep," he repeated.

In the dark, she could only make out the outline of his toned form and just a hint of his profile. Hair that she'd been pulling on earlier in the night was smoothed slightly, like he'd run his fingers back through it.

"I'd like to," she said.

"Maybe your brain just isn't tired enough to shut off completely," Kaz suggested.

He could feel the tremor rush through her at his words, her hips shifting just enough to remind him he had her exactly where he wanted her. Kaz could tell from the restlessness that had suddenly taken her over that she knew what he was implying, but in case she didn't …

"Sometimes it just takes a certain amount of exhaustion a person needs to pass out," Kaz commented, sweeping his hand up her stomach to palm her breast. A thrill shot through him at the way her back arched and he could almost see her lips part in the dull light of the moon. "Is that what you need, Violet?"

Wrapping his hand in her hair, he tugged on the strands as he sat up, keeping her steady.

He forced her gaze on him, could see the naked hunger he felt reflected back in her eyes. "Do you want me to exhaust you?"

She let out a soft moan, but didn't actually answer his question, merely nodded as though that would be enough for him. No, he wanted to hear it vocalized. He needed to hear *her*. He fucking thrived in the noises he forced out of her.

"No, you know what I want to hear. Don't make me ask again," he said, punctuating his words with a slap on her ass. Not hard enough to hurt, he'd never hurt her that way, but enough to make her nails dig into the skin

WHERE THE SUN HIDES

of his chest. "You have about a second before I make the decision for you, Violet."

She tried to hide it from him, turning her face away, but Kaz caught it before she did. He saw just the tiniest hint of a defiant smile, and that was all he needed.

Fine, if that's how she wanted it.

He shifted their positions, flipping her onto her stomach, then bringing her up to her knees. A flush swept its way down her body before his hand followed the same descent. She might not have said the words, but her body did—the way she arched into his touch, the way her fingers clutched at his sheets, and how even as her face was pressed against the pillows, he could still hear the anticipation in each breath she took.

"You know," he said conversationally, "we're going to have to work on this. When I ask something, I want an answer. Simple. But if you want, I can teach you. Right here, right now."

Maybe she was still playing at defiance.

Maybe she was overwhelmed by it all.

But either way, the game was starting.

He traced his fingers up her spine, feeling each groove before he reached the nape of her neck and her hair there. Wrapping the strands around his fist, he pulled, turning her face so that she was facing the windows, but he had a clear view of her face.

"What was my question, Violet?" he asked, letting his other hand rest on the curve of her backside. "And to give you a bit of incentive ..." He lifted and brought his hand down fast, and hard, eliciting a cry from her that made his blood run hot. "Now answer me—me fucking you depends on it."

Violet shuddered, her voice leaving her in a rush as she mumbled something unintelligible, but that wasn't good enough for him. He spanked her again, this time aiming for the spot where the curve of her ass met her inner thigh.

"Try again, *krasivaya*."

"E-Exhaust me," she said on a broken whisper.

That was enough for now. "And how do you want me to do that? Because I could do this—" he reached between her thighs, sliding his fingers down her wet center before coming back up again, using two digits to rub at her clit. "But in your state, I could get you off in three minutes, and where would the fun be in that? I, at least, want to draw it out."

He was playing a dangerous game, Kaz knew. It might have been her getting teased, but the wetter she got under his touch, and if his name fell from her lips in another breathy sigh, he didn't know how much more *he* could take before his control snapped.

Even now he was struggling with himself to keep her right where she was, and not beneath him.

"Give me your words," Kaz said suddenly, pushing two fingers inside of her and curling them up. God, it was fucking thrilling learning her body, finding the secret places that made her react violently, a keening sound scraping its way out of her throat. "Shit, Violet, I *need* them."

"Fuck me, Kaz. P-Please, I need—"

He didn't let her finish the plea before he was moving behind her, forcing her legs wider. Rational thought fled as he stroked his cock once, twice, then positioned the head at her entrance. He had fully intended on easing his way in, reveling in the feel of how tight she was, but he hadn't made it an inch before he was thrusting harder than he meant to.

But the second he was balls-deep in her, he couldn't fight himself any longer, not when he couldn't get enough of the way she felt, or how she was pressing back into him asking for more.

Pulling out, he thrust back in almost immediately, starting a pace that had her crying out loudly. It was enough to pull at the jagged edges of his sanity.

One hand was still fisted in her hair, but he loosened his hold, drawing his hand around the curve of her shoulder and to her throat, feeling the muscles there working as she drew in a ragged breath. Pulling her up, he kept his hand there, tightening his grip just slightly to make a hitch in her breath.

He wouldn't leave marks, not where anyone could see. There was nothing he wanted more than to see the evidence of their fucking, and see the lust they had fallen into. But he knew, even in his state, that wouldn't go well for her.

So the one hand he kept at her throat, her heartbeat vibrating off his fingertips, he kept gentle enough. But the other he had at her hip, forcing her back to meet his thrusts, he gripped harder, knowing by morning he would see his fingerprints embedded there.

A secret for them both.

She would feel it when she undressed, and when her fingers wandered there.

He might not have been able to claim her out there, but in his bedroom, where it was just the two of them, he made his ownership clear.

"*God.*"

He pressed her back further until his lips were at her ear, and he could hear every little sound she made even as she bit her lip to stifle them. "God? God, what?"

A *please* and a *don't stop* tumbled from her lips, the words jumbling over each other in her need. He didn't answer, he didn't have to.

Soon, he could see it, the light tremor that hadn't let up, and the way her moans had gone sharp and high. It told him that she was about to come. Shit, even he could feel it racing down his spine, making him bite down onto her shoulder, nearly losing his mind, but it wasn't helping—it only made it worse.

"I need you to come, Violet. *Fuck*."

His next words were harsh, a command for her to come on his cock, but they came out in Russian, his need too great for him to even realize, but it didn't seem to matter to Violet as she erupted almost violently. A sharp whine forced its way out of her with the harsh thrusts he made.

Almost to the second she started coming, he finally let go, holding her tight against him as he gave another brutal thrust, then two, and finally on the third, he went back on his haunches, holding them there.

They were both sweating, both fighting for breath, and he knew in that moment, he was never going to be able to let her go.

Violet added a bit more milk to the bowl of whipped eggs, lightening the yellowish color to a softer cream when she ran a fork through the mixture with fast strokes. Pouring the mixture into a hot pan, she let it settle and waited for the bubbling to begin.

The throat clearing behind her didn't startle her. She'd been working in the kitchen for a good thirty minutes, exploring the cupboards and fridge to find what she needed. And even though her companion hadn't made a noise, she knew that Kaz had been watching her for the last five minutes.

She was up early—for once. Put his shower to use, heaven that it was, and decided to cook something to eat since she had the time to actually do so with no worries about a call that would send her running again.

What was the harm, right?

She had heard the movement coming from the bedroom not long after she left, but she was already preoccupied by her work in the kitchen.

"What are you doing?" Kaz asked.

Violet shot him a look over her shoulder. "Take a guess."

"Cooking."

"Good guess," she teased.

Kaz stayed leaning against the wall, watching her in that way of his while she worked, and saying nothing. Violet wasn't so unnerved by his presence as she was his silence.

"Something on your mind?" she dared to ask.

"A bit."

Two could play that game, so Violet decided to ease him into whatever he was chewing on.

"Are you hungry?"

"Starved," he admitted.

"Find a seat."

"I like where I'm standing."

Violet gave him another look. "Why is that?"

"I'm enjoying the view. It isn't often my kitchen gets put to good use, never mind a woman that isn't my sister cooking in it."

Ah.

"Interesting," Violet murmured, turning back to her work.

She didn't even hear him move until he was right behind her. A fingertip pressed against the back of her neck, and then slowly traveled lower until it stopped at mid-spine. Having little else to wear but what she'd come in, Violet had opted to grab the dress shirt Kaz had discarded the night before. Anything to keep her decent—her panties—were a lost fucking cause.

"You look good in my clothes," he said, the words whispering against the side of her neck.

Violet grinned, keeping her attention focused on not burning the scrambled eggs. "Do I?"

"Very. And standing here doing ... *this*."

"I like cooking."

"It's very domestic," Kaz said.

Something in the lilt of his tone caught her attention. "Is that a problem? Did you want me to skip out of here before you woke up or something? I mean, I'm pretty sure I could still go on ahead and do that, but you'd be left to cook and eat the food yourself."

"No."

"No?"

"Stay," he urged quietly, moving closer to her until his chest was molded to her back and a hand landed firmly on her hip.

Violet nodded, content where she was for the moment. "I have some time, anyway. Safe time."

"Sure."

His other hand tangled into the damp strands of her hair, moving it over her shoulder, but nothing else. "Tell me there's more than just eggs, yes?"

She laughed, and took a step back. He followed the movement. Opening up the oven, she waved for him to take a look inside. Eggs and toast were the last thing to be cooked because they were the fastest. Inside the oven, bacon, hash browns, and toast sat in different dishes, staying warm.

"No worries," she told him. "I know how to cook a breakfast."

"I won't underestimate you again."

"Thanks."

Violet turned the burner down for the eggs just enough to keep them from burning as she ran her fork throughout the pan, keeping it all from sticking to the bottom. Kaz finally managed to surprise her just a bit when she felt his lips press to the back of her neck softly. Just as fast, he stepped away.

Domestic, he'd said.

She didn't think he meant it quite the same way as she took the word.

Once she was finished at the stove, and had a fair spread sitting over the island to choose from, Violet shoved a plate across the counter for Kaz to take. He did, offering her one of those smooth smiles that caught her off guard every single time.

Violet fixed her plate, and sat atop a stool when Kaz brought one around the other side of the island for her to use. He sat across from her, attention drifting between the food and her.

It wasn't awkward.

But she knew, just by the way he kept quiet, he was thinking about things. Her, maybe. The night before, likely.

"I considered taking off this morning," Violet said softly.

Kaz barely reacted to that, but he did lift a brow and stared at her over the fork he was lifting to his mouth. "I would have been severely pissed off, had you done that."

"Oh?"

"Very."

"Well, I didn't, so no need for that."

"But you thought about it," he pressed.

"Wouldn't it have been easier?" she asked.

Kaz tipped his head to the side slightly, asking, "Easier for whom?"

"This."

"And this is … what?"

Violet pursed her lips. "You don't have to make everything difficult, Kaz."

"I'm not making it difficult. I'm asking a question, Violet. You should answer it."

Fair enough.

"This," she repeated, waving a hand between them. "We hooked up once, and then again—"

"Hooking up is a one-time thing. When you start seeking the same person out to fuck again, it no longer falls into that category."

He'd said a similar thing the night before. And he had a good point.

Violet wasn't exactly able to say with confidence that it wouldn't happen again between them, because honestly, she was already wondering how she could get him back into his bedroom after he was done eating. She didn't think she would have much trouble convincing him, but she was still thinking about it.

And that in itself said a lot.

"My point was that I thought about taking off and just … letting it be what it was," she said.

Kaz stopped eating entirely, discarding his fork to the side and picking up a napkin to wipe at his mouth. He didn't look pleased at all over her statement, and for the first time all morning, he wouldn't look at her. "Is that what you want to do, then?"

She was there, wasn't she?

"I didn't leave," Violet settled on saying.

Kaz nodded once. "About last night, when you woke up."

Violet frowned, not wanting to go into specifics about why she'd woken up. It was enough that he had been able to pull details from her mumblings to make a story and go with it. She didn't have to confirm it.

"Let's not go there," she said.

"I have to."

"I don't want to talk about the dreams again, Kaz."

He chuckled, but the sound came off entirely dry and not the least bit amused. "No, not that."

"Then what?"

"I didn't grab a condom, and—"

Oh.

Violet's wide eyes and growing smile was enough to quiet him. "It's fine."

"Is it? Because I'm not sure that it is."

"Worried about making some illegitimate babies with a woman your father doesn't approve of?" she asked, smirking just enough to tell him she was teasing.

Kaz scoffed. "Babies, yes. My father, not in the least."

Violet didn't entirely believe that. "You sure?"

"Partly," he said, shrugging. "For someone else, it probably wouldn't be an issue to my father, as long as shit was handled. But since it's you … Yeah."

"Huh."

"Wouldn't be different for your father, no?"

Violet's smile melted away instantly. "Point taken."

"I thought so."

"Still, it's fine. I have regular shots to take care of that, so no illegitimate babies to worry about. My father overlooks men in my life as long as I don't … 'shame him', as he says."

Kaz's expression remained aloof and impassive as he watched her from across the island. "Shame is an interesting word to use between a father and his daughter."

"My life in a nutshell?" she offered.

It was truer than she wanted to admit.

And she could tell, just by the flashing disapproval in Kaz's gray eyes, that he didn't like it at all.

She didn't know what else to tell him.

"That's not my only concern," Kaz said quietly.

"The birth control shot?"

"Yes, that and more."

Violet didn't know what else there was. "Table's open, so to speak."

"Are you seeing someone else?"

She damn near choked on the sip of coffee she had just taken in as he asked the question. Putting the cup down to the island, she cleared her throat. "I beg your pardon?"

"Someone else. I want to know if you are fucking someone else," he clarified calmly.

"And if I was?"

"That would be a problem."

Violet steeled her spine, irritated in a blink. "We're not an item, Kaz, or a couple. You don't get a say in any other relationship I may or may not have, just because we had sex."

His tongue peeked out to wet his lips, and he laughed a husky sound. "You're right, I don't."

"Then don't ask if you know."

"But I intend to," Kaz said just as fast, his gaze cutting to hers. "Us, and this. I intend to be something with you, and I think, based on the fact you keep coming back and also last night, that's exactly what you want, too. And so, no, I won't have other men to compete with or concern myself over that you might be seeing."

Violet swallowed hard, but she appreciated his candor. "What I said still stands, though. We're not something. You don't get to ask."

"And I still want an answer."

"Kaz."

He cocked a brow at her, never wavering. "An answer."

"What if I asked you the same thing," Violet shot back.

"I would answer."

"What would it be?"

"One that would please you," Kaz said simply, still unbothered and watching her. "And probably surprise you."

Violet sighed. "What are you trying to say here?"

"Exactly what I already told you. You're going to keep coming back here. I'm going to keep letting you. And that makes us something. Answer me, please."

"There's no one else," she said, letting the confession slip out before she could think better of it.

Kaz straightened on the stool, his smug grin firmly back in place. "Good."

"Good?"

"Perfect," he said.

She didn't quite know what to think as he picked up his fork and began eating again. But she couldn't deny that his intentions were entirely too appealing.

Kaz understood far too well how quickly things could change—because of a look, a conversation, or even a thought. He shouldn't have been surprised that it happened to him and Violet, not when he knew better.

Yet, ever since their conversation over breakfast, everything had changed.

Over the span of two weeks, Kaz had made sure that he always made time for Violet, no matter when she reached out. It could have been mid-afternoon, the wee hours of the morning, and occasionally when he was in the middle of a meeting, it didn't matter. He kept his phone at his side like a lifeline, never letting it out of his sight.

"You've been busy a lot, Cap," Abram commented, glancing over at Kaz from his position in the driver's seat.

It wasn't often that Kaz let anyone drive him—most people were shit drivers in his opinion—but Abram refused to let anyone else behind the wheel of his truck. Besides, he wasn't letting the man in his own, not when Violet was regularly riding in it, and while they were careful, there was still no guarantee that she hadn't left some small trace of her presence.

"Oh?" Kaz didn't want to indulge in the conversation, but if there was one thing he knew, if Abram asked any questions, somebody else had asked them first.

"Yeah."

"I have better shit to do than to sit around asking about things that don't concern me," Kaz responded absently, his mind elsewhere.

Abram, now smiling, looked back to the road. "You see, my guess is, it's a woman. You seem like the type to keep that kind of thing pretty hush."

Were they really having this conversation? "Then why are you asking?"

"Can't hurt to try. Never be afraid to ask questions you want answers to—someone once told me that."

BETHANY-KRIS & LONDON MILLER

Kaz, feeling the beginnings of a migraine coming on, counted backward from ten in his head. "*I told you that, Abram.*"

He snapped his fingers. "Of course you did."

"Just park the fucking car so we can get this done."

"So about—"

"Fuck off, Abram."

The man had no shame, laughing even as he swung the truck into a smooth parallel park. Kaz was out in seconds, crossing the short distance into the restaurant owned by a good friend of his—Abram stayed behind to watch his truck.

The restaurant was located just a few miles outside of Little Odessa, and was one of the few places outside of his circle that he frequented on a semi-regular basis. He was a friend of the family—not a part of the *Bratva* however—that dabbled in trade. If a person needed something from another, he was the man to go to.

Kaz strolled inside, stopping at the podium where a young woman was standing, a microphone wrapped around the shell of her ear. Her gaze shifted to his left, and he realized a moment later that she was listening to someone speaking on the other end.

Then, she smiled at him, gesturing to a hallway off to the side. "Mr. Shelby will see you in his office."

There were cameras set up all around the restaurant, undetectable to anyone that wasn't looking for them. Alfred Shelby—or just Alfie, depending on his mood—was a careful man by nature, and his restaurant was no exception.

Kaz rapped his knuckles against the solid oak door at the end of the hall, stepping back so the guard he knew was waiting on the other side could get a good look at him. Once the door was open, and Kaz was inside, he smiled at one of his oldest associates.

"How's business?"

Alfie Shelby was a bull of a man, standing as tall as Kaz but much wider all around. His hair was short, but wavy, and he had the coldest eyes Kaz had ever encountered, like whatever switch he had on his emotions was always turned off.

"Not bad," Alfie said reclining back in his seat, folding massive arms across his chest. "Not bad at all. I guess I have you to thank for that."

Kaz waved his words away. "A favor between friends. Let's not speak on it."

Alfie just stared at him, seeming to gauge the sincerity of his words, before he nodded to the chairs in front of his desk. "Go on, have a seat."

Alfie waited until Kaz did just that before he spoke. "Your father won't bend on our little issue."

Yeah, Kaz had been afraid of that. His father liked to believe he knew what was best for the organization—that was his due as *Pakhan*—but he still had the mindset of the generations before him, where the *Bratva* didn't indulge in business with outsiders.

"I'll see what I can do."

That was the best he could give, and that was probably more than he should have. If his *Pakhan* dismissed a new arrangement, that was meant to be the end of it, and if Vasily knew that Kaz had known about the meeting in the first place, that wouldn't go over well.

When you wanted to do business with the *Bratva*, you went to the *Pakhan*, no one else.

"Good, now—"

Alfie paused, his head tilted to the side, and then his eyes cut to Kaz. "Your time is up. Looks like you're not the only one paying me a visit today."

Though Kaz didn't question him, he did wonder why. More than once, he had sat in the room while Alfie conducted business, and had offered insight when prompted, but never had he been asked to leave.

It, at the very least, made him curious.

Because of the position of the office, Kaz could see most of the restaurant—with the exception of the kitchens. Standing where he'd been no more than ten minutes ago was the last person Kaz had expected.

Carmine Gallucci.

He could see it, somewhat, the similarities between him and his sister—the blond hair—but the rest of him was a carbon copy of his father. And he held himself like it too, his shoulders back, his head held high as though everyone around him was beneath his notice.

Kaz couldn't remember the last time he had seen the man in person, and it was even longer since he had given him any thought. But as Carmine's gaze lifted to his, awareness making them narrow as his guard shot up, he had Kaz's full attention.

"Right, gentlemen," Alfie spoke up, stepping between them once Carmine got close. "This is a respectable place, yeah? And as much as I would enjoy watching the two of you try and beat the shit out of each other, though my money's on Kazimir here—Russians, they're fucking savages, you know?—that won't happen in here." He gestured to the door with a tilt of his head. "Outside and down the street, far away from my place, and you can do as you please. You still want to have words, Gallucci, you know where to find me. Now, get the fuck out."

Carmine looked like he wanted to argue, even more pissed off by the way Alfie casually disregarded him, but as quickly as his flare of temper showed in his face, he swept his hands over the front of his suit jacket, even going as far as straightening his tie. He tried to make himself seem taller, but next to Alfie and Kaz, he still looked like a boy playing dress up.

"Nah, I'm good. You see,"—and this was aimed at Kaz as his gaze shifted past Alfie— "we Italians don't need to act like dogs in the street. We know how to behave."

Kaz smiled at his answer. "You're right about one thing, Gallucci. I am a fucking dog, and when the day comes that you're ready to find out what that means, look me up." Clapping Alfie on the shoulder, Kaz headed for the door.

But as he passed—the two Italian guards moving to the side to let him pass without incident—Carmine started forward and bumped Kaz's shoulder hard enough to make his temper flare. Before he could quell the impulse, Kaz had his hand around the man's throat, shoved him backward, and made his head crack against the wall.

The impact was enough to silence the room, and while Carmine's guards rushed to grab their weapons, Alfie made it clear, in that silent way of his, to not do it.

"That's your one, Gallucci," Kaz said squeezing harder, feeling the muscles in Carmine's throat constrict as he fought for air. "Test me again and you won't like the results." As quickly as he had grabbed him, Kaz released his hold, laughing lightly as Carmine wheezed. "Walk away, before I give your father a real reason to start a war."

Carmine coughed, his eyes watery and angry. "Fuck you, Markovic. You're a fucking nobody. Had it not been for my family doing yours a favor, you wouldn't be standing there."

"Is that so?" Kaz asked, intrigued though he didn't mean to be.

He had already been curious about the meeting that had happened all those years ago between their families, but he had yet to question Vasily about it, not really seeing a need to. Yet, this was at least the third time in as many months that the meeting had been brought up to him, and it was clear that Carmine knew something about it.

Kaz never liked when anyone had information he didn't have.

"Why don't you enlighten me?" Maybe then he would have an answer.

But despite how idiotic Carmine looked, he wasn't about to spill secrets. "Savages, the whole fucking lot of you. We should have put all of you down, and not just that uncle of yours."

"Savages?" Kaz asked, his voice going calm. "Savage enough to cut out a heart, Gallucci?" Almost immediately, the Italian reacted to his words, his face going ashen, and in that moment, Kaz had everything he needed. "Was it you that cut out his heart?" he asked as he got in the man's face. "Did you finally get to be a fucking man, you little *suka*? Because let me explain one thing to you. I am a fucking savage—I live for that shit—and had I not been called off from coming after you, I would have found you and cut off your fingers, one by one. And only after you understood what real pain was, would I have gone for your heart."

Carmine kept his mouth shut, and was still glaring, but beneath that careful facade, Kaz saw a trace of fear, and that was enough for him.

"Careful what monsters you play with, Gallucci, I'm worse," Kaz finished, stepping back, and this time, he didn't wait for the man to give a rebuttal, but exited the restaurant, and climbed into Abram's truck.

"Take me to my place," he said when Abram was finally inside and starting the truck up.

"But what about—"

"*Zatknis'*—Shut up. Do as I said."

Abram didn't argue further.

Kaz wasn't usually one to lash out, but he was angry, angrier than he had been in a long time. And it wasn't because of Carmine bumping him, but because of what he'd said—or rather, the things he hadn't. Before, he hadn't cared enough to question Vasily about his uncle, or about the meeting, but now he needed answers.

And he would get them.

Violet stared at her reflection in the bathroom mirror, taking her time to touch up her makeup while she had the chance. She was alone in the restroom, which was unusual considering it was in a semi-busy hall of the college. But she was grateful for the privacy all the same.

Smoothing her hands down the front and sides of her dress to smooth out the lace fabric that always seemed to ride up or crinkle, her fingers hitched in their travels over her hips. It was automatic reaction—an ache pulsed between her thighs when she pressed her fingers into that one spot, because she knew what was there.

Or what had been there.

Marks. The smallest of bruises that didn't hurt at all.

His marks.

Kaz.

Violet shook her head, needing away from those thoughts as she focused back on her reflection. Her classes for the day were almost over, thankfully. She had one left, and then she was free for the evening.

Already, she was considering messaging Kaz to meet up with her somewhere safe. As long as she stayed off her father's radar, and wasn't called away, she didn't worry all that much.

And it was becoming a habit she didn't want to break.

She typed a text. Kaz answered.

She asked him away. He went.

Violet liked it more than she should. It was a stupid game to be playing with a man that was entirely off-limits to her in a big way. Whatever they were doing—whatever they were—was not something that would be able to continue on forever.

It all was going to end eventually.

She just wasn't sure this was the time.

Fluffing out the waves of her hair with her fingers, Violet leaned a little closer to the mirror. Tipping her head to the side, the blonde strands fell over her neck, exposing the tight collar of her dress that fit snugly around her throat.

He was usually so careful, she thought.

He never left something that might be seen by someone else. Not something that would be obvious, or might get them—her—in trouble.

But Kaz had left something a little too close to the column of her neck a couple of days earlier. Just a small mark on her right collarbone—his teeth.

And Christ, it had been good.

That pain was good.

Addictive.

Violet tugged the collar of her dress outward from her neck, exposing the discolored mark to her reflection. She had the means to hide it if she needed to—clothes and makeup, but she couldn't help but keep going back to it every single time she had the chance to do so without being caught or questioned.

Before she could think better of it, Violet grabbed her phone from her purse resting on the bathroom counter. She unlocked the device, opened the messages, and found the contact she wanted. Holding the phone at an angle that would keep her face hidden, she snapped a shot, making sure the mark was visible, and then sent it off.

A message quickly followed, but not from who she expected when she glanced back down at the phone.

Her father's number lit up the screen. For a moment, Violet panicked, thinking she had sent that picture to the wrong person, but she opened up the message to find it was just coincidence.

Gee will be at the main entrance of the University in ten minutes, the text read. Another followed right after. *Do not keep him waiting.*

Violet cussed under her breath, gaze cutting back to the mirror. How in the hell was she supposed to fix her grades—yet another thing her father still wasn't aware of—and manage to keep from flunking out the semester, if she couldn't even get a full day of classes in?

It didn't even matter.

She glanced back down at her phone again, waiting for a message from Kaz, responding to that picture.

It didn't come.

She didn't have the time to wonder why.

Her father was waiting.

Violet found the Gallucci mansion lit up and full of people when she arrived. The tone of her father's text message had not suggested there was a last minute party or dinner going on that he wanted her to attend, so she was confused at the sight of so many vehicles and people milling about.

That idea quickly faded away when she realized it was all men.

Her father's men.

Gee, who would usually open her door to let her out, exited the vehicle without so much as a goodbye. Violet, more confused than ever, grabbed her messenger bag and purse off the floor before leaving the backseat of the car. Inside the house, she found several familiar faces going in between rooms and chatting quietly.

Too quietly for her to really discern what was being said.

After she had put her things away—but made sure to keep her phone hidden in her dress pocket—Violet went in search of her parents. As she passed her father's men, she heard snippets of conversations she probably wasn't supposed to, but took note of anyway.

"Russian, yeah," one man said.

"Carmine was down awful deep in Brooklyn," said another.

"It could have been worse," came someone else's opinion.

Violet's brow furrowed as she took the random statements in. What exactly had happened that would cause enough of a fuss for her father to call his men to his home, not to mention her?

Passing by the entertainment room, Violet saw her friends—old friends—chatting to one another in a corner. Amelia and Nicole barely noticed her as she stopped to at least acknowledge their presences. In two weeks, they had said less than a few words to her in passing, and that was only if they had no other choice.

No calls. No messages.

No dinners or time at the clubs on the weekends.

Kaz had been right, in a way. Her friends weren't very real at all when it came right down to it. They blamed her entirely for a situation that had been caused by all three of their choices, not just hers.

But she didn't really care.

Better to move on, and let it go.

Dwelling on it wouldn't do her any damn good. Amelia and Nicole probably figured she would eventually make her way back into the folds with an apology and a willing acceptance to take all the blame.

Violet was done with those games.

Entirely.

They were not in high school anymore, and she refused to indulge their desire to act like they were.

Finally, Violet found at least one person she was looking for. Her father was in his favorite spot—his office. Leaning over his desk with palms pressed to the top and his knuckles white from the pressure, Alberto looked fit to have a spell. Her father was not a small man by any means. His larger size dominated the room in presence alone, and he often came off as intimidating to others who didn't know him well.

But she knew him.

And right then, while Alberto looked angry, she could see his worry— his panic.

Alberto nodded to a man at his side—Vito, Amelia's father, and his underboss—when Vito said something too low for the rest to hear. Across from his desk, Carmine stood with his arms crossed and a deep scowl etched on his face.

"You can't just let it go unanswered," Carmine said.

"I can do whatever I want to," Alberto snapped right back. He stood straight, brushing Vito off when the man tried to calm the situation down. "And you—what did you do in all of this to cause a scene like that?"

Carmine opened his mouth to speak, but Alberto held a hand high, stopping him.

"Do not lie to me, son," her father warned. "I will know you did. Do you think your men—those enforcers—are so loyal to you that they forget which hand has fed them for years? Don't. Lie."

"I might have knocked him a little as I passed him by in the hallway," Carmine said, "but that doesn't justify Kazimir's response, boss."

Alberto's gaze narrowed. "Men of honor hold themselves to a far higher standard than games of that sort, Carmine. And you, as a Capo, are well aware of that. Since when have I ever accepted childish taunting and antics between my men to encourage tensions, huh? When? Answer me."

"You don't."

"I don't," Alberto repeated, spitting the words out.

Violet was still trying to catch up to what she was hearing. But she understood enough. Clearly, Carmine and Kaz had a run in at some point over the day, and it did not end well.

"And now," Alberto continued, "I have men in an uproar because this is the second issue in the span of a month with the Russians."

"We could ... finish them off," Vito suggested quietly.

"What for?" Alberto asked. "And to whose gain?"

Violet figured she should probably make herself known or scarce, but she found her feet were like cement stuck to the floor.

When Vito didn't respond, Alberto turned back on Carmine.

"I know you're ... sensitive ... over the events from a couple of weeks ago," Alberto said, "but that was a choice made by me, not the Russians. And if you want someone to take your anger out on, you are more than welcome to meet me behind a closed door where we will discuss my choices as a boss and his capo and nothing more. Stay away from the Russians, Carmine. And stay the fuck away from that restaurant, regardless of the business you have with Alfred Shelby."

Carmine straightened a bit more, glared at his father and tipping his chin up. Alberto almost mimicked the pose perfectly, and it struck Violet in that moment how similar her brother and father really were.

"Are you scared of the Russians?" Carmine asked, deadly calm. "Is that it, boss?"

Alberto didn't even blink. "I have no need to be, and you will not make a reason for me. Is that understood?"

Just as quickly as her brother's defiance had shown itself, it left. Carmine gave one nod, and then moved toward the door, but stopped in his step as he saw her standing there.

Alberto noticed her then, too.

"Violet," her father said, his tone turning much softer than it had been.

Almost ... relieved.

"I didn't know we were having a party ... or whatever," Violet said, pointedly looking around at the men in Alberto's office.

Alberto waved it off. "Nonsense. No party. I just wanted to have you come over, see your face. I worry."

Oh.

Violet understood, then.

Something had happened, and her father panicked, calling her to the mansion. He wanted to make sure she was safe from any possible action—no matter how slight it was—they might face.

"Of course," Carmine said, scoffing as he tried passing Violet in the doorway.

She didn't move, confused by the bitterness in her brother's tone. Looking up at him, she found his cold, brown eyes boring down into hers.

"Always worry about poor, little Violet, right?" Carmine asked, shooting his father a look over his shoulder.

Alberto's gaze passed between his son and daughter. "Now is not the time for that, Carmine."

What had she missed?

"It's never the time, but your favorites are showing, *Dad.*"

Alberto's back stiffened like someone had shoved a stake there. "*Carmine.*"

186

Carmine sneered as he pushed past his sister. "I bet had Kazimir Markovic put his hands on your daughter's throat like he had mine, he'd already be in a grave."

Violet swallowed the lump in her throat, looking back at her father.

Alberto was watching her, too. And she could plainly see his unspoken confirmation written in his posture and shining in his gaze. Yes, if her father thought for even one second that Kaz had touched her, the man would be dead.

He didn't know it, but those hands had already been on her throat.

And everywhere else.

More than once.

"Where've you been?" Ruslan asked as he oversaw the men bringing in his new shipment of vodka—they had a tendency to go through it rather quickly.

Kaz shook his head at his brother. "Most of you gossip more than women."

Leveling his eyes on him, Ruslan said, "Any change to your routine, no matter how minute, will be noticed by somebody. Careful there, little brother, you don't want someone digging into your secrets—you won't like the result."

Kaz didn't dismiss his words as easily as he had Abram's, not when he knew how true that statement was. They had both suffered the consequences of someone being a little too curious.

Ruslan still was.

"That's not why I'm here." Avoidance was his friend at the moment.

"No? What do you want?"

Scratching at the hair covering his jaw, Kaz considered his words before he asked what he wanted to know. "Gavrill."

Ruslan frowned. "Our uncle? What about him?"

It was no secret that Ruslan had been closer to their uncle than any of their siblings. Truthfully, his relationship had been far better with Gavrill than it was with Vasily. Wherever Gavrill went, as long as there was no business involved, then Ruslan was on his heels, never too far behind.

He had been older at the time of their uncle's death, so there was a stronger possibility that Ruslan remembered the details better than he did.

"January 21st—never forget that day. It was cold as shit, and the streets were silent because of that car bomb that nearly took your life.

Someone—and even to this day we still don't know the face behind the gun, just that he was Italian—walked up to him in the middle of the street and shot him, point-blank in the face. I don't think they actually found all of his teeth."

Fucking hell. Kaz hadn't known any of that. He knew Gavrill died, or was murdered, rather, but he hadn't known it had been so brazen.

"I'm confused. Why didn't Vasily ever do anything about it? If *you* know it was the Italians, he had to know, too. Could probably find the gunman, too, if he asked the right questions."

"There was a girl, Italian, left raped and murdered behind a pizza parlor in Hell's Kitchen, all fingers pointed back to Gavrill," Ruslan said. "Whether by his word or action, Gavrill had to answer for it."

Something about the tone of his voice gave Kaz pause. "But ..."

"But?"

"You don't sound convinced."

Ruslan signed off on the slip, sending the men on their way, gesturing with a tilt of his head for Kaz to follow him inside. "Gavrill was a lot of things, but even he had limits."

Kaz shook his head, agreeing. From what he could remember of the man, he had been rather loud, quick to anger depending on who was speaking, and had a tendency to act before he thought. Was he a murderer? Yeah, weren't they all? But a rapist ... Kaz couldn't see that, nor could he ever think of a time when Gavrill had even used that as a threat.

But he had been a child ...

"And Vasily didn't question this?"

"He was more concerned with ending the war. Men were dying—*you* almost died. If Gavrill's death meant it all came to a stop, he couldn't retaliate." Rulan paused. "At least that's what Vasily says."

It didn't have to be asked whether Ruslan believed that, the contempt in his voice told his true feelings. Everything he'd said only made Kaz more curious—it wasn't meshing with the shit Carmine had said. Of course, it could have meant that he was just trying to get a rise out of him, say what he needed to push his buttons, but Carmine had been too arrogant in the way he spoke for Kaz to believe that.

"Why are you asking about all of this anyway?" Ruslan asked, peering over at him as though he could read the answer on his face.

"Had a run in with Carmine Gallucci earlier—he said some things. I was curious."

It was at that moment that Kaz's phone rang. He already had a good idea as to who it was.

"One day, you're going to go too far," Ruslan warned. "Who the hell is going to save your ass when Vasily decides to teach you a lesson?"

Digging his phone out, Kaz smiled absently. "Let's hope we never have to find out—Kaz."

"You know," Vasily began, sounding rather thoughtful, "when I asked Irina to bear my children, you were not what I hoped for."

"Someone's in a mood," Kaz said in return, already heading for his car, knowing what Vasily would tell him. "How about we skip the 'I don't know why you're calling,' discussion? Yes, I had a run in with Carmine Gallucci, and considering you're not yelling, you know that he wasn't hurt too bad—his pride, maybe. So really, what's there to discuss?"

Kaz slipped behind the wheel, and as he switched the call over to the Bluetooth radio, his phone buzzed again, this time with a text.

"Are you trying to kill me?" Vasily asked. "Is that what this is about? I don't understand. I've given you everything you could have ever wanted. Money, the best schools, the best cars ... and yet you never do the simplest of things that I ask."

"What was that?" Kaz had only been half paying attention to his father as he unlocked his phone, opening up the message.

"Kazimir!" Vasily snapped, that last little thread he had on his control breaking. "Stay the fuck away from the Galluccis. How many times must I say this?"

The image took a while to load, but when it did, Kaz grinned slowly. There was no face, just the curve of a shoulder, pale skin, and the mottled bite mark he had left some days ago. He was intrigued as to why she sent it.

Whether it was meant as a reminder that he needed to be careful as to where he left his mark, or whether it was an invitation.

He chose to go with the latter.

"I'll be in there in fifteen," Kaz said to his father, even as he typed a message to Violet. "And yeah, you have my word. I'll stay clear of Carmine Gallucci."

But not Violet. Never Violet.

The clink of a spoon hitting china lightly made Violet look up from the textbook she had spread out on the table. She found her father watching her from the other side of the large kitchen, still stirring the cup on the counter. With a smile, Alberto picked the cup up and brought it over to where his daughter was seated, pushing it across the table as he took a seat.

Violet picked up the Chai tea for a sip, and smiled approvingly. Her father wasn't the type to prepare someone else's food or drinks. He had people do that for him, and for others around him. But he had learned a while ago how to make Chai tea just the way Violet liked as a way to soften her up before a chat.

She had caught onto his games over the years.

But she still appreciated the effort.

"It's good," she mumbled around the rim.

Alberto shrugged. "As long as you like it, *dolcezza*."

Violet put the cup back to the table, flipping another page over in her textbook. With her father, it was better to let him open up the discussion, rather than coming right out and asking him what he was thinking about.

"How is school?" Alberto asked.

No better time than the present, she thought.

Her father had all but demanded she stay for supper long after his guests were gone, and even after Carmine had left. Her mother had taken to her studio office, leaving the father and daughter alone. Still, he asked her to stay, and she did.

"Actually ..." Violet trailed off, frowning.

Alberto matched the expression. "What?"

"I'm flunking two of my classes. And at this rate, I might as well just add another year—or a semester, if I'm being kind—onto my Bachelor of Art degree."

Her father's expression barely changed at all. Violet was surprised. She expected him to be angry—disappointed, even.

But, no.

Nothing.

Alberto tapped a single finger to the table. "Is college not what you want to do?"

"It is," she responded fast.

"Then why aren't you keeping up? You're not a stupid girl, Violet. You graduated top ten in your high school. What is so different about Columbia that you're struggling?"

Violet sighed. "It's a lot of things, Daddy."

"Try me."

Her phone buzzed with a text, and her gaze shot down to where her purse rested beside her chair. Still, she didn't reach for the bag to grab it. Her father surely wouldn't appreciate that at the moment, and he was being particularly kind about her bad grades as it was.

"Okay, here's one," Violet said, "today I didn't even get to finish my classes, and I had a presentation due for my last class that was meant to give me extra credit. I've been working on it for a week. That is one of the classes I'm failing."

WHERE THE SUN HIDES

Alberto nodded. "All right. Fair enough. I'm sorry."

Violet waved around her, high above her head. "And there's all this stuff going on, it seems. No one wants to talk about it, but I'm not an idiot, Daddy. I can see what's happening, okay? It's distracting when I'm brought into it or it takes me out of focusing on school."

He leaned forward in his seat. "And shall I mention the weekends at clubs, the mid-week parties, and the late nights with friends all the times in between? How about that boy you were seeing a few months ago? I seem to remember several trips out of state during times when you should have been in classes."

Damn.

Yeah, her father had her there.

"He wasn't important, just fun," she said weakly.

It was the truth.

"And the other things?" Alberto asked.

"I'm not doing those now. I'm trying to focus."

"I'm aware—your grades do show it, even if you think they're still too low. And they are too low, Violet."

She sat straighter in the chair. "What?"

"I've been keeping up with your grades for a lot longer than you think, and I hoped that you would see the downfall and start to correct it. You have, and that's enough for me to let you learn from this. So, you'll have to spend an extra year in school. That's your consequence for this last year and the mess you've been."

Violet sucked in a hard breath. Her father could have said a lot of things, but calling her a "mess" downright cut her to the bone.

"Keep focusing," her father continued to say, oblivious to her hurt. "Give me something to be proud of, hmm? Because if you do flunk out, then you're promising yourself very little but the life of a housewife with no education, dependent on her husband to carry her."

"Is that really what you think I'd be good for, marriage?"

Alberto didn't bat a lash. "A couple of decades ago, daughters of made men who couldn't make themselves useful in other ways often found themselves of use to the family."

"Meaning what?"

"Exactly what I already said. Housewives."

Violet bit hard on her inner cheek, disliking how that felt like a slightly veiled threat. She tossed a look at the clock, noting the time was well after seven. "I should get back to Manhattan. School in the morning, right?"

Alberto nodded, and stood from the table. "Remember what I said, *dolcezza*."

Right.

Housewife.

As her father turned to leave, Violet reached down for her purse. She grabbed the phone out and unlocked the screen, seeing Kaz had responded to her text earlier in the day.

She had just opened the message up when her father turned back around saying, "Oh, and Violet?"

Violet's head snapped up, heart racing. "Yeah?"

"I let Gee take the night off. Call a cab to take you back."

She nodded, glancing back down at the phone.

An ache settled deep in her stomach, traveling even lower.

Kaz had sent back his own picture. Black and white, his hand shoved down his unbuttoned pants and wrapped around the base of his length, the rest hidden where she couldn't see. She only knew it was him because of the tattoos, and damn, because she knew his body now.

Her mouth went dry.

Another message quickly followed.

An address.

A time.

Nothing else.

She took that to mean it wasn't a request.

Vasily was waiting in his office, a gun on his desk. Kaz shook his head as he entered, eyeing it. "Are you trying to send me a message, Vasily?"

His father looked from the gun to him and shook his head. "Of course not."

How easily he overlooked something as simple as his weapon being out, but Kaz? Kaz rarely, if ever, saw a gun that close to Vasily, not when he had men at his back at all times.

Ignoring it for the time being, Kaz said, "What did you need, besides the whole, avoid Gallucci thing. That's getting a bit redundant, no? After all, it's not like I actively sought out this last encounter."

"I'm sure you're completely innocent, Kazimir," Vasily said, sounding like that was the last thing he believed. "I know you better than to believe something of the sort."

"Good to know." He had thought about dismissing the incident with Carmine entirely, at least until he thought about what had been said. "He has a big mouth though."

"Oh?"

Kaz sat forward, looking around with casual disinterest at the paintings that hung on the walls of Vasily's office. "Mentioned how his family helped ours some years ago. I'd wager I was about ten? Eleven?"

Vasily scoffed. "Those Italians always believe they do more than the average man. I wouldn't place too much credence into anything the boy said. After all, he is his father's son."

It was funny, seeing how easily Vasily disregarded what Kaz was saying, especially when he didn't know what all Carmine had actually said. "True, but I did wonder what he meant by that. Oh wait," Kaz said as though he had just realized something, "he probably was talking about that meeting. You and Alberto, his daughter and I. Considering how much you actually hate the man, what made you attend a meeting with him?"

Vasily cleared his throat, sitting up just a little bit straighter as he regarded his son. "It was necessary at the time. Do you remember that bomb that nearly took your life? Who do you think set it? If you wonder *why* I hate those Galluccis, look no further than that."

"And Gavrill?" Kaz asked next. "How did he feel about you meeting with a man he wanted dead?"

There was a flash of some dark emotion in the man's eyes, but it was gone before Kaz could read into it. "The uncle you loved and the man that was *Pakhan* were two very different people. You couldn't possibly understand, not at your age. To you and your brother, he was the savior. You two treated the man like he was fucking royalty though he wasn't."

Had they? Kaz remembered Ruslan's doting, but never his own. Sure, he had looked up to his uncle, loved the man, but back then, before life and its pain came between them, Kaz had looked up to his father as well.

But even with his passionate speech, Kaz still didn't miss one important detail. "But you still didn't answer my question."

"No?" Vasily rested his fists on his desk as he stared across at Kaz, unblinking. He lacked the fatherly pride of only a few minutes ago, now replaced with coldness that Kaz had no trouble reading. "Why are you asking about this *now*, Kazimir? What has you so curious?"

Kaz had to quell his need to tap his fingers, balling his fists instead. "I hate being in the dark on certain matters—I'm sure you can understand this. Carmine Gallucci? He knows who I am, and what I'm capable of, but yet he stood toe-to-toe with me, spouting off about things I'm not sure of."

"What did he say?" There was an edge to Vasily's voice as he asked the question.

"You misunderstand. It's what he didn't say that concerns me. In one breath, he's spouting off about how his family has helped ours. In the next, he's telling me how he'll put me down, just as he did my uncle." Kaz moved to the edge of his seat. "That sounds pretty fucking strange to me."

Vasily slowly rose to his feet, the glare on his face enough to reflect his current mood. "If there is a question, ask it. My patience for this runs thin."

"The meeting in the cemetery … what were the odds that it was about Gavrill?"

"I've told you to leave it be, Kazimir. *Eto prikaz*—that's an order."

That should have been the end of it. *Should have.*

But Kaz wasn't done yet. "We know it was the Italians that killed Gavrill, I've heard you say as much. And yet, you never once tried to get back at them for it."

"I'll tell you why!" Vasily suddenly shouted, his face gone red with rage. "Your uncle was a fucking tyrant, and cared nothing for the lives of the men that had to answer for the shit he pulled. Do you think he cared that you were almost killed because of a turf war *he* started? Or even that you were practically blind for weeks? No, none of that mattered. He only cared for money and sating his bloodlust."

Very calmly, Kaz asked, "So he needed to die?"

There was a moment where Vasily's lips moved just as he was about to answer the question, but he caught himself, shaking his head as though to get his control back. "Of course not."

It took years before Kaz could see it, that tell that betrayed Vasily's thoughts.

For the longest time, he had never been able to tell whether his father was lying or not, not until he was seventeen. And his tell was not one that could be easily seen, not unless one knew to look for it, and only if they were close enough to see.

But he was close enough then, and he could clearly see that his father's eyebrows were twitching, like the muscles there couldn't be controlled.

Except, Kaz knew.

Vasily was lying.

"Right." Kaz regarded his father, taking in the details he never paid attention to in the past. "Are we done here? I've got shit to do."

Vasily waved him off. "Go."

Kaz moved to do just that, but as he hit the door, Vasily called behind him. "Careful what questions you ask, Kazimir. You won't always like the answer."

Or rather, he wouldn't like the way Vasily responded.

Leaving the unspoken threat hanging between them, Kaz left the office, then the building entirely. For once, he was ready to get the hell out of Little Odessa.

Violet stepped out of the taxi after handing over the cash for the fare. She stepped up onto the sidewalk, noting how dark and quiet the street was, like it had practically shut down for the night. It was a rare find in Brooklyn where a person could always find something open, something to do.

She checked her phone again, making sure she had given the driver the right street address that Kaz had messaged her earlier. It was.

So where was he?

Shifting the messenger bag over her shoulder, Violet took a few steps down the street, and stopped when lights flashed at her from the side. Hidden just in the mouth of the alleyway between two large buildings was a familiar Porsche.

And Kaz, leaning against the hood with his key ring in hand. He hit a button on the fob, flashing the lights at her again.

"Cute," she told him.

Kaz shrugged. "Better than standing way out in the open looking around for nothing."

"Ass."

"A little," he agreed. "Are you just going to stand there all day, or ...?"

Laughing, Violet made a beeline for Kaz. She was well aware of how much she constantly found herself thinking of him, or what he might be doing, and how that often left her missing him in one way or another. But seeing him brought it all bubbling right back up to the surface, fast and fierce.

It had yet to fail to surprise her.

She didn't entirely understand what it meant.

Violet figured as long as it felt right, it couldn't be wrong.

Kaz's arms opened the closer Violet came to where he was leaning against the hood. She dropped her bag to the ground a second before she was swallowed by a familiar, strong embrace. Her feet came off the ground before she realized it, and her backside met the hood of the Porsche.

Violet's grin and breathless laughter was muffled by Kaz when he kissed her hard, taking away what air she had left. For a moment, she was lost in him—again. It was easy to forget about the rules she was supposed to follow and the stupidity of her choice to be there with Kaz when his hands grasped tightly to her jaw, he forced her head back, and he kissed her even deeper, a smug smile growing.

"You sent me a dirty picture," he told her, dotting kisses along the seam of her lips.

Violet shook her head. "That was not a dirty picture. You sent me one with your cock in it. Totally different thing."

"Mmm, no."

"I beg to differ." Her hand landed against his chest, needing the space to think and talk. Kaz moved at her unspoken request, but he was still pressed firm enough between her thighs that she could feel the length of his erection straining against his slacks. "I showed you what you left. You—"

"Showed you what you left," he replied, smirking.

Violet had to look away to keep from smiling. "You're terrible."

"No, I'm just not going to lose this argument. That's all."

"Mine was innocent. Last word. It's final."

Kaz cocked a brow and said, "You knew damn well that wouldn't be innocent, and I wouldn't take it that way."

She had.

Violet wouldn't admit it, though.

"I see how this works," Kaz said after she stayed silent, refusing to budge even an inch.

"Good. Then we're on the same page."

His sexy grin grew into a softer smile. "Missed you, huh?"

The statement was simple enough—innocent, even.

But it still didn't feel that way.

Violet didn't think Kaz was the kind of man to just blurt out something like that for just anyone. And if he did say it, he likely meant it and probably more that he *wasn't* saying. It was just one of the many reasons why Violet was finding it especially difficult to keep distance between her and him.

When she stayed away, or tried to, something was pulling her right back in.

"Missed you, too," she said honestly.

Kaz swept the pads of his thumbs over her cheekbones, leaning down for another quick kiss. "I take it you didn't have any trouble getting down here?"

"No. I came here from Amityville, and then I'll head back up to Manhattan."

He stiffened slightly. "Your father's place?"

"Called me over before classes were out."

Violet wondered if Kaz would just come right out with the fact he had a run-in with her brother, or if he wouldn't say a thing.

He surprised her.

"I take it your brother ran to daddy, yes?" he asked.

Violet laughed dryly. "What did you do to him?"

"Very little. Less than what he deserved."

"Carmine is a little ..."

"Spoiled. Entitled. Unqualified. I have a couple more, but feel free to tell me to stop."

Violet didn't need to. "All of the above, but he's also bitter and jealous."

Kaz glanced down at her. "For what?"

"Me," she said, unfazed. "And my dad."

His fingers pressed a little firmer to her jaw, forcing her gaze back up to his. "Doesn't that bother you at all?"

"That he's jealous?"

"No, that your father has made him that way," Kaz replied.

Violet hadn't ever looked at it like that before. "Never really thought about it."

"Maybe you should."

"Why? I don't see how it matters. It's the same thing with my mother, only the tables are turned. Carmine is the golden boy and I'm the ... *leftovers*, for lack of a better word."

Kaz tipped his chin down, something flashing in his gray eyes. "That's not what I meant."

"I really don't want to talk about how fucked up my family is. It's better that no one sees it at all. We're just hiding it all behind closed doors, and sweeping it under rugs. It's always been like this."

"But your father ..."

"What about him?" she asked, feeling her defenses rise a bit at the bitter twist to his tone.

"What did he call you over for today, anyway? The run-in with your brother had nothing to do with you, no? You didn't need to be there, Violet."

"Wasn't really about that. He was worried, wanted to see me. And then we had a chat about how I'm fucking up lately with school, and can look forward to becoming the best little housewife for some man if I don't correct it and soon."

Kaz's hands dropped to her sides instantly. "That, right there."

Violet's head snapped up. "What?"

"You believe that shit."

She opened her mouth to argue the point, but something kept her quiet. Maybe it was the way Kaz watched her silently, waiting for her to say something. Or maybe it was the way she let her mind turn over conversations she'd had with her father when she wasn't performing up to his satisfaction in life.

"How often does he do that?" Kaz asked after a long while.

Violet glanced away, refusing to meet his stare. "I'm not sure what you mean."

"I think you do, *krasivaya*. It's the same damn thing as before—when you said he didn't want a daughter who shamed him. Words like 'shame' shouldn't be used between a father and his daughter. It's manipulation. It's unhealthy. And let me guess, how pissed off are you right now that I just called it out, because you want to defend him?"

She was going to deny that, too, but she couldn't. Not with the way the anger was simmering in her bloodstream. She loved her father, and he wasn't perfect, but he was hers.

And yet, Kaz had a good point.

Nothing he said was untrue.

"It's not important," Violet said weakly.

She didn't even believe her own words.

"And this is not why I came here tonight," she added, stronger than before.

"It might not be, but it's out there now," Kaz responded, unbothered at her anger. "You're close to him, no doubt. He makes it seem like pleasing him is what will further you—what makes you better. Because that's how it has been for forever, no? You make him happy, and in return he's happy with you. But when he's not happy with you, then he takes away what you want. His approval, affection, and that sort of thing. Am I wrong?"

Violet sucked in a hard breath, letting the air burn in her lungs as she held it in. "I said—"

"Don't want to talk about it. Yeah, I got that. Just answer me."

"Obviously you're wrong, or I wouldn't be here with you right now."

"Wrong," Kaz murmured. "That is only one single part of what makes everything I said right. Because you don't always do what he says, and you don't always believe what he tells you like its gospel. And sometimes it might not always feel right, but when you get someone else's voice in your head instead of his, you start seeing that things aren't colored just the way he says they are."

"Kaz—"

"Like me," he interrupted. "I am not what your father said I would be, am I?"

Violet clenched her teeth, but the word slipped out anyway. "No."

"And that pisses you off, yes?"

Right then, he was kind of pissing her off.

Violet still knew Kaz was right. Even if it hurt a lot to admit it.

"No need to continue," Violet said, blinking away the wetness starting to gather in her eyes. "The rose-tinted glasses have been pulled off, so thank you."

Kaz grabbed her waist hard and pulled her to the very edge of the hood, keeping their bodies firmly pressed together. "I didn't say it to make you angry with me."

"I know."

"But you are. Angry with me."

"More with myself," she admitted softly.

Kaz sighed, and then quickly pulled her down from the hood, snagging her hand with his own and weaving their fingers together. "Come on. Let's go do something."

"Like what?"

"I'll figure something out."

Violet didn't doubt him.

The Porsche came to a stop on wet sand, and Violet was already unbuckling her seatbelt to get out.

"The pier is closed for a week," Kaz informed, opening his door as Violet climbed out of the car. "They're doing some minor construction, and closed down the beach for about a mile either way for safety's sake, but they're lax on monitoring it during the night."

Violet looked around, noting there was no one as far as she could see. Parked right beside the pier, the Porsche was hidden by shadows, and so were they.

"And what happens if someone catches us down here?"

Kaz laughed. "They won't."

"You don't know that for sure, Kaz."

"I'm pretty sure," he countered. "And it was this or my place again."

Violet's brow furrowed as she met him at the front of the Porsche. Kaz leaned against the hood, holding a hand out for her to take. She did, letting him tug her into his side. A heavy arm rested over her shoulder, and she smiled when he kissed her temple.

"I like your place," Violet whispered.

Kaz's lips moved against her skin when he said, "I know you do, but you should see more than just the walls of my apartment. Do something with me other than hide away in my bedroom."

"I like that, too."

He chuckled, deep and heady. "Keep that up and I'll run us over there. I'm pretty confident I can get us there in under ten minutes."

Grinning, Violet pushed away from his side. He said nothing when she kicked off her suede, booted heels, letting her feet sink into wet, cold sand.

"What are you doing?" he asked.

"I want to check the water."

"It's going to be freezing."

The air had a chill as it was late fall, and winter would be coming soon, but it wasn't bad.

"Violet," Kaz said, half amused and half warning, "do not go into that water."

She wasn't listening. Before Kaz could reach out and grab her again, she was already heading toward the water lapping at the pier. Her toes hit cold water first, but her feet and ankles quickly followed when a small rush moved up the sand.

Kaz was right.

It was like ice had been poured onto her skin.

Still, Violet didn't move. Her dress rested just above her knees, high enough not to worry about it getting wet. The stinging sensation of the freezing water eventually dulled to the point it was bearable.

But she didn't care.

Spinning around, she faced Kaz.

He just shook his head, still leaning against the car and watching her like she was the most important thing to grace his presence for the day.

"How long are you going to stand out there freezing your feet off?" he asked.

"Maybe until you come get me."

Kaz made a dismissive sound. "You'll be waiting for a long time. I know how cold that water is."

"But what if the water got really high, really fast?"

"It won't."

"But what if?" she pressed.

Kaz sighed. "I suppose I would have to come out and get you."

"Don't sound so excited about saving my life, now."

In a blink, his amused features hardened, turning cold. "Violet, had I thought there was any risk to your life, you wouldn't be standing in that water in the first place."

Oh.

WHERE THE SUN HIDES

For something that was as sweet and protective as that statement had been, Kaz had spoken it rather candidly and with a sobering quality that edged the words.

Violet turned back around, watching another rush of water come in and lap at her ankles. It was enough to send her flying out of the water, as the prickling sensation of the coldness was too much on her legs for a second round. Kaz laughed at her until she was all the way back up to the front of the Porsche, and far away from the water's cold touch.

"Told you," he said, smug as fuck.

Violet shot him a playful glare as she bent down to put her shoes back on. She didn't even get the chance to grab the first shoe before she was lifted off the ground. She only realized what happened when her backside met the hood of the Porsche, and Kaz's smirk filled her vision once more.

"What are you—"

Violet's words drifted away when Kaz pulled one of her legs up, and his hands closed around her freezing foot. Over and over, he rubbed his palms against her cold skin until the stinging sensation was gone and it didn't hurt as much. He did the same to her other foot without a word, seemingly unbothered by the sand getting all over his suit and her dress.

"I may not get in the water for you, but I will certainly warm you up after," he told her.

"I'll take that deal."

By the time Kaz was satisfied he had sufficiently warmed Violet up again, he dropped her feet and stepped in between her widened legs.

"This was nice," she said.

Kaz's hands landed on her thighs, skipping up under the hem of her dress just enough to make her grin. "What was?"

"This. Pretty decent, for a second date, I think."

"I didn't say this was a date."

"It's kind of like one."

"When was the first?" he asked, a smile growing.

"The diner."

"Ah." Kaz tipped his head down, his nose touching hers a second before his lips grazed her mouth softly. "We kind of did things backward, no?"

"How so?"

"Get to know someone. Date them. That sort of thing. We did it all backward."

"I don't mind," Violet whispered against his lips.

Kaz kissed her again. "Me, either."

"By the way …"

His mouth hesitated against the path it was starting to make down her jaw. "What?"

"You were right."

"I usually am, but enlighten me."

Violet squeezed her thighs around his hips, forcing him closer. "Smartass. The picture. I sent it knowing it wouldn't be innocent for you. After all, you took far too much enjoyment putting that bite mark there."

Kaz let out a hard breath, the warmth pulsing along her neck. "Yeah."

She let her hands travel down his chest, lower to his stomach, and then grazing over the front of his slacks, barely touching where she knew he was hard and likely aching.

"Care to make me another?"

Violet smiled when she felt Kaz's teeth bare to her cheek. "Like a matching set?"

"We can go with that."

"Don't tempt me," he warned quietly.

"No tempting. Demanding. I like seeing it."

"In that case …"

Kaz's mouth crashed down on Violet's as his fingers dug into her thighs, keeping her firmly in place and her legs wide. She gasped his name in a breathy laugh, earning her a nip of his teeth to her bottom lip as his hands traveled higher under her dress.

He fisted the sides of her panties, yanking on the fabric until she lifted just high enough for him to pull them down her legs.

The cold air danced along her skin, but it was hard to notice when she was hot under Kaz's wandering hands and mouth. His lips touched down to her cheek, over her jaw, and across her neck. He tasted each and every spot he kissed with a strike of his tongue to her flesh, pulling her even closer until she rested at the very edge of the hood.

"Someone has to break this damn car in," he said, his gaze darkening as he looked her over.

Violet wet her lips, reaching for the button of his pants. "Oh?"

"Yeah."

"You haven't yet?"

"Didn't want to," Kaz said before he kissed her again.

Violet let him dominate the kiss, tilting her head back and parting her lips to let his tongue slip in with hers. There was something about the way he kissed her, so hot and hard, and always taking, that she liked the most.

She was only slightly aware of the pier, and where they were. The shadows kept her nerves at bay as he bunched her skirt up around her hips, and his hand slipped between her thighs. Firm swipes of his fingertips grazed her sex, making her rock into his hand and whimper for more.

A touch wasn't enough.

She knew exactly what he could do.

And a touch wasn't even the tip of that iceberg.

"Shh," Kaz shushed against her heated skin.

Violet sighed the second his fingers swept over her bare pussy for a second time. She found her chin in his hand, her head tipped up, and his eyes seeking hers as two of those fingers thrust into her core, fast and deep. His thumb flicked up at the same time, pressing hard to her clit. A knowing grin spread Kaz's lips as he drew her mouth closer to his, and his hand worked between her legs.

"So fucking wet," he told her.

Violet's throat felt tight, like someone was squeezing it. She didn't mind the pressure, and she didn't need to talk. He liked her sounds far better, anyway. And each little cry that escaped as she rocked into his fingers, his grin only deepened as he urged her on for more.

"Louder, Violet."

She whined low.

"Let me see it," he pressed.

Another thrust of his fingers, a quick press of his thumb, and she was there.

"*Kaz.*"

Her shout of his name echoed across the quiet beach. As fast as she had let it out, and the first waves of her orgasm began to flood her body, he muffled whatever sounds she might make next by kissing her. Violet panted into that kiss, stunned at how quickly her body had reacted to his touch.

"Shit, yeah," Kaz said, smirking as he kissed the corner of her mouth. "I don't think there's anything quite like the sight of you getting off on my car, Violet."

She blinked away the haziness in her vision, grabbing his shirt in her fist to pull him closer. His forehead rested to hers, and for a short while, they stayed still and quiet like that.

Watching.

Touching.

Silent.

When his fingers pressed into her inner thighs, Violet widened her legs, a soft moan falling from her lips.

"More?" he asked.

"More," she demanded.

Their next movements came out rushed and harsh as she worked at the zipper and button on his pants. Kaz's hands were already at the back of her neck, ripping down the zipper of her dress, and pulling the clothing over her shoulders until it pooled at her stomach.

Her heels dug into his lower back when she finally freed his cock from his boxer-briefs. She barely had his pants shoved down around his hips before he was spreading her thighs wider—wide enough to make her muscles protest and ache.

"Jesus," Violet ground out through clenched teeth.

In her palms, his cock was hard and pulsing with every fast beat of his heart. She only let go of his length when his hand wrapped around the base.

Kaz's free hand came up fast, his thumb catching her bottom lip and making her mouth open. "Palms on the hood, Violet."

She'd been watching him through her lashes, but those words made her eyes widen.

"Now," he added lower.

She didn't entirely understand why he didn't want her hands on him while he fucked her, but she listened to what he said, anyway, putting her hands down to the hood on either side of her body. She sucked in a sharp breath as he ran the head of his cock from her clit down to her entrance.

There was no pause between the brief moment when he was there, at her slit, and when he was pushing in.

One hard, deep thrust was all it took. The shock of that first thrust was brutal to Violet as he filled her full and stretched her open. She was wet enough to ease the intrusion, but it still took her breath away all the same. The slight bite of pain danced hand in hand with the bliss, and her lashes fluttered closed.

"Watch me," she heard him growl.

Violet's gaze snapped open instantly, but instead of Kaz's eyes, she was drawn down to where he was watching. Between their bodies, the sight of his cock buried almost all the way in her sex, and her arousal smeared along the base of his cock and her thighs. His hand was still holding tight to the base of his length, but a tremor skipped over his fingers.

Her fingers clenched against the hood of the car, the cold metal doing little to soothe the fire sweeping her senses.

Kaz let go of his cock, grabbed her thigh, and flexed forward, giving Violet that last couple of inches that he'd been holding back.

And it was heaven.

"Fuck," he mumbled.

Violet's gaze flew up to find his, a cry breaking free from her throat.

A long groan fell from Kaz's lips as they parted. His jaw was tight, a tick showing each time he swallowed. Violet was damn sure she had never seen him look more free, more content ... never sexier than right then, as deep as he could be inside her, fucking her on the hood of his car.

Never.

Violet pressed her heels into his lower back again. "Fuck me."

Kaz breathed deep. "Hands stay on the hood."

She nodded once, and that was apparently all he needed before he pulled out, and thrust right back in again. When his hand tangled into the hair at the nape of her neck, tugging firm enough to stretch her neck bare for him, she finally understood why he wanted her hands on the hood and not on him.

She needed support.

Something to keep her steady.

Because all he wanted to do was fuck her there like that.

Raw. Hard. *Fast.*

And it was wonderful.

"You know," Kaz said as he took a seat at the bar in his kitchen, drifting his eyes over Violet's backside as she was bent over, rummaging through his fridge, "I could get used to this."

"There's nothing in here, Kaz, besides milk that went bad a week ago and a bag of shredded cheese. How have you survived this long on your own?"

"Vera usually brings whatever I need, but now that you're coming around here, I told her I would hire someone to do it—it was a waste of her gas anyway. Now, what are you in the mood for? I know a great place that makes French toast."

"Just order me whatever you're getting. I'm going to go use your shower."

Kaz had already dialed the place, his phone to his ear, as he watched her walk past him. "Was that an invitation?"

She didn't even look back as she said, "Yep."

Violet was going to be the death of him.

Kaz finished his call rather quickly, and since they had a good twenty-five minutes before the food would show, he decided to make the best use of that time. The shower was already going, and he could just imagine her standing beneath that spray of water … but before his mind could properly seize on that image, there was a hard knock at the front door.

It couldn't be the food, no one's fucking delivery time was that great, and he knew it wasn't anyone that answered to him because they knew better than to just show up at his place unannounced.

There were only two people that would, and as he crossed the short distance between where he was sitting and the front door, he hoped that it wasn't Vasily.

Looking through the peephole, he saw Ruslan standing on the other side. He chanced a look back, still hearing the shower going.

206

One thing about his brother, he wouldn't have come up without having checked to see that Kaz's car was parked down in the lot, so he couldn't pretend like he wasn't home. He had no choice but to let him in and hope that he was there just to deliver a message.

Swinging the door open, Kaz stood in the threshold, uncaring that he was only clad in a pair of boxer-briefs. "Now's not a good time, Rus."

"When is it ever a good time for you, brother?" When he still didn't move, Ruslan frowned. "Are you going to make me stand out here?"

Reluctantly, Kaz shifted to the side, waving for him to come in as he peeked out the door to make sure he was alone.

"Is there a reason you're acting so strange?" Ruslan asked from behind him, getting comfortable on his couch. Then, almost seconds after the question was out of his mouth, Ruslan's head tilted as he listened, his smile growing. "So it's true then. You're seeing someone."

"Yes," Kaz said, not adding anything more than that. "Next time, when I'm not pressed for time, you can meet her."

But that wouldn't happen. Not ever.

If they were two different people, or maybe just in a different life, Kaz wouldn't have hesitated in introducing the two. He didn't doubt that Ruslan would have liked her, and once someone got past that gruff outer shell that Ruslan always had up, it was clear that he was a good guy.

"What's the issue?" Ruslan asked, that teasing quality to his tone fading away. "You keeping your secrets from the *bratva* is one thing, but you've never hidden anything from me. Why are you now?"

Kaz glanced in the direction of his bedroom, hearing the shower finally cut off making his heart kick up a notch. Looking back to his brother, Kaz said, "Don't ... Don't make me lie to you."

"Why would you need to? Shit Kaz, who the fuck do you—" Ruslan paused, his expression shifting. "You didn't ..."

"Ruslan, walk away."

"Fuck having to lie to me," Ruslan said as he got to his feet. "That's the least of your concerns. If who's back there is who I *think* is back there, you're begging for a fucking funeral."

"I—"

"Don't," Ruslan cut him off, not giving him the chance to get another word out. "Whatever excuse, whatever bullshit reasoning that you've fed yourself into thinking that this would work out, don't give me that. Because that ... whatever it is you have with her, it's not going to end well. For either of you. And the last thing I want to do is bury you because of it. Walk away, Kazimir, before you're not able to."

"I can't do that," Kaz said, making sure his brother heard every word. "She's under my skin, and I want to keep her that way."

Ruslan didn't say anything, not for a long time, and whatever he saw in Kaz's face had him shaking his head. "You're serious, aren't you?"

But that question didn't require an answer, not when the evidence of it was behind the closed door of his bedroom.

"Is she worth the trouble that's going to come your way?" Ruslan asked, then smiled, the sight of it breaking up the tension in the room. "Because your ass isn't."

Laughing, Kaz shook his head. "She wouldn't be here if she wasn't."

"Right. Call me later, once you're actually alone." Ruslan said opening the front door, startling the delivery man that stood ready to knock on the other side. "Be careful out there, Kaz."

Ruslan disappeared down the hall, boarding the elevator once the doors opened. Once he had grabbed the food and tipped the man, he closed the door, dropping the bag on the counter.

Standing there, it was almost like a weight was lifted from his chest. He couldn't explain why Ruslan knowing almost felt like a good thing to him.

Even as he was glad for it, it was just another reminder that this wasn't going to be easy for them.

Ruslan had reacted as Kaz expected, calmer even.

And that only meant that everyone else's reactions would be exactly as he thought.

Violent.

Violet listened in the bedroom doorway as the apartment quieted of voices. She kept clutching the large beach-sized towel around her body, not sure if she should run back to the bathroom and lock herself in, or just stay where she was for another minute or two.

Just to be safe.

In all the many times she had come to Kaz's place, no one had ever interrupted their time. Not during the evenings, and certainly not in the mornings. Sure, he'd gotten calls—work, she suspected, for his father—but it had never been so immediately important that he needed to leave her there and handle it.

Kaz had never warned her that someone might show up, either, and she strongly believed that was because he didn't think someone would without prior notice. Violet might not know every little detail about Kaz, his business, or his family, but she knew enough.

Enough to say he wouldn't put her in that kind of situation if he could help it.

"Violet?" she heard him yell from the kitchen.

She started on the spot, brought out of her thoughts with a bang.

"Yeah?" Violet called back.

"I know you're waiting back there. It's safe."

"I'm indecent at the moment."

She swore he was smirking in that fucking way of his when he replied, "And that makes a difference how?"

"Let me pull something on, Kaz."

"You're no fun this morning."

Violet let him have his complaints as she bolted back for the bathroom. Knowing she had to at least try to preserve the cleanliness of her blue lace dress from the night before—the damn thing needed to be dry-cleaned, not just shoved into a washer—she snagged a red, plain cotton T-shirt from Kaz's closet, and pulled on a pair of clean boy-shorts from her messenger bag.

At least she was remembering to keep an extra pair of those on hand, now.

Violet eventually made her way back to the kitchen, tossing Kaz a sly grin when she caught his gaze roving over her figure before she took a seat at the bar.

He already had the bags of food emptied, and the containers waiting to be opened. Violet grabbed one he pushed toward her, plucking up a plastic fork to go with it.

She couldn't help but notice how he didn't say a thing about his visitor.

"Kaz?"

"Hmm?"

"Your brother was here," she said, never taking her gaze off her French Toast.

"He was," Kaz replied at the same level.

"And I take it ... he knows now."

"Ruslan has a pretty good idea, yes."

Fantastic.

Violet didn't want to be worried about the fact Ruslan knew, given that Kaz seemed so unbothered by it all, but the panic was still welling in her gut and spilling into her throat.

One person might lead to two, and then three.

She glanced up to find Kaz watching her, and she wasn't the least bit surprised. He always watched her like that whenever he could, but especially when he thought she wasn't looking at him. Almost liked he enjoyed the sight of her when she was inside her thoughts, unaware and quiet.

Violet liked it a lot—she liked it a little more each time she caught him doing it, and he didn't look away.

She didn't have the first clue what to make of that at all.

To feel like she was important—significant—to Kaz, simply because she graced him with her very person, and her time, and he didn't ask for more.

People always wanted more.

"You know," Kaz started to say, tossing his fork into his container, "you always get a little dimple in your right cheek whenever you think too much, or you're frustrated."

Violet's brow lifted at his admission. "Do I?"

"Among other things."

"Like what?"

"We'll stick with the dimple, because it's the most obvious," Kaz said in a murmur. "And I wouldn't be very good at my profession if I weren't capable of reading body language. So what I might notice, someone else probably wouldn't, or if they did, they would overlook it as nothing unusual."

Violet licked her bottom lip, trying to relax the tension in her shoulders.

"Still there," Kaz said after a moment.

"I'm nervous."

"Because of my brother."

"Aren't you?" she asked.

"That Ruslan will run to the first person he can and spill what he knows about me? Not highly. Not at all."

Oh.

"Why?"

Kaz smiled, softer than usual. "Because I know my *brat*, that's all."

Violet had a feeling there was more to the story, but she let him have his secrets. She still had a few of her own, after all. But it seemed like all Kaz had to do was prompt and press in just the right ways, and she couldn't hold a thing back.

"Still, he's just the first person to know," Violet said softly.

Kaz's jaw tightened briefly. "You know who I am, yes?"

"Uh, yes?"

"And you know who you are, obviously."

Violet sighed. "Kaz, get to the point."

Kaz shrugged. "We've known from the beginning that this was going to continue one of two ways, Violet."

Her chest suddenly constricted with the heavy undercurrent of his words. They seemed safe enough on the surface, but had no doubt they would probably hurt if she looked a little deeper.

"Either we ended it," Kaz said, as cool and calm as ever, "or we didn't."

Violet swallowed the lump keeping her quiet. "We didn't."

"What do you want, hmm?"

"I don't understand what you're asking."

Kaz lifted a hand, gesturing to his place, and then between them. "How many times do you want to keep coming here? Staying the night? Sleeping with me, in my bed? Wearing my clothes, cooking in my kitchen? Sneaking away from your father, waking me up in the middle of the night … and I can keep going, Violet."

He could.

"So maybe I haven't seen it like that," she whispered.

"That's a lie. You see it exactly the same way, or you wouldn't do it at all because you wouldn't want to do it."

Violet hated how he always did that in one way or another. She was used to turning cheek to things she didn't want to see, or even sticking her head in the sand because it was easier.

Kaz didn't let her do that.

He forced her to look around, to take inventory and accountability.

She lived a hell of a lot more in the short time she spent with him then she ever did when she was alone.

It was good.

But it was bad, too.

"For the record," Kaz said quietly, making Violet look up at him again. "What?"

"I like you being here. Doing those things, all of those things. And the things I didn't say, too. If I had wanted you to stop, if I didn't want to see where this was going to go, then it would have ended a long while ago."

Yeah, she knew that, too.

Violet didn't understand a lot of the shit she felt and thought where Kaz was concerned, but what she did, she liked. And she wasn't ready to end it like that.

Pushing off the stool, Violet made her way around the island to stand beside Kaz. He watched her the whole while, saying nothing. Moving sideways a bit, he offered her a hand, and she took it, stepping up to sit on his lap. An arm wrapped around her waist, and his hand landed to her bare thigh.

The touch alone was possessive.

Like he intended to keep it there.

"Eat," he said, tugging her container across the counter and picking up the fork for her to take again.

Kaz's chin rested on her shoulder.

"What are we doing?" she asked.

Violet didn't feel like she had to expand on that statement.

Wasn't it obvious enough?

What were they doing with one another?

Together?

Kaz used his fork to cut a piece of her French toast, and lifted it to Violet for her to take. "Eating."

"Not what I meant."

"I think this is exactly what you meant."

It was, sort of.

The realization came hard and swift.

She wouldn't be there, otherwise. She wouldn't have crossed that distance to be closer. She wouldn't want him holding her like he was.

Intimate.

Sweet.

What was that word he'd used once?

Domestic?

"We'll figure it out," Kaz said, his words whispering along her skin.

"Will we?"

"Somehow."

One week slipped into two, two slipped into four, and before Kaz knew it, an entire month had passed in the blink of an eye. That time was mostly a blur, but the majority of it had been spent with Violet. Despite Ruslan's appearance at his place, things hadn't changed much at all. She was still coming to him, sleeping in his bed, and making his place feel like a home even though he had been living there for years now.

It had finally clicked in him, the difference her presence made. He was more relaxed, happy even, and despite that their relationship was mostly confined within those four walls, he didn't mind it. Kaz didn't need others to tell him she was his, he only needed to see the way her face lit up when she saw him to know the answer to that.

Kaz had only dropped her off a little more than an hour ago before he got a call from Vasily, telling him to come in. After their last conversation, he had done well to steer clear of his father, besides the few times they had needed to meet for *Bratva* business.

Though anytime Vasily called him for a meet, it was in the warehouse. Vasily had made a different request, texting him an address he wasn't familiar with. It was still within the limits of Little Odessa, but Kaz had never had a reason to go to that side, especially when he had no business over there. But when the boss called, even if it was the last thing he wanted to do, he went.

The house Kaz arrived at was in the middle of nowhere, land as far out as the eye could see. It was a pretty secluded place, and for the second time, he wondered what purpose his father had in bringing him here. And unlike the last time his father had called on him for a private meeting, he didn't go in unarmed.

"Good of you to finally join me," Vasily said once Kaz was inside, reclining back in one of the two wing-backed chairs in the living room.

Raj was standing in the doorway of the kitchen, looking just as imposing as ever. The last thing Kaz wanted to do was put his back to the man, because while he was sure he could take Vasily, Raj was capable of things he didn't even want to consider.

Vasily, noticing Kaz's choice to stick close to the door, smiled, though the sight of it did nothing to calm him. "Is there a problem, Kazimir?"

"Not at all. You called for a meet, here I am."

"Of course." Vasily reached for the carafe of whiskey to his left, and the glass sitting next to it, pouring himself a drink. "When you were a boy, I didn't expect great things from you. Your brother, on the other hand, he was the perfect son. Even with him idolizing Gavrill, I knew he would be exactly what any father could hope for in this brotherhood of ours. I knew the moment he'd sworn the words that he would be my successor, but that all came to an end rather quickly, no? When I caught him fucking that man."

Kaz didn't react to Vasily's words—it wasn't like this was a secret finally being revealed. He remembered all too well the night Vasily learned that Ruslan was gay. That was both the day Ruslan had come out of the closet, and Kaz had learned to truly hate the man that spawned him.

Despite the changes to the *Bratva*, and the advances their organization had made over the years, there was still one concept that Vasily had refused to let go of—no man in his *Bratva* would be gay. Kaz was sure that if it were not for the blood that ran in Ruslan's veins, his brother would be dead by Vasily's hand. He had almost done it that night, using his fists to tell Ruslan exactly how he felt about his preference in sex.

Ruslan, for reasons known only to him, had not fought back, had merely taken the onslaught of hits until he wasn't conscious anymore. Kaz had only arrived later to find the result of his father's disgust. From that day forward, Ruslan had been practically disowned within their family, forced out as though he was nothing at all. He still had his place within the organization, Vasily hadn't taken that away, but it had become quite clear that Ruslan was no longer Vasily's intended successor.

"You, however," Vasily said dragging Kaz back to the present conversation, "as defiant as you are, I was surprised you had made it to this point. I won't say that you're not good at what you do, you've obviously done quite well for yourself, but you lack discipline. You fail to realize that there are consequences to your actions and that no one, not even you, can defy me."

Kaz pushed off the wall, striding further into the room. "What are you getting at, Vasily?"

"I was curious," he went on as though Kaz hadn't spoken, "as to why you haven't been around as much lately, and when you are, you're asking questions that are of little importance. So I did some digging of my own,

Kazimir—and let me be honest, I almost wished you had the same predilection as your brother. At least that could be contained. But Violet Gallucci? I thought you knew better than that."

Vasily withdrew a picture, and even from his distance, Kaz could clearly make out his own face, along with Violet's. He still remembered that day ... picking her up and grabbing ice cream on their way back to his place, before she had spent the night. It had been a good day, but he had never suspected that he was being followed, that anyone had gotten that close to him to take pictures.

How the fuck hadn't he noticed?

"I've been lenient with you, Kazimir," Vasily went on. "I allow you your tantrums, your displays of defiance in the presence of others. You're still young, after all. But on this, I have never, and will not ever, bend. This is your last chance to heed me, boy. Walk away. Do not go near her again. This is my final warning. If she means that much to you, think of an excuse, I don't give a fuck. But when you leave this place today, I want there to be no mistake. Violet Gallucci no longer exists to you. Am I understood?"

"Yeah, I hear you," Kaz said, his voice steady, his eyes locked on Vasily. "But understand *me*. I'm not going to walk away from her because you command it."

He couldn't, even if he wanted to. She was too important to him, too ingrained in every aspect of his life for him to try and dig her out. If he did, he wasn't sure what was going to be left.

Now, it was Vasily getting to his feet, that mask of indifference slipping as the anger peeked through. "Do not force my hand, Kazimir. I am at least trying to give you the opportunity to finish this on your own."

"Why?" he asked suddenly.

"What?"

"Keeping us apart, why is that so important to you? Our families have been enemies for years, but that could end just by us being together. At the very least, it would ensure that neither attacks the other. What are you hiding that might get exposed?"

It was clear that Vasily had been expecting the question, as his mask didn't slip again. "Next time, I won't be so generous."

Kaz got close enough to Vasily to make sure his point couldn't be misunderstood. "Believe me when I say that the last thing I need is your generosity. And until you burn these fucking stars off my chest, you don't get to control who I'm with. You want to speak on Rus, then speak on the consequences of *your* actions, because the only reason I let you walk away was because he asked it of me. If you think to touch a hair on Violet's head, I'll bury you."

"Kazimir, you—"

"Over the years, you've made it quite clear where I stand with you. You want our name to continue on, and the only way you can have that is through me. If I'm going to take that seat, I'll do it the way I want. Now, do *you* understand *me*?"

Vasily was quiet for some time as he stood opposite Kaz, staring him down like he had never witnessed this side of him before. He had obviously thought it would be easy, that he would merely need to give a command and Kaz would heed it. But there was one thing about Kaz that he seemed to have forgotten. Kaz was never one to blindly follow rules.

That just wasn't who he was.

"Sure," Vasily said after a spell, "I understand completely, but I do have a question for you, Kazimir. What do you think Alberto Gallucci will do to that daughter of his once he finds out who she's spreading her legs for?"

"You fucking wouldn't ..."

Vasily held the picture up once more, waving it in front of Kaz's face. "A picture tells a thousand truths, and this ... this is just one of many that I have." He shook his head, a laugh escaping him, "You should have kept those curtains closed, Kazimir."

Violet kept her head down, attention focused solely on the silent phone in her hand, as she walked toward the entrance of her building. Like she had a hundred times earlier that day, she checked through her call log and her text messages.

She already knew what it would say.

No missed calls.

No new texts.

Violet chewed on her inner cheek, barely noticing the people passing her by on the busy street. The messenger bag hanging off her shoulder, filled with her stuff from school and her laptop, felt heavier for no reason in particular. She already had enough invisible weight wearing her down, the bag only added more.

Selecting a familiar contact on the phone log, Violet scrolled down to the last message she had gotten from the number.

One week prior.

Next time. -K.

That was it.

Violet hadn't heard a single thing from Kaz since that last message he sent after he dropped her off just beyond the Little Odessa border. She'd called a couple of times, but it rang through to voicemail, and she didn't exactly think it was smart to leave that type of message.

But he knew her number.

And so she waited for something to come back, and when it didn't, Violet started to worry that maybe something was wrong. The worry turned to anger, but that quickly bled away.

Kaz wasn't the type to drop someone—her—with nothing, not even a call at least.

Violet went back to worry in a blink.

"Miss Gallucci?"

Lost in her thoughts and concerns, Violet hadn't realized she was standing in front of her building with her attention still down on her phone, and her feet practically cemented to the ground.

Violet's head snapped up at an unfamiliar voice calling her name. She found a tall, thin man wearing a black ensemble, sunglasses included, standing right in front of her, blocking her path to her building's entrance doors. In his hand, he held a manila envelope that looked to be a foot long, the same in width, and a half of an inch thick.

"You are Violet Gallucci, yes?" he asked.

Other than his lips moving, the man's expression never changed from the stony mask he wore. Violet might have thought he was a statue had he stayed quiet, and she probably would have run right into him because of her distraction.

What concerned her more, was the familiar accent coloring his words. Russian.

There should be no Russians approaching her in front of her building.

"You can talk, can't you?" the man questioned.

Violet's gaze narrowed. "I can."

"Good. Then answer my question."

"I suspect you already know who I am if you stopped me," she replied. "How many women have walked past you in the last thirty seconds?"

That time, the man's mask did crack. The faintest hint of a sneer curved the edges of his lips upward, but it quickly fell. "Here," he said, holding out the package. "A gift for you."

Violet hesitated, not reaching to take the item. "From who?"

"Vasily Markovic sends his regards. And to your father as well, of course. Have a nice day, Violet."

She froze in place as the envelope was shoved roughly into her hand, forcing her to take it as the man passed her by without another word being said between them.

Violet could already feel the panic welling in her stomach and leaping into her throat as her hands began to shake. Her gaze flicked between the envelope, and the man disappearing into the crowd of people flooding the sidewalk.

Vasily Markovic.

The name chanted in her ringing ears.

She felt sick all over.

Grabbing the rip tab on the side of the package, Violet pulled, opening the top of the envelope. Tipping it upside down into her waiting hand, pictures fell out. She let the envelope fall to the sidewalk, uncaring of the people walking around her, as she began to slide her hand over the pictures, flipping between them.

All sorts of pictures.

Some could maybe be explained away, like the black and whites of her and Kaz walking side by side toward his car. Or even the ones of them exiting a store together.

Others, the sepia toned shots of them walking near the closed pier might be harder to explain, but possibly doable if she had a good enough excuse.

Ones, full color and close up, of her and Kaz where he was kissing her cheek, or holding her hand might not be so simple.

But the most damaging, the ones that scared her above all the others, were shots of them in his apartment. The ceiling-to-floor windows were almost always covered in the day and evenings, but she had opened them sometimes, just to watch the ocean at night. The apartment was high enough that no one directly below would be able to see inside, but …

The pictures looked like they had come from right out in the ocean.

Like someone had taken a high-grade lens and watched them.

Violet stared at the pictures again.

Four shots in total.

Her in his clothes. Her on his lap, naked then.

The other two were the same.

There was only one where her face was clearly visible, as she had turned her head just enough for the person to catch her like that.

Violet couldn't breathe.

Sends his regards …

To her father?

Had these photos been sent to her father?

Violet didn't move as a buzzing began in her hand, under the stack of photos. She pulled her hand free, staring at the number lighting up the screen.

Alberto Gallucci, it read.

There was a brief moment where Violet felt like time just stopped around her. Where there was no New York street, no busy people, and no world moving, and turning. It was just her, a stack of photos, and her father's call needing to be answered.

She ran through the last three months in her mind, and wondered ...

Were there things she should have done differently?

Would she, if given the choice to go back?

Had she done what was always wanted of her?

All her answers were the same.

No.

Her fingers still trembled when she swiped at the screen to answer her father's call. Putting it up to her ear, Violet said, "Hello, Daddy."

"You're just arriving home from school, right?" Alberto asked.

His tone was too gruff, she thought.

Too strained and forced.

Like he didn't want to frighten her, maybe.

"Yeah," Violet confirmed. "Just looking at the front door right now."

"Don't move. Gee will be there in ten minutes."

Violet swallowed hard. "Why?"

"I have something I want you to see."

She knew it then, when he didn't outright lie but he didn't tell the truth, that he was looking at the same photos she was.

Violet wasn't quite sure what she should do at that moment. Call her father out on it, or placate him as much as possible.

Alberto spoke again, forcing her hand in an entirely different manner. "And guessing by the note included in the gift that just arrived at my door, I think you know exactly what I want you to see. I thought you were doing so well, *dolcezza*. And I can see now that my blind affection has made us both fools, hmm?"

"Daddy—"

"Be in front of that building when Gee arrives. You will not like what happens if you make me come looking for you myself, Violet."

The call hung up.

Just like that.

Violet blinked down at the phone as she pulled it away from her ear. Panic settled in deep, burrowing into her bones and seeping through her nervous system.

She didn't know what to do, but her first instinct wasn't to listen to her father. His voice in her head had lessened—it didn't hold quite the same quality of law that it used to.

Someone else had told her to look around and listen more.

And so she had.

But it was still a fight for her. An internal war with one side of her brain telling her to stay put and do as she was told because she had done wrong, while her heart screamed for her to move because Kaz was *right*.

Her heart won.

Violet turned on her heel and bolted toward the street, straight for the crosswalk blinking for people to walk. She weaved in and out of people as she sent off her first text message to Kaz. A second quickly followed, more panicked than the second to the point where it was barely legible. She didn't stop moving further from her building and where Gee thought he would find her.

Blocks, three at least.

And then another two.

Finally, her phone rang.

Violet saw Kaz's number flashing across the screen, and relief swept through her blood. She still didn't stop moving, and checking over her shoulder at the same time as she answered the call.

"He knows," Violet said the second she put the phone to her ear.

Kaz was quiet on the other end, Violet almost thought that maybe he didn't hear her.

"My dad—"

"*Violet.*"

Her name always came out so smooth and deep from Kaz, but that time he said it hard and sharp enough to make her steps stumble.

"He sent pictures," Violet said, barely able to even say the words. "Your father—to me and my dad. He sent pictures of us. All sorts of pictures, Kaz. Walking. At the pier. Going into your place. And inside ..."

Kaz blew out a heavy breath. "Inside where?"

"Your place."

"When?"

"I don't know!" she cried.

"Violet, what were they of?"

She choked on nothing but air. "What do you think?"

Kaz cussed—thick and angry. "Where are you right now?"

All Violet managed to reply to that was, "Not going to my father."

The tears had started falling.

Her panic kicked up a notch.

She still heard Kaz's voice in the background of it all. He rattled off the name of an address she didn't recognize that was situated mid-Brooklyn.

"Get in a cab," Kaz said. "I'll meet you there."

Violet handed over what the taxi driver asked for, and stepped out into a residential neighborhood that wasn't exactly upscale, but certainly wasn't the slums. She kept a hand on the cab door, unsure if she was at the right spot. A small driveway led up to a modest two level home that was pretty on the outside, and had a white Bentley parked in front of the small garage.

"Miss, I got another fare to pick up," the driver shouted.

Violet hesitated. "Is this the right place?"

He rattled off the address she had given him. "I've lived and drove in Brooklyn for forty fucking years—this is the right place, girl."

She let go of the door, knowing she didn't have much of a choice. Stepping up onto the curb, she felt her phone began to ring and vibrate in her messenger bag. It hadn't stopped since she jumped into a cab and took off. Without a doubt, she knew it was her father.

Violet had checked a couple of times, just to make sure it wasn't Kaz. He hadn't called her back, or messaged, so that only left Alberto.

Guessing by the number of voicemails her father had already left, he was livid.

Beyond pissed.

She couldn't be bothered to listen to a single one.

Why should she when she knew what they would say?

As the cab pulled away, Violet stayed on the curb, still staring at the house and wondering why in the hell Kaz would send her to a place he had never taken her to before.

What was she supposed to do, just go on up to the door and fucking knock?

Violet eyed the quiet neighborhood and figured doing just that might be better than standing way out in the open where anyone might see and recognize her. She quickly crossed the driveway, and took the couple of wooden steps up to the front door. Rapping her knuckles to the glass twice, she took a step back so whoever was inside could get a decent view of her through the small clear slates in the design of the frosted glass.

She heard the footsteps approach from within, saw the light-colored shade move, and then waited another thirty seconds before the door was finally opened.

Familiar gray eyes greeted her.

For a second, Violet just took in the woman on the other side of the door. She was pretty, with her high cheekbones and her soft lines. There was a resemblance between the unknown woman and Kaz that Violet recognized almost instantly.

But where Kaz was the more masculine version, the woman was far more feminine in her features.

"Hello," Violet said.

It felt stupid because she didn't know what else to say.

The woman's hand never left the doorknob, like she was thinking about closing the door on Violet if she moved even an inch. "Hello."

"I'm—"

"I know who you are," the woman interrupted sharply. "And I don't know why you've found your way to my door, but I don't need you here causing me any kind of trouble, Gallucci."

Violet was stunned. The coldness of the woman's tone rang out in each word she spoke.

"If you know who I am, then maybe you wouldn't mind telling me who you are, or why Kaz gave me this address to come to."

For just a brief second, almost quick enough to miss it, the woman's stance softened. But just as fast, she straightened right back up like a rod had been shoved into her spine.

"Vera Markovic," she said, her gaze never leaving Violet's still form on the doorstep. "And Kazimir is my brother. But what exactly is he to you?"

Violet opened her mouth to speak, but words failed her.

She realized she didn't have a clear, good answer to give back.

Kaz was a lot of things to Violet, and he had very quickly turned those things into even more without trying at all.

He was her safe place.

A friend.

Her lover.

A confidant.

Stolen moments.

Silent conversations.

Long nights and late mornings.

How was she supposed to sum that up?

What word was good enough?

Vera cleared her throat, still looking like she was trying to decide whether or not to close the door. "So ... it's like that, huh?"

Violet blinked, warier than ever. "I don't understand what you mean by 'like that'."

"Really?"

"I—"

The roar of an engine and the scream of tires made Violet turn fast on the doorstep to find a familiar Porsche coming to a halt right in front of Vera's driveway. He didn't even cut the engine before he was getting out of the car.

Kaz rounded the front of the Porsche, his gaze zoning in on only Violet like she was the one thing he wanted to see, and just like that ...

Just like that the fucking tears started again and the pain was back. All that anxiety she had been pushing down, and the realities she was pretending didn't exist were shoving their way forefront into her heart and thoughts like they didn't have any plans to let go.

All she needed was the sight of Kaz—his fast steps, worried, angry eyes, and his hands outstretched for *her*.

Because he took, all the damn time.

From her, he took anything she didn't want to hold anymore. Stress, worries, and petty shit that she didn't have anyone to talk to about, he was the one who was there. When she had anxiety over upcoming tests for her classes, he had her books spread out over the bed. When she didn't want to just be the Gallucci girl—Alberto's daughter—she got to be just Violet with Kaz.

Violet's foot had just hit the asphalt of the driveway and Kaz was already there. His arms swallowed her whole, tightening around her so goddamn hard, enough to hurt and take her breath away, but she found that for the first time in a good hour, she could actually *breathe*.

She caught him around the middle, hugging tight when his one hand splayed wide to her back, and his other wrapped up in her hair, holding her close.

"I got you," he murmured into her hair before kissing the top of her head. "We'll figure it out, Violet."

All over again, time stopped.

There was nothing else that mattered when he was there, holding her like that.

Safe place.

Everybody had one person to be theirs. That one single person in the world that never asked for more than what was given, but always took what was too much to handle. The one person who made everything better, and made someone else better, too.

Kaz made her better, and she hadn't really thought to look beyond it because she couldn't. Not without maybe losing herself, him, or even them in the process.

She wanted to keep that safe place that he had become for her.

But it was too late.

And even if she didn't get to keep it—keep him—she knew now ...

Kaz was that one person.

For her, he was that one soul meant for hers.

And she wasn't allowed to have him.

"I moved the Bentley and put your Porsche in the garage," Vera said.

Violet looked over Kaz's shoulder to find his sister leaning in the entryway of the kitchen. Vera hadn't spoken a lot since Kaz arrived. Or rather, she said barely anything to Violet, and when she did speak, she directed everything she said to only Kaz.

It was cold and disconcerting.

Violet tried not to let Vera's attitude bother her, but it was hard. Kaz had told her once that out of all his siblings, he was closest to Vera in both age and in friendship. And it was clear that Vera didn't like Violet at all.

It was tough to swallow.

"Thank you," Kaz said, never turning around.

His finger tapped the bottom of Violet's coffee mug, silently telling her to take another drink. She lifted the tea and sipped, still watching Vera out of the corner of her eye. Kaz's gaze was firmly stuck on Violet, and she had a feeling he knew exactly what she was thinking, or he had a damn good idea. His one hand rested on the edge of the counter as he stood in front of her, close enough that he was keeping her in place and with him.

When his other hand landed on her waist with a soft touch, Violet's gaze flew to his.

Kaz smiled, but it didn't quite ring as true as it usually did. "Vera is ..."

Violet waited for him to finish whatever he was going to say, but he just left it hanging like that.

Vera huffed under her breath, and Violet watched as she spun on her heel and disappeared somewhere down the hallway outside of the kitchen. She hadn't gotten the chance to explore much of the home's layout, seeing as how Kaz had forced her into the kitchen and worked on soothing her panic attack first and foremost.

"She doesn't like me," Violet whispered.

"Vera isn't going to like anyone I care for at first unless she's hand-picked them," Kaz said, smirking just a little.

"That is not why she doesn't like me."

Kaz nodded once. "Yeah, I know."

"Then why send me here if you already knew, Kaz?"

"Because it was a safe place—Vasily won't come after Vera, no matter what happens in all of this, and I needed time."

"Time?"

"To think," he clarified.

"Oh."

Suddenly, Kaz pushed away from the counter and Violet. Instinctively, she reached out and grabbed a fistful of his jacket, tugging to pull him back. She liked him closer—there with her. Standing with her, locking her in with him.

That's where he needed to be.

"Don't go right now," she said quietly, her gaze lowering.

"I have to talk to Vera for a second, okay? Drink the tea. Don't worry."

That was much easier said than done.

Still, Violet let him go, releasing his jacket from her hold and staring out the small kitchen window as he followed the direction his sister had gone just a couple of minutes before.

Violet didn't miss how on his way out of the kitchen, he grabbed the packet of photographs that were sticking out of the top of her bag, resting on the table.

Not ten seconds later, the voices started to raise from down the hall.

"Are you serious, Kaz? Are you trying to get yourself killed—oh wait, it's too late to ask that question, considering the two of you are *here*. What were you thinking?"

"Vera—"

"And of all the women in New York, you picked the one that would piss off Vasily the most? If the situation wasn't so serious, I might have given you a pat on the back."

"Vera—"

"And how long do you think you can hide out here before Vasily arrives?"

"Will you shut up long enough for me to speak?" Kaz asked dryly.

"Oh, I'm sorry. Please, enlighten me on how you expect to get out of this one without our mother having to bury you ... I'll wait."

"Jesus, when did you become so pessimistic?"

Clear as day, Vera said, "The day my brother brought the one female to my door that would surely get him a bullet to the forehead. How do you want me to act, Kaz? Should I go out there and smile pretty, make sure she's happy and comfortable? Wait until her psychotic father sends some of his people to kick in my door trying to get her back?"

"Don't, Vera," Kaz said with an edge to his voice. "Don't blame her for the decisions I made."

"No, you're just as guilty as she is, but at the end of the day, she may get no more than a slap on the wrist. You, Kaz … they're going to bury you for this."

Violet clenched the cup a little harder in her hands, wondering how much truth was in Vera's words.

Probably more than she wanted to admit.

They had gone into this whole thing so stupidly. Together, sure, but dumb all the same. The innocence of it was quickly wiped away by the fact it had always been hidden, quiet, and secret. That alone was enough to say it was wrong, and they knew it was.

And yet, here they were.

Violet lifted her cup for another sip as Kaz strolled back into the kitchen, his expression a blank slate. He stopped at the table, and one by one, dropped the pictures down as he looked through them. She wasn't quite sure what to say, so she let him do whatever it was he was doing.

Finally, when he came to the last one—the most revealing of them all—Kaz scowled and tossed it down, too. "These were not included in the one Vasily showed me."

Her heart stopped. "What?"

"The one photograph he showed me was innocent, and he alluded to more, but nothing to this …" Kaz's jaw clenched before he finished with, "*Extent.*"

Anger and betrayal swirled fast in Violet's emotions, warring with one another for attention. "You *knew* he—"

Kaz spun around, a hand raising slowly. "Don't do that with me right now."

Violet dropped her unfinished tea into the sink, the cup clanging loudly against the metal. She took a step forward, hurt and so angry. "Don't do this? Like what, like I shouldn't be angry with you that you already knew?"

"You're assuming. Don't assume."

"Don't talk to me like I'm a child, Kaz."

"I'm not. You're angry, and you're worried. You're lashing out at me instead of listening to me."

Violet had all she could do to stay where she was, knowing he had a point. It didn't help her fury a great deal. "Go ahead, then, explain to me how you knew he had pictures of us, and you couldn't be bothered to pick up a phone and at least *tell me* that he had them!"

"Have you thought ... Oh, I don't know, in the last fifteen or so minutes—maybe since you got the pictures—that this was exactly why I didn't call you?"

How was he so calm when she was clearly pissed?

"You're doing it again. Patronizing me. Stop it."

Kaz sighed, and raked a hand down his face. "I knew he had the pictures, yes, but he also made it clear that if he caught me running around with you again, that he would send them to your father. I was waiting for his attention to cool down enough that I might be able to get away with meeting up with you. This wasn't something I wanted to do over the phone, Violet. But let's not forget how he had someone following me for weeks."

Violet snapped back at the sudden heat in Kaz's tone. "I—"

"Weeks," he repeated sharply. "And obviously, by the looks of those last few, we can safely fucking assume I get so entirely distracted by you that I don't even notice when someone is photographing me from outside *my* goddamn home!"

"Don't blame me. It wasn't just me."

Kaz let out a short, dry laugh. "Oh, Violet. I don't blame you for very damn much. Some things, yes, but not this mess."

Violet wasn't sure what he meant by that, but his posture softened and that calm mask fell away. He was in no better shape than her, and that left her lost.

Because she was okay to panic.

Kaz would stay calm.

She could rage.

He wouldn't.

This wasn't right at all.

"I'm sorry," Violet said.

"God, for what?" Kaz asked.

"I don't know. Assuming, I guess."

"Yeah, I get it."

Violet wrapped an arm around her middle, feeling like she just needed to hold herself together in a different way or she was going to fall apart all over the fucking floor. "But you do blame me for something."

Kaz shook his head, letting out a hard breath. "Don't do that, either."

"Well, you said it."

"You're looking into something that's not there—seeing it all wrong."

"You said it!"

Kaz crossed the space between them in a flash, grabbing her waist with one hand, her jaw with the other, and pulling her close. With no warning, he closed that little bit of distance too, kissing her hard and fast, letting her find that familiar heat of his and how it soothed her like nothing else.

Violet sucked in a ragged breath when Kaz finally pulled away, rested his forehead to hers, and stroked her cheek with his thumb.

"I don't blame you for this mess," he said again, his tone much softer than she'd heard him speak before.

And maybe she knew it then …

What Vera had meant on the doorstep.

It was … like that for them.

"I blame you for being you," Kaz murmured. "And who you are made it so easy for me to love you. And I blame you entirely for that."

Violet felt a sliver of wetness escape from the corner of her eye, but Kaz quickly swiped it away with the next stroke of his thumb.

"You shouldn't cry when someone tells you they love you," he said.

"Should you cry if you're just figuring out that you love them, too?"

Kaz smiled. "I don't know. I've never been here before."

"Yeah, me either."

She still wasn't sure if it was going to end well for them.

And that colored everything that should have been beautiful a little black.

Violet fingered the soft detailing on the silver comforter as Kaz paced the length of the spare bedroom.

"What are we doing?" she asked.

"I'm thinking," he replied. "You're …"

"What?"

"Helping."

Violet scoffed. "By sitting here?"

Kaz's pacing stopped abruptly. "Yes."

"That doesn't seem very helpful of me, Kaz."

"You don't seem to understand the importance of your presence. That, or you undervalue it a lot more than you should. And I partly blame that on your father because clearly he has it stuck in your head that your only use is to be pleasing and to his standards."

Violet didn't deny what he said.

It was true.

It just took her a while to see it, too.

"It might help if, instead of telling me why I am this way—something I already know, thanks—you could try explaining why I help you by just being here."

Kaz's icy gaze melted a bit. "I said that wrong, no?"

Violet shrugged. "Maybe just the wrong way."

Instantly, he moved toward her, dropping down into a crouch, his hands finding her bare knees. After yet another snapping match between him and Vera, his sister had pointed out that she had a spare bedroom—if they wanted to use it—but that they needed to figure something else out and soon. Violet, wanting to get back into her safe place for at least a little while, had stripped out of her clothes and snagged Kaz's shirt when he had jumped into the shower.

"You help me," he started to say, "because even if you distract me a great deal of the time, that also means I'm focusing on only you. And right now, that's where I need to focus. On you, Violet."

"Okay."

"That's it?"

"If it's what you want, then whatever."

She didn't have to pretend to understand him to love him. It just … was.

Kaz chuckled, and then leaned forward, resting his head on her lap. She trailed her fingers through his hair, taking that silent moment as there didn't seem to be nearly enough of them.

"You're one of my earliest memories," Kaz said.

Violet's fingers stilled. "What?"

"That day in the graveyard when you were four and I was ten. I have other memories of being younger than that, but that one day is so clear for me, above all the rest. I couldn't see a thing, not good enough for it to be worth mentioning, anyway."

"And what?"

"There's no fuzziness around it. I remember things surrounding that day, and even going to the graveyard. But nothing was quite as clear and as bright as you. Everything was hiding from me in a way, because I couldn't see it. I saw the sun that day, Violet, and it was you."

Violet let her fingers start to wander and thread through his hair again. "I didn't know you looked at it like that."

Kaz laughed. "You jumped off the bench and told me we would do this again. I think I've been waiting for that day to come for a long time."

"I was … precocious. Or that's what everyone says."

"You were—are—something else," he said, pressing a soft kiss to her thigh.

Violet shivered when his lips touched down to her skin again … higher the second time, and then higher again the third time. Her hands slid down from his hair to his shoulders as he kissed a path over her thigh, and then her hip. His fingers worked at the two buttons she had done up at the middle of the dress shirt before he was pushing the clothing off her shoulders and kissing a slow trail from her navel to the lace covering her breasts.

Kaz's hands cupped her neck and jaw, and his mouth came to a stop at the hollow of her throat. She felt his breath stutter against her skin, like he was chewing on what he wanted to say, but not sure he wanted to say it.

"I don't know what's going to happen," he finally whispered.

Violet blinked away the wetness in her gaze, letting her fingers stroke his bare back, feeling his muscles jump under her touch. "Does it matter right now?"

"I want to tell you that I have it figured out—that it'll be better tomorrow. I want to do that for you right now."

"Kaz—"

His fingers pressed into her skin, rough but sweet, quieting her.

"I don't want to lie to you," Kaz said.

Violet hugged him. "So, don't. Tell me something that's not a lie. Something that's true."

Kaz kissed her collarbone, making a tremor race down her spine. His mark there had long gone away and faded, as had the other one on the other side. But she swore she could still see it every time she looked at it, and when she touched the spot, it was like every nerve was attached to that one part of her skin for a brief moment.

"Something true?" he asked.

Violet slid her hands from his back under his jaw, tilting his head up so she could see his eyes. Love stared back, and that was enough for her. "Yeah."

"I would rather show you what you already know, Violet."

She tipped her head down just enough to capture his mouth with hers. The soft, steady sweep of his lips, and the stroke of his tongue against the seam of her lips had her deepening the kiss. She wanted more of him then—more of him to taste, and to feel.

All of him.

Kaz never broke the kiss as he lifted enough from the floor to push Violet back to the silky comforter. He was already shoving his undone pants down along with his boxer-briefs a second before he met her on the bed. She widened her legs under his urging hands, hooking them around his waist.

When he finally tore his mouth away from hers, she only had one quick moment to take in a breath, and then he was there ...

Violet felt his hand between their bodies, and his cock sliding against her slit. She wasn't surprised that he was already hard. How could she when she was already gasping for air and wet from just the need to have him, and nothing more?

With one sharp flex of his hips, Kaz took Violet deep. The immediate rush of relief washed through her, and sent her head tipping back to the bed, exposing her neck to his mouth again. His groan buried into her skin, right along with the imprints of his teeth as her first cry came out broken and loud.

God, she ached for this man.

"Kaz ..."

He grabbed onto her waist, and lifted up from her just enough that he could catch her kiss again. His tongue struck against hers hard, but it was the only roughness between them.

Their fucking had always been hard and fast. No matter where or when it had happened, it usually left her sated and tender, but still demanding more.

And this wasn't the same at all.

But it still killed her just the same.

Slow, long thrusts that filled her, and took her higher with each one. His fingers raking down her skin while she traced the lines of his face and watched him from up above. The only sounds registering to her ears were the slap of skin, his shuddering exhales, and her whispers.

Violet tightened her legs around his waist, needing Kaz closer than what he was, if it were possible. She wanted to stay like that for a moment, chasing bliss, and watching him love her.

All that blackness she had seen coloring their world began to bleed away. Her fingernails dug into his back, raking lines over his skin.

"Love you," he breathed.

She felt his lips tremble against hers with the words.

The tears fell, and he caught them.

"Love you," Violet told him.

She was pretty sure she had never said anything more honest in her life.

And she probably wouldn't ever find anything more true to say than those words to him.

Another slow stroke of his body into hers, and she was flying high, and crashing down at the same fucking time. It hit her when she wasn't expecting it to, and that made it so damn good.

Good enough that she shook, and colors burst behind her clenched lids when she shut her eyes and her back bowed off the bed. Kaz's mouth came down on hers, hiding the cry that crawled its way out of her throat. He pushed harder into her once, and on the second thrust, she felt him shudder as he came, her name muffled against her lips.

"Love you," he repeated.

Violet let more tears fall.
She knew he did.
But they were still a little lost.
And that blackness was seeping back in.

Kaz couldn't sleep, not when Violet had finally relaxed enough to go under tucked into his side, or the three hours he had lain there awake after, struggling to find peace in his thoughts.

They were out of time.

He knew that the moment she called him, nearly too afraid to put into words that Vasily had given her father more than enough ammunition to send him gunning down for Kaz. But he wasn't concerned with what Alberto had planned for him, but rather his plans for Violet.

He didn't doubt that her father was going to punish her for being with him. And considering the way the man treated her when she was in his good graces, he couldn't imagine how he was going to react now.

As he knew, Vasily didn't make idle threats. When he gave a warning, it was up to the person to understand that that would be the only one they got.

Hubris. Kaz had thought he would be able to maintain the relationship, as well as keeping it a secret from both their families. Even as careful as they had been, they still weren't careful enough, and now ... they were out of time.

Lost in his thoughts, he gently stroked Violet's hair, finding peace within the movements. How many times had he done this very action, but took it for granted?

She, every part of her, was worth committing to memory, so in his darkest hours, he could have something that brought him calm.

After some time, however, Kaz must have fallen asleep as the next thing he knew, Vera was swinging the door open, startling them both awake as the wood hit the wall.

"You need to get dressed and leave. Now. I just got a call from a friend, letting me know he's seen some of the Gallucci family in cars heading my way."

This wasn't very surprising. Even if Vera didn't agree with the life they were brought up in, she still learned quite a few things, and one of those was having friends everywhere.

Kaz was on his feet in seconds, grabbing the clothes he'd worn the day before off the floor, and pulled them on. "Where's—"

"Here. Have her put these on," Vera said, shoving Violet's clothes in his arms before turning on her heel and hurrying back down the hallway.

Violet was already sitting up, the sheet clutched to her chest as she turned terrified eyes on him. He didn't know who of the Gallucci family would be showing up, ready to cause mayhem if it meant dragging her away from him, but he knew that whoever did show up, it wasn't going to be good for either of them.

But even as the situation was dire, Kaz forced a smile for her. "Don't worry about it. No one is going to die today."

At least not where she could see …

"Let's go."

She was out of the bed, pulling on her own clothes as he grabbed his wallet and his gun, leaving his cell phone for last. There were a couple dozen messages, most from Ruslan asking what the fuck was going on, but as he was running low on time—and he was sure Vera had explained all or some of what was going on—he left them unanswered.

He grabbed hold of her hand, leading the way down the stairs, but as he was passing the windows, he paused at what he saw outside of them. There were cars already waiting, one blocking the driveway. The tinted windows hid the passengers, but if Kaz had to guess, there were at least two in each car, and if that was the case, they were outnumbered by at least six.

"*Shit.*"

Kaz's gaze shot to Violet, recognizing the terror in her eyes as she stared down at the fleet of cars. They were an ominous sight, a reminder of their reality.

"It's fine," he said drawing her to the side, forcing her to face him and not what awaited them. "I've got it under control."

"How do you want to handle this, Kaz?" Vera asked from her position at the base of the stairs, her arms folded across her chest.

She didn't look the slightest bit afraid that her house was practically surrounded by the very same men she was brought up to fear. But while Vera minded the lines, she didn't cower when she walked the streets of Brooklyn—if there was one thing she'd inherited from their father, it was her bravado.

"I haven't thought that far," Kaz responded as he and Violet walked down the last few steps. "But she's—" He pointed to Violet, "—staying in here."

"Then I'll go with you," Vera said, already reaching to pull the door open.

"No. You can stay in here with Violet. And call Rus."

Kaz didn't know where Vasily was, or whether he was planning a surprise visit, too, but he didn't want to know. After all, he was the only one that could have possibly told the Italians where to find them—which was saying a lot, considering he usually went out of his way to keep their business away from Vera's doorstep.

"I should be with you," Violet argued. "They won't shoot me to get to you."

"Right now," Kaz said. "I don't know what they're capable of. I'm not putting you at risk for—"

"This isn't up for discussion, Kaz."

Though he was tempted to argue this point with her, he just didn't have the time. The last thing he needed was one of Violet's overzealous relatives to step out of line and hurt Vera while trying to get to him—his reaction would probably have him apologizing to Violet later—but Vera had a mind of her own, and more, she could handle herself if the need arose.

Shifting his attention to Violet, he placed a hand at the small of her back, giving her a slight push away from the front door, and ordered, "Stay inside."

"Kaz, they're opening the doors …" Vera said, turning the lock, her hand on the knob.

"Be careful," Violet whispered against his lips, finally drawing away though her hand lingered at his side, like she was afraid to let go.

Pressing his lips to her forehead, he stayed there for a long moment, wishing that he could take that look of fear from her face. The last thing she should be was afraid when with him.

The moment his back to her, Vera looked to him, conveying everything he needed to know with one look. She opened the door for him, staying slightly hidden behind it, and as he crossed that threshold, he was careful not to look back. He hoped Vera would keep Violet safe and inside the damn house.

Most of the men that stood next to the cars, Kaz didn't recognize, but as his gaze shifted over every man in turn, he paused at the car parked farthest to the south. One door opened slowly and out stepped Carmine. Unlike the last time they were in the same vicinity, today he looked rather smug as he casually strolled forward as though he had every right to.

There was no fear in him, not this time.

Kaz wasn't entirely sure what to make of that.

Either Carmine had something up his sleeve, something that made him unafraid, or the man was a fool.

"I've come to collect what belongs to my father," Carmine said, his tone never wavering.

Kaz sneered, tipping his head to the side just a bit. "First off, there's nothing here that *belongs* to Alberto."

"We both know that isn't true."

"True as the fucking blood I bleed."

Violet wasn't a possession to own, and her father wasn't her master. Besides that, over his fucking dead body was he going to hand Violet over to someone who claimed to be there to *collect* her like she was property.

"Give that a few minutes," Carmine said, chuckling. "And we might get to see that blood, scum."

Kaz let that comment roll off his shoulders. He'd been told worse. "As I said, there's nothing here that belongs to your father, so be a smart little prick, and go."

"Not until you give me what I've come for, Kazimir. My sister—now."

"No," Kaz replied, unfazed.

If this was the only thing Carmine had to toss at Kaz, the fool was going to be surprised at the outcome.

"You're not walking away from this one, Markovic," Carmine said, never taking his gaze off Kaz for a moment. "If I were you, I'd get on my knees and beg for a bullet."

"That's because you're weak, Carmine. Unlike you, I don't get on my knees for anyone."

Carmine smirked, his voice lowering just enough as to not be heard by the men feet away. "Seems there is a particular slut you'll get on your knees for, huh?"

It was the "slut" that made Kaz's eye twitch. He couldn't ever picture calling one of his sisters that, but Carmine had done it easily, with relish almost.

Words rarely bothered Kaz, not when he had called himself worse during his darker times, but hearing Carmine say that about Violet? It made him snap.

Before he could even check the impulse, his fist was flying, landing with almost perfect precision across the man's jaw, just as he'd been about to say something else. It was at the perfect angle that as soon as his knuckles met Carmine's face, he felt the crack of bone.

Even Carmine couldn't contain a grunt of pain as his head jerked to the side with the force of Kaz's hit. He had barely drawn his fist back when he heard the unmistakable sound of guns being drawn.

But his attention wasn't focused on the weapons aimed in his direction, but rather to the car where a door was being opened. Kaz knew, even before the first hint of the man's dark head showed above the roof, that it was Alberto Gallucci. And though they looked quite similar, there was definitely a difference between father and son.

While Carmine played at being a boss, it was clear that Alberto was one. He had yet to even say a word as he took his time walking past the cars, but he didn't have to use his words to announce that he was the man in charge. It was just a known fact. Though the men never took their eyes from Kaz, they all stepped out of the way as Alberto neared.

Kaz, on the other hand, was not impressed. "I don't think we've had the pleasure, Gallucci."

"No, I'm glad to say we haven't." Alberto came close enough to be just a couple of feet away from Kaz, and barely gave his injured son a second glance. Lowering his voice just enough to not be heard by all watching, he said, "Not with you being an adult, anyway. Although I must say, I liked you better as a boy, before you thought to chase after my daughter."

"I seem to remember that differently, then."

Alberto rubbed his hands together, as if he was wiping dirt from them. "Oh?"

"I liked her quite well then, too, no?"

The Italian boss stiffened, but that was his only show of irritation. His face remained as cold and impassive as ever as he looked Kaz over once more, then his gaze swept to the house behind him. "I will give you one more chance to give my daughter to me and this all goes away, Kazimir."

"I don't know what you're talking about, but I can assure you that if you storm my sister's home like you own the place, you might not like what Vasily does."

Alberto smiled then—small and dark. "I think you will soon come to find you have no idea what your father will do."

Kaz felt the brief urge to reach for the gun at his back, but he beat it down. It would do him no good at that moment, given the weapons still trained on him.

"Two minutes," Alberto continued, "and she had better be clothed."

"I told you—"

Alberto held up a hand, stopping Kaz. "I may not like your kind, but there is one thing we Russians and Italians have in common in our business, and that is learned respect. You have, in the highest of regards, disrespected me, Kazimir. And you will either bring me what is mine, or I will take it from you."

Kaz's fist clenched with the need to strike another man. He had the feeling that hitting Alberto would not end as well as it had when he hit the man's son.

"She's not yours," Kaz said cooly.

She was his.

Alberto sighed, passing another look over Kaz's shoulder. It took all Kaz had not to turn around and make sure his sister and Violet weren't watching from the windows where they could be seen.

"*Topina*," Alberto called loudly, "*venire*. Now."

Kaz didn't move, he barely even breathed. He wasn't sure what the Italian had said, but it couldn't have been too threatening, considering it was only a couple of words.

When Alberto didn't get the desired reaction from within the house that he clearly wanted, his calm mask slipped a bit when his gaze narrowed.

"Fine, Violet," Alberto said, still loud enough to carry over the yard and into the dark house. "We will do this your way, *ragazza. Il prossimo scatola apparterrà al suo cuore.*"

"What did you just say?" Kaz demanded.

Alberto said nothing to Kaz, simply held his hand down to his side, and opened his palm to his still groaning son. "Take my hand and get up off the ground, Carmine. I have let you whimper down there long enough. Any more and you will turn into a sniveling puppy. Get up. *Adesso.*"

By the time Carmine was on his feet again, his broken jaw being cradled by his hand, Alberto's attention was back on the front door of the house.

"Twenty seconds, Violet," Alberto informed like he was breaking bread. "I have the knife already sharpened, *dolcezza.*"

Kaz's brows drew together at his words, trying to understand what the man was getting at, but he didn't have time to ponder it for long, not when Violet came running out of the house, frantic eyes on her father even as she stopped next to Kaz.

He didn't think he had ever seen her look so torn.

But he didn't reach for her ... merely stood at her side. Whatever choice she made, he wasn't going to force her hand either way.

"Violet," Alberto said, his tone having softened as he offered his hand. "It's time to leave."

Her eyes shifted over the men, as though seeing them all for the first time. Kaz was sure that she would have tucked her head, walked away with them, and accepted whatever punishment her father saw fit for her relationship with him—at least until he felt her fingers slide against his, twining them as she held tight.

"I'm not leaving."

Kaz was careful to keep his face neutral, though the surprise he felt internally was reflected on Alberto's face as he turned to face his daughter, like he had never considered that she would defy him.

Alberto was still trying to maintain that calm demeanor though his eyes spoke a different story as he said, "Do not push me on this. Get in the car. Now."

But even still, she remained next to Kaz, her hand in his.

She refused to move.

Not after he asked again, then asked once more.

One minute Alberto was content with merely asking, but in the next breath, all decorum fled as he snatched Violet by the arm, thick fingers digging into her flesh, enough to make her wince in pain as he attempted to draw her to his side.

Except, she had barely taken two steps before Kaz had his own gun in hand, the barrel pointed straight at one of the men in the state that he really *shouldn't* pull a gun on.

He could feel everyone tense as they waited. A made man pulling a gun on their boss could potentially be a death sentence, but the enemy doing it?

He was practically asking to die.

"Let her go before me pulling this trigger is the last thing you see."

Alberto wasn't afraid, not that Kaz had expected him to be, but he thought he might have seen a touch of admiration in the man's eyes. "If only you were Italian, my boy. Now, you would be wise to move that gun out of my face."

Kaz's arm didn't even twitch as he repeated himself, saying, "Let her go."

When Alberto's gaze shifted just slightly, Kaz was too late to see the fist coming his way. Blood filled his mouth almost instantly, and he could feel the sting of his split lip. He could hear Violet screaming, the sound of it felt like it was tearing him apart—he only belatedly realized it was his name she was yelling.

The hits still rained down on him, but Kaz no longer cared, swinging his arm, he brought the butt of his weapon across the man's face. But he didn't linger to see his good work, instead he headed to the street, walking into the center where the car was now trying to pass.

Even with the tinted glass, he could still make out Alberto Gallucci, Carmine on one side, Violet on the other.

"She walks away, or you don't," Kaz warned, aiming at the windshield, making sure Alberto could see just how serious he was. "And before your driver gets any great ideas, know that I can still kill you before he even makes contact."

BETHANY-KRIS & LONDON MILLER

Kaz was so focused on the man that he didn't hear the sirens, or see the flashing lights, not until they were upon him, three officers climbing out of a squad car with weapons drawn.

"Kazimir Markovic! Put down your weapon!"

Kaz kept his gun exactly where it was, but did lift his gaze just far enough to take in the officers. He didn't recognize them, and doubted they were his father's men, who could be bought off for the right price … so how did they know his name?

It dawned on him quite slowly at first as he took in the scene around him, realizing how it made him look. He was the only one standing there with a gun at that very moment, and as quickly as he had been surrounded just moments prior, the men had already climbed back into their cars.

This time, Kaz did smile.

He'd been fucking played.

"Markovic, we will not ask again! Drop your weapon and put your hands where we can see them!"

Turning that smile to Alberto, he didn't take his eyes off the man as he did what he was told, placing his gun at his feet before holding his hands, palms out for them to see.

"This isn't over, Gallucci. This won't ever be over."

He could almost see Alberto frown as his words penetrated, but Kaz lost sight of him as he was grabbed and shoved onto the hood of the car, his arms wrenched behind his back. He thought he heard Violet's cries as one of the officers read him his rights; he could almost imagine he heard her pleading for him, but as he was forced up, and pushed toward the squad car, he knew he would never be able to get that sound out of his head.

Officer Barnes, from the name on his tag, had a hand to Kaz's head and was about to push him down into the car when they all paused at the sight of Vera running out the house. At first, Kaz thought she was coming for him, but then he noticed her attention was on something past him.

And more, her curses and words weren't spoken in English.

But Russian …

Kaz turned to look over his shoulder, trying to see who his sister was yelling at, but knew with a gut feeling who it would be.

It didn't make sense otherwise.

How could they have known he and Violet were at Vera's place at all?

There were only two people that knew where Kaz would go if he was in trouble, it had been that way since they were children, but only one of those two people did Kaz know would not give that information to anyone.

He didn't know how he had his fingers dipped in this one, but Kaz didn't doubt that his father was behind this.

He only got a glimpse of Vasily before he was being forced into the car, the door slammed shut after. Already, the fleet of cars that belonged to the Gallucci family were vanishing out of view.

Kaz didn't have time to reflect on that, not when the officers were climbing in the car themselves, it was only moments later when they were pulling off.

"You're lucky the boss's daughter was there," Barnes said from the front seat, glancing back at him. "He went easy on you for her sake."

Boss? Kaz was trying to piece together what the man was saying when it clicked. The reason why he didn't recognize them was because they worked for the opposite side.

They were on Alberto's payroll.

Shit. Why hadn't he thought of that before?

The panic must have shown in his face because the one driving laughed.

"Don't worry, Markovic," the officer said looking away from the rearview mirror as he pulled onto the interstate. "You're not going to die tonight."

Violet yanked her arm out of her father's grasp, turning in the seat to stare out the rearview window. It killed her—*killed her*—to watch the police shove a handcuffed Kaz into the back of a police car. It wasn't long before her view was obstructed by moving cars, and then their vehicle was taking a corner, leaving the scene behind.

She felt the hot tears crawl down her cheeks, her breaths coming out hard and fast with each one.

The man who had attacked Kaz—she hadn't seen him rush in from the side until it was too late. She should have warned Kaz somehow.

"Turn around," Alberto said, calm and seemingly happy.

Violet didn't listen.

Carmine was too busy holding his broken jaw, cursing in a mumbled way every so often, to care about his sister or his father.

The next box I hold will belong to his heart.

That's what her father had said.

It was the only reason she came out of the house, even knowing she shouldn't.

That fear—the terror—sent her running.

But it wasn't quite enough to make her go when her father demanded she should. She didn't belong with her father, she wanted Kaz.

"Violet, turn around and sit," Alberto said.

She still didn't give him what he wanted.

Without warning, her father grabbed her arm and twisted, making pain shoot through her shoulder as he forced her to sit in the seat properly.

Alberto didn't let her go, his fingernails digging into her skin.

Violet hissed. "Let me go."

"There, that's better," Alberto said like she hadn't uttered a thing.

"Daddy—"

For the first time since she had come out of the house, she saw a real anger flash in her father's eyes and settle deep into the scowling lines of his face. "Do not call me that like you want to find some sympathetic part in me. You are twenty-one, not a child. You know how to follow my rules. And I will no longer keep treating you with the kid gloves I have in the past, Violet. You …"

Violet blinked, feeling another swell of tears fall from the corners of her eyes. "What?"

"You couldn't have hurt me more—betrayed me more—than how you did with that Russian."

"Kaz."

Alberto didn't give a thing away when he asked, "What?"

"He is not *the Russian*, his name is *Kazimir*."

"You are being foolish," Alberto spat. "A foolish, stupid girl who spread her legs for a pretty man and nothing more."

He could have slapped her and it would have felt better.

Violet refused to show how his words cut her. "Then why not leave me to be with him, huh? If I shamed you so much, why not let me *go* and be the whore you clearly think I am?"

Stay, she had wanted to say. *Stay with Kaz.*

A man who loved her.

Who would protect her at all cost.

Who never treated her like her father did.

"Because you are not his," her father said sharply, his fingers digging in harder on her arm. "You are *mine*."

"I'm not," Violet whispered. "Not after this."

Alberto's gaze narrowed, but he finally let her go. "Fix your face."

She didn't make a move to do what he said, letting her tears stain her cheeks even more.

Her father waved a hand at the driver. "Chris, take us around to the Kitchen."

The driver glanced at Alberto in the rearview mirror. "Boss?"

"The Kitchen—to the Black Hall," Alberto demanded.

Violet didn't know what her father was talking about, but it couldn't be good considering even Carmine had lifted his head and was staring at Alberto like the man had grown a second head.

"What?" her brother mumbled.

"Make it fast," Alberto said, never taking his gaze off Violet.

What was going on?

Violet watched streets fly by and eventually become more familiar, until they were in the bowels of Hell's Kitchen and coming to a stop at what looked like a rundown, decrepit building that might, at one time, have been an apartment building.

"Stay in the car, I do not need you for this," Alberto told the driver, and then Carmine. He grabbed Violet's arm, pulling her with him as he exited the back of the car. "Keep quiet, and keep up, darling."

She didn't like how he'd used that endearment with just a hint of sarcasm and condescension, but chose to do as he said.

At that point, it wasn't like Violet had much of a damn choice.

It wasn't long after they entered the shamble of a building before Violet figured out why her father had called it Black Hall. Darkness enveloped the entire place but when a small, flickering light bulb was turned on, black halls stared back at her from every direction.

Alberto pulled her along, opening a door to another set of halls, and a staircase. Again, the place was black all over, even with the bit of light.

Violet couldn't understand why they would paint the place black like it was, and it almost felt like the walls were fucking closing in on her because it seemed so small. Her heart rate picked up, thundering. Anxiety simmered through her bloodstream.

"What—"

"Shut up," Alberto said.

Violet snapped her mouth shut, letting her father continue to drag her along like she was a doll and nothing more. The more she breathed in the air of the building, the sicker she felt. It stunk with a musky, earthy tone, but also with something she couldn't describe. Something that smelled like rotting meat and garbage.

Finally, her father pushed open a door at the end of yet another long, small black hallway. His hand found her shoulders, and he shoved, pushing her inside first.

Violet spun on her heel to face her father, and he slammed the door shut, and flicked on another tiny light bulb that barely did the job of lighting the small space.

All over again, the walls seemed to close in on Violet.

"You never liked the dark when you were a child," Alberto said, taking one step away from the door.

Violet forced her panic down, keeping her gaze on her father and not the black walls surrounding her. "I'm not a child now."

"Clearly. But I'm not quite sure what to think of you now, either. A lady doesn't seem to fit what with your recent behavior. No lady would go on acting as you did with that Russian."

She beat down the urge to correct Alberto again.

"Why am I here?" Violet chanced a look at the dark walls, wishing the room was bigger. She didn't like small spaces, either. "And what is this place?"

Alberto smiled, but it came off cold.

She had no doubt he meant for it to.

"This, Violet, is the Black Hall. And I wanted to show you it."

That answered nothing.

"*Why*? To frighten me with it because it's small and dark?"

Alberto chuckled, waving a finger at her. "Smart, but it's actually much bigger than you think. And there are chains on every exit door. The walls are so thick that no one can be heard screaming when they're brought here, and even better, no one would say a thing if they were heard. But no, that isn't why I brought *you* here."

Violet clenched her fists at her sides, confused and wary. "I don't understand."

"All it takes is a room like this, and a few days to ruin a man's mind."

"So?"

"I want you to take a good look around you right now, imagine it being cold, dark, and small. Then consider the only light you get is when someone comes in here to beat you at least once a day, but sometimes twice if they're in the neighborhood."

Violet backed up a foot, wanting to be further away from her father. She didn't know this man at all—he was not who she knew.

"Careful," Alberto said when Violet's back almost hit the wall. "Don't touch, it's probably still wet."

She didn't look over her shoulder, but did ask, "With what?"

"Take a guess."

"No."

Alberto shrugged. "Your mind will do it for you. And believe me, that is more than enough."

It already had, but Violet refused to even go there. This was just another one of her father's games—a head game to mess with her mind, and trick her into compliance.

She didn't want it to work but she wanted *out* of this fucking building.

"I want to go home," Violet said.

"Soon," Alberto promised. He waved a hand high, gesturing at the room, but maybe he meant the building. "I wanted you to see, Violet."

"See what?"

"What I will do to Kazimir Markovic before I kill him, should he ever put his hands on you again."

With guards on either side of him, hands on their guns as though they had to worry what Kaz's next move would be, he was walked down the hallway, bypassing a number of cells, where inmates were shouting, or otherwise asleep. Though smaller and far younger than a number of the men that made up the block he was housed in, no one bothered him.

While his name felt like a burden sometimes, this was not one of them.

As they continued on, they didn't stop at the first door to the left where the large room was where the inmates were allowed visitation, but kept going, finally stopping at another door where Kaz's guard to the left had to look up at the camera in the corner of the wall before a buzz could be heard, and they were allowed inside.

Through there, and the corridor adjacent to it, Kaz's shackles were finally unlocked, giving him the chance to rotate his wrists, after having the metal rubbing against them for so long. His guards stepped to the side, but one said, "You got ten minutes," before he gave the door opposite him a push, and gestured for Kaz to walk outside.

Breathing in the fresh air, Kaz dug into the pocket of his uniform for his cigarettes, plucking one from the pack then bringing it up to his lips.

"Those things are going to kill you, Kazimir."

He turned slightly, just enough that he could see Vasily waiting for him, standing out of view of the cameras that lined the roof—or maybe he had someone to shift the angle for the time being.

"Maybe so," Kaz said with a shrug. "But it could be worse."

Vasily's brows lifted as he said, "Oh? How so?"

"You could be standing at my back."

Kaz almost grinned as Vasily's humor fled. He'd had enough time in the thirty days he had already been locked inside to think on just how he had ended up here. The right people could have been easily bought off in a matter of days for a weapon's charge.

And yet, nothing.

Kaz had no choice but to take the deal they offered, knowing that because he already had a felony on his record, he could have been facing a number of years behind bars, as opposed to just the six months he ended up with.

But six months in a cell was still fucking torture for him.

"You came here for a reason, Vasily," Kaz said, taking a drag from his cigarette. "What do you want?"

"I'm offering you a chance for you to move on once you're out—to focus on what's important. If you want it, your position will still be yours, and there will be no bad blood between us and the Galluccis. Alberto is willing to let you be free."

Laughing without humor, he shook his head. "And what makes you think I give a fuck what Alberto Gallucci is *willing* to give me?"

"Kazimir—"

"Understand something. The second you arranged this," Kaz said gesturing to the number stitched on his uniform, "was the very second you were dead to me. Did you think you were punishing me? Sticking me in here for a few months? Was this supposed to be my *lesson?*"

"Your actions have consequences, Kazimir—whether you like it or not," Vasily retorted, that familiar fire entering his words. "You are not above my rules, boy, or have you forgotten your place? This was nothing new. Playing the victim will get you nowhere."

"Is that what you think this is?" Kaz asked. "Me playing the victim?"

"No, I think you're acting like a child that got his favorite toy taken away."

It took great focus to keep his emotions in check, but Kaz had had a full month to prepare for this face-to-face, and he wasn't ready to tip his hand just yet.

"I honestly believe that's what you think, too. Violet was never a toy. She wasn't a fucking possession that I fucked around with when I was in the mood. She meant something to me."

"Meant?" Vasily questioned. "Does she not mean anything to you now?"

"Why did you come here, Vasily?"

"Is it such a foreign concept that a father would want to check on his son?"

Kaz smirked. "Only when that father was the one that did it to him." Taking one last drag from his cigarette, he flicked the butt across the yard, watching it skip along the pebbles before settling. "You're a fan of your warnings, no?" Kaz asked as he looked back to his father. "Here's one for you. When you looked into the abyss, it didn't stare back—it winked."

Vasily shook his head. "What does that mean?"

Kaz tapped his throat on either side with two fingers, smiling even as Vasily glared. "Watch your back."

Leaving him standing there, Kaz headed back into the building, holding his arms out so the cuffs could be put back on him, and he could be taken back to his cell. He didn't doubt that he had gotten his point across.

Besides the meeting with his father, the rest of his night was rather uneventful, much of it spent counting down the minutes, first until dinner was over, then showers, and finally, when it was lights out.

Then there was always that hour in between that felt like it took the longest, that the money he'd been shelling out ultimately meant nothing. But just as the thought crossed his mind, he heard footsteps, then saw an arm appear in front of the bars, slipping the device through them.

Kaz had the small cell phone in his hand, dialing the only number added as a contact inside before the guard could even walk off.

His heart beating fast, his mind in shambles, he waited, listening to each ring like it would be the last, and then finally, after the fourth ring, the call connected.

The voice was soft, tentative, almost afraid, but the sound of it was enough to make him feel like he could breathe again. "Kaz?"

Smiling, he rested his head against the cinderblock wall, closing his eyes as he said, "It's good to hear your voice, *krasivaya.*"

Bios

Bethany-Kris is a Canadian author, lover of much, and mother to three very young sons, one cat, and two dogs. A small town in Eastern Canada where she was born and raised is where she has always called home. With her boys under her feet, a snuggling cat, barking dogs, and a spouse calling over his shoulder, she is nearly always writing something ... when she can find the time.

With a degree in Creative Writing, London Miller has turned pen to paper, creating riveting fictional worlds where the bad guys are sometimes the good guys. Her debut novel, In the Beginning, is the first in the Volkov Bratva Series.

She currently resides in Atlanta, Georgia with her husband and two puppies, where she drinks far too much Sprite, and spends her nights writing.

Made in the USA
Las Vegas, NV
29 April 2021

22213845R00146